"Force's skill is also evident in the way that she develops the characters, from the murdered and mutilated senator to the detective and chief of staff who are trying to solve the case. The heroine, Sam, is especially complex and her secrets add depth to this mystery... This novel is *The O.C.* does D.C., and you just can't get enough."

—*RT Book Reviews* on *Fatal Affair* (4½ stars)

"Force pushes the boundaries by deftly using political issues like immigration to create an intricate mystery."
—*RT Book Reviews* on *Fatal Consequences* (4 stars)

"The romance, the mystery, the ongoing story lines... everything about these books has me sitting on the edge of my seat and begging for more. I am anxiously awaiting the next in the series. I give *Fatal Deception* an A."

—*TheBookPushers.com*

"The suspense is thick, the passion between Nick and Sam just keeps getting hotter and hotter."
—*Guilty Pleasures Book Reviews* on *Fatal Deception*

"The perfect mesh of mystery and romance."
—*Night Owl Reviews* on *Fatal Scandal* (5 stars)

The Fatal Series
by *New York Times* bestselling author
Marie Force
Suggested reading order

MARIE FORCE

Fatal IDENTITY

HQN™

ISBN-13: 978-0-373-78995-5

Recycling programs
for this product may
not exist in your area.

Fatal Identity

For questions and comments about the quality of this book,
please contact us at CustomerService@Harlequin.com.

www.HQNBooks.com

Printed in U.S.A.

For Uncle Bobby
1933–2016
Love you always.

CHAPTER ONE

STANDING BEFORE THE Internal Affairs Board that would determine her fate, Detective Lieutenant Samantha "Sam" Holland was at peace. If they busted her down a rank or two, so be it. Her life would be a whole lot less complicated with someone else in charge of the Homicide unit. Sure, she'd rather be the boss, but having been the boss for more than a year now, she wouldn't cry over letting someone else do it.

Of course, knowing there was no one else who *could* do it at the moment added to her peaceful, easy feeling. Her number two in command, Detective Sergeant Tommy "Gonzo" Gonzales, had understandably been a mess since his partner was gunned down right in front of him, and as he was the only one the brass would even consider for the top spot, Sam wasn't worried.

Would there be some sort of hell to pay for punching Sergeant Ramsey in the face? Probably. Would she do it again if she had it to do over? *Abso-fucking-lutely.* He'd had it coming after what he'd said. *I would've thought Stahl had taken some of the starch out of you...* That any member of the department could make light of what their former colleague had done to her was beyond reprehensible. And besides, how was it her fault that Ramsey had fallen down the stairs, broken his wrist and given himself a concussion? The guy needed to learn to take a punch.

Deputy Chief Conklin cleared his throat, and something about the way he wouldn't look at her made Sam nervous for the first time. "Lieutenant, we've reviewed the testimony provided by you and Detective Sergeant Ramsey about the incident in question. While we agree that Sergeant Ramsey's comments were unfortunate and unnecessary, your actions amount to conduct unbecoming an officer of your rank and stature."

Sam kept her expression blank even though her insides began to quiver like a bowl of gelatin. *Crap. Here it comes, the reduction in rank. It's okay,* she told herself. *It'll be okay.* This, right here, was why police officers commonly referred to IAB as "The Bureau of Proctology."

"The board has agreed that you are to serve a fourday unpaid suspension effective immediately. Your first day back will be next Wednesday at zero seven hundred. Furthermore, you'll be requested to make a onethousand-dollar donation to the Widows and Children's Fund. Finally, you should be aware that U.S. Attorney Forrester is considering criminal assault charges. That concludes this hearing. We're adjourned."

Conklin stood to leave the room, while Sam remained riveted in place, at once relieved and filled with dread over the possibility of criminal charges. She'd really stepped into a steaming pile this time, but she still didn't regret punching that mouthy son of a bitch.

"Lieutenant."

At the sound of Captain Malone's deep voice, Sam looked up at her commander.

He took her by the elbow to lead her from the hearing room. "Could've been much worse," he said in a low tone that only she could hear.

"How serious is Forrester about criminal charges?"

"The question is how serious *Ramsey* is about wanting to see your ass in a sling. He's the one forcing Forrester's hand by demanding he press charges."

"Of course he is. As far as I'm concerned, Ramsey can kiss my ass."

"You shouldn't have hit him, Sam."

"You would've hit him too if you'd been there."

"Possibly."

"Definitely."

They walked back to the detectives' pit where most of her squad was waiting for the results of the hearing.

Detective Freddie Cruz, Sam's partner and close friend, jumped up when she and Malone entered the pit. "Well, what'd they say?"

"You'll be glad to know you're rid of me for the next four days, but like the flu, I'll be back."

His relieved expression was almost comical. "Thank goodness."

"Lieutenant," Detective Jeannie McBride said, "while you were at the hearing a man was here asking to speak with you. He said it was very important, and he would only talk to you."

"Who was it?"

"He refused to leave his name," Jeannie said. "But he was very insistent about speaking only to the vice president's wife."

"He asked for me that way?" Sam said. "That almost guarantees I won't see him."

"That's what we told him. I think he's gone now."

"Um, Lieutenant," Malone said, "I believe you were on your way out?"

Sam scowled at him and then went into her office to shut down her computer and grab her coat, purse and gloves. Then she closed and locked her door before addressing her squad. "Hold down the fort while I'm gone, and call me if you need me."

"Don't call her about police business, however," Malone said, "because she can't help you with that for the next four days."

"They know that," she said. "Don't you?"

Mumbled replies of "yes, ma'am" followed her question.

Speaking only to Cruz, she said, "Where's Gonzo?"

"No-show," he said softly.

She gave his arm a squeeze. "I'll check on him."

"Let me know."

"I will."

Malone walked her out.

"Have you been assigned to escort me from the premises?"

"I volunteered."

"Lucky me." She glanced up at him as they went toward the lobby and main exit. "You'll keep an eye on my squad for me, won't you? They're all a bit fragile these days after losing Arnold, and Gonzo is in no condition to be put in charge."

"We know. I'll be overseeing Homicide until you return. What do we know about where Sergeant Gonzales is today?"

Sam had hoped he wouldn't notice Gonzo wasn't in the pit. She should've known better. "We don't know anything, but I'm going to find out what's up as soon as I can."

"I've noticed he's been absent a lot lately."

"He refused to take leave after Arnold was killed, but he's called out sick a few times, and between you and me, I suspect it's bottle flu more than actual sickness."

"So he's drinking."

"I think so, and I can't say I blame him. What he saw, right in front of him… And he blames himself because he let Arnold take the lead to get him to shut up. In the few times I've actually gotten him to talk to me, he says it should've been him."

"He didn't do anything wrong."

"We both know that, but there's no telling him."

"Has he been keeping his appointments with Trulo?" Malone asked, referring to the department's psychiatrist.

"Yeah, but I don't see where it's doing any good. He seems to be getting more withdrawn all the time."

Malone sighed. "I know. We've all noticed."

"I'll give him a call and see what's up today. This is the first time he's actually failed to show up for a shift without getting in touch with me."

"You can check on him as a friend, of course, but not as a supervisor."

"Believe it or not, Captain, I've been suspended before, and I know how this works."

They were nearly to the door when he stopped her with a hand to her arm. "I have to tell you, Lieutenant, that in your place, after what you went through with Stahl, I probably would've clocked Ramsey for what he said. But—"

Sam rolled her eyes. "How did I know there was a 'but' coming?"

"I want to see you rise through the ranks and be rewarded for your hard work and service to the department. I can almost guarantee that's not going to happen if you get suspended again."

Sam thought about that for a second before she replied. "I appreciate your candor, as always, but if I never go any further than lieutenant, I will have done a thousand times better than I ever expected after coming in here with dyslexia and my father's legacy to live up to. It's been a great career. I wouldn't change a single thing, even the stuff that got me suspended, because the first time I got Nick out of it, and the second time I got to deck Ramsey and then listen to him squeal like a baby. Life is good, you know?"

Malone grunted out a laugh. "You're too much, Holland."

"I know. You guys tell me that all the time."

"Be gone with you, and don't let me see you around these parts until Wednesday."

"Ahhh," she said with a dramatic sigh, "bubble baths and bonbons for *four whole days*. Punish me please. Maybe Nick can punch the president and get himself suspended from the White House. I'll have to ask him if he's got any scores to settle, because this would be a great time to get it done."

"You're taking this surprisingly well, Lieutenant."

"I almost died in that basement with Stahl. It takes a lot to rattle my cage after that."

"Possible criminal charges are no laughing matter. You might want to talk to one of the union attorneys while you're off, just in case."

"I'll think about that. Can you imagine the headlines? Vice President's Wife Charged With Assault. Something tells me the White House communications people have never dealt with that particular headline."

"Safe to say they've never dealt with the likes of you."

"Aw, Captain, you flatter me. I'd better get out of here before someone hears I'm still here and I get in more trouble. Take care of my people for me."

"I will."

Sam pushed through the double doors and into cool, crisp winter air that smelled like snow. She'd had a conversation yesterday with her son, Scotty, about how air can smell like snow. Scotty said it wasn't possible to *smell* snow, even after she got him to take a few deep breaths to see what she meant. He remained skeptical, but she had a few more weeks of winter to prove her point.

"Mrs. Cappuano."

Sam turned toward the man who'd called to her. He was in his late twenties or early thirties, handsome with dark blond hair and brown eyes. The panic she saw in his expression put her immediately on alert. "That's me, although they don't call me that around here. And you are?"

"Josh Hamilton."

Sam shook his outstretched hand. "What can I do for you, Josh?"

"I need your help."

"Okay."

"This… It's going to sound sort of crazy, so bear with me." He took a deep breath. "Today I was bored at work, so I started surfing the web, you know, just clicking around aimlessly."

As a technophobe of the highest order, Sam didn't know because she'd never done that and certainly not at work, where she was usually too busy to pee, let alone surf.

Josh took another deep breath, and Sam's anxiety

ramped up a notch. "I saw this story about a baby who was kidnapped thirty years ago. They had this age-progression photo showing what he'd look like now, and…" He gulped. "It was *me*."

"Wait. *What?*"

With trembling hands, Josh retrieved his cell phone from his pocket and called up a web page, zeroing in on a digitally produced photo that did, in fact, bear a striking resemblance to him.

"Those photos are produced by computers. They're not exact."

"*That's me!* And it explains why I've never felt at home or accepted in my family. What if they *took* me?"

"Hang on a minute. What evidence do you have to suspect that your parents participated in a criminal act to bring you into their family?"

He seemed to make an effort to calm down. "They're extremely accomplished people and so are my siblings. My brother is a board-certified neurosurgeon. He went to Harvard for undergrad and medical school. My sister is an attorney, also Harvard educated, Law Review, the whole nine yards. And then there's me. I barely made it out of state college after having spent most of my five years there on academic probation. After four years working for the federal government, I'm a GS-9 at Veterans Affairs, where I shuffle paper all day while counting the minutes until I can leave. The only reason I have that job is because my father, who has never approved of a thing I said or did, pulled strings to get me in. They're all Republicans while I'm a liberal Democrat who fully supports your husband. I hope he runs in four years, by the way."

"None of that proves your parents kidnapped you."

"Will you take my case? Please? I need to know for sure. This would explain so much of why I've felt like a square peg in my own family my entire life."

Sam held up a hand to stop him. "I'm a homicide cop, not a private investigator, but if you really believe a crime has been committed, I can refer you to someone within the department—"

"No." He shook his head. "I want you. You're the best. Everyone says so."

"I'm honored you think so, but I'm on a leave of absence for the next few days, so I'm not able to take your case personally."

"It *has* to be you. You're the only one I'd trust to do it right."

"The Metro PD has plenty of very qualified detectives who could look into this for you and help determine whether a crime has been committed, Mr. Hamilton."

"You don't understand. It can't be any random detective. It can only be you."

"Are you going to tell me why?"

He took another series of deep breaths, appearing to summon the courage he needed to tell her why. "It's… He's… Well, my dad, you see… He's Troy Hamilton, the FBI director."

CHAPTER TWO

HOLY BOMBSHELL, BATMAN! Sam's mind raced with implications and scenarios and flat-out disbelief. "You can't honestly believe that your father, one of the top law enforcement officials in the country, *kidnapped* a child thirty years ago."

"I wouldn't put it past him," Josh said.

"He's one of the most respected men in our business. He's revered."

"Believe me, I know all about how *revered* he is. I hear about it on a regular basis." He looked at her beseechingly. "You have to help me. I don't know who else to turn to. Besides some of the people who work for my father, I don't know any other cops, and you're the best. And...I'm scared." The last two words were said on a faint whisper.

Sam wanted nothing to do with the snake pit this case could turn out to be, but the detective in her was far too intrigued to walk away. "How'd you get here?"

"I took the Metro."

She took a look around to see if anyone was watching, but the parking lot was deserted, and the usual band of reporters that stalked the MPD were taking the day off. They tended to do that when it was freezing. "Come with me." She led him to the tricked-out black BMW her husband had recently given her and gestured for Josh to get in the passenger side.

Though she had no idea what she planned to do with him or the information he'd dropped in her lap, she couldn't walk away from what he'd told her. "Tell me more about this website where you saw the photo."

"It's a blog run by parents of missing children."

"How did you end up there?"

"I read a story about a baby who was kidnapped from a hospital in Tennessee the day after he was born and how his parents have never stopped looking for him. The thirtieth anniversary of the abduction is coming up, so they've gotten some regional publicity. There was a link in the story that led to the blog where the age-progression photo was."

"So the photo hasn't been picked up by the media?"

"Not that I could tell, but I was too freaked out by what I was seeing to dig deeper, especially since my thirtieth birthday is next week. I told my boss I had an emergency. I left the office and came right to you."

"Why me?"

"Are you *serious*? After what you did at the inauguration, the whole country knows what an amazing cop you are. Who else would I go to with something like this?"

Sam winced at the reference to her crowd surfing stunt during the inaugural parade. She wished people would forget about that and move on, but the media attention on her and Nick had been even more relentless than usual since the inauguration and since their interview last week with one of the network morning shows. They'd hoped the interview would diffuse the interest, but that had backfired. Andrea, her White House communications director, had been inundated with hundreds of new interview requests for Sam, all of which she'd declined. The last thing she needed was *more* attention focused on her.

"You realize that accusing the FBI director of a capital felony is not something you do without stacks of proof that he was involved."

"That's where you come in. I need proof, and I need it fast before that picture gets picked up by the wires or social media and flung around the country. I need proof before he knows that *I* know."

Sam had to agree that time was of the essence before this thing blew up into a shitstorm of epic proportions. With that in mind, she started the car, pulled out of the MPD parking lot and into weekday afternoon traffic that clogged the District on the way toward Capitol Hill.

"Where are we going?"

"My house."

She glanced over at him and saw his eyes get big. "For real?"

"Yes, for real." She paused before she continued. "Look, if you want me to dig into this, I have to do it at home. I'm serving out a suspension for punching another officer."

"Whoa."

"As you can imagine, I'd prefer that not be all over the news in light of who my husband is, and I've gotta stay below the radar on this or my bosses will be all over me."

"No one will hear it from me."

After a slow crawl across the District, Sam pulled up to the Secret Service checkpoint on Ninth Street. Normally they waved her through, but she had to stop to clear her guest. "They'll need to see your ID."

Josh pulled his license from his wallet and handed it to her.

She gave it to the agent, who took a close look before returning it to her. "Thank you, ma'am. Have a nice day."

"You too."

"What's that like?" Josh asked. "Being surrounded by Secret Service all the time?"

"About as much fun as you'd expect it to be."

"Why don't you have a detail?"

"Because I don't need one. I can take care of myself." Thankfully, he didn't mention the recent siege in Marissa Springer's basement as an example of her inability to take care of herself. Sam liked to think that was a onetime lapse in judgment, never to be repeated.

Outside their home, her husband's motorcade lined the street. What was he doing home so early?

She parked in her assigned spot—everyone who lived on Ninth Street now had assigned parking spaces—and headed up the ramp that led to their home.

"Why do you have a ramp?" Josh asked.

"My dad's a quadriplegic. He lives down the street. My husband installed the ramp so he can visit."

"Oh, that's cool. Sorry about your dad, though."

"Thanks."

Nick's lead agent, John Brantley Jr., met her at the door. "Lieutenant."

"Brant. What's he doing home so early?"

"The vice president isn't feeling well."

"Say what?"

He gave her a "you heard me" look that nearly made her laugh, except she was too concerned about Nick to laugh. Her invincible husband didn't get sick the way other mortals did. In all the time they'd been together, she'd never known him to have so much as a cold.

"What's wrong with him?"

"He didn't say, and I didn't ask."

She used her thumb to point to her guest. "This is Josh—he's with me."

"Yes, ma'am."

She hated the way the agents insisted on calling her *ma'am*, as if she were seventy years old or something, but she'd chosen not to fight that battle. She wanted to say, *if you can call me* ma'am *why can't you call me* Sam? Close enough, wasn't it? But Nick had asked her not to make an issue of it, so she didn't. But she wanted to.

"Have a seat." She directed Josh to the sofa while she tossed her coat over the back of it. "I'll be right back."

"Okay."

Sam dashed upstairs to their bedroom, anxious to see what was wrong with Nick, who'd been fine earlier. She found him in bed, curled into the fetal position, and was instantly concerned. Leaning over the bed, she pressed a kiss to his forehead, which was on fire. "Babe."

"Mmm."

"Hey, what's wrong?"

"Don't know. Was fine and then I wasn't."

"You're burning up. Did you take something?"

"Couldn't. Stomach."

"I'm calling Harry."

"No, I'm fine."

"You're not fine, and I'm calling Harry."

He mumbled something that sounded like "don't bother him," but to hell with that. She was bothering him. Withdrawing her cell phone from her pocket, she found the number for one of their closest friends, who happened to be a doctor, and made the call.

"Madame Vice President," Harry said. "To what do I owe the honor?"

"Nick is sick. Can you come over?"

"Sick with what?"

"I don't know. He said it came on out of nowhere, and now he's burning up and says his stomach hurts too bad to take anything."

"Sounds like the flu. Keep your distance."

"Way too late for that warning." Sam winced when she thought of the sex they'd had last night and again this morning. Not getting too close to her husband was usually the last thing she wanted to do.

"Figures with you two," Harry said with a huff of laughter. "I'll be there as soon as I can. Can you clear me through security?"

"Yeah, I'll let them know."

"Try not to worry. He's an ox. He'll be fine."

Sam usually took Harry's assurances to heart, but she was worried. She'd never seen Nick this way and had no idea what to do to make him feel better. She hated feeling powerless. Then she remembered Josh was downstairs waiting for her to figure out what to do about his suspicions.

So much for a nice, peaceful few days "off."

Sam ran her fingers through Nick's hair, which was sweaty from the fever. "Babe, I have to go downstairs and take care of something. I'll be right back up, okay?"

He had gone back to sleep and didn't respond.

Sam bent over to kiss his cheek, trying not to notice that he already felt hotter than he had a few minutes ago. She ran back downstairs to where Josh was waiting right where she'd left him. His leg bounced as he bit his nails.

"Sorry about that."

"No problem."

Their assistant, Shelby Faircloth, came into the room

from the kitchen, carrying a cup of tea and holding her iPad under her arm.

"Hey, Sam, what're you doing home? And why is Nick here?"

"He's sick, and I'm off for four days," she said with a meaningful glance.

"Ahh, gotcha." Shelby knew Sam was due to hear the results of the IAB hearing today.

"Could I borrow your iPad for a minute?" Sam asked. "Oh, and this is Josh. I'm helping him out with something. Josh, Shelby, our assistant."

"Nice to meet you, Josh." Shelby punched in her code and handed the iPad to Sam. "What's going on?"

Without telling Shelby about Josh's connection to Director Hamilton, Sam told her about the photo Josh had found on the Internet.

"Oh my," Shelby said, dropping into a chair.

Sam gave the iPad to Josh. "Show me the site where you found the photo."

He did some typing and poking at the screen until he landed on the site. "Here."

Sam took it from him and scanned the text that accompanied the photo. A newborn male by the name of Taylor Rollings had gone missing from a maternity ward in Franklin, Tennessee, located twenty miles outside of Nashville in Williamson County. According to the article, the baby's kidnapping had been the lead story for weeks in the *Williamson Herald* and had been picked up by papers and TV news channels around the state.

His parents—Chauncey, a farmer, and Micki, a homemaker—were now in their sixties but had never given up hope of finding their missing son.

"He was taken right out of his bassinet while I was

sleeping," Micki said in the article, "and we've never seen him again." The reporter noted that Micki still weeps when she speaks of the son who disappeared on a cold winter night three decades ago. "I'll never stop looking for him. As long as I have a breath left in me, I'll look for him."

Touched by Micki's sorrow, Sam skimmed the rest of the article, planning to read everything she could find on the case later. "If you really think you're the missing son of this family, we could reach out to local law enforcement in Williamson County."

"What would happen then?"

"They'd probably request DNA and run it against Mr. Rollings to see if it's a match. That might be a good place to start."

"But what if it doesn't match? They've been through so much. I'd hate to get their hopes up."

"That's a very real concern and one you'll need to weigh carefully if you're determined to go through with this."

"What would you do?"

Sam tried to put herself in his place. "I'd want to know, but that's my nature. I always want to know everything. I guess that's why I'm good at my job. I'm not satisfied until I know the truth."

"I don't know what to do. You saw what they said about Taylor's mom, how she still cries when she talks about him thirty years later. What it if turns out not to be true, and I get their hopes up?"

"What if it turns out to *be* true? What if you're their missing son? Think about the peace and comfort you could bring them."

He dropped his head into his hands and sighed.

"May I ask a question?" Shelby said.

Josh raised his head to nod.

"What's your gut telling you? I'm a big believer in trusting my gut."

"Me too," Sam said.

"There's something to this," Josh said. "I know there is. I don't know if I'm this missing kid, Taylor, or not, but when I saw the picture? I felt like I'd been struck by lightning."

"You should listen to that feeling," Shelby said.

"I agree," Sam said. "Maybe there's a way we can test the DNA without getting the parents involved until we know there's a match." She flipped open her phone and scrolled through her contacts to find Dr. Lindsey Mc-Namara's number.

"Hey, Sam," Lindsey said. "Heard you were off for a few days."

"Is that how it's being played?"

"Well, actually I heard you were suspended for punching Ramsey."

"I still say he had it coming."

"You won't hear any argument from me. So what's up?"

"I need an off-the-books favor. I have a friend who needs a DNA test done. Do you think you could come by my house and take care of that for him?"

"Um, sure. I'm leaving for lunch shortly. Could I do it then?"

"That'd be perfect. And if you could keep this between us, I'd appreciate it."

"Of course. No problem."

"I'll clear you through security."

"See you soon."

"Hey, Brant," Sam said when she ended the call with Lindsey. "Would you please let them know outside that Drs. Harry Flynn and Lindsey McNamara will be coming over shortly?"

"Sure, thing, Mrs. Cappuano. No problem."

"Thanks."

"Who was that you called?" Josh asked.

"The District's Chief Medical Examiner, Dr. Lindsey McNamara. She's a friend and a colleague. I trust her to be discreet."

"I thought medical examiners worked on dead people."

"Usually they do, but she's also a medical doctor and handles DNA testing for us." She glanced at the stairs. "I need to check on my husband. He's not feeling well. I'll be right back down."

Sam went upstairs to the bedroom, where Nick was exactly where she'd left him. She placed her head on his face and was stunned by how hot he felt. Running back downstairs, she called Harry again and got his voicemail. "Harry, it's Sam again. He's scary hot. I'm worried. Let me know if you think I should take him to the ER."

Sam's phone rang, and she pounced on it, hoping it was Harry. "Mrs. Cappuano, this is Mrs. Perry at Eliot-Hine. The school nurse asked me to call to let you know Scotty's not feeling well. He has a fever of one hundred point two. Is it okay if we send him home with his detail?"

Sam's heart sank at the news that Scotty was sick too. While she'd rather pick him up herself, the agents could get him home faster. "Yes, please. Send him home."

CHAPTER THREE

SCOTTY NARROWLY MISSED throwing up on Sam when she met him on the sidewalk in front of the house. Fortunately, she saw what was happening and jumped out of the way in time for him to puke on the street rather than on her. She patted his back and took tissues from Darcy, one of his agents, to wipe his mouth when he was done.

"Sorry," he muttered. His face was so pale he barely resembled her robustly healthy son.

"Don't be sorry. You can't help it, buddy. You okay for now?"

"I think so."

Sam wrapped her arm around him to lead him inside. "How long have you felt lousy?"

"About an hour. I was fine and then my head was spinning and my ears were buzzing. Then my stomach started hurting, and I felt really hot."

"Whatever it is, your dad has it too, and Harry's on his way."

Scotty closed his eyes and leaned his head against her. "Okay."

"Oh my goodness," Shelby said when Sam brought him inside.

"You need to get out of here while the getting is still good," Sam said. "Whatever they've got is the last thing you need."

"I can't leave you to deal with this by yourself."

"Yes, you can. *Go*, Tinker Bell. That's an order."

"If you're sure," Shelby said tearfully. Everything made her cry these days.

"I'm very sure this is no place for a pregnant woman."

"All right, I'm going. I'll check in after a while."

In a low voice only Shelby could hear, Sam added, "Please don't say anything to *anyone*, even Avery, about what Josh told you." Sam wanted to say *especially* Avery, but she showed some restraint. The last thing she needed was Shelby's FBI agent fiancé catching wind of possible accusations against his boss. Shelby hadn't put Hamilton plus Hamilton together to get Troy Hamilton, but Avery was apt to.

"I won't. I promise."

"Um, should I go too?" Josh asked, eyeing Scotty warily.

"No, you stay. I'll be back down as soon as I can." With her arm still around Scotty's shoulders, she guided him to the stairs. "Come on, pal. You gotta help me out here."

"Sorry." He climbed the stairs in slow steps. By the time they reached the top, he'd broken into a sweat.

Sam wrangled him into his room, helped him out of his coat and sweater. "Do you want to do the jeans?"

"You can," he said in the smallest voice she'd ever heard from him.

That her thirteen-year-old wanted help with his pants said a lot about how sick he really was. A pang of fear struck her heart. Where the hell was Harry?

She got Scotty out of the jeans and into a pair of flannel pajama pants that had the Batman logo all over them. He was asleep before she finished dressing him.

Sam pulled the comforter up and over him, tucking him in. She'd no sooner gotten him settled when she heard retching noises from her own room. She ran for the hallway.

"Is he okay?" Darcy asked from her post outside Scotty's door.

"I don't know. Doc is on his way."

Sam went in to help Nick, who'd fortunately made it to the bathroom. Wetting a washcloth, she bathed his face and cradled his head against her chest between bouts of vomiting.

"Scotty has it too."

He moaned. "Haven't felt this bad ever."

"I'm scared for you guys."

He wrapped an arm around her, thinking of her first as he always did, even when he felt like hell. "Don't be. Just the flu or something."

It was the "or something" that scared the crap out of her.

"What happened at the hearing?" he asked.

"Suspended for four days, but don't worry about that now. It's no biggie."

"Yes, it is. You're not upset?"

"Nah. This too shall pass. I'm not sorry I slugged him. He had it coming."

"He certainly did."

"You ready to go back to bed?"

"So ready."

It took both of them to get him up off the bathroom floor and back into bed. Sam tucked him in and sat next to him, stroking his hair and thinking about what to do with Josh.

With Nick asleep again, she crept out of the room and placed a call to Freddie.

"Hey, did you talk to Gonzo?" he asked.

"Jesus, I totally forgot. You won't believe what's been going on since I left HQ earlier." She brought him up to speed on the situation with Josh Hamilton.

"Holy cow," he said softly. "Director Hamilton's son is accusing him of being a *kidnapper*?"

"We don't know anything yet, other than Josh Hamilton closely resembles the age-progression photo the family released to mark the thirtieth anniversary of the kidnapping, and his thirtieth birthday is coming up. That's *all* we know. Lindsey is coming to take a swab, and I'll ask the lab to rush it. I'm going to reach out to the Williamson County people to let them know we might have a lead for them. Once we have the DNA, we'll send it to Williamson County to see if it's a match to the missing baby's parents."

"What if it is?"

"One thing at a time."

"What can I do?"

"It's kind of a big thing, but I need someone on Josh until we know what we're dealing with. I'm sure you have plans this weekend—"

"Actually, Elin is going wedding dress shopping with her friends for the weekend, so I'm on my own."

"How do you feel about hunkering down in a hotel with him until we know more?"

"I'd much rather hunker down in a hotel with Elin, but since that's not happening this weekend, I can do it."

"Are you sure? I'm technically not allowed to ask you to do anything, and I'm not sure how the OT will work. I'll clean it up later with Malone."

"Don't sweat it. It all comes out in the wash."

"In case I forget to tell you, you're the best."

"Yeah, yeah, so you say until you get mad with me and I'm not the best anymore."

"When was the last time I was mad with you?"

"Um, when I tuned up Elliott?" he asked of the man who'd assaulted his fiancée.

"That was a very specific instance of you doing something stupid."

"Sort of like you punching Ramsey?"

"Just like," she said with a laugh. "Touché."

"Where's Josh now?"

"My living room."

"Seriously? You brought him *home* with you?"

"Where else was I supposed to take him? HQ is off limits to me at the moment, and I wanted him somewhere that no one could get to him. This place is like Fort Knox these days, so where better?"

"I'll come get him."

"Enter at your own risk. Nick and Scotty are down hard with something that could be the flu but more closely resembles the bubonic plague."

"Ah, damn, that's too bad."

"Puts a damper on my plans for a restful break," she said as she looked in on Scotty and then Nick. Both were sleeping peacefully—for the moment.

The doorbell rang, and Sam headed for the stairs, praying it was Harry. "I gotta go. I'll see you when you get here."

"I'll be there within the hour."

"Thanks again."

"No problem."

It was a huge problem and an even bigger imposition,

but he wouldn't say so, and that made him the best partner she'd ever had. He did whatever she asked of him, no matter how outrageous the request.

She reached the living room as Brant ushered Dr. Harry Flynn into the house. "Thank God you're here. My boys are sick as dogs."

The handsome, dark-haired doctor kissed her cheek. "Boys plural?"

"Scotty came home with the same thing Nick has. They're both scary sick."

"Dr. Harry's on the job. Lead the way."

"Be right back," Sam said to Josh as she took Harry upstairs, first to Scotty, who hadn't budged since she tucked him in.

Harry took his temperature with a thingie he swiped over the boy's forehead. "One-oh-three. That's one heck of a fever. Did he mention any symptoms other than the vomiting?"

"He could barely hold himself up, let alone talk."

"And he was fine this morning?"

"They both were—and then they weren't."

"It's going around. We've seen it in the office."

Sam felt slightly better to hear her guys hadn't been taken down by something random.

"It's usually a miserable day or two before they start to rebound." He finished examining Scotty. "Let me take a quick look at Nick."

"Right this way."

Nick woke up while Harry was taking his temperature. "What're you doing in my bedroom?"

"I came to seduce your wife since you're not capable at the moment."

Nick groaned and attempted a smile. "Hands off. She's all mine."

"One-oh-two," Harry said, reading from the LCD. "How did it come on and what're your symptoms?"

"I was in a meeting and my head started to buzz and my stomach started to hurt and within five minutes, I felt like I was going to pass out. Fortunately, Melinda saw it happen and was all over it. She and Brant got me out of there before I could puke in the White House."

"Did she have her hands on you?" Sam asked of the blonde bombshell agent she called Secret Service Barbie.

"Relax. I didn't feel a thing other than the need to puke."

"I love how she's jealous even when you're sick as hell," Harry said with a laugh.

"That's my girl," Nick said, his eyes closing. "True blue." His hand found hers, and he linked their fingers.

No matter what the circumstances, he always knew how to handle her, and Sam didn't mind being handled as long as he was the one doing it.

"I don't think either of them needs more than rest and fluids. Unfortunately, it's got to run its course. If they get any worse, don't hesitate to call 911 and get them to the hospital."

"That's it? That's all we can do?"

"For now. I'll be checking in with you, and we'll keep tabs on how they're doing. Try not to worry. I know it's hard to see them so sick, but you should see a big improvement by tomorrow. The most important thing is keeping them hydrated. Push the fluids."

"All right. If you're sure."

He kissed her forehead. "I'm a phone call away if you need me. I promise they're going to be fine."

For the first time since she'd seen Nick looking like death warmed over, Sam relaxed ever so slightly. She wouldn't completely relax, however, until they were both back to normal.

After she and Harry checked once more on their sleeping patients, she walked him downstairs and gave him a hug at the door. "Thanks for coming."

"Anytime. Don't hesitate to call me if they get any worse, okay?"

"You'll be the first to know."

He passed Lindsey McNamara on the ramp, and they exchanged a few words before Brant admitted Lindsey.

"Is it safe to come in?" Lindsey asked.

"Enter at your own risk," Sam said. "We're down hard with the flu."

"Yikes."

"At least my suspension is well-timed. I'm needed here for the next few days."

"Silver lining," Lindsey said with a smile. She glanced at Josh, who sat on the sofa, his leg still bouncing nervously. "Are you going to tell me what this is about?"

"I can't. Not yet anyway. But suffice to say it's a matter of paternity, and if it turns out to be something, it's gonna be huge."

"Say no more."

Sam introduced her to Josh, and Lindsey explained the process of obtaining a cheek swab to test his DNA.

"How long will it take to get results?" he asked.

"I'll put a rush on it, but it could be four or five days."

"How will you know if someone is a match to my DNA?"

Lindsey glanced at Sam before she replied. "The basic DNA fingerprint or profile that we use for law enforcement or human identity purposes is called the nuclear or autosomal STR profile. STR means short tandem repeat, which describes repeating segments of DNA code at particular locations on the human genome."

Josh's eyes glazed over as Lindsey explained the technicalities.

"We'll be looking for a match to your biological father," she said when she seemed to realize she'd lost him. "The Y chromosome is passed down from father to son. The Y-STR profile for a father and a son should exactly match, except in rare cases of mutation. So this wouldn't work for identifying a daughter, because a girl wouldn't have the Y chromosome. The lab will rely upon a combination of information from autosomal STRs and the Y-STRs to make a determination of father/son. You see?"

Judging by his baffled expression, he didn't see. He didn't see at all. But he said, "I think so. Thank you for explaining."

"No problem."

"Thanks so much for coming, Lindsey." Sam walked her to the door. "Let me know the second you have anything."

"You know I will. Even with a rush it'll be a few days." Lindsey glanced at Brant guarding the door and lowered her voice. "I don't know what you're up to here, Sam, but you need to be careful. I heard Forrester is seriously considering assault charges."

"So I've been told. And don't worry. I'm being careful. This isn't an official MPD case. He asked me for a favor. That's all it is."

"You've involved me, which involves the department."

"No one knows that but you and me."

"Be careful."

"I hear you."

"I'll get back to you as soon as I have anything."

"Thanks again, Lindsey."

Sam returned to the sofa and sat next to Josh. "So here's what I'm thinking. I'm going to reach out to law enforcement in Williamson County as a professional courtesy. I'll tell them what I know so far and that we've taken DNA. I'll strongly suggest they refrain from contacting the family until we know for sure there's a match. That way if you're not a match, we haven't raised their hopes for no reason."

"What do I do in the meantime?"

"We're going to put you in a hotel with police protection until we know what we're dealing with."

"Is that really necessary?"

"If I didn't think it was, I'd never ask you to do it." Sam chose her words wisely. "If this turns out to be true, you're sitting on a powder keg because of who raised you. If he was complicit in this, it'll be the biggest BFD in the history of BFDs. You got me?"

"Yeah." Arms on knees, he dropped his head and sighed. When he looked up at her, she saw his anguish. "You don't really think he'd harm me or anything, do you?"

"If you'd asked me this morning if Director Hamilton had possibly raised a child kidnapped from another family, I would've said no way. And I remain ninety-nine percent skeptical that'll turn out to be true. But if the one percent pans out…I have no idea what'll happen, and I want to ensure your safety."

He ran his fingers through his hair repeatedly.

"The choice is definitely yours, Josh. If you don't want to be under police protection, you don't have to be. But if I were in your shoes, I wouldn't take any chances, especially since it's only a matter of time before that photo goes viral."

"You really think that'll happen?"

"People are always interested in missing kids."

"I wish I hadn't seen it."

Sam leaned in to put her hand on his arm. "If it turns out to be true, will you still feel that way?"

"I don't know how to feel about any of this. Before I saw that picture, it never occurred to me that something like this was even possible. Now… Well, now I'm wondering if my whole life has been a lie. Did they just pretend to care about me when they were lying to me the whole time?"

"You'll know soon enough, and until then, I recommend you let us keep you safe."

"You and who else?"

"My partner, Detective Freddie Cruz. I trust him implicitly. You'll be in very good hands with him, and as soon as we have the DNA results, we'll get you some answers."

"Fine. Okay. I'll go with your partner."

"I think that's the wisest choice, especially since this place is overrun with the flu."

"And you'll let me know what's going on?"

"I'll be in touch with you the second we have anything concrete. I promise."

With his face set in a grim expression, he nodded, seeming pacified for now. Sam entered his phone number into her contacts and gave him her number in case he needed her for anything. Freddie arrived a short time later, and Sam introduced him to Josh.

Josh shook his hand. "Nice to meet you. I guess we're going to be roommates for the next few days."

"Looks that way," Freddie said. "You like the Skins?"

"Of course I do. Born and raised right here in D.C."

"It's Cowboys weekend, so at least we have something fun to watch."

"I'll spring for the beer." Sam handed her credit card to Freddie. "Put the room on that too."

"Your personal card? Will they let me do that?"

"Have them call me if you need to."

"I could use my department card."

She shook her head. "I'm keeping this separate for the time being. I'll work out the expense side of it later."

"You're the boss."

"Not right now, I'm not. Check in with me later."

"Will do."

CHAPTER FOUR

AFTER THEY LEFT, Sam went upstairs to look in on Scotty and Nick. They were both sleeping soundly, so she went downstairs to get something to eat while she could. Shelby had left a big salad and a pot of meatballs on the stove, so Sam had some of both along with a glass of water when she'd much rather have had a diet cola.

While she ate, she picked over the details of the case Josh had dropped into her lap. Though she probably should've *technically* declined to help him in light of her suspension, there were no rules she knew of that dictated personal favors outside of work. And technically, it wasn't even an actual case, so she wasn't violating the terms of her suspension.

Calling Lindsey might've crossed the line, but Lindsey's connections with the lab would ensure a speedier turnaround than they would've gotten from an outside doctor. With the possibility of Director Hamilton's involvement or culpability, she needed to do things by the book. At some point, the chain of custody on the DNA might matter, and who would care then that Sam had technically been suspended when she requested the swab?

You're justifying yourself, baby girl. Sam smiled at the sound of Skip Holland's voice in her head. Thinking of him made her want to talk to him, so she called down the street to see what he was up to.

"Hi, honey," her stepmother said. "How're you?"

"We've been struck by the flu over here. First Nick, then Scotty."

"Oh no, are they okay?"

"They're asleep for the moment, but they've both thrown up."

"Poor guys. I'll make some soup for when they feel up to eating again."

"I'm sure they'd appreciate that it came from you rather than me."

Celia laughed. "Probably."

"Is Dad up for a chat?"

"He sure is. Let me get him for you."

"What happened at the hearing?" Skip asked.

"Hello to you too."

"Spill it."

Sam smiled at his sauciness. She expected nothing less from him. "Suspended for four days and a thousand-dollar donation to the widows and kids."

"That ain't bad, all things considered."

"I guess. I hear Forrester is considering assault charges, but I'm not worrying about that until it happens."

"You should worry. He's got a valid case, and you know it."

"Maybe so, but I'd do it again. And don't tell me I'm better than him and should've risen above it. I heard you the other ninety times you've said that."

"It's true."

"I've got bigger fish to fry with both my guys down with the flu."

"Aw, crap, that's too bad. Wish I could come help you take care of them."

"You're far better off over there away from the germ pit. I sent Shelby home to get her out of here."

"Probably for the best in her condition."

"So I caught an interesting new case today. Or a potential case."

"How's that possible when you're suspended?"

Sam filled him in on Josh Hamilton's story and his connection to Director Hamilton.

Skip's low whistle came through the phone loud and clear. "Are you *shitting* me?"

"Would I shit you, Skippy?"

"*Holy*... Sam, you gotta be *so* careful here—you know that, right?"

"Yes, Dad, I know that."

"What's your plan?"

"First step was getting the DNA. Next I'm going to call Williamson County and give them a heads-up that we have a guy who closely resembles the composite. We'll go from there."

"God, those poor people. Thirty years wondering where their kid is."

"I know. It's unimaginable. You think it's possible Director Hamilton could've been part of something like this?"

"Shit, I don't know. I only know what I've read about him, but he has a good reputation in law enforcement circles, as you know."

"Yeah, Avery thinks the world of him."

"I can't even begin to get my head around the implications of what this guy is saying."

"Neither can I. But the picture... The resemblance is uncanny."

"There's a whole lot of speculation involved in the

production of those age-progression photos. Just remember that."

"I'm operating on the presumption that Josh Hamilton is not Taylor Rollings until I have proof otherwise."

"Good plan, but you also need a plan for what you're going to do if he *is* Taylor Rollings."

"What would you do with that info?"

"I'd go directly to Farnsworth. Don't pass Go, don't collect two hundred dollars. Don't do *anything* but go right to him."

"Right. I agree. That's what I'll do."

"This might be the craziest thing I've ever heard, and I've heard a lot of crazy shit in my life."

"I know—me too. Well, I'd better go make that call to Tennessee."

"Keep me posted, baby girl, and be careful not to get yourself into another pot of hot water with the department over this."

"I do so love a good hot bath."

"Sam."

"Yes, sir. I hear you. I'll be careful."

"Let me know how Nick and Scotty are later."

"You got it. See ya, Skippy."

"Bye, baby."

Before she made the phone call to Tennessee, Sam went upstairs to look in on Scotty, resting her hand on his forehead, which was still burning hot.

He opened his eyes. "Hey."

"How're you feeling, honey?"

His eyes went wide all of a sudden, and Sam wondered if he was going to be sick again. "What is it?"

"I, um, that's what my mom—my first mom—used to call me."

"Oh, sorry. I shouldn't have—"

"No, it's fine." He forced a weak smile. "I like it."

Her heart had never actually *ached* with love the way it regularly did for this sweet boy. She returned his smile and brushed the hair back from his forehead. "You need anything?"

"Some water maybe."

"I'll be right back." She went downstairs and brought two glasses of ice water back up. Leaving Nick's on Scotty's bedside table, she helped her son sit up and take some sips.

"Was Harry here, or did I dream that?"

"He was here, and he said that despite how bad you feel, you're going to live."

"That's good."

Sam kissed his feverish cheek. "That's very good."

"How's Dad?"

"Out cold the last time I checked."

"I hope he's okay."

"He'll be fine, and so will you."

His eyes went wide all of a sudden. "TJ's party! It's *tomorrow* night. I have to go! *Everyone* is going."

Sam hated to disappoint him, especially after all the hoops they'd had to jump through with the Secret Service to make it possible for him to attend. "Let's see what tomorrow brings before we decide anything. You wouldn't want your friends to get sick if you go out too soon, would you?"

"No, but..." His chin quivered ever so slightly. "I *really* want to go."

"I know. Maybe you'll feel a thousand times better by tomorrow."

"I hope so."

"Me too. Now get some sleep, and call me if you need anything. I'll be close by."

"Okay, thanks."

Sam leaned over to kiss his cheek again before tucking the comforter in around his shoulders.

"You're a good mom," he said so softly she almost missed it.

Her heart skipped a beat. "Really?"

"Mmm-hmm. The best."

"You make it easy for me."

His eyes were closed, but his lips curved into a smile.

Taking the other glass of water with her, Sam left his door propped open so she could hear him if he called for her. She went into her room where Nick was exactly where she'd left him—curled up on his left side sound asleep. Other than their honeymoon, when they'd done nothing but eat, drink, sleep and have sex, she'd rarely seen him asleep at this hour of the day. It was unsettling to see her unstoppable husband felled by anything, let alone something as pedestrian as the flu.

At times, she'd wondered if he had superpowers that he kept secret from her. How else to explain the way he managed to get so much done while also taking excellent care of her and Scotty? Sam kissed his cheek, and even though she knew she shouldn't, she kissed his lips too.

"Mmm, not tonight, babe."

Sam laughed out loud.

His eyes popped open.

"I think that's the first time you've ever said no to me."

Clearing his throat, he said, "I take it back. I never say no to you."

"You're allowed to today. How you doing?"

"Never better."

"Now you're lying to me?"

"Don't want you to worry."

"Too late for that."

"How's the boy?"

"Worried about TJ's party."

Nick winced. "Ahh, crap. That's tomorrow, right?"

"Yep."

"What are the odds that we're going to be free of this plague by then?"

"Slim to none."

"He'll be so disappointed."

"We'll make it up to him—somehow."

"I've got to go make a call, and then I'll come back and tell you a story you won't believe."

"'K." His eyes were already closed, his breathing heavier, his muscles relaxing as he drifted back to sleep.

Sam went into the bedroom they now used as an office, since the Secret Service had commandeered their downstairs study. She fired up Nick's computer, then knocked a few of his rigidly organized files out of alignment, smiling at the thought of him discovering her handiwork when he felt better. She did a search for Williamson County law enforcement, clicking on the link to the Franklin, Tennessee police department.

The age-progression photo Josh had seen online and a paragraph about the photo being released on the thirtieth anniversary of Taylor's kidnapping appeared on the department's home page. The write-up ended with the phone number to call with information about the case.

Sam felt unusually nervous as she placed the call. Rarely did her work cause jitters, but everything about this situation was odd—from Josh happening upon the photo on a random website to the way he'd singled her out to investigate. And then there was his connection to Director Hamilton.

"Franklin Police."

"I'd like to speak to the detective in charge of the Taylor Rollings case, please."

"Who's calling?"

"Lieutenant Holland, Metro PD in Washington, D.C." Dead silence.

"As in the *vice president's wife*?"

"As in Lieutenant Holland, Metro PD."

"Ah, I got it. So you don't play the VP card, huh?"

This guy was lucky Sam wasn't his boss, or his ass would be grass and she'd be the lawn mower. "Could I please speak to the detective?"

"You sure can. Just hang on one second. And may I say it was an honor to speak to you?"

Since her head was about to explode with aggravation, she decided it would be wise to remain silent. The phone clicked to hold music that was even more annoying than the MPD's, and that was saying something.

"Detective Watson."

"This is Lieutenant Holland, Metro PD in Washington, D.C. Are you the detective in charge of the Taylor Rollings case?"

"I am."

"I may have something for you."

After a long pause, he said, "Define *something*."

"A possible match for the age-progression photo you circulated. I've had someone make contact who believes it's possible he may be the person you're looking for."

"Can you send me a picture?"

"Not yet. We've taken a DNA swab and will have a report for you in the next few days. If there's a match, we'll proceed from there. You'll understand that he's not interested in raising the hopes of the Rollings family without definitive proof."

"I do understand, and that's the last thing I want either, believe me. I appreciate the call and the heads-up. Is there anything else you can tell me about him?"

"Just one thing—his thirtieth birthday is next week, so the timing lines up. But if the DNA doesn't match, there'll be no point in discussing it any further."

"I'll be waiting to hear from you." He shared his email address and cell phone number. "If you'd give me a call when you send it, I'd appreciate it."

"I'll do that. Could I ask if there've been any other leads resulting from the photo?"

"Lots of calls, but nothing that's panned out. We're following up on everything the way we always do when this case gets new attention, usually around the anniversary of the abduction." He sounded exhausted and frustrated, which gave him tons of credibility with Sam. Most detectives she knew spent a vast majority of their careers exhausted or frustrated, often both.

"How long have you been on the case?"

"Fifteen years. The original detective literally worked himself into an early grave looking for Taylor. His wife left him, his kids stopped speaking to him and he turned to the bottle for comfort."

Sam felt for a guy she'd never met. Sometimes the job took everything you had to give and then asked for more. "And the parents…"

"Toughest people you'll ever meet. True salt-of-the-earth types. I don't know how they do it, but they never give up hope. They speak of Taylor in the present tense.

MARIE FORCE 47

Micki says that until she has proof to the contrary, she believes her son is alive."

"Wow."

"Yeah, they amaze me and everyone else who knows them."

"I need to warn you, if this guy turns out to be their son, it'll be the lead story on every TV station and in every newspaper in the country for the foreseeable future."

"Why? What the hell? Who is he?"

"It's more about who his father is."

"I'm not going to like this, am I?"

"None of us are."

CHAPTER FIVE

SAM SPENT MOST of Friday night and early Saturday morning running between her puking son and her puking husband. She was about to fall over from exhaustion when she crawled into bed next to Nick after changing the sheets on Scotty's bed for the second time.

She'd no sooner closed her eyes when her cell phone rang. That only happened at this hour when she was on call, so she was immediately concerned about her dad. "Hello."

"Sam."

She groaned loudly and then regretted it when Nick stirred. Rubbing his back to settle him, she said, "What do you want, Darren?"

"I heard you were suspended for assaulting a fellow officer, and Forrester is considering charges. I wanted to give you a chance to comment before I go with it."

How in the hell had a reporter from the *Washington Star* caught wind of her suspension? That was supposed to be an internal department matter, thus the term *internal affairs*.

"Sam?"

"No comment, other than to say if you run that I've been suspended when I haven't, that might be embarrassing for you."

"So you haven't been suspended?"

"I'll neither confirm nor deny. Now leave me alone. I'm sleeping." She slapped her phone closed and put it on the bedside table. If it weren't for her father's precarious health, she'd turn the thing off.

"What's that about?" Nick muttered.

"There's a very good possibility that the headline in the *Star* tomorrow will be 'Second Lady Suspended After Assaulting Fellow Officer, U.S. Attorney Forrester Considering Charges.'"

"He had it coming."

"And that, right there, is why I love you so much."

"Why? What'd I say?"

"You still say he had it coming even though it could turn into a firestorm for your team."

"They get paid to put out fires. What about your staff? Should you give them a heads-up?"

"Crap, you're right. Lilia shouldn't hear about it on the news. I keep forgetting I have a staff." Another thought occurred to her. "Ah damn, I never checked on Gonzo today."

"Today is now well into tomorrow, and you need some sleep. You can check on him later and call Lilia."

"He blew off his shift yesterday. Never does that."

Nick reached for her hand and gave it a squeeze. "He's grieving. It's going to take a while."

"Worried about him."

"I know, babe. Me too."

TOMMY GONZALES COULDN'T SLEEP. He couldn't eat. He couldn't breathe without pain rippling through his chest in agonizing waves. He couldn't play with his toddler son without breaking down in tears because his late partner would never experience the exquisite joy of fatherhood.

He couldn't bear the touch of his fiancée while knowing that Arnold would never drop to one knee and propose to the love of his life.

The only relief Gonzo got from the unrelenting pain was found in a bottle of whiskey. He and Jameson had become very close friends since the dreadful night in January when his partner had been gunned down.

If you shut the fuck up, I'll let you take the lead.

Those words would haunt him for the rest of his life. Of course, if he hadn't let Arnold take the lead that night, Gonzo would be dead. His son would be fatherless, and his fiancée bereft. The thought of those scenarios was only slightly less agonizing than the loss of Arnold had been. He didn't like to think of Alex or Christina grieving him, but he'd almost rather be dead himself than have to live with the way his partner had died.

The gurgling sound of blood in Arnold's throat gave Gonzo nightmares in the rare instances when he actually slept. In a career filled with things he'd much rather forget than remember, it was the single worst sound Gonzo had ever heard, the sound of life leaving his partner, one desperate gasp at a time.

He shuddered, thinking of it now and reached for the bottle that was never far from his grasp. The whiskey burned on the way down, his empty stomach protesting its arrival. Powering through the gut pain, he took another gulp, looking for the sweet oblivion he only found at the bottom of a bottle.

It was almost five now, and he had to work at seven. He'd missed his shift yesterday. That was a first. Under normal circumstances, he'd be freaking out about screwing up at work. Under these circumstances, he couldn't find the wherewithal to give a shit about his fucking nightmare of a job. He could no longer remember what he'd ever loved about it.

In what other career could you be gunned down on a sidewalk simply because you carry a badge? In what other career did you risk your life every day for people who didn't give a shit about you?

These days, cops were viewed as the enemy because of a few bad ones who couldn't control themselves. Did anyone other than his family and friends and colleagues in blue even care that a young man named Arnold John "AJ" Arnold had been gunned down on a sidewalk simply because he'd approached a suspect on a cold, dark night?

Life had gone on for everyone else. Six weeks later, it was like it never happened for the rest of the world. Despite his best efforts to carry on, to be brave and strong for the people who were counting on him at home and at work, Gonzo could still hear the echo of the gunshots, smell the blood, taste the fear and panic of knowing there was nothing he could do. He could still hear that god-awful gurgling noise.

Gonzo had about twenty—or maybe it was thirty—unanswered calls from the department shrink, reminding him he needed to make his next appointment. Like the last time Gonzo had seen him, Trulo would make him talk about it when that was the last freaking thing he wanted to do. How in the hell would that help anything? Let's tear the scab off the wound and poke a sharp stick in it because that'll surely make everything better. So he was avoiding Trulo and all the other do-gooders who wanted to "help." As if there was anything anyone could do.

"Tommy." Christina's soft voice jarred him. He hadn't

seen her coming. His reflexes weren't what they used to be if she could sneak up on him in the dark.

"What?"

"Are you coming to bed?"

"No." It wasn't her fault. None of this was her fault. He told himself that a thousand times a day as she hovered over him, her care and concern wearing on his already-frazzled nerves. It was hard to believe that only a few short weeks ago, they'd been talking about making time to get married. And now he wanted to tell her to leave him alone. He wished everyone would just *leave him the hell alone*. But they didn't. In addition to Christina, he had his family and colleagues around his neck too.

If Cruz called him one more time to "check in" he was going to tell him to fuck off. What did they *want* from him anyway?

"Will you please come to bed? You need to sleep."

"No, I don't need to sleep." Sleep brought nightmares, and the last fucking thing he wanted was to relive it—again. "I need to be alone." On the outer edges of his mind, in the place where the man he used to be lived, he knew he was making an extraordinary mess of the most precious relationship in his life. But he couldn't bring himself to care.

Christina knelt on the floor in front of him, her hands flat against his thighs. There'd been a time, not that long ago, when that would've been enough to fire him up. Now he felt nothing for her or his son or his family or his friends. He felt absolutely nothing but pain.

"You're scaring me, Tommy. You can't go on this way. You need help. You have to let us help you."

"I don't have to do anything. You don't know what you're talking about."

"I can't possibly know what you went through that night, but the Tommy I know and love—"

"Is dead. That guy died on a sidewalk right along with his partner. So if you don't like the new and improved Tommy, maybe you should cut your losses and get out."

Her face went slack with shock, tears flooding her eyes. "You don't mean that."

"Maybe I do."

"Tommy…"

"Don't make this harder than it has to be. We had a good thing, but it's over now."

"You… Alex…"

"Take him. Take him and just go. Leave me alone."

"I'm not leaving you, Tommy," she said as sobs shook her petite body.

Once upon a time, her tears would've moved him. "Then I'll go."

"No. You're not going, and neither am I. We're a family, and if you won't fight for our family then I will."

"Knock yourself out." He reached for the bottle.

She grabbed it from his hand, and it went flying, smashing into the glass coffee table and shattering it.

The sight of her surrounded by shards of glass cleared the fog in his brain, making way for a moment of clarity. "Don't move."

As tears continued to rain down her face, she whimpered.

Standing, he reached for her and lifted her up and off the floor.

Christina wrapped her arms around his neck and curled her legs around his hips. She trembled violently, her tears wetting his face.

"You're okay. I've got you." His heart beat fast and hard as fear sliced through the numbness.

"Please don't let me go, Tommy." Her chest heaved from the strength of her sobs. "I'd never survive it."

He tightened his hold on her, blinking rapidly to stop tears that suddenly couldn't be contained. His chest ached as the dam broke, flooding him with a barrage of emotions he was unequipped to handle. Fear and grief and love and despair... All of it poured forth as Christina clung to him. He'd never cried like this before. Not when his grandparents died or when he found out he had a son he didn't know about or when Arnold was killed right in front of him.

Something about the sight of Christina surrounded by broken glass had done what nothing else could. It had broken *him*. Leaning against a wall, he slid down, taking her with him, until they were on the floor. She never let go, holding him through the storm the way she had from the beginning.

He had no idea how long they were there before he found his voice. "I... I'm sorry. I shouldn't have said those things. I didn't mean—"

Cradling his face in her hands, she kissed him and wiped away his tears. "We need help, Tommy. We can't do this alone. *Please*. Before we lose us..."

He hesitated but only for a second. "Okay."

SAM SHOT OUT of bed, going from asleep to running in the blink of an eye when she heard Scotty cry out. Fearing another vomit-astrophe, she steeled herself as she turned the corner in his room and found him sitting up in bed, weeping.

"Buddy, what's wrong? Are you feeling sick again?"

She'd never seen him cry like this, as if his heart were breaking. Sam sat on the bed and wrapped her arms around him. The heat from his body radiated through the thin T-shirt he wore, but he didn't feel quite as hot as he had during the night.

"I still feel awful," he said between sobs. "I can't go to the party."

"I'm so sorry, and so is Dad. We know how disappointed you are." And she knew that under normal circumstances, Scotty would never cry over such a thing. "But Dad said last night—and it's true—there'll be lots and lots of chances to have fun with your friends and lots of other parties."

"I wanted to go to this one."

"I know." Desperate to find a way to comfort him, she settled him back on his pillow. "How about we have our own little party right here? We'll watch whatever movie you want and play video games."

His shoulders lifted ever so slightly.

She was no substitute for his friends, but she'd do whatever she could to fill the void. "You want to get up and try to eat something?"

He shook his head. "No, thanks. Not yet."

"Let me know when you're ready." She tucked him in and kissed his forehead.

"Thanks," he said, "for taking care of me and stuff."

"It's my pleasure."

"Sure," he said with the tiniest hint of a smile. "Cleaning up puke is a pleasure."

"Being your mom is a pleasure. The good, the bad and the ugly. I love it all."

"Something's wrong with you if you like the ugly."

"I hear that every day." She left him with a smile and

went back to her room, crawling in bed next to Nick, who hadn't stirred. When she placed a hand on his back, the heat of his body alarmed her. She felt his forehead and launched out of bed to find the thermometer Harry had left for her. Running it over his forehead, she gasped when it registered at 104.5. *Dear God!*

"Nick." She shook his shoulder. "Babe, wake up. You've got to take something for the fever." Kissing his cheek, she said, "Nick, wake up." He didn't respond, even when she shook him vigorously.

Frantic, Sam grabbed her phone from the bedside table and called Harry. "Nick is at 104.5, and he won't wake up," she said the second Harry answered.

"Call 911. Right now. I'll meet you at GW."

"I can't leave Scotty with only his detail!"

"Call Tracy to stay with him."

"Okay. I'll do that. Harry—"

"Make the call, Sam."

Her hands shook as she called 911 and requested an ambulance. In the hallway, she said to Darcy, "I called rescue for Nick. He's unresponsive."

"Oh my God! I'll let them know downstairs."

After nearly dropping the phone in her haste, Sam found Tracy's number and willed her sister to answer the phone. "Trace! I need you to come over here. Hurry. Nick and Scotty are sick, and I have to take Nick to GW—"

"What? Okay, I'm coming. I'll be there in a few minutes."

"You have to stay with Scotty." Her voice broke and tears flooded her eyes. "I can't wake him up, Trace. Nick. He won't wake up."

"I'll be right there."

Sam went to Nick and shook him again, looking for something, anything. "Please," she whispered. "Wake up."

But like before, he didn't move.

She laid her hand on his chest where the strong beat of his heart was the best thing she'd ever felt. Then she noted the rise and fall of his breathing. Those were good signs, weren't they?

It seemed to take hours for the paramedics to arrive when it was probably only minutes. Everything moved very quickly. They had him on an IV and strapped to a gurney in a matter of seconds and were whisking him out of the house, escorted by the Secret Service.

Sam was torn in two very distinct directions—go with Nick or stay with Scotty until Tracy arrived. She looked in on Scotty, who'd gone back to sleep. The fact that he was sleeping through this cemented her decision.

"My sister Tracy is coming to stay with him," Sam said to Darcy. "If he wakes up before she gets here, tell him I took his dad to see Harry. Don't say anything about ambulances or paramedics."

"Of course. I hope the vice president is okay."

"So do I."

Sam ran out of the house without a coat and bolted down the ramp to the back of the ambulance. The sight of Nick, unmoving and strapped to a gurney, his face ghostly pale, made Sam stagger under the weight of her fear. Thankfully, Brant took hold of her arm and helped her into the ambulance before she tripped and fell.

"Why won't he wake up?" she asked the paramedics when they were on their way to GW.

"We think he's severely dehydrated. We're pumping fluid into him, which ought to help."

Dehydrated. She could work with that.

"But he's going to be okay, right?"

"He should be."

Sam clung to those three little words on the rapid trip to the hospital, where he was taken straight into an exam room. One of the nurses put an arm around Sam's shoulders and guided her out of the room. "Let me find a place for you to wait where you won't be bothered, Mrs. Cappuano."

"I want to be with him."

"Give us a chance to get him stable, and we'll get you right in with him."

"He's not stable now?"

"We're still assessing his condition. It'll be a few minutes."

Harry came rushing in, and Sam had never been so happy to see anyone in her life.

"They're telling me I can't stay with him."

"I'll get you in there as soon as I can." He gave her a quick hug. "Go with Nancy. She'll get you settled somewhere to wait."

"Harry, please… *Please*."

"He's going to be fine. I promise."

Those were, without any doubt, among the best words she'd ever heard. While Brant and another member of Nick's detail stood watch outside the exam room, Sam let Nancy lead her to a private waiting room. She wanted to ask why the agents could stay but she couldn't, but she already knew the answer to that.

"Is there someone you could call to come sit with you?" Nancy asked.

The only person Sam wanted was Nick. "I, um, I could call my sister."

"Would you like me to do it for you?"

Angela would freak out if she got a call from a nurse at the GW Emergency Room. "Thank you, but I'll do it."

"Is there anything I can get you? Water, coffee?"

"A stiff drink?" Sam said with a small smile.

"Wish that was on the menu."

"I'm fine, thank you. Please let me know the second you hear anything."

"We will. I just want to say… All of us here, we think you and the vice president make for a beautiful couple, and we admire you both so much."

Sam blinked rapidly, overcome with emotion. "Thank you. That's very nice of you."

"He's young and strong and healthy. Have faith in all those things."

Sam nodded because she didn't trust herself to speak.

Nancy left her alone, and Sam took a moment to get herself together before she called Ang.

"Hey, what's up? I was going to call you later."

"Ang."

"What? What's wrong?"

"Can you come to the GW ER? Please? Nick is here, and he's really sick. I don't know what's wrong with him—"

"I'll be there. Hang tight."

"Thank you." Thank God for her sisters, Sam thought. They always came running when she needed them. Her phone dinged with a text from Tracy saying she was at Sam's house, and Scotty was still sleeping.

Let me know when you hear anything about Nick.

I will. Harry is with him now.

He's in very good hands.

Sam tried to take comfort in that, in knowing Harry cared about him as much as anyone did, anyone other than her, that is. No one cared more about Nick than she did. She couldn't sit still. She paced from one end of the small room to the other, worried about Nick, worried about Scotty waking up to Tracy rather than her. If anything happened to Nick…

That thought had her dropping into a chair because her legs were too wobbly to support her. If this was what he went through every time she walked out the door to go to work or got herself into a jam on the job, it was a wonder he could function.

Her phone rang and she took a call from Nick's dad. "Hi, Leo."

"Hey, Sam, I tried to reach Nick, but his phone goes right to voicemail. I know how busy he is, so I figured I'd call you about coming up for dinner this weekend."

"Oh, um, he's sick, Leo. He's got the flu. In fact, I'm at the GW ER with him right now. They think he's severely dehydrated."

"Oh no! I just talked to him yesterday."

"It came on him and Scotty out of nowhere."

"Should I come down?"

"I don't think you need to," she said with more confidence than she felt. "They said he's going to be fine, and I can keep you posted. No sense exposing you or Stacy and the kids to what they've got."

"If you're sure…"

"I'll tell him you called, and I'll text you."

"Tell him…" Leo hesitated, but only for a second. "Tell him I love him."

"I'll do that." She wiped tears from her eyes. Under normal circumstances, tears pissed her off. Today she couldn't care less about them.

Angela arrived twenty minutes after Sam called her. Wearing yoga pants and a sweatshirt without a coat, she rushed into Sam's outstretched arms.

"Thank you so much for coming."

"How is he?"

"I haven't heard anything since I talked to you. I'm losing my mind."

"So what happened?"

Sam relayed the story of how Nick and Scotty had come home sick the day before, and while Scotty seemed a tad bit better after a rough night, Nick was worse. "I couldn't get him to wake up, Ang. I've never been so scared in my life." Even when she'd been at Stahl's mercy in that basement, she hadn't been nearly as frightened as when she couldn't rouse Nick. Being scared for herself was a whole lot different than being scared for him.

CHAPTER SIX

TIME SLOWED TO a crawl. Sam experienced every minute as if it were an hour. Her heart ached with worry and fear and the agony of being separated from him when he needed her. If the roles had been reversed, he'd be raging at anyone who tried to keep him away from her. She headed to the door to start raging, and nearly ran into Harry.

"How is he?"

"He's conscious but badly dehydrated and a little confused due to the dehydration. We're pumping him full of fluid, and he should be much better in a couple of hours."

The flood of relief was so profound that Sam ended up in Harry's arms sobbing.

He held her until she got it all out.

"Sorry," she said, embarrassed by her meltdown.

"Don't be. I was pretty freaked out myself when you said he was unresponsive."

"Glad it wasn't just me."

"It definitely wasn't just you. You want to see him?"

"Yeah." The understatement of a lifetime.

"Come on." He gestured for Angela to join them as they walked through the ER to Nick's room, where Brant and one of the other agents, whose name escaped her at the moment, were standing watch.

"Good to hear he's doing better," Brant said.

Sam nodded in agreement. In the room, a nurse typed on a computer. Nick was asleep, and when she looked extra close, she saw a tad bit more color in his cheeks than he'd had earlier.

Her cell phone rang, but she ignored it to go to him, to run her hand over his face, to brush the hair back from his forehead so she could kiss him there. "How's his fever?" she asked the nurse.

"It was down to 102.5 the last time we checked it. He's getting something for that in the IV."

"Good, that's really good."

"He'll be fine," the nurse said. "It's just going to take a day or two."

Sam's phone rang again, and since Nick was sound asleep, she looked at the caller ID. Terry O'Connor. She took the call from Nick's chief of staff. "Hi, Terry."

"What's going on? I heard from the Secret Service that he's in the hospital."

Sam filled him in on what'd happened.

"Jesus. I was with him when it came on yesterday. Never seen anyone go down that hard or that fast. Scared the shit out of me and everyone else around here."

"Scared me too. I've never seen him with a cold, let alone something like this."

"The press is going crazy wanting to know what's wrong with him. What would you like me to tell them?"

"Do we have to say anything?"

"I'd recommend we give them a little something to stop the feeding frenzy. I saw one comment online that people are speculating he was poisoned."

Sam's stomach dropped. "For real?"

"Afraid so."

"Hang on a second."

To Harry, she said, "Terry wants to say something to the press about what's going on. How would you describe it?"

"A nasty bout of the flu."

Sam relayed the information to Terry and gave him the green light to tell the press the vice president had been hospitalized due to the flu.

"Got it," Terry said. "I'll take care of it. What else can I do? Anything for you or Scotty?"

"Scotty has it too, and my sister Tracy is with him. I think we're set, but I'll let you know later how he is."

"Please do. Tell him we're thinking of him."

"I will."

"I suppose I probably ought to clear his schedule for the next few days."

"Make it the next week."

"Okay, will do." He paused and then said, "Before I let you go, I should mention I talked to Christina, and she said Tommy isn't doing well at all. I thought you might like to know."

Sam closed her eyes and took a deep breath, ashamed to realize she'd forgotten all about Gonzo and getting in touch with him in the madness of the last twenty-four hours. "You're right. I do want to know. I'll reach out to him later today."

"Sounds good. Take care, Sam, and let me know how Nick is."

"I will." She stashed the phone in her pocket and took hold of Nick's overly warm hand, bending her head over his chest when the tears started up again.

Angela squeezed her shoulders.

"You don't have to stay, Ang," Sam said. "You must've had other plans today."

"I don't mind staying. Spence is with the kids, and they'll make him appreciate and worship me, so it's all good."

Sam wouldn't have thought she could laugh right then, but Angela proved her wrong. Then she was crying again, her head propped on Nick's hand. Her cell phone rang, and Angela took it from her to answer it. Sam heard her sister talking, but couldn't bother to care who she was talking to.

"Hey, Sam, Freddie really needs to talk to you. I told him where we are and what's going on. He said it's urgent."

Sam took a deep breath, wiped away her tears and stood to take the phone from her sister. "Hey, what's up?"

"Angela told me about Nick. I hope he's okay."

"He will be. What's going on?"

"Director Hamilton is calling Josh every fifteen minutes like clockwork."

"Since when?"

"Early this morning. Josh says he's called him more today than in the last five years combined."

"Shit, he's probably tracking the phone by now so he knows where Josh is." Sam's brain was so muddled with worries about Nick that it was hard to think about anything else. "Get him out of there right away. Move to another hotel outside the city and have him power down the phone. Tell him to let work know he's got an emergency to contend with and won't be in this week. Don't let him make any contact with the outside world until we say otherwise."

"What do I do with him when I have to go to work?"

"Leave him locked in the room and tell him he has to stay off the radar until we know what's going on. The fact that his father is looking for him has me thinking he knows about the photo. *If* they had anything to do with taking him, that photo will send them into a panic. If they panic, they may do something stupid that might involve him getting killed. You see where I'm going with this?"

"Yeah, I do, and I don't like it, Sam. This has the potential to blow up like a nuclear bomb in our faces, and frankly, after recent events, neither of us can afford that."

He was right. She knew he was right, but what was she supposed to do? As if she'd conjured him, she heard her father's voice in her head. *Go to Farnsworth. Go directly to Farnsworth.*

Sam blew out a deep breath. "Listen, if you don't want to be involved, I understand. Let me know where you stash him, and I'll take it from there."

"I didn't say I don't want to be involved. I merely mentioned the potential for nuclear-level fallout."

"I'll take it to Farnsworth and turn it over to the department."

"Um, before you do that, you should know that Josh told me last night that if anyone but you—and me by extension of you—is involved, he's going to disappear. He seems really agitated since his father started calling. So you might want to hold off on involving the department."

"Rock, meet hard place." Sam glanced at Nick, who was still sleeping. She rarely found herself at a loss for what to do in any given situation, but this was a tough one. She was torn between what she *should* do to look out for herself—and now her partner too—and what was best for Josh. "What do we do?"

"My better judgment is saying go to Farnsworth, but if Josh bolts, this could get really complicated, especially when it comes out that we had him in custody."

"Shit, fuck, damn, hell."

"What you said."

Sam was well aware that Freddie would take his lead from her, even if it meant venturing into murky gray area. "Get him settled somewhere else and then punch out of this situation. I'll take it from here." As she said the words, she didn't have a plan beyond getting through the next hour with Nick. She'd figure something out for Josh. She always did.

"I don't want to punch out. I'm in it for better or worse at this point. I'll do some digging and see if I can get anything useful from him."

"I can't protect you if this goes nuclear."

"I don't expect you to."

"If you're going to dig, dig carefully."

"Don't worry. I will. I'll let you know if I get anything, and I'll shoot you a text about where Josh is. Keep me posted about how Nick is doing?"

"Yeah, I will, and thanks."

"No problem."

Though he said it was no problem, this situation could turn into a huge problem for both of them unless they managed it carefully. But what was she supposed to do at this juncture? Go to her brass with the possibility that FBI Director Hamilton's son could or could not be a child kidnapped from a family in Tennessee thirty years ago? She was already on thin ice with the department. If she opened that can of worms only to find out it wasn't true, what then? And if Josh found out she'd taken his claims to the department, he'd bolt.

"What the hell is going on?" Angela asked when Sam had stashed the phone in her back pocket.

"A really weird new case."

"I thought you were suspended."

"Heard about that, huh?"

"Everyone knows. It was in the paper this morning."

"Ugh, goddamned Darren."

"It wasn't just him. It was all over the place—in the papers, on TV, talk radio."

"Great." Her phone rang and she removed it from her pocket to check the caller ID. Her White House chief of staff, Lilia Van Nostrand's name showed on the screen. Since Nick was still asleep, Sam took the call. "Hi, Lilia."

"I just heard about the vice president. Is he all right? Are you?"

"He's been felled by a nasty bout of the flu. I'm told he's going to be fine. My nerves are shot, but otherwise, I'm okay."

"Oh, thank goodness! I couldn't believe what they were saying on the news about him being transported by ambulance to GW."

"Jeez, nothing gets by the Washington press corps, huh?"

"No, and that's the other reason for my call."

"I heard my name is above the fold today."

"It is, and I'm wondering how you wish to handle it."

"Why do I have to handle it?"

"We're getting slammed with requests for statements, as is the vice president's office."

"I spoke to Terry a few minutes ago, and he didn't mention it."

"Probably because he's concerned for the vice president's health at the moment, as am I. We wouldn't want you to think our priorities lie anywhere other than with both of you."

"I understand, and I appreciate the fact that you're

being slammed. You could say that the second lady has no comment on the suspension, which is an internal MPD matter."

"How about the fact that U.S. Attorney Forrester is considering assault charges?"

"You can get a statement from him about that. If or when it happens, I'll have no choice but to deal with it. Until that time, it's speculation, and I don't comment on speculation."

"Can we say that in the statement?"

"Sure, knock yourselves out."

"I'll have Andrea put something together for you," Lilia said of Sam's communications director. "We'll run it by you before we release it."

"No need. I trust you guys to handle it."

"We'll take care of it, then. If you have a chance later, let me know how the vice president is doing—and how you're doing."

"I will. Thank you, Lilia."

"Anytime."

"I still can't believe you have a chief of staff at the White House," Angela said as Harry returned to the room to check on Nick.

"Can you imagine being her chief of staff?" Harry asked. "I need to meet this saint of a woman."

"Bite me," Sam said, though she was relieved he was making jokes. That must mean Nick's situation wasn't as dire as it had seemed for a while there.

"Who's she biting now?" Nick muttered.

CHAPTER SEVEN

SAM HAD NEVER been so relieved to hear him speak. She sat on the edge of the bed and ran her hand over his face. "Only you, babe."

"Better be only me." His eyes opened slowly, and his brows knitted as he took in the room. "What the hell?"

She glanced at Harry before she filled Nick in on where he was and why. "You wouldn't wake up. Scared the living hell out of me."

"And me," Harry said. "I was afraid she'd sue me for saying you'd be fine in a couple of days."

"Andy has agreed to take my case pro bono," Sam said, smiling at Nick.

"That traitor," Harry said of his and Nick's mutual friend.

"Scotty," Nick said in a low rumble.

"Is home with Tracy and doing better than you are."

"That's a relief. When can I get out of here?"

"Probably tomorrow or the next day," Harry said.

"Aw, come on," Nick said, groaning. "I feel a lot better. Let me go home."

"Dude, you were out cold an hour ago," Harry said. "You're not going anywhere."

Sam pointed a thumb at Harry. "What he said."

As if it was too much effort to keep them open, Nick closed his eyes. "Thought you guys were my friends."

Sam leaned forward to kiss him. "We're your best friends."

"You might want to cut out the kissing unless you want what he's got," Harry said.

"Too late to worry about that."

Nick's arms came around her, keeping her right where she wanted to be—close to him.

"They're hopeless," Harry said to Angela.

"They certainly are. We'll remind her of this when she's barfing her guts out in a couple of days."

"Worth it," Sam said.

Nick tightened his hold on her and for the first time since he wouldn't wake up earlier, she was able to take a deep breath. He was okay, and that was all that mattered.

HOURS LATER, NICK ordered Sam and Angela to go get something to eat. They'd talked to Scotty by FaceTime on Angela's phone so he could see that Nick was doing better and they could see that he was fine. Tracy had gotten him to eat some of the soup Celia sent over, and he'd even asked for ice cream.

Nick, on the other hand, wasn't interested in food of any kind yet. "You guys go grab something. I'm not going anywhere."

"Are you sure?" Sam messed with his blankets until she was happy with the way they covered him. They'd fielded another call from his dad, as well as Graham and Laine O'Connor. Nick's adopted parents were also concerned about him.

He put his hand over hers. "I'm sure."

"Come on," Angela said, tugging Sam's arm. "I'm starving."

She'd kept them entertained with the increasingly desperate texts she'd received from Spencer as the day progressed. The kids were making a man out of him, or so Angela said.

They went to the cafeteria where Sam forced herself to choke down a turkey club even though she didn't really want it. Angela said she'd be no good to anyone if she didn't take care of herself. In deference to the day from hell, Sam indulged in a rare diet cola. Desperate times called for desperate measures.

"Best thing I ever tasted," she said of the icy-cold soda.

"So I was going to call you today about something else."

"What's up?"

Angela dipped a French fry into ketchup and popped it into her mouth. "Mom's in town and she wants to see you."

Sam shook her head from the word *town* on. "Not now."

"I think you need to see her. She has some news you should hear from her."

"What kind of news?"

Angela shook her head. "It's not mine to tell."

"Seriously?"

"You know I would if I could."

Sam blew out a deep breath. "This is just what I need right now with all the other crap I've got going on."

"What was that thing with Freddie earlier?"

"Something for work that fell into my lap after I was suspended."

"Is it something that's going to get you into deeper shit than you're already in?"

"Perhaps, but it could be such a huge big deal that no one will care about my role in it."

"I know you've got a lot going on, but you need to see her. I wouldn't ask you to if it wasn't important."

"Does Tracy know about this too?"

"Yes."

"Great, so everyone knows but me."

"That's the way you wanted it when you cut Mom out of your life, Sam. We chose not to go that far. What do you want me to say?"

Her mother had left Skip for another man the day after Sam, their youngest child, graduated from high school. Sam had sided with her dad, and she'd do the same thing again if she had it to do over. Lately, however, especially after what'd happened with Stahl, she'd been thinking it might be time for a ceasefire with her mother. She'd yet to follow through on those thoughts, but Angela had presented her with a golden opportunity.

"How long is she in town?"

"The rest of the week."

"Set something up for a couple of days from now. Let me get my guys out of the woods first."

"I'll take care of it and let you know."

During fifteen years on the job, Sam had had her share of scrapes and close calls, but nothing like what her ex-colleague had put her through in the basement of Marissa Springer's home. The incident had served as a wake-up call that life is short and grudges are pointless.

Though she'd probably never again be close to her mother, it was time to put down her sword and allow her mother back into her life. Having Scotty's adoption finalized was another good reason to bridge the chasm with her mother. He had asked a few times about her mom, and his curiosity had cemented her resolve to make a move—eventually. She hadn't expected to make that move today.

Nick was sleeping when they returned to his room, so Angela offered to stay with him while Sam took Angela's car home to check on Scotty.

"He fell asleep about twenty minutes ago," Tracy whispered when Sam came in to find Scotty sleeping next to Tracy on the sofa. Tracy ran her fingers through Scotty's hair as he slept, and the sight of her sister tending to her son made Sam weepy again. Enough with the waterworks today!

Sam rested a hand on his forehead, which was cool. "Thank you so much for staying with him."

"He's a pleasure to be with, and he was so glad when you guys called earlier and he could see for himself that Nick is fine. That helped to take some of the sting out of missing his friend's party."

Sam bent over to kiss Scotty's cheek. "What a long, crazy day."

"Nick's doing better?"

Sam sat in one of the upholstered chairs. "Yeah, he's pissed that Harry is making him stay the night. I hope they let him out tomorrow, or he'll be beside himself."

"Now you know what we deal with anytime you're injured."

Sam stuck her tongue out at her sister. "So, Ang told me something's up with Mom."

"I wondered if she would mention that."

"Is it bad?"

"It's not good news, but it could be worse. She really wants to see you, Sam."

"I know. Ang is going to set it up."

"Really?"

"Yeah, it's time."

"I'm so glad to hear you say that."

"Do you want to go home? I can take over from here."

"I figured you'd want to be with Nick at the hospital. I had Mike bring me a bag so I could stay with Scotty."

"I'm not sure where I belong right now. I've never felt so divided."

"Welcome to motherhood," Tracy said, smiling. "Scotty is fine with me, and you want to be with Nick, so go. We've got it covered here."

"You must've had plans for this weekend."

"Nothing that couldn't be shifted around."

"Thank you. You and Angela are the best. Always there when I need you."

"Right back at you. I'll never be able to pay you back for everything you did for Brooke last year."

"I was just doing my job."

"You did way more than your job, and we both know it."

"All that matters is that she's doing great and finishing up her senior year and going to college."

"UVA of all places," Tracy said. "I'm so proud of her."

"We all are. I'm going to grab a quick shower and change before I head back to the hospital. But first, let's get my big boy up to bed."

They woke Scotty, who brightened at the sight of Sam. "How's Dad?"

"He's cranky about being in the hospital."

"That's good. That means he's fine."

"I'm going to tuck you in and head back to be with him. Tracy will spend the night, okay?"

"Sure, you should be with him."

"I should be with both of you."

"Until we clone you, that's not possible."

"Dear God," Tracy said, shuddering dramatically, "do *not* clone her. One of her is more than enough."

"No kidding," Scotty said.

"Hey, I'm in the room," Sam said, while hiding her pleasure at her son's teasing. She much preferred that to the tears of the night before.

He was still weak and droopy, so they helped him into pajamas and got him tucked into bed.

"I'll see you in the morning, buddy."

"Will Dad get to come home tomorrow?"

"I fear for Harry's safety if he doesn't spring him."

"I hope he gets to come home."

Sam leaned over to kiss his cheek. "Me too. Get some sleep and don't worry about anything. He's fine."

His eyes closed. "It's hard."

"What is?"

"When you care more about someone else than you do about yourself. It's hard when something happens to them."

Sam had to swallow the huge lump in her throat before she could reply. "Yes, it is." She kissed him again and left him to sleep. After a quick shower and a change into yoga pants and a sweatshirt, she was on her way back to GW to spend the night with Nick.

She sent Angela home to Spencer, who had gotten both kids into bed and raised the white flag on the day. He'd sent a hilarious selfie with a six-pack of beer sitting next to him on the sofa.

"He's getting so lucky tonight," Angela said after sharing his comical texts with Sam.

"He got lucky the day you said yes to him."

"Remember that night when I went to meet him? The night you met Nick for the first time?"

"I remember that night like it was yesterday."

"Funny how that was such an important night for both of us. I think all the time about how Spence might've gotten away while I was busy mourning my relationship with Johnny the douche bag. And you having to put up with all that crap with Peter to get to what you have now with Nick…"

"I don't like to even think about him."

"He's been quiet lately."

"Ever since his 'suicide' attempt you mean?" Sam made air quotes around the word *suicide.*

"He must've been so disappointed when you didn't come running."

"Whatever. Those days are long over."

"Better be," Nick said.

"He is such an eavesdropper," Angela said, laughing.

Sam gave her a hug and sent her on her way. "You really are a terrible eavesdropper," Sam said to Nick when they were alone.

"Come here."

"I'm here."

"All the way." Without opening his eyes, he held out his arms to her, and she crawled into bed with him.

"There. Much better."

"You do seem much better."

"I'm outta here in the morning. I don't care what Harry says."

"You'll do what you're told, which is what you always say to me when I'm in this place."

"Hate when my own words come back to haunt me. How's Scotty?"

"Feeling much better and worried about you. He said

it's hard when you care about someone else more than you care about yourself."

"Did he now." Nick sighed. "Wow."

"I knew that would get to you."

"Right here." He rubbed his chest. "Now, how about you fill me in on what happened yesterday? It was only yesterday, right?"

"Yeah, it was. Feels like a lifetime ago, though." She told him about the results of the IAB hearing, Josh Hamilton and what he'd uncovered on the Internet.

"So he just happened to see an age-progression photo that was of *him*? What're the odds of that?"

"Astronomical."

"Imagine seeing one of those photos, and it's *you*. Jesus."

"You haven't even heard the real kicker yet. Guess who his father is?"

"Who?"

"Troy Hamilton."

"As in the *FBI director Troy Hamilton*?"

"One and the same."

"Holy shit. Sam, seriously… Are you kidding me right now?"

"Would I do that?"

"What's your plan?"

"To keep him alive while we wait for DNA proof that he's Taylor Rollings."

"So you think he is?"

"I think he could be. The resemblance to the photo is uncanny. It's like someone drew a picture of *him* and posted it. His thirtieth birthday is next week, so the timing works. And according to Freddie, who I've got babysitting him, his father has been calling every fifteen minutes, which is more than he's called his son in the last five years."

"So Hamilton knows about the photo—and he knows that *Josh* knows."

"Yeah, that's the theory. How well do you know Hamilton?"

"Not very well. From what I've seen at hearings on the Hill and in a few meetings at the White House, he's a cool customer with an ego the size of Texas."

"It's well earned. He's a legend in law enforcement circles."

"And in his own mind."

"So you don't like him."

"I don't know him well enough not to like him, but something about him is off-putting. Can't put my finger on it."

"You think he'd be capable of kidnapping someone's child and taking him home to raise as his own?"

"Hell if I know. I can't imagine how anyone would be capable of such a thing. Those poor people. They've been through hell for thirty years. It sure would be something if you could give them some peace."

"If Josh turns out to be Taylor, I fear that peace will be the least of what I'm giving them, and the frustrating part is that there's not a damned thing we can do from an investigative perspective until the DNA comes back."

"You could look into where Hamilton and his wife were the day Taylor went missing."

"How can I do that without bringing down the wrath of Hamilton on me and the department?"

"Carefully."

Sam could hear how tired he was in the way he said

that one word. "You need to sleep now. We'll talk more about this tomorrow."

He didn't protest, which was unlike him, especially since he had such a complicated relationship with sleep. His insomnia had been awful since he became vice president, which was one of many challenges they'd faced after he accepted the president's offer to replace the ailing Joe Gooding.

"Thanks for waking up earlier," she whispered.

His hand moved in small circles on her back. "Sorry I scared you."

"You really did. Sorry for all the times I've scared you."

"Love you, baby."

"Love you too. So much." If anything ever happened to him… No, she couldn't think about that or she'd go mad. There were two agents stationed right outside the door to ensure that nothing happened to him. But they hadn't been able to prevent severe dehydration. Her stomach ached from the fear of the many things that could happen to someone she loved that no one could prevent.

"Stop," he whispered. "I can feel you spinning. Everything is fine. I promise."

Sam took a deep breath, closed her eyes and carried his assurances to sleep with her.

CHAPTER EIGHT

NICK WAS RELEASED from the hospital the next afternoon. With the hospital surrounded by photographers hoping for a glimpse of the ailing vice president, the Secret Service arranged for him to be released through a loading dock.

"I've been officially reduced to cargo," he said when they were settled in the back of one of the big black SUVs.

Sam took hold of his hand. "Precious cargo." Though he looked a thousand times better than he had yesterday, he was moving slowly and his face was still paler than Sam had ever seen it.

They were whisked through the streets of the city with the kind of efficiency only the Secret Service could provide in the notoriously clogged District. On the way up the ramp to their house, Nick waved to the photographers that had gathered outside the Secret Service checkpoint on Ninth Street.

"I predict that photo will be on the front page of every paper in the country tomorrow," Sam said.

"Maybe they'll stop frothing at the mouth now that they know I'm going to live."

"Too soon for jokes." Her cell phone rang, and after a brief glance at the caller ID, she ignored the call from

Darren Tabor. He was on her shit list after publishing the article about her suspension.

Melinda, the agent on duty, opened the door for them. "Welcome home, Mr. Vice President. Good to see you looking well."

"Thanks, Melinda."

Sam wanted to tell Secret Service Barbie to get her filthy eyes off her husband, but she held back that urge. One of these days…

Scotty came rushing toward them, hurtling himself into Nick's outstretched arms, which cleared Sam's mind of every thought that wasn't focused on her family.

"So glad you're home," Scotty said.

"Good to be here." Nick smiled at her over Scotty's head as he hugged their son for much longer than usual since Scotty had become a teenager and began recoiling from most forms of parental affection. "You're feeling better?"

"A lot better today. How about you?"

"Same. Still not perfect, but better."

"This would be a good day to binge watch *Star Wars*," Scotty said.

"I can't think of anything I'd rather do," Nick replied.

They went upstairs to the master bedroom, and Sam got them settled in bed with remote controls and tall glasses of ice water. She'd been taught a big lesson about the perils of dehydration and was pushing the water hard.

"Move over and let me in," she said to Scotty.

"You hate *Star Wars*."

"True, but I love you, and I need some snuggles."

He curled up his lip at the word *snuggle*, but he moved closer to Nick to let her in.

She had just gotten settled when her phone rang again.

Prepared to tell Darren to fuck off and leave her alone, she flipped open the phone.

"Sam, we've got a problem," Freddie said. "You need to get over here."

"What kind of problem?"

"Josh is going off the rails. He's terrified his father is going to have him killed."

"*What?* He said that?"

"He's been ranting about it all morning. I tried to talk him down because I know you're dealing with Nick and the flu and everything, but he's losing it. Nothing I say gets through to him."

The last freaking thing she felt like doing was leaving the nice warm bed and her two favorite people, but she couldn't let Freddie twist in the wind alone with Josh. "Where are you?"

"Crystal Gateway. He's paranoid about me calling you. He's convinced Hamilton is probably having you followed."

"How would Hamilton even know I'm involved?"

"Josh says he knows everything." After a brief pause, Freddie added, "In case there's any truth to it, shut your phone off before you leave so he can't find you."

"So you're buying into the conspiracy theories?"

Lowering his voice, Freddie said, "There's something about how fearful he is that's resonating with me. I'm getting a gut check."

Sam had taught him to trust his gut, so the comment had her moving a little quicker to put on the shoes she'd only recently kicked off. "I'll be there shortly."

"Thanks."

While Scotty's gaze remained glued to the action on the TV, Nick was watching her. "What's up?" he asked.

"Josh is melting down. Gotta do some damage control. I shouldn't be long."

"Be careful."

She went around the bed to kiss him, which had Scotty making retching noises.

Nick smiled and curled his hand around her neck to keep her there for a moment longer. Into her ear, he whispered, "Watch out for Troy Hamilton. Be extra careful."

"I will. Don't worry."

"That'll be the day."

Mindful of Freddie's warning, she powered down her phone and put it in her pocket. Though she was suspended, she still unlocked her bedside table to retrieve the weapon she never left home without, except when running after the ambulance carrying her husband. She stuck her badge into her back pocket just in case she needed it, not that she expected to.

"Scotty, you're in charge," Sam said. "Make sure he does nothing but rest."

"Got it," he said, eyes still glued to the TV.

Though they were both a lot better than they'd been, she still hated to leave them, even for a couple of hours. And when she stepped outside the bedroom to see Melinda positioned in the hallway, she hated leaving them even more.

"They're not to be disturbed for any reason," Sam said.

"Yes, ma'am."

Sam wanted to snap back at her, to tell her not to call her ma'am, but that would be pointless. As the second lady, she was *ma'am* to the Secret Service whether she wanted to be or not. There were battles that could be fought and won, but that wasn't one of them. Besides, she had enough on her plate at the moment without taking on Nick's detail.

Was it petty to let the woman bug her? Of course it was. Melinda was only doing her job, but why had her young, sexy husband warranted a young, sexy *female* agent on his detail? Sam wondered if there was someone she could complain to and get Melinda reassigned. But she'd never do that, especially as a law enforcement officer herself. It was hard enough working in the old boys' club without making life difficult for a female colleague.

So she would keep her mouth shut and put up with Melinda's presence in her home and her eyes on Nick, but she didn't have to like it.

Traffic was light on Sunday afternoon, and she made good time on her way to Arlington, keeping half an eye on the rearview mirror looking for a tail that didn't materialize. If Hamilton was having her followed, he wasn't being obvious about it. There was no way anyone could get near her car outside the house with the Secret Service all over the place, and the car had been home since she brought Josh there the other day. For once, having the place crawling with Secret Service was coming in handy.

Well, that time they stopped Stahl from killing her on her own doorstep had been rather convenient too.

She kept an eye in the mirror as she took the 14th Street Bridge out of the city into Northern Virginia and headed for the Crystal City exit. That the Crystal Gateway Marriott was right next door to the Crystal City Marriott perplexed her as it always did. Who'd had the big idea to give two hotels practically the same name? Freddie had said *Gateway*, hadn't he?

She pulled up to the main door and flashed her badge to the valet on duty. "I won't be long."

His eyes bugged when he recognized her.

Sam was long gone before he stopped gawking. Inside, she used a house phone to ask the operator to connect her with Freddie Cruz's room. He answered on the first ring.

"Yeah."

"It's me. Where are you?"

"Room 718."

"On my way."

"Were you tailed?"

"Not that I could tell."

"Okay."

Sam took the elevator to the seventh floor and followed the hallway signs to the room. She knocked once, and Freddie opened the door. With one look she could see he was harried and annoyed.

"Thank God you're here," he said in a low growl. "He's driving me *nuts*."

Josh was pacing the small room, energy coming off his body in waves that were nearly visible. With his face a scary shade of red, he looked like he was about to blow from the pressure building inside him.

"Josh," Sam said, since he hadn't seemed to notice her arrival.

Whirling around, he said, "You gotta let me out of here. He's going to find me. I'm like a sitting duck here."

"Calm down—"

"*Don't tell me to calm down!* You don't know him! You don't know what he's capable of!"

"Why don't you tell me?"

His lips tightened as he shook his head. "Take my word for it."

"I wish I could, but I just met you on Friday, and his

reputation is legendary, so you'll have to forgive me if I need more to go on."

He took a series of deep breaths, obviously trying to calm himself down. "He raised me, and I'm terrified of him. What else do you need to know?"

"Specifics. Why are you terrified of him?"

"He's ruthless. Nothing I ever did was good enough for him. If I screwed up, he beat the shit out of me. If I mouthed off, he beat the shit out of me."

"Just you, or your siblings too?"

"I don't know if he ever hit them. They're older than me, and by the time I was old enough to be his punching bag they were out of the house."

"And you never asked them?"

Shaking his head, he said, "Until now, I've never told anyone that he hit me."

"Did your mother know?"

"I think she did, but she never said anything, and she certainly didn't try to stop it."

"So she wasn't in the room when he hit you?"

"Never. It was only ever the two of us."

"Why didn't you tell me this the other day?"

"Because! It's not something I just blab about. I know who he is and what people think of him. Who's going to believe me over him?"

"I believe you, Josh."

He stopped moving, and his shoulders sagged, as if he'd been relieved of a weighty burden. "You do? Really?"

"Yeah, I do. I've been in this business a lot of years, and I know the difference between someone who's playing the sympathy card and someone who's been the victim of violence."

At that, he stood up straighter again. "I am *not* a victim. I'm a *survivor.* Huge difference."

"You're right. There is a huge difference."

"I can't stay here. He's going to find me, and when he does, he'll kill me."

Sam exchanged glances with Freddie, who looked as tense as she felt. "Give me a minute to talk to my partner, okay? We'll figure something out."

Josh didn't acknowledge her question or her statement, so Sam turned and took Freddie by the arm. "Hallway."

They stepped outside the room.

"You've got a key?"

"Yeah."

She nodded toward the alcove next to the elevators, which was just around the corner from the room. "What's your take?" she asked when they were out of earshot of the room.

"I believe him. He's legitimately terrified."

"I agree. I think it's time to call in the brass on this. I didn't want to until we were sure we had something, but his fear is enough for me to involve the department. This is *way* above my pay grade."

"I'm glad to hear you say that. How do we explain what we've done so far?"

"I'll figure that out on the way to Farnsworth's house."

"You're going to his *house*?"

"That's where I'm most likely to find him on a Sunday afternoon, and PS I grew up going to his house, remember?"

"Since I wasn't actually there, no, I don't remember."

"Very funny. I'm suspended, so they have to cut me out of this, but you'll keep me in the loop, understood?"

"Of course. What do we tell Josh?"

"That I'm going to talk to my chief to figure out how to keep him safe while investigating his claims."

"He's gonna freak. He's been ranting that people are going to find out the truth about Troy Hamilton and how someone's going to kill him."

"You think he's mentally ill?"

"No, I think he's truly terrified. When the calls from his father started, he did a one-eighty. Before that he was calm, we were chilling, watching TV. After the calls, he was unhinged. I've seen nothing that smacks of mental illness, and I'd recognize it if I saw it." The comment was a reminder that Freddie's father, who'd recently re-entered his life after a twenty-year absence, suffered from bipolar disorder.

"I'll talk to him and explain the plan. Your job is to keep him calm until I get back."

"Lucky me." They rounded the corner and Freddie withdrew the keycard from his pocket to open the door to an empty room. "Aw, shit, he's gone."

"Check the bathroom," Sam said, her heart sinking.

"Gone."

"Fuck." She rushed out of the room and ran for the stairwell at the end of the hallway, well aware that he had a decent head start on them. Freddie's pounding footsteps followed behind her. They went down seven flights and burst into the lobby, startling an older couple.

"You're the second lady!" the man said.

Ignoring him, Sam said to Freddie, "Take the back." She ran for the main doors, hoping for a glimpse of Josh before he disappeared, but there was no sign of him. *Motherfucker.* She jogged to the corner of Fifteenth Street, but he wasn't there either. *Goddamn it.*

Freddie came out the front door and ran over to her. "Anything?"

"No."

Sam powered up her phone and tried to call Josh, but the call went straight to voicemail. She left a message, begging him to call her, to trust her to keep him safe, and then slapped the phone closed.

"So what now?"

"Now I do what I probably should've done on Friday," she said grimly. "I'm going to Farnsworth."

"What should I do?"

"Grab your stuff and anything of Josh's out of the room and go home.. I'll call you after I see the chief."

"You were trying to help him, Sam. You didn't do anything wrong."

"Maybe so, but if he turns up dead, that's on me."

"No, it's on the person who kills him."

"Let's hope we can find him before anything happens."

"Since I've got nothing going on at home until later when Elin gets back, I'm heading to HQ. Hit me up there when you know what the plan is."

"What do I tell the Rollings family if he turns out to be their son and I can't find him?"

"We'll find him."

As Sam trudged to her car, her stomach aching the way it used to when she was strung out on diet cola, she wished she shared his certainty.

CHAPTER NINE

JOE AND MARTI FARNSWORTH lived in a modest home in the city's Kingman Park neighborhood, known for its brick-fronted townhouses and social activism. The chief believed in living among the people he served, and they had resided in the same house for more than thirty years. Sam and her sisters had been frequent guests there, for holidays, barbecues and even an occasional sleepover.

Uncle Joe and Aunt Marti had been like family to the Holland girls, which is why Sam didn't think twice about going to the chief's home on a Sunday afternoon. Marti answered the door, her face lighting up with pleasure at the sight of Sam. They'd last seen each other at Nick's inauguration.

Sam returned Marti's warm embrace.

"What a lovely surprise! Joe and I were talking about you and Nick last night. We heard he was in the hospital! Is he all right?"

"He's much better. He and Scotty have been laid low by the flu."

"Aww, the poor guys."

"The good news is I finally have definitive proof that Nick is not superhuman."

Marti laughed as she linked her arm through Sam's to lead her into the family room where Joe was face-first in the Redskins game. "Earth to honey, we have a visitor."

Joe tore his gaze off the TV and did a double take when he saw Sam with Marti.

"Sorry to bother you at home, sir."

"Oh, stop that, Sam," Marti said. "He's Uncle Joe here."

"He's always *sir* to me now, ma'am."

Though Marti scowled, her eyes glimmered with amusement.

"If I have to be called *ma'am* in my own house, so do you," Sam added.

"Fair enough," Marti said with a laugh. "I assume this isn't a social call, so I'll leave you to talk to your uncle Joe. I'm off to the grocery store." She gave Sam a kiss on the cheek. "Don't be a stranger around here, okay?"

"I won't. Sorry it's been so long since I stopped by."

She swept away Sam's apology with the wave of her hand. "No apologies needed. You're the second-busiest lady in America these days, and I'd venture to guess Gloria Nelson's schedule hasn't got anything on yours."

"Your words, not mine."

Marti laughed. "Spoken like the wife of a politician. You take care."

"You too, Aunt Marti."

Marti kissed her husband before she left through the kitchen.

"You two are still honeymooning, huh?" Sam asked as she took a seat, propping her elbows on her knees. Her family had always teased the Farnsworths about their adorable PDA habit.

He eyed her shrewdly and muted the game. "Is that why you're here? To tease me about kissing my wife?"

"No," she said with a sigh. "We have a situation."

"How's it possible that you have a *situation* when you're suspended?"

"Well, it's sort of like this." Making use of the department-issued tablet that sat on his coffee table along with files he'd brought home from the office, she showed him the age-progression photo, explained how Josh Hamilton had sought her out and everything that'd happened since then, concluding with the information that he was now on the run. As she spoke, Farnsworth's normally amiable expression hardened.

"So let me get this straight—while you're serving out a *suspension*, you took on a new case involving the *son of the FBI director*, you called in the District's chief medical examiner to take a swab that will be processed through the District's lab and asked Detective Cruz to provide protection for Mr. Hamilton—"

"At my expense."

"Still, you involved Detective Cruz, and now the man you were trying to protect has gone missing. Do I have the facts correct?"

It took everything she had not to squirm under his intense glare. "You do."

He stared at her for a long time before he shook his head in apparent dismay. "You do *not* make it easy, Lieutenant."

She was about to ask him what he meant by that but she didn't have to.

"You're always coloring outside the lines, and it's becoming increasingly more difficult for me to defend your actions."

Ouch. That hurt. "I don't expect you to defend me or to understand why I do the things I do. You want results. I get you results. Every time."

"You'll never hear me deny that. But the means to the end, Lieutenant, is where we have a problem."

To hear him say they had a problem raised all sorts of alarms within her, but now was not the time to worry about alarms. "You have to understand the spot I was in—Josh refused to deal with anyone but me, and if it turns out that he is this missing kid, how could I *not* try to get those answers for the poor parents who've spent thirty years looking for him?"

"I do understand the spot you were in, and I hope you understand the spot you've put *me* in. You've got a man accusing the FBI director of kidnapping, and you didn't think I needed to know that the second it happened?"

"No one has accused Director Hamilton of anything."

"Semantics, Lieutenant. The second you involved Dr. McNamara you involved the department, and you *know* it."

"So what do we do now? Hamilton is on the run, and he's convinced that if his father finds him, he'll kill him."

"He said that? Those exact words?"

"Those exact words."

"Jesus. And you believed him?"

"Both Detective Cruz and I believe he was genuinely afraid for his life."

Farnsworth reached for the landline extension that sat on the coffee table and dialed a number, keeping his steely stare fixed on her. "This is Chief Farnsworth. Put me through to Conklin." After a pause, he said, "Hey, it's me. I'm with Holland and we need an APB for Josh Hamilton." He provided a description based on the photo Sam had shown him. "I want everyone looking for him. Notify Maryland and Virginia State Police. He was last seen on foot in the Crystal City area just over an hour ago. If we find him, take him into protective custody."

After a pause, he said, "Yes, she knows she suspended. I'll fill you in later. Ask for hourly reports from Patrol."

He ended the call and put the phone on the table.

"What do we do now?"

"*You* are doing nothing. You're going home to tend to your sick husband and son."

"Josh Hamilton trusts me, Chief."

"He trusts you so much he ran from you, Lieutenant."

Sam forced herself to remain calm. "When you find him, you'll want me there. He knows I'm on his side."

"You're not on anyone's side! You're on suspension. This matter no longer involves you—and I hate to point out the obvious, but it never should've involved you."

"But—"

"Go home, Lieutenant. Do yourself—and me—a big favor and stay home until Wednesday morning at zero seven hundred. Do I make myself clear?"

She bit back the retort that was dying to get out. "Yes."

His brow lifted.

"Yes, sir."

"You ought to know that I spoke with Forrester yesterday. He's going to request a meeting with you tomorrow. I'd recommend you have an attorney present. Ramsey's not letting it go, and frankly, I don't blame him. I expect better from you than how you handled that situation."

"I'm sorry to disappoint you, sir." Not even his disappointment, which mattered greatly to her, could change the fact that Ramsey had gotten exactly what he'd deserved.

"You want to know the only reason Forrester hasn't already filed charges?"

Not really, but she couldn't say that, could she? "Um, sure?"

"Because you're the second lady, and he's not looking forward to the feeding frenzy that'll erupt if he charges you."

"Don't let that stop him," she said drily.

"You think this is funny, Sam?"

"No, I don't. I think it's ridiculous."

"Did you or did you not assault a fellow officer?"

"I did. I absolutely did. And I'd absolutely do it again in light of what he said and how he said it. In fact, I'm so certain that he deserved it, maybe I'll just plead guilty and save Forrester the trouble of prosecuting the second lady."

"If you plead guilty to felony assault charges, your career as a police officer is over."

"So be it."

"You don't mean that."

"What if I do? My life would be a whole lot simpler without this job, and I could focus on my duties as a mother and the second lady without having to worry about chasing down killers or people taking me hostage or gunning down my officers simply because they carry a badge."

"Your squad has had a rough go of it lately. We're all painfully aware of that. For what it's worth, I urged Forrester to take that into account as he weighs whether or not to formally charge you."

"I appreciate your efforts on my behalf, Chief."

"I also want you to know that Ramsey will face disciplinary action for what he said to you, which was so far out of line it's not even funny."

"No, it wasn't funny, and as far as I'm concerned, a broken wrist and a concussion are the least of what he deserved."

"On that we may agree, but I can't and won't condone this kind of behavior from officers of your rank and stature."

"Understood. Hopefully, I'll never again have reason to lay out one of my fellow officers."

"Let's hope not. I'll see you Wednesday?"

"Yeah."

"Let me know what happens with Forrester."

"I will."

He walked her to the door. "Give Nick and Scotty my regards. I hope they feel better soon."

"Thank you."

Sam was walking to her car when her phone rang. She took the call from Darren Tabor, prepared to rip him a new one for reporting on her suspension, but she never got the chance.

"Why have you guys issued an APB for the FBI director's son?"

For a second, Sam thought about telling Darren why they were looking for Hamilton's son, but the chief's words echoed loudly in her mind, reminding her she had no right to speak on the department's behalf. Not today anyway.

"Why're you asking me? As you've already told the world, I'm suspended."

"But you know why, don't you?"

"No comment."

"Is he in trouble?"

Sam could almost hear the young reporter salivating over the possibility of one of the nation's top law enforcement officers having a son in trouble. "No comment."

"Come on, Sam, you gotta give me something."

"No, I actually don't, especially since you screwed me on the suspension thing."

"Other people already had it. That was happening with me or without me."

"I've got to go, Darren."

"How's the vice president?"

"Better."

"Can you tell me anything about this situation with Hamilton's family?"

"Nope."

"Not even off the record?"

"Nope."

"You're killing me, Sam."

"You'll survive." Sam slapped the phone closed and got into the car, cranking the heat as she tried to figure out her next move. She had a million questions about the Hamilton family and the abduction of Taylor Rollings and whether the two were somehow related. Under normal circumstances, she might head to HQ for a few hours to do some digging. But that wasn't an option today.

She'd heard every word the chief had said, and was well aware that his patience with her was waning. Uncle or not, he had a job to do, and her recent actions had made that job more difficult for him. She regretted that aspect of what she'd done. It was never her intention to cause him heartburn. The heartburn seemed to find her whether she toed the thin blue line or not. How was that her fault?

While she took the chief's annoyance seriously, the fact remained that her suspension didn't extend to online research she might do on her own. With that in mind, she headed home.

Her phone rang while she was stopped at a red light.

"Are you freaking kidding me?" Captain Malone said when she answered.

"Hello to you too, Captain."

"Hamilton's son thinks he was kidnapped from a family in Tennessee thirty years ago?"

"That's about the gist of it?"

"Holy fucking shit."

"My thoughts exactly."

"I know him a little bit."

"Who?"

"Director Hamilton. I shadowed him for a month years ago when he had Hill's job," Malone said, referring to Special Agent-in-Charge Avery Hill, who oversaw the Bureau's Criminal Investigation Division. "The shadowing was part of an interagency coordination effort."

"What do you think of all this?"

Malone hesitated for a couple of seconds. "Meet me at your dad's in thirty minutes." The line went dead before Sam could reply.

"Well, alrighty, then."

The half hour Malone had given her allowed for time to stop at home and check on her patients, both of whom were sound asleep as war raged on in a galaxy far, far away. She worked the remote out of Nick's hand and shut off the TV before tiptoeing from the room.

In the hallway, she sent a text to both their phones. I'm at Dad's if you need me. Sure, she could tell the agents on duty where she'd be, but she refused to run her family life through the Secret Service.

She zipped up the coat she'd left on for the check-in at home and went down the ramp to the sidewalk. To her right, she glanced at the reporters who had gathered outside the checkpoint, probably hoping for another glimpse of the vice president. She wanted to tell them to go get a life, but chasing the big story was their lives. Poor bastards. What a way to make a living.

Three doors down from her house, she went up the ramp to her father's home, entering after a brief knock on the door.

"Hi, honey," Celia said from her post on the sofa, where she was curled up with her e-reader.

"Hi there. What goes on around here?"

"Tracy and the kids were here to visit. You just missed them."

Sam took off her coat and dropped into a chair. "No sign of the flu in anyone else's house?"

"No, thank goodness."

"Hope it stays that way. It was nasty, but they're both better. They're out cold at the moment."

"Glad to hear they're doing better. We were so worried about Nick."

"Me too. What's Dad doing?"

"He's in his room watching the game."

"Captain Malone is on his way over. He wants to talk to both of us."

"What's going on?"

"I can't really say—yet. I'll tell you when I can."

She raised a brow. "I thought you were suspended?"

Sam shrugged. "I am."

Smiling, Celia said, "Suspended but still in the game?"

"Something like that," Sam said, grinning.

"Could I ask you…" Celia shook her head. "Sorry, none of my business."

"What?"

Celia's pretty face flushed. "I'm venturing into territory that's technically off limits to me by asking if you've heard your mother is in town."

"I heard that, and she wants to see me."

"I might've heard that too, and I wondered how you feel about it."

"I'm going to see her because it's time, not because I'm dying to mend fences or be best friends with her."

"How come, then?"

"When I was in that basement with Stahl, it occurred to me that I should've fixed the rift with her at some point. I thought I was going to die, and I was sorry I hadn't done that."

"Sam." Celia blinked back tears. "I hate to think about that awful day."

"So do I."

"For what it's worth, I think it's good you're going to see her and clear the air."

"It's worth a lot, especially coming from you."

"Why do you say that?"

"Because you've more than filled the mother void for me the last few years, and even if I kiss and make up with my mother, that doesn't change anything between us. You got me?"

Celia swiped at tears. "Now look what you've done."

Smiling, Sam got up and went to hug her stepmother. "Add it to the long list of ways I'm in trouble at the moment."

Celia held on tight for a second before she released Sam. "Go see your dad. He so looks forward to your visits."

"Send the captain back when he gets here?"

"Will do."

CHAPTER TEN

SAM WENT THROUGH the kitchen into her father's room in what used to be the dining room. Skip was in his recliner with the Redskins game on TV. It had been a while since Sam had seen him anywhere other than in his wheelchair or bed, but since the surgery to remove the bullet in his spine, he'd been spending more time in the specially outfitted recliner, which was a sign of progress, albeit limited progress.

"Hey there," she said.

His face lit up with pleasure at the sight of her. "Hey, baby girl. How's it going over in the infirmary?"

"Much better today."

"Glad to hear it."

Sam bent to kiss his forehead. "How's the game?" she asked, though she already knew the Skins were losing.

"Different week, same story. What're you up to?"

She sat in the other recliner. "So the situation with Hamilton's son has gotten complicated."

"How so?"

"Hamilton started calling Josh every fifteen minutes this morning, which is apparently more than he's called his son in the last five years combined. That freaked out Josh, and he bolted from protective custody. We're looking for him."

"I was going to call you because I just saw an alert on

TV that the director has issued a statement saying his son is mentally ill and off his medication, and the family is looking for him."

Sam felt light-headed all of a sudden. "He said *what*? Josh is not mentally ill. He's terrified his father is going to find him and kill him."

"He should be," Malone said as he came into the room looking flustered. "There's a world of difference between Hamilton's public image and his true self. The guy's a ruthlessly ambitious son of a bitch, and I wouldn't put it past him to kill his own son if it suited his agenda."

Shocked by Malone's unusually forceful statement, she said, "Is he capable of kidnapping someone else's child and raising him as his own?"

"I spent a month shadowing him, and I wouldn't put anything past that guy."

"How is it possible that I've never heard anything but praise and adulation where he's concerned?" Sam asked.

"Because that's what he wants you to hear. Troy Hamilton's public image is a carefully crafted work of fiction."

"Jake's right," Skip said. "I remember when you shadowed him and came back with stories about the only thing bigger than his arrogance was his ego."

"Exactly."

"We need to rip his life apart," Sam said. "Dig into his past. I want to know where he was thirty years ago this week when Taylor went missing."

Malone frowned at her. "I hate to remind you that you're suspended—"

Sam waved him off. "I'll do it on my own time and my own dime." Her phone rang and she removed it from her pocket to check the caller ID. "It's Hill."

"Take the call and get him over here," Malone said.

"Hi, Avery."

"You want to tell me why you people are looking for my director's son?"

"Come over to my dad's, and I'll tell you why."

Unprepared for her easy capitulation, Hill said, "Oh, um… Okay. I'll be there in ten."

Sam slapped the phone closed. "He's on his way."

"Is this going to blow up in our faces, Jake?" Skip asked, speaking of the department—as he always did—as if he were still an active member.

"It all depends on how quickly we can locate Josh and what Hamilton does when he finds out we've got him in custody."

"He took off without his wallet or any of his stuff," Sam said. "He does have his phone, though."

"Then he won't get far," Malone said. "We need to figure out who his friends are and who he might go to for help."

"From what he told us, he's not really close to his family," Sam said.

"How about colleagues?"

"He worked for VA. I can try to find out where and see if I can talk to some of the people he worked with."

"On your own time, of course," Malone said.

"Of course. I wouldn't dream of doing anything on the department's time while serving out my suspension."

Malone grunted out a laugh. "Sure you wouldn't."

"Is he insulting me?" Sam asked her father. "I think he's insulting me."

"He's speaking the truth, baby girl."

Sam scowled playfully at her father. "I expect better from you than that."

"A few more hours in the woodshed might've been

time well spent with this one, Skip," Malone said, using his thumb to point at Sam.

"She came out this way. I did what I could with her."

Sam was saved the bother of coming up with a witty retort to that when Avery Hill came into the room, looking pissed off. "That was quick." Though she had absolutely no interest in him whatsoever, she was struck nonetheless by how incredibly good-looking the agent was, especially when wearing well-faded denim, a navy-blue sweater and black ski jacket. His golden-brown hair was windblown and his face red from the cold.

"I was at Eastern Market with Shelby when I got a text from one of my people saying you guys issued an APB for the director's son. You want to tell me what that's about?"

"Where's Shelby?"

"In the car."

"Tell her to come in!" Sam said. "She can't sit in the cold."

"She's fine. The heat is on, and she's talking to her sister on the phone."

"Lieutenant," Malone said, "you want to bring Agent Hill up to speed on why we're looking for Josh Hamilton?"

Not really, Sam wanted to say, but instead she cleared her throat and forced herself to meet the golden gaze that had once looked at her with much more than collegial interest. Thankfully, he'd backed off on that bullshit since he got engaged to Shelby.

"Josh Hamilton came to HQ on Friday looking for me. He said he would only talk to me. As you and the rest of the world know, I was suspended. He waylaid me as I was leaving and told me he'd been surfing the net at work and stumbled upon an age-progression photo of a missing child who was a dead ringer for him."

Other than his eyes widening ever so slightly, Avery's expression didn't change.

"Do you know Josh?"

"I've met him a couple of times."

"Captain, may I borrow your phone?" Sam asked.

Malone rolled his eyes, mocking her refusal to upgrade from her trusty flip phone, and handed over his smartphone after punching in the code.

Sam went to the browser and found the link to the photo and showed it to Avery.

"Holy shit," he said in a whisper.

"That's what Josh said too. He was totally freaked out and came right to me."

"Why you?"

"Um, well, you might not have heard, but I have a bit of a reputation for being pretty good at my job."

Avery groaned. "Christ, I walked right into that, didn't I?"

"You asked."

"Children," Malone said sternly. "Get on with it."

Sam told him everything that'd happened since she encountered Josh Hamilton on Friday, culminating with the news that he had bolted from protective custody and was convinced his father was out to kill him.

"Seriously?" Avery said. "And you *believe* him?"

"Detective Cruz and I agreed that his concerns seemed legitimate."

"Do you honestly believe that *Troy Hamilton*, one of the most revered and well-respected men in law enforcement, would be capable of *kidnapping and murder*?"

Sam chose her words carefully, knowing how difficult it had to be for him to hear this about his illustrious director. "I'm sorry to say, Agent Hill, that in my line of work, you quickly discover that just about everyone is capable of murder under the right circumstances."

"Troy Hamilton is not capable of murder. He's spent his entire adult life working to apprehend criminals and to make this country safer for all of us. That you would even *imply* such a thing is so far beyond egregious I don't even have a word for it."

"I understand how you feel—"

"Do you? Do you really? How could you possibly understand when you have no relationship with him, when you haven't worked for him for more than a decade and seen him in action on a daily basis? You have no earthly idea how I feel. How would you feel if I insinuated that your beloved uncle Joe was capable of murder?"

Touché. "Look, I hear what you're saying, and what I meant to say is I know how difficult it is to hear this, but the fact remains that his son was scared shitless that his father was coming after him and was convinced that if Troy caught him, he'd kill him. He told us Hamilton used him as a punching bag every chance he got when Josh was a kid."

"Hamilton said the kid is mentally ill and off his meds."

"Yes, he said that."

"You don't believe it?"

"I spent hours with him on Friday. Detective Cruz was with him Friday night through this afternoon, and not for one second in all that time did we pick up on anything that smacked of mental illness. Cruz's father is bipolar. As he said, if the guy was mentally ill, he'd have noticed. There were no indicators of that whatsoever."

"Having a bipolar father doesn't make him an expert on mental illness."

"Granted. But it does make him more acutely aware of certain behaviors that might indicate an underlying issue. The only underlying issue we detected from Josh Hamilton was abject fear."

Avery ran a hand through his hair, as he processed what Sam was telling him. "If you accuse him of this, and you're wrong, the nightmare you'll bring down upon yourself and your department, not to mention the implications for your husband, will be epic. You know that, right?"

Sam had to admit she hadn't given the first thought to how this situation might affect Nick, but he would tell her to do her job and not worry about him. "I get it. Don't shoot the messenger. I'm only passing along the facts as they've been presented to me."

"Fucking hell," Avery muttered. "I can't believe we're even having this conversation."

"We're waiting on DNA before we accuse anyone of anything. In the meantime, we're looking for Josh because he was concerned for his welfare, not because we necessarily think Director Hamilton is going to have him killed."

"This whole thing is nothing short of preposterous."

"Unless," Skip said, "the DNA is a match for Taylor Rollings and the director raised a kidnapped child as his own. Then it won't seem so preposterous."

Avery's face reddened. "You can't honestly believe that *Troy Hamilton* kidnapped someone else's child and raised him as his own!"

"I never imagined the speaker of the House or a ranking senator would be involved in a prostitution ring,"

Sam said, "or that one of the top candidates for president would murder the wife of the current president's deputy chief of staff because she stopped providing information. I never would've thought a Supreme Court nominee would be gunned down by his own brother. Shall I go on?"

"No," Hill said, his expression stony. "But this is *Troy Hamilton* we're talking about."

"I know," Sam said with a sigh, "and I respect how shocking it is for you to hear this, but please don't tell me it's impossible that he had anything to do with it."

"Fine, I won't," he said testily. "What's your plan?"

"We're going to find Josh Hamilton, make sure he's safe and lean on the lab to get us those results ASAP," Sam said. "After that, I don't have a plan."

"You'll keep me posted?" Avery asked. "As a courtesy."

Since she was technically suspended and not on the case in an official capacity, Sam glanced at Malone.

"We'll keep you posted," Malone said.

"And you'll keep what we've told you here under wraps until we have cause to take this to Hamilton?"

"Yeah," Hill said gruffly. "I won't say anything. I'm going to take Shelby home. Let me know if you hear anything about Josh or the DNA."

"We will," Sam said.

He nodded and turned to leave the room.

"He's in denial," Skip said after they heard the front door close behind Hill.

"He worships Hamilton," Malone said. "Most of the people who've worked for him do. He's a magnetic, powerful leader who's transformed the Bureau during his tenure as director. If the DNA is a match, we're going to get huge pushback from the Feds on this, so we have to make sure our *i*'s are dotted and *t*'s are crossed every which way to next Tuesday."

"The proof will be in the DNA," Skip said. "His many fans can't quibble with a match."

"Hill is right about one thing," Sam said. "If it gets out that we're looking at Troy Hamilton for kidnapping before we have proof, and it turns out to be untrue, we'll be screwed, glued and tattooed."

"Let's not allow that to happen," Malone said.

Sam put up her hands. "I'm suspended. Not much I can do."

"I want you on this behind the scenes," Malone said, shocking the shit out of Sam. She hadn't expected him to say that. "Josh Hamilton came to you once. Maybe he will again. If he does, you're on the case."

"And you'll clear that with the brass?"

"I'll take care of it."

Sam's phone rang and she glanced at the caller ID, startling when she saw Josh's name pop up. "It's him," she said, as she flipped open the phone to take the call. "Holland."

"It's me," he said in a small voice. "Josh."

"Where are you?"

"I'm close to your house."

Sam began walking toward the front door, grabbing her coat off the chair in the living room before she went outside. "Come toward the Secret Service checkpoint, and I'll meet you. We'll bring you to my house where no one can touch you. I'll personally guarantee your safety."

If the Secret Service hadn't turned her home into a fortress, she'd never consider bringing him there. But it was the second most secure home in the District and thus the best place for him right now.

After a long pause, she said, "Josh? Are you coming?"

"Yeah, I'll come."

"Good." She expelled a deep sigh of relief. "You'll be surrounded by Secret Service. No one will touch you." Sam was kicking herself for taking him out of her house to begin with. She should've let him stay there, even with the flu running rampant. Oh well, hindsight was always twenty-twenty. "Keep talking to me. Where are you now?"

"Seventh."

"Two more blocks." She was waved through the checkpoint and walked toward Seventh Street, where she could see him in the distance. Jogging as she held the phone to her ear, she covered a block in a matter of seconds. When she reached his side, she slapped her phone closed and jammed it into her coat pocket. "Come on." As she hooked her arm through his, she noticed his eyes were red and raw, as if he'd been crying. His clothes were dirty and disheveled, and one of the sleeves on his coat was torn.

"I didn't know where else to go," he said in a despondent tone. "He's coming for me. I know he is."

"You did the right thing calling me. I'll keep you safe."

"You have to tell the Secret Service not to let him in. If he finds out I'm with you, he'll come here, and he'll strong-arm them into letting him in."

"They don't let anyone in unless we ask them to, and we won't let him in. I promise."

At the checkpoint, Sam vouched for Josh since he didn't have his ID on him. She noted the agent's recognition of his name. The agent had probably seen the APB.

"Is everything all right, Mrs. Cappuano?" the agent asked warily.

"Everything is fine. I'd like some additional security posted at both ends of Ninth Street."

"Any particular reason?"

"I want to make sure my guest feels as safe as possible."

"Yes, ma'am. We'll take care of it."

"Thank you very much." Taking Josh by the arm again, she led him to her house, where Malone waited for them at the foot of the ramp. Sam introduced Josh to him and the agent on duty admitted the three of them into the house.

Malone called HQ to cancel the APB for Josh.

Josh released an audible sigh of relief when the front door closed behind them. "Thank you," he said softly.

"No problem. I should've kept you here to begin with. I'm sorry I didn't."

"You were—and are—under no obligation to protect me."

"The minute I put you in my car on Friday, I've felt an obligation to protect you." She gestured for him to have a seat on the sofa. "What happened to you after you left the hotel?"

"I wandered around for a while. I ended up in Rock Creek Park and fell down a hill. That's how I got dirty." He jumped back up and began to pace. "How long do I have to stay here? What happens now? Will someone tell my father to leave me alone?"

The rapid-fire questions, the jerky pacing and the trembling of his hands put Sam on alert. "Are you on something, Josh?"

He stopped short. "What? Why would you ask me that?"

"You're extremely jittery."

"My father, *the director of the FBI*, wants me *dead*. Wouldn't you be jittery if you were me?"

"Is it possible you're wrong about what he wants from you?" Malone asked.

"No, I'm not wrong."

"Why do you say that?" Sam asked.

"Because he's a ruthless bastard. If this is true, if he took me or paid someone else to do it or however it happened, he'll kill me before he'll admit to having had anything to do with it."

"It won't matter if he kills you now, Josh," Malone said. "We've got your DNA. If it's a match to Taylor Rollings's family, then your father will have to answer to how you came to be in his custody, whether you're alive or dead."

Josh stopped pacing and turned to face Malone. "He... He doesn't know I gave DNA."

"I think it might be time for you to return his calls," Sam said, playing a hunch.

"You're sure that's a good idea?" Josh asked.

"I'm sure it'll send the message to your father that you're cooperating with the investigation," Sam said, "and that it won't matter now what he does. We've got the info we need to make a connection to Taylor Rollings, if a connection does in fact exist."

"He needs to know that," Malone added. "It would also give you a chance to ask him if he knows anything about Taylor or his abduction."

"If he does, he'll deny it," Josh said.

"Still won't hurt to ask," Malone said.

They waited for Josh to mull it over. He sat on the sofa, the frenetic energy of a few minutes ago giving way to a weary resignation. After a long moment of silence, he withdrew his phone from his pocket and placed the call quickly, almost as if he was afraid to take even another second to think about it.

"Put it on Speaker," Malone said.

Josh did as he asked, and they listened to the phone ring and ring before voicemail picked up.

"This is Troy Hamilton. I can't take your call right now, so please leave a message, and I'll get back to you as soon as I can."

"Um, Dad, it's me, Josh, calling you back. Call me when you get this message." He ended the call and looked up at them. "What now?"

"Now we wait for him to return your call," Malone said.

CHAPTER ELEVEN

AVERY DROVE SHELBY home to the townhouse they now shared in the District's Adams Morgan neighborhood, his mind whirling with what Sam and Malone had told him about Troy Hamilton. There was no fucking way on God's green earth that Troy Hamilton *kidnapped a child* and passed him off as his own for thirty years. No way.

He couldn't deny, however, that Josh Hamilton bore a striking resemblance to the age-progression photo. But that didn't prove a goddamned thing, and even if Josh turned out to be Taylor Rollings, that didn't mean Troy took him or had any knowledge of a kidnapping.

The whole thing was so far beyond preposterous as to be laughable.

"Are you going to tell me about it?" Shelby asked as they made their way through streets congested by cars heading to the Capitals home game at the Verizon Center.

"I'm still trying to process what I just heard."

"Can I help?"

He glanced at her and then back at the road, wanting to tell her but conditioned to keep his work to himself.

"If it makes any difference, I already know about Josh Hamilton's possible connection to the missing kid in Tennessee."

"How do you know that?"

"I was at the house the other day when Sam brought

him home. I didn't know then that he was your director's son, but since we heard about the all-points bulletin earlier, I put two and two together to get holy moly."

"Yeah, that's putting it mildly."

"What're you thinking?"

"That there's no fucking way that Troy had anything to do with kidnapping someone else's kid. There's just no way."

"If it's true that Josh is really Taylor, maybe there's some sort of reasonable explanation for how he came to be in the Hamiltons' custody."

"What kind of explanation would be reasonable? No matter how it came to happen, if it's true, his career is over and his reputation will be shredded."

"Knowing how much you look up to him, I can't imagine how you must feel after hearing their suspicions."

Avery tightened his grip on the wheel. "Everyone in the Bureau looks up to him. He's a god to us. It's not true. There's just no way it's true."

"I'm sorry you're upset."

He took a deep breath and tried to shake off the shock of what he'd been told by Sam and Malone. Today was his day to spend with Shelby, and she deserved his complete focus. If there was anything he knew for certain it was that Troy Hamilton could take care of himself. He'd find a way to deflect these accusations away from himself and the Bureau.

"You want to get something to eat?" he asked.

"I'm more tired than hungry. I was thinking about a nap."

Knowing she tired easily in her second trimester, he said, "Whatever you want."

She took hold of his hand and kissed the back of it. "I was hoping you might join me for a rest."

Which was code for afternoon nooky. Under normal circumstances, Avery was on board for any kind of nooky she wanted, but today… "Sure, honey."

"Are you okay, Avery?"

"I'm…" He'd been about to say he was fine, but he wasn't. He wasn't fine at all. "I'm on edge about what this is going to mean for Hamilton and the Bureau. I'm sorry. Today is our day. No more work."

"I understand why you're upset. If you need to go to the office, we can postpone our plans for another day."

Avery thought about that for a minute. "Thanks, but there's really nothing I can do. It's not like we have an active case to pursue or anything. This is the weirdest situation I've ever encountered, and that's saying something in my line of work. Sam has Josh under protective custody—"

"I thought she was suspended."

"She was—or is—but that's not stopping her. Her captain was at her dad's, so he's aware that she's involved. Apparently, Josh was willing to talk to her and only her, which made it necessary for them to involve her."

"It's ridiculous that they suspended her anyway."

"She did assault a fellow officer."

"Who asked for exactly what he got."

"You don't hear me arguing."

Shelby looked over at him. "Do you think the U.S. Attorney will actually charge her for assault?"

"Hard to say. He's in a tough spot on this one in light of who she is to the department and the country."

"Can you imagine the second lady being charged with *assault*?"

"No, I can't, and I'd be surprised if the administration isn't leaning on Forrester to go easy on her."

"Nick would never condone that."

"It's probably coming from above him."

"Wow. You really think the *president* is involved?"

"I have no way to know that for certain, but I'd be surprised if he wasn't. Having his vice president's wife charged with felony assault isn't going to look good for any of them. If Nelson can keep it from happening, I'm sure he will, especially since Forrester is a Nelson appointee."

"People would go crazy if she gets charged. She's so popular—not just here anymore but everywhere after what she did during the inauguration."

"There's a lot to consider beyond whether she hit Ramsey or whether he deserved it. I don't envy Forrester this situation."

He parked at the curb outside their townhouse and cut the engine. "Wait for me to come around," he said as he got out of the car. Ever since she'd fallen a couple of months ago, he treated her as if she were made of spun glass, or at least that's what she said. But with the sidewalk coated in a thin layer of ice, he wasn't taking any chances. He opened the passenger door and held out a hand to help her up and out of the car.

"Thank you." She curled her hand into the crook of his elbow to climb the stairs he'd salted earlier in the day. "Spring can show up anytime now."

"Going to be a few more weeks, I'm afraid."

"Ugh, enough already with this cold weather."

"I'll remind you of that when you're sweltering through the last weeks of pregnancy in the dog days of summer." Inside, he unwound her puffy pink scarf and used the two ends to draw her closer to him.

She looked up at him expectantly.

Sometimes he still had to marvel at the series of events that had led to where they were now—engaged, living together and expecting a child. Whether or not that child was biologically his was of no consequence to him, and that thought led Avery right back to Troy Hamilton and the baffling situation with his son.

"What?" Shelby asked, reminding him that he'd been about to kiss her.

"Nothing." He shook off his worries about Hamilton to focus on her, leaning in to kiss her. "You mentioned a nap?"

A smile lit up her adorable face. "I did." She took him by the hand to lead him upstairs to the room they now shared.

He put up with pink throw pillows on his bed because he loved having her in it, but he'd drawn the line at allowing any other pink in his bedroom. Whenever she teased him about his willingness—or lack thereof—to compromise, he referred to the pink pillows on his bed that were now flying through the air as Shelby prepared for their nap.

Smiling at her haste, Avery pulled his sweater over his head and dropped his jeans to the floor, kicking them aside. He got into bed and propped his head on his up-turned hand to watch her undress. She was effortlessly sexy. Everything she did, every move she made, every word she said turned him on.

She removed her sweater, revealing the gentle swell of her abdomen and the breasts that were getting bigger by the day, much to her dismay.

He had no complaints. He loved her. He loved their life and the plans they'd made for the future. But goddamn if he didn't still react to Sam Holland every fucking time he saw her. Today had been no different. What the hell was wrong with him? How could he be in love with a woman who was perfect for him in every possible way but still be drawn to someone he could never have?

He didn't *want* to want Sam. He'd never wanted it, knowing all along she was permanently off limits to him. And yet... The reaction today was because he hadn't seen her in a few weeks, or so he told himself. During that time, he'd barely given her a thought. He'd been too busy with his work and his life with Shelby to think about Sam. Yesterday he would've said he was well and truly over whatever he'd once felt for her.

Then he walked into her father's home, she looked at him with those eyes that saw everything and, as always, he felt like he'd been struck by lightning. Why did that happen every time? *Why, why, why?* It wasn't like he wanted to react to her. He didn't. He wanted to put that madness in the past where it belonged. He wanted to focus on the life he had now with Shelby and the life they were anticipating with the baby. Nowhere in that life was there room for his fascination, or whatever you wanted to call it, with another woman. He'd gone so far as to wonder if he needed to be hypnotized or exorcised or something—*anything*—that would make it stop once and for all.

Shelby removed her jeans and panties, putting an extra wiggle in her motions for his benefit, and crawled into bed with him. The feel of her soft skin rubbing against his had an immediate and predictable effect on him.

She curled her hand around his erection. "Is this all for me?"

The question hit him like a gut punch. It was all for her. Of course it was. "You know it, sugar."

"Mmm, that accent. You could read the phone book to me, and it would turn me on."

"Is that so?"

"God, yes." Tightening her grip, she stroked him the way he loved it best, her small hand moving quickly up and down his shaft.

"I do love your naps, Shelby Lynn."

Her lips curved into a smile, and then she peppered his chest with kisses.

Avery ran his fingers through her long blond hair, determined to give her everything she deserved. He had no doubt that she loved him with her full heart and soul. She showed him that every day in a million little ways. Whether it was serving him a perfect cup of coffee fixed just the way he liked it or picking up his shirts from the dry cleaner or… Ah, *fuck*… She gave one *hell* of a blow job.

He was tempted to let her finish him off, but he needed the connection to her. He needed the reminder of who he loved and who he'd vowed to spend his life with. Giving a gentle tug on her hair, he said, "Sugar."

She tightened her lips on his cock and gave a final deep suck that was nearly the end of him. "Yes?" Her innocent expression made him groan.

"Come here." He helped her get settled on top of him. Then he reached around to unhook the bra she'd left on because she was self-conscious about her blossoming breasts. They fell hot and heavy into his waiting hands. He ran his thumbs over her nipples, which were more sensitive than ever, and she jolted from the sensation. "Take me in, sweetheart. Ride me."

She was so wet and hot and tight. God, it was heaven to be inside her.

Grasping her hips, he tried to control her, but she wouldn't cede to him. Instead, she flashed a wicked smile that let him know she planned to torture him. He loved her like this, uninhibited, smiling, her eyes dancing with joy and looking at him with so much love. It was humbling to know that she loved him as much as she did, and after fighting so hard to win her over, he wouldn't do anything to dim the light that shone so bright inside her.

The thing with Sam was ridiculous. He'd be the first to admit it. His reactions to her were involuntary, so how could he be held responsible for feeling the way he did? This, right here, was his real life. Shelby was his real life, and as she rode him to an explosive orgasm, he vowed to keep his focus where it belonged—right here at home with her.

Her pussy tightened around his cock, milking a second wave of pleasure from him as she came hard, her head falling back and her breasts flushing with a rosy glow. She was so sexy, so sweet and adorable. He loved her. He truly did. And as she collapsed onto his chest, he told her so.

"Love you too," she whispered. "So much."

This was what mattered. And he would keep telling himself that until the involuntary reactions ceased to occur every time he laid eyes on Sam Holland. He stroked Shelby's back, making her shiver from the light caress of his fingertips over her skin. She was always so sensitive after they made love.

Then she gasped and sat straight up.

"What?"

"The baby! I felt something!"

Avery was immediately alarmed that they'd somehow managed to harm their unborn child. "Something bad?"

"No, a flutter." She took his hand and placed it flat against her abdomen. "Here. Do you feel it?"

At first, he felt nothing more than the heat of her skin against his palm, but then, sure enough, there was a ripple of something.

She gasped again and tears filled her big eyes. "Oh my God! There he is!" Though she had no proof to back her claims, she'd convinced herself the baby was a boy. Her hand covered his as their eyes met and held, her smile so bright it could light up the world.

Avery hardened inside her, and when the fluttering finally stopped, he gently turned them so he was on top.

"That was amazing," she whispered. "I'm so glad you were with me the first time I felt the baby move."

"So am I. It was incredible."

"I can't wait to meet him."

"Neither can I." She'd been undergoing fertility treatments when they got together, hoping to become a mother. They didn't know if the baby was his or a result of the treatments, and he honestly didn't care either way. The baby would be *theirs*. He began to move, slowly, reverently, gazing down at her expressive face as he made love to her.

She caressed his face and chest, looking up at him with wonder in her big eyes.

He bent his head to draw her nipple into his mouth, and her moan traveled straight to his cock. Sucking on the tight nub, he picked up the pace until they were both coming with deep groans. Afterward, he gathered her in close to him and closed his eyes as his heart continued to beat fast and hard.

The next time he opened his eyes the room was dark, and Shelby was fast asleep in his arms. He took a deep breath and released it slowly, his brain coming back to life to focus on the situation with Director Hamilton. Hours later, he had the same thought he'd had earlier: it couldn't possibly be true.

Moving carefully, he disentangled his limbs from Shelby's embrace and got up to shower. As the hot water rained down upon him, he decided he needed to know. He had to see Troy, to find out what was going on and ask how he could help. That was the right thing for him to do, even if it might be difficult.

And what if the worst was true? What if Troy had been involved in the kidnapping of Taylor Rollings? What if he had knowingly raised a child who belonged to someone else? If Josh was actually Taylor, Troy couldn't have known that. Someone had fooled him into raising the child. Except... The Troy Hamilton he knew and admired was nobody's fool. It didn't add up or make sense.

Avery stepped out of the shower, dried off and got dressed in the same jeans and sweater he'd had on earlier. When he stepped into the bedroom, Shelby stirred, looking up at him.

"I need to run a quick errand." He leaned over to kiss her cheek and then her lips. "I'll bring something for dinner when I come home."

Her eyes closed. "'K."

He went downstairs to his office where he retrieved his badge and weapon from the locked desk drawer and headed out. Troy lived in a big house in the city's Northwest quadrant, near the vice president's usual residence.

As everyone knew, the current vice president had chosen to remain in his Ninth Street residence so his wife could be close to her paralyzed father.

But he was not thinking about *her* right now. No, he was thinking about his director and his pregnant fiancée and his own damned life.

Avery had been to Hamilton's house several times in the last year, most recently for the holiday get-together the director had held for the Bureau's top people. He'd been amazed to realize he was among the top people, one step outside the director's inner circle. He had admired Hamilton from afar long before he joined the Bureau. The dynamic director had been a big reason Avery had chosen the FBI over other agencies that had expressed an interest when he left the military after ten years as an Army Ranger.

Being handpicked by Hamilton to lead the Bureau's Criminal Investigative Division had been the highlight of his career. Thinking back to the day he'd been summoned to Hamilton's office reminded him that he'd intended to put in for a transfer far from D.C. and the beguiling detective. Hamilton had changed his plans with the offer to head up CID, and Avery's path continued to cross hers on a regular basis.

With hindsight, he probably should've turned down the director's offer and gone with his original plan. By now he'd be far away from the source of his continuing vexation. But he also wouldn't be engaged to Shelby and preparing to be a father to her child.

Tightening his grip on the wheel, Avery wondered if perhaps he needed intense therapy or something to rid his brain of thoughts about a woman who didn't belong in his head. He did not *want* her there. *She* did not want to be there. Her husband would kill him—or have him killed—if he knew how often Avery still thought of her. Not to mention what it would do to Shelby to find out that he still reacted to Sam the way he always had, despite the amazing relationship he now had with Shelby.

He'd never in his life faced a challenge as confounding as this one. How could he be madly in love with one woman and still thinking about someone he'd never had *anything* with?

"Fucking hell," he muttered as he brought the car to a stop at the curb a block from Hamilton's red brick mansion. "It's got to fucking stop, and it's going to stop right now. Today. That's it."

He got out of the car and walked the short distance to the director's front gate, surprised to find one side of it open. Avery knew the director had declined any sort of government security for himself or his home, preferring to take care of himself rather than have a detail, so it was surprising to see the gate standing open.

A tingling sensation rippled down his spine. Avery had learned to pay attention to the sensations that alerted him to potential trouble. Looking around, he saw that the street and sidewalk were all but deserted. Other houses on the block were aglow with lights, but Hamilton's place was dark.

He walked down the driveway to the portico where Hamilton's silver Jaguar was the only car in the driveway. The tingling intensified when he went up the stairs to the wide veranda and noticed the front door was ajar. Pausing for a second, he contemplated calling for backup, but hesitated. The last thing he wanted was to draw any more attention to the director or his family, especially if there was no reason for it. He rang the doorbell and listened to the loud chimes echo through the house.

After waiting a few minutes, he knocked on the door. When no one came, he drew his weapon and nudged the door open with his shoulder. The house was so dark he could barely make out the shape of a table in the front hall. His foot slipped on something on the floor. Withdrawing his phone, he turned on the flashlight to find a shattered vase that had contained yellow flowers. Water had spilled all over the marble floor.

He should retreat, call for backup, get the hell out of there. Though he knew all these things, he pressed on, deeper into the house, using his flashlight to guide him. In the sitting room to the right of the foyer, a lamp had been knocked off a side table. Avery walked around the fallen lamp and into the room the director used as a home office. He'd taken Avery and others inside to show off the office during the holiday party. Avery recalled being impressed by the lineup of photos showing Hamilton with the last four presidents, countless senators and numerous world leaders.

Following the beam of his flashlight into the office, the first thing he saw was a foot on the floor. The tingling in his spine was now a cascade of nonstop sensation, his better judgment telling him to get the fuck out of there right now. But he had to know. He had to see with his own eyes.

Using his elbow, he pushed the right side of the double French doors open to reveal Hamilton, lying in a pool of blood. *"Fuck."* Avery knew it was him by the size of his frame and the width of his shoulders. His face had been beaten to a bloody pulp by a golf club that had been left on the floor next to the body. Under normal circumstances, he would've checked for a pulse, but there was no point. The director was dead and had been for some time.

Confusion and despair mixed with grief and anger that someone, anyone could've killed this giant of a man, a man Avery had looked up to for most of his adult life. He sent the beam around the room, making sure it was clear before he extinguished it and, knowing the situation was out of his hands now, called it in.

CHAPTER TWELVE

SAM HEATED UP Shelby's meatballs and boiled pasta for dinner. Nick and Scotty were much better, but still not that interested in food. They ate the soup Celia had sent over while she and Josh had the pasta and meatballs.

Josh pushed the food around on his plate, not showing much interest in the meal.

Nick glanced at Sam, his brow raised in question, as if to ask what the hell Josh was doing here.

Though she'd explained the need to keep Josh safe, bringing him here had been a questionable decision at best. But what was she supposed to do? Where else could she have taken him where there was no chance the most powerful law enforcement official in the nation would find him?

Her home was the safest place for him. No doubt about that, but it was a lot to ask of Nick—and Scotty, who tried to engage Josh in conversation.

"Do you like sports?" Scotty asked.

"Some."

"Which ones?"

"Baseball, but my dad always said it was boring as shit. He hates it."

"My dad and I love baseball. We go to lots of Feds games and last year we saw the Red Sox play at Fenway. That was so cool."

"I'd love to go to Fenway sometime," Josh said wistfully.

"You should. It's awesome. We sat in the Green Monster seats, and I got to see Big Papi. He's my favorite player. I liked Willie Vasquez from the Feds, but he got murdered."

"I know. I liked him too."

"All because he dropped a ball."

Sam didn't mention that there was a lot more behind Willie's murder than the error he'd made on the field. The loss of one of her son's favorite ballplayers had been traumatic enough for him at the time. There was no need to revisit that now.

"Do you have homework you need to do before you go back to school?" she asked.

Scotty frowned. "I don't know. Probably."

"You ought to check in with some of your classmates so you can find out what's due."

"I'm sick. I don't have to do it now."

"You'll have to do it eventually," Nick said. "If you do some now and some later, it won't be as awful."

"I guess. I'll see if I can find out." To Josh, he said, "Do you like Xbox?"

"I guess."

"You wanna play?"

Josh glanced at Sam, who nodded. "Sure," he said.

"I'll get the dishes," she said. "You guys go ahead."

"Thanks for dinner," Scotty said, taking his bowl to the sink.

"Yeah, um, thanks," Josh said as he too delivered his plate to the sink.

They left the room, and Sam forced herself to meet Nick's questioning gaze.

"This is weird," he said.

"I know, and I'm sorry, but this place is like a fortress with the Secret Service surrounding us. It was the best place for him until we figure out what's going on."

"This might be the strangest case you've ever been involved in, and that's saying something in light of some of the crap you've dealt with."

Sam poured herself a glass of wine. "It's bizarre. I'm hoping the DNA will be back tomorrow so we can get some answers for Josh—and the Rollings family."

"You haven't told them anything yet, have you?"

She shook her head. "I talked to the detective in charge of the kidnapping case, and we agreed to keep it between us until we had proof one way or the other. I let him know about Josh as a professional courtesy."

"It would be quite something if you could help to solve the mystery for Taylor's family, but the possibility of Hamilton being involved in something like this is…"

"It's hard to comprehend."

"Yeah."

Sam got up to deal with the dishes and was standing at the sink when his arms encircled her waist, making her smile.

He nudged her hair aside and delivered a series of kisses to her neck as his erection pressed against her back.

"Someone is feeling better."

"Much better."

"I'm so glad. I don't like it when you're sick. It's scary."

"Sorry you were scared, babe."

Sam dried her hands and turned to face him, taking in the scruff on his jaw, the paler-than-usual face and the hazel eyes that burned with desire for her. "Nice to have you back."

He bent his head to kiss her softly. "I'm still feeling a little achy in some places. I could use some TLC from my wife tonight."

She laughed at his blatant come-on. "Your wife has been afraid to go near you for fear of contracting the plague."

"I'm no longer communicable." Raising his hands to her face, he kissed her more insistently as his erection pressed against her.

All he had to do was look at her and she wanted him, but when he kissed her and touched her this way, she was lost to him every time. But he'd been so sick only yesterday, and her better judgment took over. "Not yet."

"Hmm?" His lips moved softly over her neck, feeding the fire.

It took all the willpower Sam could muster to gently push on his chest.

"What?" he asked, sounding perplexed because she hardly ever pushed him away, and it was the last thing she wanted to do now.

"You were so sick only yesterday."

"I'm fine now."

"No, you're not."

He rubbed his erection against her, his fingers digging into her hips as he tugged her into his embrace. "I'm *fine*, Samantha."

She shook her head. "No."

"You're not seriously saying no to me."

"First time for everything, my love."

"No way. I can change your mind."

"I have no doubt you could, but you're not going to. One more day won't kill you."

"It just might, and think about how bad you'll feel if it does."

Sam rolled her eyes. "Shameless manipulation will get you nowhere tonight."

His low growl made her laugh.

"I've spoiled you rotten in our first year of marriage," she said, "and now you're downright unmanageable."

He took her hand and pressed it against his cock. "I'm very manageable. Give me what I want, and you'll see just *how* manageable I can be."

She leaned in close to him, so close that her lips nearly touched his. "Not. Happening."

"This is cruel and unusual punishment."

"No, this is me being a good wife and making sure you're totally healed before I ravage you."

He scowled. "You can't say no in one breath and then talk about ravaging me in the next. Not fair."

"It'll give you something to look forward to tomorrow. And PS, pouting is not an attractive quality for a vice president."

"I'm not the vice president right now. I'm a horny husband with an uncooperative wife."

"Whatever! I'm the most cooperative wife in the history of the *world*."

"Most of the time…"

Before she could respond to that, her phone rang. She checked the caller ID, saw Avery's name and took the call.

"I'm at Hamilton's house. He's been murdered."

At first, his words didn't compute. And then they registered, taking her breath away in a whoosh. "How?"

"Someone took a golf club to him. His face is unrecognizable."

"Who else knows?"

"Only you so far. It's your jurisdiction, and even though it goes against everything I believe in as a federal agent to hand this off to someone else, it'd be a conflict for us to be involved. I want this done right, Sam."

"I understand. Stay put. I'm on my way."

"Are you allowed? Aren't you still suspended?"

"I'll clear it with Malone. We'll be right there."

"Okay."

"Are you all right, Avery?"

"Yeah, I'm great," he said grimly before he ended the call.

"What does he want?" Nick asked.

"He found Director Hamilton murdered in his home."

Nick's mouth opened and then closed as his eyes widened. "Seriously?"

"Unfortunately." Sam eyed the closed kitchen door, thinking of Josh on the other side of it and how she should handle this with him. Tell him or wait until they knew more? What more did they need to know? His father was dead.

"What if it was him?" Nick asked, using his thumb to point to the other room.

Recalling Josh's disheveled appearance when he arrived earlier, Sam's stomach twisted with anxiety. "There was no sign of blood on him. I would've noticed that. And murder by golf club would be messy."

"Still, you can't say for sure it wasn't him. He certainly had motive."

With her brain whirling with details and implications,

Sam blew out a deep breath and placed a call to Captain Malone.

"Hey, what's up?" he asked.

"Troy Hamilton is dead. Avery found him bludgeoned with a golf club in his house."

"Fucking hell." After a short pause, Malone said, "Call in your troops and meet me there." The phone went dead before Sam could say, "Yes, sir," and before she could ask him what she should do about Hamilton's son, who was currently playing video games with her son.

"He wants me there," Sam told Nick, who was leaning against the counter, arms crossed and brows knitted in concern.

"And what am I to do with the son who may or may not have wanted his father dead?"

"I don't know, Nick!"

"He doesn't need to stay here anymore since the so-called threat has been neutralized."

"We don't know that. Whoever killed Troy might be gunning for Josh next."

"Sam, come on. I want him out of here."

Keeping her gaze fixed on Nick, she called Dispatch and asked them to recall her squad to Hamilton's address.

"Yes, ma'am," the dispatcher said after a short pause, during which Sam had no doubt the woman was wondering why Sam was issuing orders while suspended. Luckily she didn't ask so Sam didn't have to tell her to mind her own business. She slapped the phone closed and stashed it in her pocket.

"I know it's a lot to ask."

"Yeah, it is. The guy was running from the threat of murder, so you brought him here."

"I wanted to keep him safe!"

"By endangering us?"

"There's no danger to us with the Secret Service all over this place."

"So now my detail is convenient to you when most of the time you hate it?"

"Are you fighting with me because I said no to having sex with you tonight?"

"Are you seriously asking me that?"

"No, I guess I'm not." She went to him, flattening her hands on his chest. "I know it's an awful lot to ask, and I'm sorry I brought him here. He was so damned scared. Freddie and I both saw it, and I didn't know where else to take him that Hamilton couldn't get at him."

"This whole thing is fucking crazy. You know that, don't you?"

"Yes, I do, but now I've got a homicide to contend with, and it's going to be the hottest case we've had in years."

"Which is saying something," he muttered. "I don't want him alone with Scotty."

"Okay."

"One night, Samantha, and then he's out of here. Are we clear?"

"Yes, thank you. I agree that I need to figure out something else for him, and I'll take care of that as fast as I can. I promise."

"I want to bring Brant in on what's going on. He can't protect us if he doesn't know."

She hesitated as she considered that. It was her natural tendency to keep things to herself, but Nick was right. Brant couldn't do his job without all the information, and since Brant's job was to protect the two most important people in her life, she nodded. "Fair enough." She went up on tiptoes to kiss him. "I love you. I'm sorry I brought this situation into our home, and I'm sorry I had to say no to you for the first time ever."

His lips curved into a small, sexy smile. "You'll make it up to me." He leaned in close to brush his lips against her ear. "On your back, with your legs on my shoulders, your ass red from my hand and—"

"Stop it," she said, shivering from the desire that instantly heated her core. "Right now. I've got to go to work."

Chuckling, he released her. "Hurry home, and be careful out there, Samantha. Whoever decided to kill the FBI director won't think twice about killing again."

"I'm always careful. Don't worry."

"Right. You may as well tell me not to breathe."

"Don't do that. I need you alive and well when I get home so I can make it up to you."

"It's not fair. You're suspended and you still have to work. I was sort of looking forward to having you all to myself for a few days. Should've known it was too much to hope for. But you'll pay. Yes, you will. When you get home and when we get to Bora Bora at the end of the month. You will pay."

Smiling, she kissed him again. "Can't wait."

"Me either." He stole another kiss from her. "Love you so much. Please be careful."

"I will. I promise. Hold down the fort, and keep an eye on our guest." She patted his chest one last time and left the kitchen, deciding in that moment to keep the news about Troy from Josh until she knew more. They'd keep it on lockdown so there was no way he'd hear it online or anywhere else until they were ready to release the news.

In the living room, Scotty and Josh were playing

a driving game on the Xbox, racing through winding mountain roads.

"I have to go out for a while," Sam said as she put on her coat. "I'll see you guys in the morning."

"Bye, Mom," Scotty said without taking his eyes off the screen.

Josh glanced up at her. "Thanks again for letting me stay here."

"Sure, no problem." Sam had spent most of her career dealing with murderers, and if Josh had murdered his father, he was being awfully calm in the aftermath. Most of the time, a regular person who was driven to kill would be agitated, nervous, afraid of being caught. She'd seen none of that behavior in Josh. If he'd had anything to do with his father's murder, he was doing a hell of a job hiding it.

On the way down the ramp, she took a call from Freddie.

"We just got called to a homicide in Northwest."

"I know. I'm on my way."

"I thought you were suspended."

"I am."

"Ahhh," he said with a chuckle. "I see."

"This is big, Freddie. It's Hamilton."

Gasping, he said, "Josh?"

"No, Troy."

"Holy smokes."

"I was thinking more along the lines of holy fucking shit myself."

"Yeah, that too. You don't think…Josh…"

"I don't know, but Nick mentioned that possibility. He showed up disheveled earlier and said he'd fallen in Rock Creek Park. I didn't see anything on him that looked like blood, and a murder like this would've been messy. But he certainly had motive."

"This is the weirdest case ever."

"And it's just gotten a whole lot weirder."

"No kidding. See you there."

"On my way." She pressed on the accelerator, dodging what little traffic there was at that hour on a Sunday and headed for the city's Northwest corner. On the way, she placed a call to Lindsey McNamara.

"Hey, I was just going to call you," Lindsey said. "I got word that the DNA report is back. What do you want me to do with it?"

"Email it to me?"

"Will do."

"We've got a body," she said, giving Lindsey the address. "And not just any body. It's FBI Director Hamilton."

"Oh my God."

"I know, and you're probably not on call, but I want you on this one. Can you come?" Sam gave her the address.

"Yes, of course. I'll call in my team and meet you there."

"We're keeping a tight lid on this for obvious reasons."

"Where's his son?"

"On lockdown at my house. He's been there for hours, but was in the wind for a period of time earlier today. I'm going to be very interested in the time of death."

"Are you on the case? I thought you were off."

"I am, but Malone called me in. See you in a few."

Not surprisingly, the Hamiltons resided in one of the swankier areas of the city, and the street was lined with cars and emergency vehicles by the time Sam pulled in behind Freddie's rattletrap Mustang. The neighbors had begun to wander out to see what was going on.

Sam walked down the long driveway to the huge porch where Freddie greeted her. "We've got gawkers out there," she said. "Get Patrol here to set up a perimeter."

"Already done."

"Someone trained you right."

"Yeah, I can't remember the name of the guy, but he did a good job."

"Yes, *she* did." She followed him inside, through a foyer that was the size of her first apartment after the academy, into a sitting room that led to the office where Hamilton lay in a pool of blood, a golf club on the floor next to him. His face was unrecognizable, which seemed deliberate, as if the killer had wanted to erase his identity.

Avery Hill stood watch over his director, arms crossed, expression tense. When he looked at her, however, Sam saw the despair.

"Any sign of forced entry?" Sam asked, sensing that engaging Hill in the investigation would help.

"Not that I could see, but I didn't do a full search. The front door was ajar when I arrived."

Sam glanced at Freddie, and he nodded, leaving the room to see to her unspoken order to do a full search of the premises to check points of entry and to make sure no one else was in the house. She squatted for a closer look at the victim and noted the blow that had caved in the side of his skull and likely ended his life. Lindsey would confirm that, but in cases like this, it didn't take an autopsy to determine cause of death.

"You touch anything?" she asked Hill.

He shook his head. "I used my shoulder to push open

the door and the only thing I've touched since I got here was my phone to call you."

The rest of her team began to arrive—Dominguez and Carlucci, McBride and Tyrone and then Lindsey, Malone and Farnsworth.

Freddie returned. "Clear," he said of the rest of the house.

"Where's Gonzo?" she asked in a low tone that only he could hear.

"Not here."

"Call him." To the others, she said, "Listen up. Our victim is FBI Director Troy Hamilton."

Her announcement was greeted with shocked expressions and gasps of surprise.

"Wait," Tyrone said. "Weren't we looking for his son earlier today?"

"You were," Sam said. "Here's what we know so far." She began with her encounter with Josh on Friday and quickly took them through the sequence of events over the weekend that had culminated with Avery finding Hamilton's body an hour ago.

"What brought you here, Agent Hill?" Malone asked while the others processed what Sam had told them.

"After I saw you and Lieutenant Holland earlier and you informed me about what was happening with the director's son, I went home and tried to wrap my head around the possibility that the director could've been involved in a kidnapping of all things. After a couple of hours, I realized I needed to see him, to talk to him, to try to get to the bottom of what was going on. So I came here."

He paused before he continued, seeming to gather his thoughts. "I rang the bell and knocked on the door, which was ajar. When no one answered, I nudged the door with my shoulder and stepped inside, calling for the director. I noticed a vase shattered in the foyer and a lamp on the floor in the room to my right. I've been here before, so I knew where the director's home office was located. Upon approach to the doorway, I saw his foot on the floor and then the rest of his body in a pool of blood. I called the lieutenant after confirming he was dead."

"Did you touch him?" Farnsworth asked.

"I didn't need to. It was obvious he was long gone."

Lindsey McNamara's team arrived in a flurry of activity and began to prepare Hamilton's body for transport to the morgue.

"Who was his next of kin?" Sam asked Avery.

"His wife, I suppose."

Sam withdrew the notebook she carried with her from her back pocket. "What's her name?"

"Courtney. He also has three children—Josh, Mark and Maura. Only Josh is local. Mark lives in Chicago, and Maura is in Boston."

"Where might we find Courtney?" Sam asked.

"I have no idea." He met her gaze. "You could ask Josh."

"I suppose we'll have to."

"Is Josh a suspect?" Freddie asked.

"Doc, can you tell how long he's been dead?" Sam asked Lindsey.

"I'm guessing until I get him back to the lab, but upon visual inspection, I'd say it's been a couple hours."

To Freddie, Sam said, "I don't know if he's a suspect, but he was off the grid for a period of hours, during which time his father was murdered. I'd say we need to have a conversation with him about exactly where he went after he left the hotel."

"He was scared shitless that his father was going to kill him," Freddie said. "I find it hard to believe he would've come anywhere near here."

"Or maybe he wanted us to *think* he was scared shitless so we wouldn't look at him for this," Sam said.

"I suppose that's possible," Freddie conceded.

"All I know," Sam said, "is we can't rule him out for this, and right now he's with my husband and son. I'm going home."

"I'm going with you," Avery said.

"Let's make it a party," Farnsworth added.

"Cruz, wait for Crime Scene and then you can join us at the lieutenant's home," Malone said.

"Yes, sir."

"The rest of you start a canvass," Sam said. "See if the neighbors report anything suspicious, but don't give them any details about what happened to Hamilton. Very tight lid."

Murmurs of "yes, ma'am" preceded their departure.

"Did you reach Gonzo?" Sam asked Freddie.

"Right to voicemail."

She had to hunt down her sergeant tomorrow and figure out what to do for him before his grief fucked up his once-promising career.

Sam took a final look around the director's study, noting the desktop devoid of clutter the way Nick's was, the framed photos on the wall of the director with presidents, world leaders and other luminaries, the awards, the certificates, the accolades. The room was a shrine to his career, but nowhere among the pomp or pageantry did she see a photo of his wife or children.

Interesting. The first thing anyone would notice on her husband's desk was the gorgeous, intimate photo from their wedding and a second one of them with their son. There would be no doubt of where his priorities lay.

Hamilton would take his secrets to the grave with him, but Sam was going to figure out what those secrets were, and if she had to shred his vaunted reputation in the process, well, so be it.

CHAPTER THIRTEEN

SAM LEFT THE director's home less than an hour after she had arrived, placing a call to her husband as she walked to her car. "The cavalry is coming," she said when he answered.

"What do you mean?"

"Farnsworth, Malone, Hill. They want to talk to Josh."

"Um, okay."

"I'm sorry I brought this situation into our home. That was a mistake."

"Hang on. I'm going into the kitchen." She heard him moving around. "No, it wasn't. At the time you thought it was the right thing. You had no way to know his father would end up murdered and you'd be wondering what, if anything, Josh had to do with it."

"I am wondering. He was off the grid for a few hours today. That's one of the things we need to talk to him about. When we're done, I'll have Malone set up a new place to keep him until we figure this out."

"I was hoping you'd say that. Brant told me he has a weird feeling about the guy. He's been watching him like a hawk."

"Brant is paid to trust those feelings," Sam said with a sigh. "I really fucked this up. I'm sorry."

"Stop apologizing, babe. This is your home too and you can invite anyone you want to come here."

"I shouldn't have brought my work home with me. If it wasn't for this goddamned suspension, I wouldn't have had to."

"How bad was the scene at Hamilton's house?"

"Golf-club-to-the-face bad."

"Jesus. How could someone get at him? Didn't he have security?"

"Nope."

"He was arrogant to think he didn't need it."

"Like someone else you know?"

"Your words, not mine," he said with a laugh.

"I'm almost home. Do me a favor and send Scotty up to bed?"

"Yeah, will do. He's yawning his head off anyway. See you in a few."

She closed her phone and stashed it in her coat pocket as she pulled up to the security checkpoint and opened the window. "I've got some of my colleagues on the way over. MPD Chief Farnsworth, Captain Malone and FBI Special Agent Avery Hill. They're all on my visitor list, so please let them through."

"Yes, ma'am."

Scowling at that dreaded word, she accelerated through the checkpoint to her parking space. As she took the ramp to the front door, she tried to decide how best to approach Josh. Tell him now when it was just the two of them or wait for the others. Because she had only a split second to make that call, she decided to tell him now and let him know the others were on their way to talk to him.

The agent on duty opened the door and nodded to her. "Evening, ma'am."

"Evening." Sam wondered what they truly thought of the way she came and went as she pleased. It was probably better if she didn't know their thoughts about her. Tossing her coat over the back of the first chair she encountered, she went over to where Josh sat by himself, game controller in hand, clicking away.

"Hey," she said as she sat with him. "Could you pause that for a second?" Out of the corner of her eye, she saw Nick come downstairs and head for the kitchen. Brant stepped out of the home office and followed Nick. Sam had no doubt they both had eyes on her as she talked to Josh.

"What's up?" Josh asked. The room had gone oddly silent without the screech of tires or manic game noise.

"I'm afraid I have some news that may be upsetting to hear."

"The DNA isn't a match?"

"No, it's not that, although the results are back, and I'll be sending them to the detective in charge of the kidnapping in the morning."

"Then what?"

"Your father has been murdered." She watched him carefully, gauging his reaction.

His brows furrowed, but his expression otherwise remained passive. "Murdered," he said slowly. "How? Where?"

"He was bludgeoned at home." She purposely omitted the weapon used in the killing. For now, only the killer and the police—and Nick, who wouldn't breathe a word of it—had that information, and she planned to keep it that way. That tidbit could come in handy later.

Josh expelled a deep breath that sounded a lot like relief to her. "He's dead? He's really dead?"

"Yes."

Propping his elbows on his knees, he bent his head and

his shoulders began to shake. At first she thought he was crying, but then she realized he was laughing.

"You think it's *funny* that your father was murdered?"

"Yeah, kinda, in light of who he was. Nice to know he was human after all."

"Josh, I've got to be honest with you. This isn't looking all that great for you. You were missing for a couple hours this afternoon, around the time the medical examiner estimates your father was murdered. There was no sign of forced entry, which leads us to believe he knew the person who attacked him or the person had access to the house. And when I told you the man who raised you was murdered, you laughed. Can you see how this might be a problem for you?"

His eyes went wide with what looked like shock. "You think *I* killed him?"

"I think you had opportunity and possible motive, which are two factors we look at closely in homicide investigations."

"Let me save you some time and trouble. I didn't do it."

"If I had a dollar for every time I've heard those words, I'd be rich."

"This time, they're actually true. I wanted nothing to do with him. That house was the last place you'd ever find me. Ask anyone who knows me. I haven't been there in years. I had nothing to do with him being murdered, but I'm not sorry he's dead. He was a narcissistic asshole who made my life a living hell. You won't see me crying at his funeral."

Strangely enough, Sam believed him, but they'd still have to establish his whereabouts for the missing hours to eliminate him as a suspect. "I need to get in touch with your mother. Can you tell me where she might be?"

"I take it she wasn't at home?"

"There was no one there but your father."

"I don't know where she is. I haven't talked to her in a couple of weeks."

"Would you mind calling her now?"

As he reached for his phone on the coffee table, the Secret Service admitted Farnsworth, Malone and Hill.

"Don't tell her your father is dead. We'll take care of that. I just need to know where she is."

While he made the call, Sam got up to greet the others. "He says it wasn't him, he hasn't been to the house in years and won't cry at the funeral. I asked him to reach out to his mother, which he's doing now."

Listening to his side of the conversation, Sam deduced that his mother was relieved to hear from him.

"I don't know what medication he was talking about," Josh said. "I'm not on anything." After a long pause, he said, "I don't know, but who ever knows with him? What're you up to?" He listened. "Is she okay?" Another pause. "It's going around. I know some other people who've had it." He wrapped up the call, telling his mother to tell his grandmother he hoped she felt better and saying he'd call again soon. "Love you too."

Josh looked up at Sam. "She's at my grandmother's in Chantilly. My grandmother is sick. It sounds like she has the same thing your family had."

"Did she say how long she's been there?" Sam asked.

"You can't honestly think she had anything to do with my father's murder."

"I didn't say anything about her having something to do with it. I asked if she said how long she's been there."

"No, she didn't, but I got the sense she's been there awhile. My grandmother is pretty sick."

"Do you know your grandmother's address off the top of your head?"

He eyed her for a long moment before he rattled off the address.

Sam wrote it down in her notebook.

"Mr. Hamilton, I'm Chief Farnsworth with the MPD. I've made arrangements for you to be escorted home now that the perceived threat to your safety has been neutralized."

Josh glanced at Sam and then at the chief. "Perceived? There was nothing *perceived* about it, and when word gets out that he's dead, his henchmen will be looking for me."

"I think it's possible you've been watching too much television," Farnsworth said. "You were afraid of your father. Lieutenant Holland went to extraordinary lengths to keep you safe, and now your father is no longer a threat. We believe it's safe for you to return to your own home at this time, providing you remain local and available during our investigation."

"I disagree." He stood and turned to face the chief. "Lieutenant Holland told me the DNA results are back. I'd like to know those results before I go home."

"And we'd like to know exactly where you were after you left the hotel this afternoon," Malone said.

"I told Lieutenant Holland. I walked around. I ended up in Rock Creek Park and took a fall, which is why my coat was dirty and torn when I got here."

"Rock Creek Park isn't exactly around the corner from Arlington," Avery said.

"I walked for a long time. I was scared he was going to find me, so I went to the park. I thought I could hide there until I figured out what to do next. I'd left my wallet in the hotel, so my options were limited."

"Did you see anyone? Talk to anyone?"

Josh shook his head. "I didn't talk to anyone. I just walked."

"Take a seat and let us make a plan," Sam said.

Seeming resigned, he returned to his seat on the sofa, the controller in hand, but the game remained frozen on pause, like his life since Friday.

She turned to her commanders. "What do you want to do?"

IN THE KITCHEN, Nick kept an eye on the goings-on in the other room. He trusted Sam's instincts about people implicitly, but he didn't like having Josh Hamilton in his house and neither did the Secret Service. After hearing about the APB that had been issued for Hamilton earlier in the day, Brant had gone so far as to ask when he would be leaving.

When Nick's cell phone rang, he withdrew it from his pocket to check the caller ID, and took the call from Christina, his former chief of staff. "Hey, what's up?"

"I'm sorry to bother you when you're sick. I'm trying to get in touch with Sam, but her phone is going to voicemail."

"No worries. I'm much better, and she's dealing with something for work right now."

"Oh, um, I don't know what to do."

She sounded as if she were about to break down.

"What's wrong, Chris?"

"Tommy… He—he's asleep, really asleep, for the first time since AJ was killed. I took his phone out of the room so he wouldn't be disturbed. I just got out of the shower and noticed that he'd missed a recall to work. He's going to be furious, especially with Sam suspended, but I can't bring myself to wake him. He needs the sleep so badly." Her voice caught on a sob.

"I'll tell Sam, and she'll smooth it with the brass. She's working the case, so let him sleep."

"Thank you," she said softly, her sobs echoing through the phone.

"Are you okay?"

"I'm trying to be. It's been rough. Really, really rough."

"What can I do for you? Name it. Anything."

"You're sweet to offer, but I've talked him into counseling. I'm pinning all my hopes on that. We have an appointment tomorrow with Trulo."

"That's a good first step. He helped Sam a lot after what happened with Stahl. I don't know that she would've found her way back to work without Trulo."

"I'm worried about him, Nick. He's wrecked."

"It's going to take some time, but he'll get through it. He's tough."

"Usually, yes, but this… I've never seen him like this."

"If you need us, you know where we are. Always."

She blew out a deep breath. "Thank you."

"Do you need some company? I could come sit with you or help with Alex or something."

"You can't just come over the way you used to, but it's nice of you to offer."

"I can come, and I will if it would help."

"I thought you were on lockdown with the flu."

"I know how to escape if need be."

She laughed. "I love you for offering, but you stay home and get better. I'll be okay."

"Call me tomorrow? Let me know how you guys are doing?"

"I will. Thanks again, Nick. Tell Sam to call me if she needs to."

"You got it."

Sam came into the kitchen as Nick was ending the call with Christina. "We're trying to relocate Josh. I wanted you to know."

"That was Christina. She said Tommy is sleeping—really sleeping for the first time since AJ died—and she took his phone out of the bedroom. That's why he missed the recall. She was freaking out that she might've done the wrong thing."

"No, she didn't," Sam said with a sigh. "It's good that he's sleeping. I'll let Malone know."

"Can I tell her it's okay?"

"Yeah, do that."

He fired off a quick text to Christina, conveying Sam's message.

She wrote right back. Thank you both. xo.

"She also said she's talked Gonzo into seeing Trulo. They have an appointment tomorrow."

"That's good news. Let's hope it helps."

Nick put his arm around her and kissed her temple. "What's up with the case?"

"We're figuring that out now." She looked up at him. "How're you feeling?"

"Totally fine."

"That's not possible. You were in the hospital yesterday."

Tipping her chin up, he kissed her. "I. Am. Totally. *Fine*." Raising his brows, he added, "And ready to get back to *normal* around here."

She smiled. "Message received. Let me see what's what out there."

"Could I say something you might not want to hear?"

"Um, I guess?"

"You're suspended. That means technically, this case isn't your problem."

"Technically, you're right, but I'm invested, and I want to help, especially with Gonzo out for who knows how long."

"I understand, but I *need* my wife. You cleared my schedule for the next few days. You're suspended. You know what this means, right?"

"Ummm—"

"It means you're mine. All mine. For *days*."

"I thought that was our plan when we go to Bora Bora."

"So you're saying no to unexpected bonus days?"

"Definitely not saying no. I'm saying let me figure out a few things and get back to you."

"You know where to find me."

"Yes, I do." She patted his face and kissed him. "Go to bed. You need your rest."

"That's not what I need."

"I'm going to have to dial it back in year two if this is how you're going to behave when you hear the word *no*."

"You're not dialing back anything. We're perfect exactly the way we are."

Smiling up at him, she said, "You've got to let go so I can get rid of the people in our living room."

He dropped the arm he had around her. "Make it snappy," he said, punctuating his words with a light slap to her ass that had her looking over her shoulder at him, eyes ablaze. God, he loved when she looked at him that way. Yes, he knew he was being pushy and maybe a little obnoxious, but they were always so insanely busy. They had to take full advantage of every chance they got to spend time together.

He watched her go through the kitchen door and caught the way Hill's gaze immediately shifted to her when she entered the room. Nick wanted to poke the guy's eyes out of his head so he would stop looking at her that way. Until Sam had come back into his life, Nick would've said he didn't have a jealous bone in his body. But Hill's obvious attraction to Sam made Nick crazy, and it infuriated him on Shelby's behalf. What right did Hill have to look at Sam the way he did when he had an amazing woman like Shelby waiting for him at home?

Nick was well aware that none of these thoughts were particularly dignified or vice presidential, but when his precious wife was involved, dignity was the least of his concerns. Resigned to waiting for her, he left the kitchen and went into the living room.

"Mr. Vice President," Malone said with a cheeky grin, knowing how much Nick hated to be called that in his own home. "Nice to see you up and about. You had us worried."

Nick shook hands with Sam's captain and chief, pointedly ignoring the third man in the room. "Thanks for the concern."

"You're feeling better?" Farnsworth asked.

"Much," he said, sending a meaningful glance to Sam.

"Sorry to overtake your home," Farnsworth said. "We'll be out of your hair shortly."

"Take your time." Nick kissed his wife's cheek. "You know where to find me when you're done."

The glower she directed his way nearly made him

laugh out loud, knowing how much she despised overt displays of affection in front of other people, especially other people who happened to be her bosses. Fuck it. What did he care if they saw how much he loved her? He had no desire to hide that from anyone, least of all the FBI agent who had taken an interest in his phone the minute Nick came into the room.

Nick had no doubt he would pay for that kiss later. He couldn't wait.

CHAPTER FOURTEEN

"WE'VE ARRANGED A safe house for Josh until we figure out the next steps in the investigation," Malone said after Nick went upstairs. They spoke in low voices so Josh couldn't hear them.

Sam would deal with her husband and his habit of staking his claim on her in front of Hill after everyone left. "Who's going to see the director's wife?"

"I will," Hill said.

"We're coming with you," Farnsworth said of himself and Malone.

"That's fine," Hill replied. "I need to speak to my deputy director and make him aware of what's happened. He'll assume command of the Bureau until a permanent director can be named, so he needs to know what's going on."

"Make the call," Farnsworth said, "but let him know the MPD is leading the investigation into Hamilton's death and will keep the Bureau apprised as a courtesy."

Sam loved the way the chief cut through the bullshit to establish jurisdiction. The Feds would want in on it, but that wasn't happening. She also loved the way Avery's golden eyes flashed with anger that he wisely kept under wraps.

"I'm well aware that it would be a conflict for the Bureau to investigate the murder of our director," he said with a testy edge to his normally honeyed Southern accent. "That's why I called the lieutenant when I found him rather than my own people."

"Excellent," Farnsworth said. "Glad we're all on the same page."

Sam almost laughed at that, but thankfully managed to control herself, knowing Hill wouldn't appreciate it. "In the morning, I'm going to jump all over the Rollings case and any connection Hamilton might've had to Tennessee during that era." She would've already done that if her husband and son hadn't been sick all weekend.

"I can tell you what connection he had," Hill said. "He was the agent in charge of the Knoxville Field Office in the eighties."

Sam felt like she'd been sucker punched. "Holy Christ."

"I… I know it'll sound like I'm defending him," Hill said, "but in my wildest dreams I can't conceive of Hamilton kidnapping someone's child and raising him as his own."

"If I've learned one thing in more than thirty years in this business," Farnsworth said, "it's that people are capable of anything under the right circumstances." His words echoed hers from earlier. They'd both seen a lot during their careers and had learned to keep their minds wide-open to all possibilities.

"What *circumstances* could've led him to kidnapping someone else's child?" Hill asked, becoming more flustered by the second.

"Until we know we have a match on the DNA, the kidnapping should take a backseat to the homicide investigation," Sam said.

"How can they not be related?" Malone asked. "The timing can't be coincidental."

"Agreed," Sam said. "But our priority right now needs to be notifying Hamilton's wife and working the homicide. We'll know more about the kidnapping and whether the DNA is a match tomorrow or the next day." She handed the address Josh had given her for his grandmother to Hill. "That's where you'll find Mrs. Hamilton."

He took it from her without comment.

Sam asked for a moment with Malone and brought him up to speed on Gonzo's whereabouts.

"Good to know he's getting some sleep," Malone said.

"That's what I thought too. Christina's concerned about whether she did the right thing. I'd like to put her mind at rest…"

"Yes, tell her I agree with you, and we'll see him when he feels up to returning to duty."

"I will. Thank you, Captain."

"I can't say I understand what he's going through because I've never had a partner gunned down right next to me."

"Same. I hope I never do."

Speaking of her partner, the agent working the front door admitted Freddie Cruz, and Sam's heart ached at the thought of losing him the way Gonzo had lost Arnold. She couldn't go there, not even for a second.

"We're all set, Detective?" Farnsworth asked.

"Yes, sir," Freddie said. "I spoke with the Patrol commander and they'll be providing overnight security at the house."

"Very good, thank you." To Josh, Farnsworth said, "Mr. Hamilton, Detective Cruz will escort you to a safe house that's managed by the MPD. You'll be under the protection of the department until we know more about what happened to your father and whether there's a connection to the Rollings family."

"It's the same place we kept Selina during the Lightfeather investigation," Freddie said to Sam.

She nodded. "Good. Thanks. Did you get anything from the canvass of Hamilton's neighborhood?"

"One neighbor reported seeing someone running from the house at around three-thirty. Carlucci and Dominguez are taking the statement at HQ."

"Do we have any cameras in that neighborhood?"

"Archie's on that," he said of Lieutenant Archelotta, who headed the department's IT division.

Sam's cell phone rang, and she retrieved it from her pocket, scowling at the sight of Darren Tabor's name on the caller ID. He was becoming a regular pest. "What?"

"What're you guys doing up at the FBI director's house?"

"How would I know? I'm suspended."

"You were seen there earlier."

"No idea what you're talking about, Darren. I'm not allowed to conduct MPD business as you and everyone in the city knows thanks to your reporting."

"Who's covering for you while you're out?"

"Malone."

"Where's Gonzo?"

"Gotta go, Darren. Nice to catch up." She slapped the phone closed. "He's going to call you," she said to Malone, whose phone rang. He ignored it. "He's digging into what's going on at Hamilton's house. We're on borrowed time to notify the family before the press gets the story."

"Let's go." Hill headed for the door, with Malone and Farnsworth following.

"I'll call you in the morning," Malone said to Sam over his shoulder.

She wanted to go with them so badly she could taste it. This was the kind of case she lived for, but thanks to fucking Ramsey and his big fucking mouth, she was relegated to the cheap seats while the others got to work the case. There was still a lot she could do from the cheap seats, but there was nothing like the front lines when it came to a homicide investigation.

Resigned to her fate for the time being, she turned her attention to Josh, who was putting on his coat.

"Thanks for letting me come here," Josh said. "Sorry for any trouble I caused."

"You were no trouble. Hopefully we'll have some answers for you in the next day or two."

"I don't know what to hope for anymore—that I'm Taylor or that I'm not. It's all very confusing."

"I'm sure it is. Let me ask you… Did your father ever talk about the time he spent in Tennessee as the field office director in Knoxville?"

Josh's brows knitted in confusion. "He didn't live in Tennessee."

"Special Agent Hill confirmed that he was the agent in charge of the Knoxville Field Office in the eighties."

"I don't think that's right. I've never heard him talk about living in Tennessee, and he talked about everything when it came to his career."

"Well, maybe Agent Hill was mistaken."

"Must've been."

"Let's get you out of here and settled for the night," Freddie said. To Sam he added, "I'll call you."

She waved him over before he went through the door. "Christina called Nick. She said Gonzo was sleeping for the first time since Arnold was killed, and she let him sleep rather than telling him work had called."

Freddie shuddered. "Remember when Elin did that to me and I ended up getting shot?"

"A. Elin did it because she wanted a booty call. B. You got shot because you were stupid. Two very different situations."

"Gee, thanks, Lieutenant. Appreciate the reminder of my stupidity."

"I'm always here for you, Detective. Now get out of my house. My husband wants a booty call."

"Ugh."

Sam cracked up laughing at the face he made.

"Unnecessary."

"It's actually very necessary. Call me in the morning. I want to be kept in the loop on every aspect of this investigation. Let the others know too."

"Okay."

To Josh she said, "We'll be in touch as soon as we know anything about the DNA."

"Thank you for everything you've done. I'm sorry to have dragged you into this."

"I'm glad you came to me, and I'll see it through to whatever conclusion it leads to. I promise."

Nodding, he preceded Freddie out the door.

"Are you expecting other visitors, Mrs. Cappuano?" the agent asked.

"Not tonight."

"Very good. Have a nice evening."

"You too." She shut off the lights in the kitchen and living room and went upstairs to the bedroom, expecting to find Nick already in bed. But he wasn't there or in the adjoining bathroom. Sam smiled when she realized where she would find her husband. Though she was still concerned about his health, she knew by now how convincing he could be when he wanted her. So she took a quick shower, shaved her legs and applied the vanilla-scented lotion that drove him wild, not that she needed any help when it came to driving him wild. He was easily driven where she was concerned, which was one of many reasons she loved him so much.

Her mind refused to shut down, spinning through the events of the day. This was one hell of a time to be hit with a case of this magnitude, with her on suspension, Gonzo spiraling and the Homicide unit already short-handed due to the loss of Arnold. Those worries had her placing a call to Malone.

"Didn't I just see you?"

"I'm thinking…"

"Always a dangerous pastime for you, Lieutenant."

"Ha, ha."

"What's on your mind?"

"This huge case falling into our laps at a time when we're ill prepared to cope with it."

"Your thoughts match mine."

She realized he was choosing his words carefully because he was in the car with Hill. "The chief could lift my suspension, and I could serve out the rest after we close this case."

"Again, your thought process and mine are aligned. I'll discuss it with him and get back to you in the morning."

"Great, thanks." Sam was nearly giddy at the thought of being brought back to deal with the Hamilton investigation, not to mention imagining Ramsey's reaction to hearing that she was back on the job because she was so essential to the department.

"You can stop your gloating now, Lieutenant," Malone said with a chuckle.

"Who's gloating? Have a good night, Captain."

"You do the same."

Sam ended the call and did a jig around the bedroom. It sure was nice to be *essential* to so many people, including her husband, who was getting so lucky tonight, even if she wasn't convinced he should be exerting himself after being sick. He said he was fine, and she chose to take him at his word.

She crossed the hall to the room she used as a closet and changed into some of the sluttiest lingerie she owned before tying a big, bulky, unsexy, safe-for-Secret-Service-to-see robe over the ensemble.

She stepped into the hallway to find Secret Service Barbie giving her the eye. *Eat your heart out*, she wanted to say to the other woman. *I'm going to get it on with the sexiest vice president in the history of the world right now.* Of course she couldn't actually say *that*, so instead she said, "Good night, Melinda."

"Good night, ma'am."

Sam felt the agent's eyes on her back as she checked on Scotty, who was sleeping soundly, and then made for the stairs that led to the third-floor loft her loving husband had put together as a getaway for them. If the agents knew what went on up there, they never let on, but Sam was sure they had their suspicions. Let them wonder. It was bad enough that their house was overrun with people these days. The time they spent alone up there belonged to her and Nick and no one else.

On the way upstairs, she was greeted by the scent of coconut that took her right back to the blissful days and nights of their honeymoon. As she shut and locked the door behind her, she saw that he'd lit the candles, turned on music and was asleep on his side, the sheet pooling around his narrow hips, leaving his muscular back exposed. She licked her lips at the sight of him, torn between wanting him and not wanting to disturb his badly needed sleep.

Sam removed the robe and the lingerie since he was asleep, tossed her clothes over the end of the double lounge chair, put her cell phone on the bedside table and slid in next to him, tugging the covers up and over her.

His arm immediately encircled her waist, making her squeak inelegantly as he tugged her in close to him.

"I thought you were asleep!"

"That's what I wanted you to think," he said, laughing.

Her heart beat fast with adrenaline from being surprised and the ever-present desire that flooded her senses whenever he was nearby. She'd never reacted to any man the way she did to him, and she was addicted to the way he made her feel.

He propped himself up on an elbow and gazed down at her, as if seeing her for the very first time.

"What?" she asked, unnerved by his intense scrutiny.

"Just looking at what's mine."

"You put on quite a show downstairs."

"When?"

"Don't play dumb with me. You know exactly what I'm talking about."

"*Why* does he still look at you that way when he has Shelby waiting for him at home with his ring on her finger?"

"I don't know what you're talking about. He doesn't look at me any way."

"The second you walk into the room his eyes are on you. Every. Single. Time."

"Why do you let it bother you? It has no bearing on us."

"It pisses me off."

"Sort of like it pisses me off that Secret Service Barbie looks at you like you're a great big banana split with an extra helping of nuts?"

He lost it laughing.

"Why is that funny but your shit about Hill isn't?"

Wiping tears from his eyes, he said, "Because she's *paid* to look at me, and he's just hot for you."

"No, he isn't. And PS, I came up here hot for *you*, but I'm cooling by the second."

His hand landed on her thigh as he nuzzled her neck. "We can't have that, now, can we?"

"I don't know. You tell me. Are you going to keep pulling this alpha-dog crap every time he's around? Because with his director bludgeoned to death, I'd venture to guess he's going to be around."

"You love when I'm your alpha dog."

"No, I don't!"

"Yes, you do." As if to prove his point, he anchored her arms above her head with one of his hands around her wrists and settled between her legs, the hot press of his cock against her sex leaving no doubt in her mind what he wanted. "You love it when I do this, for example."

She turned her face away from his kiss even though that was the last thing she wanted to do. "No, I don't."

"I'm feeling the evidence to the contrary."

It was on the tip of her tongue to say that Hill's attention had made her hot, but she knew better than to make that particular joke.

His lips made a path from her throat to her jaw, further reducing her to putty in his hands. "Now, that's what I'm talking about."

Sam was powerless to resist him, and he knew it. "Let go of my hands."

"In a minute."

Sighing, she closed her eyes and gave herself over to him, jolting when his teeth closed around her nipple as he slid a finger into her. Sam's mind cleared of anything that didn't involve the intense sensations spiraling through her body.

He kissed his way down her center, releasing her hands as he went lower, his hands skimming over her belly.

"Nick."

"What, baby?"

"I want you."

"You'll have me. In a minute. Or two."

She groaned as he raised her legs to his shoulders, making his intentions clear.

"Relax," he said, the whisper of his breath making her shiver in anticipation. "Open for me."

He made her feel madly vulnerable when he touched her this way. Their physical connection, always incendiary, was more so tonight after the scare he'd given her yesterday. "Yes, like that," he said. "Mmm, so wet and so hot." He sank two fingers into her and gave her his tongue in teasing strokes that had her immediately on the verge of release. "Not yet," he said, retreating as she groaned.

He kept that up until she was about to lose her mind or beg for relief or both.

"Nick, *come on!*"

"Is this what you want?" he asked. Then he sucked on her clit and made her explode.

She might've even screamed, which she tried not to do these days with a house full of Secret Service agents.

He crawled into her arms and kissed her with lips and a tongue that tasted of her. His kisses were wild and heated, and she clung to him, so thankful to have him back to normal after a frightening few days.

"What're you thinking about?" he asked, gazing down at her. Propped on his elbows, he used his thumbs to brush the hair back from her face.

"About how badly you scared me yesterday."

He brushed his lips over hers. "Sorry about that."

"Don't do it again."

His smile lit up his gorgeous hazel eyes. "I'll try not to."

"It made me realize how much I put you through."

"Yes, you do, but you know what makes all the stress worth it?"

"What?"

"This." He entered her in one deep stroke, flexing his hips to ensure maximum impact.

Sam gasped and clutched his back as she struggled to accommodate his thick length.

Dropping his head, he kissed her neck. "Every second I get to spend inside you more than makes up for the time I spend worried about you."

She wrapped her arms and legs around him, wanting him as close to her as she could get him. For a long time, they stayed just like that as he pulsed inside her, making her squirm under him.

"This is all I need to be happy, Samantha," he whispered. "You're all I need."

"I need you so much that it scares me sometimes."

He raised his head to meet her gaze. "Why does it scare you?"

"Because." She would've looked away, but he wouldn't let her. "All that need makes a girl…needy."

"I like when you need me." He withdrew almost completely before pushing deep again. "I fucking *love* it."

"Mmm, me too. I love everything with you."

After that, there were no more words. No words were needed to convey the love Sam felt in every touch, every stroke, every kiss. When he picked up the pace, Sam knew he was close and allowed herself to go with him, swept away in a sea of desire and love.

CHAPTER FIFTEEN

NICK COLLAPSED ON top of her, breathing hard, his skin slick with sweat, and she was immediately concerned that he'd overexerted himself.

"Stop," he said. "I'm fine."

"How do you know what I was thinking?"

"Because I know how your brain works."

"I guess you're superhuman after all," she said, caressing his back in small circles. "Look how fast you bounced back from being so sick."

"I'm resilient." To make his point, he flexed his hips, letting her know he was ready to go again.

"No way, mister. One and done tonight." She pushed on his hips trying to dislodge him, but he was unmovable.

"Don't hurt yourself, babe," he said with a low chuckle.

"I mean it, Nick. We're not doing it again."

"Okay." He ran his fingers through her hair as Sam floated on a cloud of contentment.

She loved the weight of his body on top of her as their bodies pulsed with aftershocks.

"I have to tell you something you're not going to like," he said, ending her contentment with one sentence.

"What?"

"Nelson wants me to go to Iran to help broker the new arms deal."

Despite the heat of his body and the heat they had generated together, she went cold all over at the thought of him so far from her in a place that wasn't exactly known for its love of Americans.

"Why you?" she asked.

"I think he's punishing me for my new higher profile."

"I told you those six million Twitter followers would come back to haunt you."

He smiled down at her. "Exactly."

"But won't sending you to Iran *raise* your profile?"

"Maybe, but I think he wants me out of his hair for a couple of weeks, and he certainly doesn't want to go."

"A couple of *weeks*?"

"Apparently, that's the best-case scenario."

"Can you refuse to go?"

"I suppose I can do whatever I want."

"Then don't go. Stay here and continue to do what you're doing to raise the profile on issues that matter right here. Gun control and immigration reform and middle-class families—"

He stopped her with a kiss. "All important things, no doubt, but what good is all that if we aren't focused on national security first and foremost?"

"Why does it have to be you? Doesn't he have a secretary of state to deal with stuff like that?"

"She'd be there too."

"So why can't you go and shake some hands and leave the heavy lifting to her?"

"I suppose I could do that." He kissed her again. "I didn't tell you this to upset you. But I didn't want you to hear about it from Darren or another member of the press corps or Lilia."

"Does that mean you're going?"

"It means I'm considering it while wishing I'd never

left the Senate. Things were much less complicated there—for all of us."

Sam shook her head. "If you'd stayed in the Senate, you'd be wondering what-if about being the VP. You made the right move at the right time."

"You can say that even with our home overrun with Secret Service and hardly any privacy and women paid to watch me who you can't stand?"

"Woman. Singular. As in *one* woman I can't stand. And you can wipe that smug grin off your face before I slug you."

"What smug grin?"

She traced the outline of his mouth with her finger. "That one." Glancing up, she saw his eyes heat with desire the way they did no matter how she touched him. "I have to tell *you* something you're not going to like."

"What's that?"

"Malone wants me to come back to work the Hamilton case and serve out the remainder of my suspension after."

Nick withdrew from her and turned onto his back, staring up at the ceiling.

Sam raised herself up on an elbow so she could see his face. "Are you mad?"

"No, of course I'm not mad. I know how much you want to be smack in the middle of something like this."

"But?"

He shook his head. "Nothing."

"Clearly you've got something on your mind or you wouldn't be all the way over there, so don't say it's nothing."

Taking hold of her hand, he brought it to his lips. "I'm just being selfish. I see an opportunity to have some alone time with you, and I want it. That's all."

"We're alone right now."

"It's never enough."

"We have ten days in Bora Bora coming up very soon. That'll be here before we know it." She dropped her head to his chest, and he snuggled her in next to him. "Believe it or not, I don't relish the idea of working this case. It's sure to be a shitshow of epic proportions. But we're shorthanded without Arnold and with Gonzo out for who knows how long. My squad needs me to walk them through this."

"Malone could do it."

"He could, but he's been on desk duty a long time. He's rusty around the edges. He'd tell you that himself." She ran a finger over Nick's well-defined pectorals and then down to explore his abs, loving the way his muscles quivered under her touch. "The department has taken a lot of hard hits lately. We have to seriously nail this one so the chief can hold on to his job. We've got Arnie Patterson in prison claiming he was framed by the MPD. Bill Springer blamed the chief for the death of his son, who was a cold-blooded murderer, but those accusations are outliving Springer. The story of Stahl taking me hostage and our longtime animosity has been all over the national news in recent months, and now the shit with me and Ramsey. It's been a lot of bad press, some of it involving me, and this is our chance for retribution."

"There's been good press too. Like you crowd surfing during the inaugural parade and nabbing Arnold's killer."

"That was one high moment in a sea of lows."

"It's not up to you to single-handedly change the story."

"I know that, and I'm not insinuating that I even *could* single-handedly change the story, but the fact is, the story hasn't been great lately, and Hamilton's murder is a big opportunity for us to do what we do best. I'd still be working right now if I hadn't been suspended." In fact, she needed to check in with McBride and Tyrone to see what they had so far. She reached for her phone on the bedside table and fired off a text to Jeannie asking for an update.

Nothing new to report yet. Lindsey has transported the body to the morgue. Waiting for Hill to notify the wife and the FBI deputy director so we can issue a statement. Working with the Public Affairs people on that and wishing you were here.

I may be able to come back. More to come tomorrow.

Fingers crossed.

Keep me posted.

Will do.

It was good to know her team missed her and wished she could be there to guide them through the early stages of the investigation.

Sam returned the phone to the table and relaxed into Nick's embrace. The outside world was always tugging at them, but for now they could pretend, at least for a few more hours, that they were alone in paradise.

STILL REELING FROM the sight of Troy Hamilton's dead body, Avery drove through the darkness on Route 66 on the way to Chantilly, while wishing he was home with

Shelby watching a movie or one of her mindless cooking shows. Anything would be better than trying to process the loss—especially under such bizarre circumstances—of a man he'd admired and respected.

"I need to call the deputy director," Hill said. "I don't feel right waiting to tell him. He won't understand why I did that, especially when he hears I found the body."

"You've handled everything by the book," Farnsworth said from the front seat.

"Agreed," Malone said.

"I still need to tell him."

"Go ahead and make the call," Farnsworth said, "but ask him to keep a lid on it until we can notify the wife."

Dustin Jacoby's number was in Avery's list of contacts, so he used the voice assist feature on his phone to make the call. He'd worked directly for Jacoby at one time and considered him a friend. After four rings, Jacoby's voicemail picked up.

"Dustin, it's Avery Hill. Give me a call as soon as you get this message. It's urgent." If he didn't hear from the deputy director within the hour, he'd go through official channels to track him down.

The GPS led them to Mrs. Hamilton's mother's house in Chantilly, twenty-five miles outside the city in the western part of Fairfax County. The two-story brick colonial was located on a street made up of similar houses. Outside the house in question, a porch light was on over the front door and lights were on inside, which was a relief. If they had to deliver devastating news, at least they wouldn't have to wake her up to do it. The three men approached the door, and Hill rang the bell.

He retrieved his badge from his coat pocket, and showed it to Courtney Hamilton when she came to the door. She was a petite blonde who was known for her love of tennis, martinis and philanthropic activities in the D.C. area.

"Special Agent Hill, Mrs. Hamilton. This is Chief Farnsworth and Captain Malone from the Metro D.C. police department. I wondered if we might have a few minutes of your time?"

"Of course." Eyeing them warily, she stepped aside to admit them, giving no indication she recognized Avery. them, giving no indication she recognized Avery. "What's this about? I talked to Josh earlier, and he's fine. I don't know why you were looking for him or what Troy was thinking issuing that statement. Josh isn't on any medication that I know of."

She's nervous, Avery deduced. The run-on sentences and jerky movements were out of character for the woman Avery had met a number of times at Bureau events and get-togethers at the director's home, where Avery had found her to be a smooth, elegant, gracious hostess. The perfect wife for a high-ranking government official.

They took seats in the living room, and Courtney lowered the volume on the television.

"Mrs. Hamilton," Avery said, hating his job passionately in that moment, "I'm afraid we have some difficult news."

"Not Josh! I just talked to him!"

"It's not Josh." Avery forced himself to continue, to say the words, to put it out there and let her begin to deal with the unimaginable loss. "It's your husband."

"What about him?"

"He was found dead in your home earlier tonight."

She tipped her head, as if trying to make sense of what he'd said. "Troy's not dead. I talked to him earlier too. He was doing paperwork and going to bed early."

"What time did you speak with him?" Malone asked.

"I don't know exactly." As she spoke, her hands trembled. "It was this afternoon sometime. I'm sure he's fine. I can call him now for you if you'd like."

"Mrs. Hamilton," Farnsworth said, saving Avery from having to do it. "I'm afraid Agent Hill is correct. Your husband was attacked and killed in his home. His body was found on the floor of his study."

She shook her head. "That's just not possible. Not Troy. He can take care of himself. He always says there's nothing to worry about." Tears slid down her cheeks. "He can't be dead. He's *Troy Hamilton*." She said that as if he weren't as human as the rest of the world's population.

"Did you know of any problems he was having with anyone who might want to harm him?" Malone asked.

"There was always someone unhappy with him. That was the nature of his work. He told me there was nothing to worry about, so I didn't worry." She looked up at Avery, heartbreak etched into her pretty face. "I should've been worried. Why didn't I worry about him?" She used her sleeve to mop up the tears. "Is this why you were looking for my son earlier? You don't think he had something to do with it, do you?"

"This is not why we were looking for him," Malone said.

"Is he a suspect?" she asked.

"Not at this time. Do you have reason to believe he'd be capable of harming his father?"

"No, of course not. He and Troy never saw eye to eye, but Josh couldn't harm a flea, let alone the man who raised him."

The man who raised him. The peculiar choice of words

set off alarms for Avery, and apparently for Farnsworth and Malone too, because the two men exchanged glances.

"Mrs. Hamilton, may I ask what might seem to be an odd question?" Avery said.

She nodded as she continued to wipe away tears.

"Is Josh your biological child?"

"No," she said hesitantly. "He's adopted. I was unable to have more children after my daughter was born, so Troy and I adopted him. We'd always wanted a big family and were disappointed when we couldn't have more than two of our own."

"Does Josh know he's adopted?" Malone asked, sitting now on the edge of his seat.

She looked down at her hands. "No, he doesn't. Troy didn't want him to know, and I went along with what he wanted because it seemed so important to him."

Avery felt like he'd been struck by lightning. What the fuck was going on here? He could sense that Farnsworth and Malone were equally riveted by the revelations.

"What do you know about Josh's birth parents?" Farnsworth asked.

"What does this have to do with my husband being murdered?" she asked.

"We're not sure yet, but it might have everything to do with it," Malone said.

"I... I don't know much about them. The mother was an administrative assistant in my husband's office. She got pregnant outside of wedlock and couldn't afford to keep the baby, so we took him in."

Avery forced air into lungs starved for it. "Did you know her name or anything else about her?"

"Her name was Danielle. I can't recall her last name off the top of my head. It was a long time ago."

Avery exchanged glances with Farnsworth and Malone.

"In a conversation with Josh about your husband's career, it came up that you all once lived in Knoxville," Avery said. "But Josh was adamant that you never lived there. Do you know why that would be?"

"We... Troy and I... We had some marital problems during those years. It was a difficult time in our lives, so we rarely talked about living there. That's probably why."

Avery found that explanation curious, to say the least. "Have you been with your mother all day today, Mrs. Hamilton?"

"Yes, since she called me this morning to tell me she was feeling poorly."

"And your other children are where?"

"Mark is in Chicago, and Maura lives in Boston. Why?"

"Establishing the whereabouts of the immediate family is routine in a homicide investigation," Malone said. "Do you know if they're both at home today?"

"I... I don't know. I haven't spoken to them."

Hill produced a notebook and pen. "We'll need their phone numbers."

She took it from him with hands that were trembling more violently now. "You don't honestly think they'd harm their father? They adored him!"

"We have to explore all possibilities, ma'am," Malone said.

"Why isn't the Bureau investigating?" she asked. "In light of recent events, I'm not sure I trust the MPD to handle it."

To his credit, Farnsworth didn't react to the insult. Rather, he said, "We have jurisdiction because of where the crime occurred, and it would be a conflict of interest for the FBI to investigate the murder of its director."

"Is that true, Agent Hill?"

"It is."

"Dustin will need to be notified. Troy would want him involved."

"I have a call in to the deputy director, ma'am," Hill said. "If you could please write down the contact information for your children as well as a number where we can reach you, I'd appreciate it."

With her jaw set in a stubborn expression, she did as he asked and handed over the notebook. "What happens now?"

"The director's body is with the city's Medical Examiner, who will perform an autopsy. When that is completed, the body will be released to the funeral home of your choice. The ME will call you when she has completed her work."

Mrs. Hamilton nodded.

"Thank you for your cooperation," Malone said. "We'll be in touch."

She saw them out the door and shut off the porch light, the dead bolt clicking loudly.

When they were in the car and on their way back to the city, Farnsworth said, "Did anyone else find it interesting that she didn't ask how he was murdered?"

"I found it very interesting indeed," Malone said. "And she didn't ask to see him. Family members almost always ask to see the victim, like they need to see it with their own eyes before they'll believe it's true."

"How about her referring to Hamilton as the man who 'raised' Josh, rather than as his father?" Avery asked.

"Parents of adopted children are almost always extra particular about those semantics."

"We need to look more closely at her, and we need to notify the media," Farnsworth said. "If there's anyone you should tell within the Bureau before we go public with this, now is the time. I've asked my Public Affairs people to get the media to HQ within the hour."

Hill withdrew his cell phone and tried to reach Dustin, getting his voicemail again, so he contacted his director supervisor, Leslie Monroe, the executive assistant director for the Criminal, Cyber, Response and Services branch.

"Agent Hill," she said when she answered. "What can I do for you?"

"Director Hamilton has been murdered."

After a gasp, she said, *"What?"*

"I've been trying to reach Dustin, but I keep getting his voicemail."

"Have you got a team at the scene?"

"It's not our scene. The murder occurred in the director's home. The MPD has jurisdiction."

"Not this time they don't. He's ours. We'll see to it."

"Leslie, we can't, and you know it." He liked and respected her—most of the time. She left him alone to run his division the way he saw fit, and got involved only when he asked her to. But she was dead wrong on this, and he was prepared to dig in if need be.

"How did you hear about it?"

"I was the one who found him."

"And you didn't call us first? What the hell, Avery?"

"I followed procedure, and when you take a minute to think it through, you'll realize that."

After a long pause in which he wondered if he'd ended

his own career by criticizing his boss's judgment, she said, "What were you doing at the director's home on a Sunday?"

Avery filled her in on what'd been going on with Josh, the APB that had been issued, the subsequent statement that had come from the director and the reason he had gone to the director's home. He wanted to ask what rock she'd been living under all day to have missed the events from earlier.

"We had my daughter's birthday party today," she said, answering his unspoken question. "I've been off-line. Was Josh located?"

"Yes, the MPD has him in protective custody until we figure out what's going on with the kidnapping case."

"I'm trying to understand what you're saying about that. You honestly believe that it's possible a young man Troy Hamilton raised as his son was *kidnapped* from a family in Tennessee thirty years ago?"

"I'm saying only that Hamilton's son bears a striking resemblance to the age-progression photo that was released by the family. The DNA results are being sent to the Franklin police tomorrow. We'll know very soon if we have a match. That, coupled with the director's odd behavior today, has us operating under the assumption that he knew something about the kidnapping."

"What's the plan if there's a DNA match?"

"Then I guess we'll have to figure out how Taylor came to be in Hamilton's custody."

"I'm trying to wrap my head around this."

"I've been trying to do that all day."

"You should've called me the minute you heard about this, Avery."

"There was nothing to tell you other than a man raised

as Hamilton's son looked like an age-progression photo of a missing kid."

"What's the plan for announcing the director's murder to the media?"

"The MPD chief is calling a press conference within the hour."

"I'll try again to call Dustin, and if I can't reach him, I'll issue a Bureau-wide alert to let people know before it goes public." Pausing, she added, "There'll be a lot of questions in light of the APB and the director's statement about his son."

"You could be preemptive by saying the MPD is working to resolve a situation with Hamilton's son that arose earlier in the day, and it's unclear at this time if there's a connection between the two events."

"But there has to be, right? How can it not be related?"

"I don't know if it is or isn't. I've told you everything I know."

"And the MPD is keeping you in the loop?"

"I'm with Chief Farnsworth and Detective Captain Malone right now. We're on our way back to the city after notifying Mrs. Hamilton, who was in Chantilly with her sick mother."

"That poor woman. What she must be going through."

For some reason, Avery chose not to mention to Leslie that the poor woman had shown a distinct lack of curiosity about how her husband's life had ended.

"I'll get the alert out," Leslie said. "Keep me posted on every development."

"I will."

When they arrived at the MPD headquarters thirty minutes later, they were met by Patrol Captain Hernandez. "We've got a situation, sir," he said, speaking directly to the chief.

"What now?" Farnsworth asked.

"Detective Cruz's car was found running and abandoned at a stoplight at North Carolina Ave and 14th Street Northeast. The driver and passenger doors were open. There was no sign of Detective Cruz or Mr. Hamilton."

CHAPTER SIXTEEN

SAM HAD NO sooner fallen asleep than she was awakened
by her alarm. She smacked at the bedside table, looking for the snooze button until she remembered she was
suspended and hadn't set an alarm. The noise was from
her cell phone, which was ringing. At two-thirty in the
morning.

With her heart racing, she grabbed it and flipped it
open. "Yeah."

"Lieutenant," Malone said, "Cruz is missing."

Sam sat up in bed. "What?"

"He and Josh never arrived at the safe house. His car
was found running and abandoned, doors open at the in-
tersection of North Carolina and Fourteenth Northeast."

Once again, Sam felt like she'd been punched. She
forced air into her lungs. "Cameras?"

"We're working on it."

"Witnesses?"

"None so far."

"I'm coming in."

"Technically—"

"*Fuck technically!* He's my partner! I'm coming in."

"I'll see you when you get here."

Sam got up and was running for the stairs when she
remembered she was naked. She turned and went back

to grab her robe, nearly screaming in frustration when one of the sleeves was inside out.

"What's wrong?"

"Freddie is missing." This could not be happening again. Not to him.

"What do you mean?"

"He was taking Hamilton to the safe house, but they never arrived." She tied the robe around her waist with jerky movements. "His car was found idling at a light, doors open."

"Ah God." Nick got up and came to her, but when he tried to put his arms around her, she shook him off.

"I can't. I just… I can't."

"Okay, babe. I'll talk to Brant. I'll get there as soon as I can."

"What do you mean? You don't have to—"

"I'm coming, Samantha, and I'll do anything I can for you."

His kind insistence nearly broke her. Because she didn't trust herself to speak, she only nodded.

"And I won't let it be a circus, I promise." He kissed her forehead. "Go on. I'll be right behind you."

"Scotty."

"I'll call Shelby in the morning. He'll be fine here with his detail until then. Go."

Bolstered by his love and assurances, she went down the stairs and into her closet, grabbing jeans and a sweater and shoving her feet into socks and running shoes, telling herself all the while that Freddie was fine, he knew how to protect himself. She'd taught him well, had given him the tools…

Her eyes burned with tears that she refused to indulge.

That was not what he or Josh needed from her right now. They needed her best, and she'd give it to them.

She went into her bedroom to retrieve her weapon, badge and cuffs, jamming her notebook into her back pocket out of habit as she ran down the stairs and through the dark living room, stopping only to grab her coat from the chair where she'd left it. The agent on duty stood when he saw her coming.

"Ma'am? Is everything all right?"

"I'm going to work."

"Give me a second to disarm the system."

"Hurry."

Listening to the maddening beeps and dings of the security system disarming, she about lost her mind. It took every ounce of self-control she possessed not to scream her head off at the agent, who was only doing his job. She experienced the same level of frustration waiting for the agents working the Ninth Street checkpoint to let her through. Okay, so they weren't expecting to see her at two-thirty in the morning. Deal with it!

She raced through the quiet streets on her way to HQ, her mind spinning with possibilities and scenarios, her muscles tight with fear. When forced to stop at a red light, she called Malone.

"Trace his cell phone," she said.

"Tried that. It's off."

"Trace Hamilton's."

"We're working on it, Sam."

"Who knew they'd be together?"

"No one, other than a few people from our department and Hill."

"Where is he?"

"He's here, working the case with us."

"Who did he tell that we were moving Hamilton to a safe house?"

"Only Josh's mother, and they were taken before she knew. We looked for them for a couple of hours before we called you."

"Why would someone grab them? What would be the motivation?"

"We're working it from every angle."

"I'm dying a thousand deaths, Cap."

"So am I. We're going to find them. I'll see you when you get here."

Sam pressed the accelerator, not caring what laws she broke or who she ran down on her way to HQ. The only thing that mattered was finding Freddie before something awful happened. Another something awful.

Because they needed all the help they could get, she called Gonzo.

Christina answered. "Sam?" she said, sounding sleepy.

"I need to talk to him."

"He's asleep."

"Wake him up."

"I'm not going to do that."

"Christina! It's an emergency. I need to talk to him."

"I'm very sorry, Sam, but he's not available right now. He's sleeping for the first time in weeks. I won't disturb him."

She wanted to crawl through the phone and beat the hell out of Christina, but she'd probably feel the same way if the roles were reversed. "When he wakes up, tell him Freddie is missing." She slapped the phone closed and pulled into the parking lot at full speed, ducking into the first available spot.

Sam ran for the main door, pushing her way through the media that had gathered for the chief's press conference, which had apparently been delayed.

"Lieutenant, what do you know about the murder at Director Hamilton's house?"

"Who was killed?"

"Where is the director?"

"Where is Josh?"

"Was Josh kidnapped?"

That one stopped her cold. How did they know about that? Though the question surprised her, Josh's case was the least of her concerns right now. She blasted through the main doors and headed straight for the chief's suite, having no doubt that Freddie's disappearance was being handled at the highest level.

The door to the chief's office was open so she went in. "What do we know?" she asked.

In attendance were Farnsworth, Malone and Hill, who weren't surprised to see her, Deputy Chief Conklin, Captain Hernandez from Patrol and Captain Roback from Vice, all of whom seemed shocked that she was there.

"Someone tell me what's going on!"

"We have people looking for them all over the city, and Lieutenant Archelotta's team is reviewing the security footage in the area—"

"I've got something," Archie said as he came into the room carrying a flash drive. He went around the chief's desk to insert it in his computer, calling up images that stopped Sam's heart.

Freddie's beat-up Mustang, stopped at a red light, approached by three men with assault weapons. The whole thing happened quickly. Freddie and Josh were overtaken before they could react and were led to a white van that idled half a block away. Sam watched, horrified, as her partner and Josh were thrown into the van, which was moving even before everyone was in.

"The plate," Sam said, swallowing the fear so she could function.

"One step ahead of you," Archie said. The next frame showed a close-up view of the plate. "I put a trace on it." He reached across the desk to hand her a piece of paper with an address on it.

Sam headed for the door.

"Sam, wait," Malone called after her. "We have to do this right."

She kept moving.

"Lieutenant! *Stop!* That's a direct order."

Only because he'd rarely ordered her to do anything did she stop, even though everything in her wanted to go to where Freddie was being held. If anything happened to him…

"Give us ten minutes to get our shit together. I promise you I want him back as much as you do."

"I doubt that."

Wearing jeans and a sweatshirt and looking like the best thing she'd ever seen, Nick came through the main doors, Brant following right behind him. Her husband came to her, putting his hand on her shoulder. "What's going on?"

"We've got something."

"We're mobilizing SWAT and preparing to go after him," Malone added.

"I want to be there," Sam said. "You have to let me go."

"You're not going," Farnsworth said.

Sam spun around to plead her case, but the words died on her lips when she saw the stony expression on his face.

"You're suspended. You shouldn't even be in this building."

"He's my partner! My friend. My…" He was the little brother she'd never had, and Sam loved him. "You can't ask me to stay away."

"I'm telling you that's what you're going to do, or you'll face much greater consequences than your current suspension. You're wasting time that could be better spent finding Detective Cruz."

The chief walked away, leaving Sam reeling.

"Sam." Nick took hold of her arm. "Don't."

Thankfully, Nick was there to keep her from completely flipping out and doing something she'd probably regret. Like telling off the chief…

Hill gave her a sympathetic look as he followed the chief.

Sam wanted to punch the sympathy off his face. She had no idea what she was supposed to do with the energy that was exploding through her, needing an outlet. How was she to sit idly by with her partner in potentially mortal danger? Standing in the middle of the lobby with her husband, she felt the eyes of every officer currently in the building on her. They were wondering why she was there.

"Let's get out of here," she said to Nick.

He took her by the hand and gestured for Brant.

"Let's go out through the morgue," Brant said. "It's a mob scene out there."

With the press already ravenous for information about what'd happened at Hamilton's home, they'd want to know why Nick was there too.

Brant mobilized the detail and hustled them through the morgue door and straight into a waiting SUV.

"My car."

"We'll get it tomorrow."

"I'm losing my mind."

He put his arm around her. "He's going to be okay."

"They had assault weapons. Whoever took him meant business."

"The chief and captain won't let anything happen to him."

Sam tried to take comfort in that, but she was too aware of what could go wrong, even with the best people looking for him. "I should call Elin."

"Do you think that's wise?"

"No, but it's what he'd want me to do."

"Are you sure?"

"No!" Her voice broke. "I'm not sure of anything except he's missing, and I'll die if anything happens to him."

"It's okay, babe." He tightened his hold on her. "He's tough and he's smart and he was trained by the best cop I know. He'll get through this."

Sam held his hand and clung to his assurances. They were all she had at the moment. Thanks to the efficiency of the Secret Service, they were home within minutes.

The waiting was agonizing. She stared at her phone, willing it to ring, but it stayed stubbornly silent.

"Can I borrow your phone?"

Nick handed it over.

Because she wanted to keep her line open, she used the contact info on her phone to call Elin on his.

"It's Sam," she said when Elin answered. "There's something going on that you need to know about, but I don't want you to panic." She was panic-stricken enough for both of them. "Freddie would want you to know that he was taken hostage earlier tonight."

Elin's sharp gasp came through the phone like a shot-gun blast.

"We've narrowed down where we think he's being held, and teams are being dispatched as we speak."

"Why aren't you with them?"

"I'm suspended."

"He needs you, Sam!"

The words struck her heart like sharp arrows. She dropped her head into her hands. "I tried, but they wouldn't let me."

"Sam, oh my God! You can't let anything happen to him!"

Sam's chest felt like it was being squeezed in a vise. "We've got our best people on it. If you want to come to my house, you can wait for news with us."

"I… Um, okay. I'll do that."

"Take a cab so you don't have to drive. I'll tell them to let you in."

"He's going to be okay, isn't he?"

"I really hope so."

"I'll be right there," she said on a sob.

"Brant, will you please let them know outside that Elin Svendsen will be arriving by cab? Tell them to let her in."

"Yes, ma'am."

"Thank you."

Nick sat next to her on the sofa, his arm around her shoulders. "Lean on me, babe."

For the first time ever, she didn't want him to touch her. She didn't want him to comfort her or speak to her in that soothing voice that usually worked wonders on her nerves. Before she could do something stupid like shake him off, she stood, wrapped her arms around her torso and began to pace.

She felt his gaze on her, watching over her the way he always did.

The front door opened and Shelby came rushing in, stopping short at the sight of them. "I got your text," she said to Nick, "but I didn't think y'all would be here."

"I didn't think so either," Sam said. "Freddie is missing. I got sent home because I'm suspended, and now I'm losing my shit."

Shelby took off her coat, dropped it over the sofa and came to Sam. "What can I do?"

"There's nothing any of us can do because *I'm fucking suspended.*"

To her credit, Shelby didn't react to Sam's harsh tone. She knew by now how much Freddie meant to her and how panicked she had to be at the thought of him in grave danger.

"Sorry to drag you out in the cold for no reason, Shelby," Nick said. "I didn't think we'd be home so soon."

"I don't mind at all. It's good to see you up and around again. You gave us a heck of a fright."

"Sorry about that."

"I'll make some coffee."

Sam resumed her pacing, stopping only to grab her phone off the table.

Wearing pajama pants and a sweatshirt, Elin came running in a few minutes later, going directly to Sam, who hugged her as she sobbed. "It's okay," Sam said even though she had no idea if it was. It just seemed like the right thing to comfort her.

"I can't lose him, Sam."

"We're not going to lose him," Sam snapped, immediately regretting her sharp tone. "Any minute now we're going to hear that he's fine." She only hoped that was true.

CHAPTER SEVENTEEN

AVERY STOOD WITH MALONE, Conklin, Farnsworth and Roback while the SWAT commander, Captain Nickleson,
quickly briefed them on the plan for gaining access to a
freestanding home on First Street Southwest, located just
off Potomac Avenue between the Anacostia River and the
Washington Channel. Standing outside the house, Avery
stared at the windows, wondering what they'd find when
they went in. Was Cruz dead? Was Josh?

Upon hearing Nickleson's plan, the chief nodded in
approval. "Do it."

"Green light," Nickleson said into his radio.

Dressed all in black, SWAT commandos appeared out
of the darkness to batter their way into the house through
windows and doors. The sound of glass shattering preceded cries of surprise from people inside the house.

Over the radio, Avery heard one officer after another
say "Clear" as they went through the place room by room.

"I've got something in the basement" were among
the best words he'd ever heard. He wasn't prone to praying, but he sent up a request to the Almighty that Freddie Cruz and Josh Hamilton would be found unharmed.
He couldn't imagine Sam without Freddie, and he didn't
want to. And if Josh was Taylor Rollings...

"I've got Cruz. No sign of Hamilton. Get the paramedics in here."

Avery was cautiously relieved. If they were calling for EMS and not the ME, Cruz wasn't dead.

As the paramedics, who'd been on standby, rushed into the house, SWAT team members brought three men out in handcuffs.

"Someone needs to call Sam," Avery said.

"I'm on it," Malone said.

Avery heard him telling Sam that they had Cruz, that he was injured and on his way to the GW ER.

"I don't know," Malone said. "EMS is with him." After a pause, he said, "Yes, you're allowed to go to the ER, and no, we can't send you home from there." He rolled his eyes at the chief as he said the words.

Avery smiled at her feistiness. He'd feared she would actually explode in the HQ lobby when the chief told her she couldn't help look for Cruz.

"There was no sign of Hamilton," Malone said. "I'll let you know if I hear any more." He ended the call and said to Farnsworth, "Cruz's fiancée is with Sam. They're heading for GW."

The EMTs rolled Freddie out five minutes later, their haste ramping up the tension in the group of officers that had been relegated to the sidelines. Avery was able to see his face as he went by and realized he was unconscious with dried blood on his forehead and face. Shit.

Nickleson came out after the EMTs. "He was zip-tied in the basement. They did a number on him, but he was breathing on his own."

"How do you want to proceed?" Malone asked the chief.

"I'll go to GW with Detective Cruz," Farnsworth said. "You get to HQ and find out what you can from them." He nodded to the two Patrol cars that contained the three men who'd been arrested. "We need to find Josh Hamilton. Fast. Brief the media on Troy Hamilton's murder and Josh's abduction."

"Yes, sir."

Avery rode with Malone to HQ. "What're you thinking, Captain?"

"I have no idea what the hell to think of any of this."

"No question the murder of Troy and the abduction of Josh are related."

"I'd be hard-pressed to deny that, but what's the motive?" Malone asked.

"If I had to guess, I'd suspect we're going to learn that Josh is Taylor Rollings, and whoever took him thirty years ago is covering his or her tracks."

"That's a good guess and a decent theory to start with."

"What do they accomplish by eliminating Troy?" Avery asked.

"He must've known something that they feared would be revealed when it was proven that Josh is Taylor."

"So why take Josh? We've already got his DNA, and we don't need him to investigate how he ended up with the Hamiltons thirty years ago."

"I don't know." The captain sounded tired.

"When was the last time you slept?"

"I don't know that either. Crazy couple of days with my top two Homicide detectives out."

"You guys should bring Holland back to work this case."

"It's not my call."

"You have influence with the chief. You need her on this."

"I don't disagree, but he's dug in on keeping her off the job until her suspension is up. He's got to think about the officer she assaulted."

"Who's a douche bag."

"Agreed, but…the chief can't keep cutting her breaks when she screws up, or he'll have issues with other officers crying favoritism. She doesn't need that any more than he does. She won't see it this way, but he's doing her a favor by digging in on this. If he relents, everyone will say it's because of who she is to the chief, who her father is, who her husband is, and she'd hate that."

"Yeah," Avery said. "She would."

They were met by Detectives McBride, Tyrone, Carlucci and Dominguez when they arrived at HQ, where the three arrested men were being booked.

"Freddie," Jeannie McBride said. "He's all right?"

"We're not sure yet," Malone said. "He was unconscious when he was brought out. They roughed him up pretty good."

Carlucci sighed audibly. "He has to be okay."

Dominguez put a comforting arm around her partner. "Is Elin with him?"

"She's with the lieutenant, and they're on their way to GW. In the meantime, we have work to do. What do we have on Troy Hamilton?"

"Archie is dumping his phone," McBride said, "and Crime Scene is still there. Dr. McNamara is conducting the autopsy. They both said they'll have more for us in the morning. We had one witness who saw someone running away from Hamilton's home earlier, but he wasn't able to give us too many details other than that he saw the person around three-thirty. Archie's team is reviewing our cameras in the area and we're working with the company that provides the security at Hamilton's house to get footage."

"Crime Scene is also processing Cruz's car," Tyrone said.

The sergeant overseeing Central Booking let them know the three men were available for questioning.

"Get them into rooms," Malone said. "McBride and Tyrone, you take one. Carlucci and Dominguez take the second. Hill and I have got the third. Let them think the others are talking. You know what to do."

"Don't bother," Conklin said grimly when he joined them. "They've lawyered up. They're not talking."

"Brant, we need to get to the GW Emergency Room right away," Nick said.

"Oh, um, I don't think that's a great idea, sir."

"We're going. With you or without you."

Sam reached for Nick's hand and smiled up at him. "Thanks."

His jaw pulsed with tension as he nodded. She knew how much he hated the restrictions his new job put on his ability to move freely.

Elin had been sobbing since she heard that Freddie was hurt. "Can we go? I want to be there when he arrives."

"You guys go ahead," Nick said, his frustration apparent in every word. "I'll be right behind you."

"I'll take you all," Brant said. "I just hope you can find a job for me somewhere after I lose this one."

Nick's entire disposition changed when he heard he'd be able to accompany them. "I'll take care of you. Don't worry."

YOUR PARTICIPATION IS REQUESTED!

Dear Reader,

Since you are a lover of our books – we would like to get to know you!

Inside you will find a short Reader's Survey. Sharing your answers with us will help our editorial staff understand who you are and what activities you enjoy.

To thank you for your participation, we would like to send you 2 books and 2 gifts – **ABSOLUTELY FREE!**

Enjoy your gifts with our appreciation,

Pam Powers

SEE INSIDE FOR READER'S SURVEY

For Your Reading Pleasure...

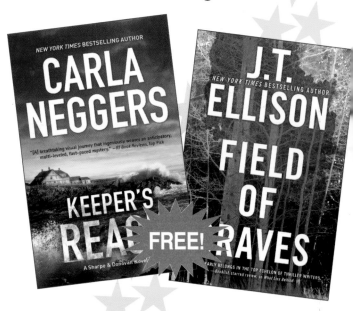

YOUR READER'S SURVEY
"THANK YOU" FREE GIFTS INCLUDE:
- ▶ **2 FREE books**
- ▶ **2 lovely surprise gifts**

PLEASE FILL IN THE CIRCLES COMPLETELY TO RESPOND

1) What type of fiction books do you enjoy reading? (Check all that apply)
- ○ Suspense/Thrillers   ○ Action/Adventure   ○ Modern-day Romances
- ○ Historical Romance   ○ Humor   ○ Paranormal Romance

2) What attracted you most to the last fiction book you purchased on impulse?
- ○ The Title   ○ The Cover   ○ The Author   ○ The Story

3) What is usually the greatest influencer when you <u>plan</u> to buy a book?
- ○ Advertising   ○ Referral   ○ Book Review

4) How often do you access the internet?
- ○ Daily   ○ Weekly   ○ Monthly   ○ Rarely or never.

5) How many NEW paperback fiction novels have you purchased in the past 3 months?
- ○ 0 - 2   ○ 3 - 6   ○ 7 or more

YES! I have completed the Reader's Survey. Please send me the 2 FREE books and 2 FREE gifts (gifts are worth about $10) for which I qualify. I understand that I am under no obligation to purchase any books, as explained on the back of this card.

191/391 MDL GLDN

FIRST NAME	LAST NAME

ADDRESS

APT.#	CITY

STATE/ PROV.	ZIP/POSTAL CODE

▼ If offer card is missing write to: Reader Service, P.O. Box 1867, Buffalo, NY 14240-1867 or visit www.ReaderService.com ▼

BUSINESS REPLY MAIL

FIRST-CLASS MAIL   PERMIT NO. 717   BUFFALO, NY

POSTAGE WILL BE PAID BY ADDRESSEE

READER SERVICE
PO BOX 1867
BUFFALO NY 14240-9952

NO POSTAGE
NECESSARY
IF MAILED
IN THE
UNITED STATES

"We'll have two other cars with us, so just give me one minute to make that happen."

"Thanks, Brant." To Elin he said, "Sorry to hold you up."

"It's okay. I'd be freaking out by myself. It helps to be with you guys."

Sam hugged her. "It's going to be okay. He's young and strong and…" Her voice faltered when she thought about the possibility that he might not be fine.

Nick's hands landed on her shoulders, providing the support she needed to comfort Elin.

"He's going to be fine," Sam said firmly as if that would make it so. "I know it." Any other alternative was not worth considering.

It took ten minutes, but Brant worked his magic and had them on the way to the ER in a smaller-than-usual motorcade.

"You have to go through this to go anywhere?" Elin asked.

"Unfortunately, yes," Nick said in the irritated tone that had become more familiar to Sam since he took the new job.

"That kind of sucks," Elin said.

Nick laughed. "It sucks balls."

"It beats the alternative of someone deciding to harm him simply because of the office he holds," Sam said.

"That's true." Elin stared out the window, her big blue eyes shiny with unshed tears. "Should I call Freddie's parents?"

"Probably," Sam said. "They'd want to know."

"Would it be better to wait until we know what's wrong with him?"

"That might be best," Nick said.

"I don't know how to handle this," Elin said, her eyes filling again. "When he got shot last year, we had just started seeing each other. But now we're engaged and..."

"Everything is different now," Sam said, "and you're handling it the way he'd want you to. You're staying calm and thinking things through. You'll be an excellent cop's wife."

"You think so? Really?"

"I do."

"That means so much to me coming from you. Freddie... He thinks the world of you."

"The feeling is entirely mutual," Sam said. "I love him." Before the incident with Stahl she wouldn't have said such a thing out loud. But now she refused to hold back. After Stahl took her hostage, and after Arnold was gunned down, she knew life could be taken in an instant, and she wanted the people she loved to know how she felt. She reached for Nick's hand, linked their fingers and held on tight to the love of her life. He and Scotty were everything to her, and having him right there next to her made whatever she had to face with Freddie more bearable.

Of course he knew that, which is why he'd insisted on coming.

She smiled up at him, hoping he knew how much she appreciated his support.

He looked down at her with warm, sexy eyes that told her everything she needed to know. He was there for her now. He would be there for her always, and there was such comfort in knowing that, in having faith in it.

They arrived at the Emergency entrance at the George Washington Hospital Center, which Sam often joked was her home away from home. They were forever patching up her or a member of her team—and only yesterday, they'd patched up Nick.

Chief Farnsworth was with several Patrol officers when Sam ran in with Nick and Elin by her side. She went right to the chief. "What do we know?"

"He was still unconscious when we arrived, and we're waiting to hear more."

Hearing Freddie was still unresponsive, Elin covered her mouth to hold back her sobs.

Sam put an arm around Elin and held her while she cried.

They waited a long time until a doctor came through the doors looking for the family of Frederico Cruz.

"I'm his family," Elin said. "We all are."

"He's awake and asking for Elin and Sam."

"That's us," Elin said.

"Right this way."

They followed the doctor into the cubicle area. When Elin saw Freddie in bed, his eyes open and alert, she rushed to his side, all but crawling onto the bed to get closer to him.

He put the arm without the IV around her. "I'm okay, honey."

Overwhelmed by relief at the sound of his voice, Sam studied his pale face and the abrasion on his forehead. He met her gaze over Elin's head.

"What can you tell me?"

"Happened really fast. We were at the light and they surrounded us. They were heavily armed, so I didn't try anything."

"You did the right thing."

"Where's Josh?"

"He wasn't in the house. We're looking for him now."

"What the hell is this, Sam?"

"I don't know, but we're sure as fuck going to find out."

BEFORE SHE LEFT Freddie in the capable hands of Elin and his parents, Sam sent a text to her entire squad letting them know he was on the mend and would be spending the night in the hospital. They were watching him for a possible concussion. He didn't remember anything following a blow to the head knocked him out shortly after he was shoved into the van.

I'm asking everyone who's available to be at my house at zero seven hundred to work this case. I can't go to you, but you can come to me and bring me everything you've got. It's your call to come or not. This is not an order.

One after the other, her squad members replied with relief to hear that Freddie was okay and to say they'd be there in the morning. The only one she didn't hear from was Gonzo, but at least she knew why.

Confident that Freddie was in good hands and that a plan was in place to manage the case, Sam went to find Nick. He was sitting in the waiting room with the chief. They stood when they saw her coming.

"How is he?" Nick asked.

"He's got one hell of a headache, and they're keeping him for observation, but he's going to be fine."

"Thank God for that," Farnsworth said.

"Yes, thank goodness," Nick said.

Every set of eyes in the busy waiting room was on them. It was still unnerving the way they were recognized everywhere they went. Of course the Secret Service agents sprinkled throughout the room didn't help to lower their profile.

"We can go home," Sam said, eager to get away from the prying eyes.

"Look," the chief said, pointing to the TV in the corner. Malone was briefing the press, and they moved closer so they could hear.

"At approximately eighteen-thirty, Troy Hamilton, director of the Federal Bureau of Investigation, was found dead in his Northwest home. The MPD is working the case in cooperation with federal authorities. We'll release more information on the director's murder as it becomes available."

"How does this relate to the APB that was issued earlier for Hamilton's son?" one reporter asked.

"We're looking into the connections," Malone said.

"What happened with Detective Cruz?" Darren Tabor asked.

"How does he know *everything*?" Sam asked.

"Detective Cruz and a passenger were taken hostage by a group of armed men who are now in custody. Detective Cruz has been located and is receiving medical attention."

"Was this related to the director's murder?"

"We don't know."

"And the passenger?" Darren asked.

"Dogged little bastard," Sam muttered.

"We're looking for the passenger."

"Who was the passenger?" another reporter asked.

"We're not releasing that information at this time. I'll have more for you in the morning. That's it for now."

When the local anchors came back on, the FBI director's murder was the top story.

"Mr. Vice President," Brant said. "We're ready."

"Sam?"

She took his outstretched hand. "Let's go."

They rode home in silence, the comfortable kind of silence, the kind in which no words were required. She needed only the heat of his body next to hers to feel grounded, to clear her mind, to think through the case from all angles. There were times, especially on days like this one, when she wondered how she'd managed to function before she had him and his calming effect in her life.

"Thanks for coming with me to the hospital," she said.

"Nowhere else I'd rather be than wherever you are. Sorry it's always such a production."

"I'm all for keeping you safe. Whatever it takes."

"Sometimes it's too much for me. It really is. I feel like a circus animal locked behind the gilded cage."

"It's an adjustment. In a year, it'll be old hat, and you'll be used to it."

"I hope so, because four months in, I'm ready to break out and run for it."

"Don't you dare."

His low chuckle made her smile. "Reminds me of the first time I wore a tie and felt like it was literally choking me to death. I couldn't stop touching it, looking for relief."

Because he seemed to need the distraction and because Brant was riding in the front seat, Sam cupped Nick's groin. "I know that feeling. I can't stop touching it, looking for relief."

His bright smile lit up his eyes. "Are you trying to change the subject, my love?"

"Just trying to get your mind off the confinement. Is it working?"

"You tell me."

"Hmm," she said, stroking him through his jeans until he was hard as a rock under her hand. "It seems to be having the desired effect. A whole different kind of confinement."

"If you build it, you must tend to it."

"Is that a rule?"

"A new rule."

She glanced at the front seat and then tugged at the button to his jeans.

He stopped her with a hand over hers. "Not here."

"Come on. They'll never know."

"*Not* here."

She made a pout face at him. "You're absolutely no fun."

"You know otherwise." He kept his hand over hers, pressing her palm against his hard length. "I'm feeling terribly depressed and confined. I need you to take my mind off my troubles the minute we get home."

"The minute?"

"The very second we walk in the door."

"Someone ought to warn poor Shelby."

CHAPTER EIGHTEEN

NICK LAUGHED AND kissed her neck, which sent shivers spiraling down her spine. Apparently shivers on her spine led to an ache between her legs. How did he do that so easily? That was one of the great unsolved mysteries of her life, one she was more than happy to keep mysterious.

As they got out of the car at home, she noticed how he kept his coat strategically positioned over the front of him, and a tight grip on her hand. They were ushered into the house by the agent at the door.

Shelby was asleep on the sofa.

Sam took off her coat and tossed it over the sofa, earning a glare from her neatnik husband. "Can I take your coat, honey?" she asked with a cheeky grin.

"I'll keep it on, thank you."

Sam laughed, which earned her another furious glare as he tugged her through the house. "Shelby—"

"Let her sleep. She's perfectly comfortable where she is, and Hill's working anyway. She's better off here than home alone."

"Said the world's horniest vice president."

"Keep talking and laughing at me, and you'll give me no choice but to spank your sexy ass until it's bright red."

Sam stared at the back of his head, stunned that he would say such a thing out loud in a house full of Secret Service agents who watched their every move—except in the bedrooms and bathrooms. Oh, and their third-floor loft. Those spaces were strictly off limits.

Melinda was sitting outside Scotty's room. Of course she was. "Good evening Mr. Vice President, Mrs. Cappuano."

"Evening," Nick said gruffly as he went into their bedroom, towing her behind him, and slammed the door.

"Why don't you just announce what we're going to—"

His lips came down on hers as he lifted and pressed her back against the door he'd just closed.

Oh. My. Sam loved him like this, unhinged, undone and nothing at all like the calm, cool customer he was to the rest of the world. She loved that only she got to see him this way, that she'd driven him to it with some harmless flirting.

He devoured her with his lips and tongue, biting down on her bottom lip until the painful pleasure had her crying out. "Shhh, you don't want your friend Melinda to hear us."

"Not here."

He pushed his hard cock into the V of her legs. "Right here. Just like our first time. Remember?"

"How could I ever forget?"

"I relived that a million times in the years we spent apart."

"So did I. That was an incredible night, and this will be too, but I can't do it here, with her on the other side of the door. I just can't."

Groaning in aggravation, he cupped her ass and picked her up to carry her to the other side of the room, to the farthest wall from the hallway. "Better?"

"Much."

"I'm putting you down for five seconds. Get your clothes off."

"Only if you do the same."

His shirt flew over his head, making her laugh at his haste.

"Are you laughing at me again?"

"Would I do that?"

"I believe you would. You'd do it just so I'll spank your sweet ass."

The very thought ignited her desire. "No, don't do that."

"Now you're telling me what to do?"

What did it say about her that she, who was dominant in every aspect of her life, absolutely loved when he dominated her in the bedroom?

"Please, Nick. I'll behave."

"No, you won't," he said, laughing.

When they were both naked, he lifted her, cupping her ass in his big hands and bringing her down on his hard cock.

Sam gasped at the impact and held on tight to him, knowing he'd never drop her but unnerved by the position nonetheless.

"Relax," he said, tuned in to her as always. "I've got you."

She loved the play of his muscles under her hands as he moved in her. She loved his confidence and the way he watched over her as he made love to her. She loved everything about him.

He played her body like a maestro, and had her on the verge of climax when he stopped, withdrawing and putting her down.

It took Sam a moment to catch up. "What… What're you doing?"

"I want you on the bed, on all fours. Right now."

The authoritative way in which he said that made her skin tingle and her blood heat as she made her way to the bed to do what he'd asked.

"Down on your elbows," he said in the gruff tone he saved only for her.

In a previous life, Sam would've been self-conscious about having her naked ass in the air for a lover's inspection, but with him, there were no thoughts of things such as vanity. Not when she knew he loved and worshipped every inch of her—and told her so frequently. His adoration set her free from the chains of the past, and allowed her to give in to the powerful desire.

She felt the bed dip behind her and then his hands were on her cheeks, squeezing and shaping them. Though she knew it was coming, it still came as a surprise when he spanked the right one and then the left one. God, she loved that. It turned her on like nothing else ever had.

He drove into her as he spanked her again, sparking an epic release that detonated deep inside and radiated through her entire body, driving every thought from her mind that didn't involve him and the magic they created together.

She came back down from the incredible high to discover he was still hard inside her, still keeping up a relentless pace.

Nick ran his hand over one of the heated spots on her ass, turning the ache into heat that had her climbing again.

Before him, before them, once was a miracle. Now, the word *multiple* was a regular part of her sexual vocabulary.

"Shhh," he said, making her realize she was express-ing her pleasure a little too loudly.

"I hope she's listening," Sam said.

That earned her another slap to the ass. God, he was killing her, one deep thrust at a time. Then he reached around to caress her clit and she came hard—again—this time taking him with her. With him hot and heavy above her, she collapsed onto the mattress, her entire body quiver-ing. When he would've withdrawn from her, she took hold of his arm to keep him there a little while longer.

"I'm not crushing you?"

"I like being crushed by you."

"Are you okay? I was a little rough…"

"I loved it, and I'm fine." She squeezed her inner mus-cles, drawing a deep groan from him.

"Keep that up, and you'll be looking at round two."

"You're supposed to be resting and regaining your strength, not gearing up for round two—or is it round four?"

He pushed his hips against her ass. "I declare myself fully recovered. So that's a yes for round four?"

Sam groaned and then laughed. "When are you going to start acting like the old married guy that you are and have sex with your wife once a week like a normal hus-band?"

"Never," he said, biting the back of her shoulder just hard enough to ensure he had her full attention. "As long as I've got the hottest wife in the world in my bed, noth-ing about this marriage is ever going to be normal." He withdrew from her and turned her over. "This time I want to see your gorgeous face." Brushing the hair back from her forehead, he gazed down at her as he entered her again.

Sam curled her legs around his hips and her arms around his neck.

"I love my wife."

"I love my sexy husband."

And she loved the smile that lit up his beautiful eyes. As he moved in her, she could spare no thoughts for the case, her heartbroken squad, her injured partner or anything other than the exquisite pleasure she found in her husband's arms.

FILLED WITH ENERGY after her passionate night with Nick, Sam was up early to make coffee and pancakes for her squad. The blanket that had covered Shelby was neatly folded on the sofa, but she was nowhere to be found. Sam assumed she'd gone home.

While the pancakes cooked, she checked her email, found the DNA report from Lindsey and forwarded it to Detective Watson in Franklin with a request for notification as soon as he knew whether it was a match. She sent Watson a text to let him know about the email but didn't mention the part about Josh currently being missing.

"What's gotten into you?" Nick asked when he came downstairs dressed in a suit and tie. "Other than me." He laughed at his own joke.

Sam poured him a cup of coffee. "Very funny, and why are you dressed for work?"

"Um, because I'm *going* to work?"

"I called you out sick for the week, so you'll have nothing to do. You may as well stay home with me and help me figure out what the hell is going on with this case."

Nick thought about that suggestion for a second and then reached for his tie, unknotting it and pulling it off before releasing the top two buttons on his dress shirt.

Smiling, Sam went to him, looped the tie around his neck and drew him into a kiss. "You were so uncorruptible when I first met you, and look at you now."

"I don't think that's actually a word."

"Don't try to dodge the truth."

"I'll admit to being easily led when my beautiful wife wants me to be bad."

Scotty came into the kitchen wearing his grumpy morning face and scowled at the sight of them kissing. "Knock that off. I haven't had coffee yet."

Sam lost it laughing. "You don't drink coffee."

"When will I be old enough for coffee?"

"Talk to me when you're fifteen." She served him a plate of pancakes and the syrup she'd warmed.

"Did you actually make these?" he asked as he lathered the pancakes with butter before dumping a healthy amount of syrup on them.

"I did."

He looked to Nick. "Did she really?"

"Is he accusing me of lying?" Sam asked her husband.

"I think it's more a matter of him pointing out an unusual and unprecedented level of domesticity on your part."

Scotty snorted with laughter. "What he said."

"See if I ever get up early to cook for you guys again," she muttered, even though she loved that Scotty was comfortable enough in their home to tease them.

"Why is your tie around your neck rather than where it belongs?" Scotty asked Nick between bites.

"I'm staying home today. Still not feeling a hundred percent."

"Neither am I, but I have to go to school. How is that fair?"

"You know what happens when you miss a day of school, buddy," Nick said. "It piles up on you. If you get there, and you really don't feel good, you can come home, okay?"

"I guess."

A knock on the door preceded Brant into the kitchen. The poor guy had learned the hard way to knock before he entered a room in their home. "Are you ready to leave, Mr. Vice President?"

"I've decided to give it another day before I go back."

"Very well."

"Brant, would you please let them know outside that my squad will be arriving shortly?" Sam said.

"Yes, ma'am."

"Thank you." Under her breath she said, "Don't call me ma'am."

Jeannie McBride was the first to arrive, and like Scotty, expressed amazement that Sam had made breakfast.

"I'll remember this at annual review time," Sam said.

"I hope you'll remember only how *impressed* I was," Jeannie said with a smirk as she loaded her plate with pancakes and sausage.

The others filtered in, razzed her about cooking and then devoured the pancakes and guzzled the coffee. At seven-fifteen, Sam took a call from Captain Malone.

"Would you happen to have any idea where my Homicide squad might be this morning?"

"Oh, um, I made them breakfast. Sorry, I should've invited you."

"What're you up to, Holland?"

"I'm up to my elbows in pancake batter. You want some?"

"I know what you're doing."

"What am I doing?"

"You've called your squad to your house to work the case from there since you're not allowed to come here."

"Captain! I would never do something like that."

The others shook with silent laughter as they listened to her side of the conversation while he growled in frustration.

"You're welcome to join us for breakfast if you'd like. And if you wanted to bring any new information that came in overnight about the murder of Troy Hamilton and the disappearance of Josh Hamilton, that'd be an excellent hostess gift."

She heard the captain's snort of laughter before the line went dead.

"Is he coming?" Tyrone asked.

"We'll see."

Her phone rang again with a call from Avery Hill. "Good morning, Agent Hill."

"What's the plan?"

"I don't have a plan. I'm suspended."

"Cut the shit, Holland. You always have a plan. What is it?"

"Would you like to join my squad and me for breakfast at my house?"

After a brief pause, he said, "Yeah, I'll be there."

Sam had no sooner ended that call when her phone rang again, this time with a call from Lilia. "Good morning."

"Good morning, Mrs. Cappuano. I trust the vice president is feeling better?"

Sam smiled to herself as she eyed her insatiable husband. "He's feeling much better."

The comment earned her a sly, intimate smile from Nick.

"That's such a relief. The White House switchboard and communications staff have been inundated with calls inquiring about his health."

"Oh. Well." Sam glanced at Nick, who was talking to Tyrone and Carlucci. "I'm sure he'll want to issue a statement to put fears to rest. I'll mention it to him."

"That'd be great, thank you. The reason I called, though, was to tell you that we have a draft of your speech for Friday completed, and we hoped we might run through it with you later today."

For a moment, Sam's mind went totally blank. Then she remembered she'd agreed to give the keynote address at a convention addressing women's health and fertility. The event had seemed like a long way off when she'd agreed to do it. How could it be *this* Friday? "I could come in around noon if that would work."

"Shall I send a car?"

"Only because that's easier."

Lilia chuckled. "Got it. I'll send a car for you at eleven forty-five."

"See you then."

Nick crossed the room to her. "Where are you going at noon, babe?"

"Apparently, I'm going to the White House to go over my speech for Friday."

"That's *this* week?"

"My thoughts exactly."

"How're you feeling about it? You still want to do it?"

"Not really, but I said I would and I will." She rubbed

her hand over her abdomen. "My stomach suddenly feels like I swallowed a dozen bats."

Smiling, he squeezed her shoulder and gazed into her eyes. "You're going to kill it. I know you are, and think of all the good you'll do for a cause that's near and dear to us." The speech was part of their plan to use the national stage to advance their own agenda on a number of issues.

"I know all that. I just hope I don't puke on the stage or something equally embarrassing. And do not laugh at me!" She poked his hard-as-a-rock belly when he laughed anyway. "Eat up, everyone! It's time to get to work! I need some threads to pull!"

CHAPTER NINETEEN

As HE DID upon awaking every morning, Gonzo reached for his cell phone on the bedside table. It wasn't there. What the hell? He glanced at the clock, which read seven-thirty, and sat up straight in bed. He was late for work. Again. At this rate, he wouldn't have a job to go back to if and when he got his shit sorted out.

Running his fingers through his hair, he tried to establish some order. His body ached after the longest stretch of sleep he'd had since Arnold was killed. He went into the bathroom, took a leak, brushed his teeth and went in search of Christina and Alex. They were having breakfast when he emerged from the bedroom.

Christina eyed him in the wary, guarded way she had for weeks now. It pained him to see her walking on eggshells around him, but he supposed he couldn't blame her.

"Morning," he said as he poured some coffee and then went to kiss his son. "Where's my phone?"

"I have it." She seemed extra nervous as she tended to Alex.

"Why do you have it? And where is it?"

"You were sleeping," she said beseechingly. "For the first time since AJ died, you were actually *sleeping*. I didn't want you to be disturbed, so I took the phone out of the bedroom."

He held out his hand for it, his anxiety growing as it became apparent that something had happened while he was out cold.

"Please don't be mad at me, Tommy. I did what I thought was best for you."

Continuing to stare her down, he waited for her to put the phone in his hand. He clicked on the power button and it came to life to reveal a flurry of text messages from his colleagues and several missed calls from Dispatch. *"Fuck,"* he whispered under his breath so Alex wouldn't hear him and repeat the word. Scrolling through the texts, his heart began to beat super fast, and he felt light-headed at the realization that he'd missed a Homicide call. Son of a bitch.

"Tommy." Christina laid her hands on his shoulders.

He flinched and shook her off. "How could you do this to me? Do you know how much trouble I'll be in for missing a Homicide call?"

"You're not in trouble. I talked to Sam and she talked to Malone. They agreed that you needed the sleep more than you needed to go to work. We did what we thought was best for you."

Though he was furious—at her, at Sam, at Malone, at the man who'd gunned down his partner, at Arnold for dying the way he had—he kept a lid on it so he wouldn't frighten his son. If the lid ever blew off, he hated to think about how epic the explosion would be. The last text was from Sam, calling everyone to her house to work the case. He ran for the shower.

Christina followed him. "Tommy, the meeting with Dr. Trulo is at noon today."

"I'll meet you there." Maybe it was the eight hours of uninterrupted sleep or maybe it was the rage that fueled him. Whatever it was, he wanted back in the game, and he wanted in right now.

"LET'S START WITH what you learned from the men who took Freddie and Josh," Sam said when Malone and Hill had arrived and after Sam and Nick sent Scotty off to school with his detail. "Captain?"

Reading off the suspects' names, Malone said, "They refused to talk without lawyers present, so we got nowhere with them. We're hoping to have the chance to talk to them today."

"And what did Crime Scene get from Hamilton's house and Cruz's car?"

"We got some decent prints off the golf club at Hamilton's that are with the lab. They're still working on the car."

"What're we doing to find Josh?" Sam asked.

"We've done all the usual things," Malone said. "We've issued a second APB, alerted the airports, train and bus stations to be on the lookout and we've asked the local media to publicize his photo. We're doing everything we can to find him, but because of the way he was taken, it's safe to assume that whoever took him doesn't want him found."

"Are we thinking he's dead?" McBride asked.

"I really hope not," Malone said. "Especially if it turns out that he's Taylor. Imagine those poor parents looking for him all this time only to learn five minutes after they find him that he's dead."

Avery looked up from his phone. "We may have a secondary issue. It appears that FBI Deputy Director Dustin Jacoby is missing too. No one has heard from him since early Saturday. Our people are trying to track his phone and credit cards. He and Hamilton were tight. They came up through the ranks together, and Hamilton handpicked Jacoby for the deputy's job."

"This case is getting crazier by the second," Sam said.

"The attorney general has named the associate deputy director, Gillian MacKenzie, the acting director," Avery added. "We've got people at Jacoby's house and talking to his family and friends, trying to track him down."

"Correct me if I'm wrong," Sam said, "but it's unusual for someone with Jacoby's job to be off the grid for more than twenty-four hours, even on a weekend. Am I right?"

"You are," Avery said, nodding. "He and Hamilton and their top management team are on call 24/7."

"Are you thinking that something has happened to him too?" Malone asked.

"I don't know what to think," Avery said. "This entire situation is unprecedented. People within the Bureau are on edge, to put it mildly."

"Have there been any threats against the Bureau in recent weeks?" Carlucci asked. "Anything out of the ordinary?"

"Nothing more than the routine stuff, and I would've heard if there was something more." After a pause, Avery added, "Since we spoke to Courtney Hamilton last night, I've been thinking about the administrative assistant who worked with Hamilton and Jacoby in Knoxville. I did some digging, and I found that she still works in the Knoxville office. I'm thinking about going there to talk to her."

"I'll go with you," Sam said.

Nick gave her a look of fierce annoyance that pissed her off.

"On my own dime and my own time, of course," Sam added for the captain's benefit.

"Of course," Malone said drily.

"I'll get my assistant to put us on the next flight," Avery said, typing on his phone.

Sam could *feel* Nick's eyes boring holes in her head and was afraid to glance in his direction. There'd be hell to pay for this, of that she had no doubt. But whatever. The trip to Knoxville would allow her to participate in the case while suspended. She wasn't passing up that opportunity, no matter how angry it made her husband. "What else do we have?"

"We're speaking to the witness who saw someone running from Hamilton's house again today," Dominguez said. "We're hoping to get something more we can use."

The front door opened to admit Lieutenant Archelotta. "Had a feeling I'd find y'all here," he said with a grin.

Once again Sam was grateful that she'd never mentioned her brief fling years ago with the IT lieutenant to her husband. She could only imagine how that information would add to his current ire.

"What did you get from Hamilton's phone?" Sam asked.

"A whole lot of nothing. No calls in or out after he issued the statement about his son being off his medication."

"How is that possible?" Malone asked. "The MPD is looking for his son. He takes the time to issue a statement, and *no one* calls him about that?"

"I thought it was weird too," Archie said, "so I checked to see if he might have a second phone and hit pay dirt. The one we dumped is his FBI-issued phone. The second one is his personal phone, and that's where all the action was yesterday."

He handed out stapled pages to each of the detectives.

"We'll go through this today," McBride said.

"We'll help you," Carlucci added.

"Can we talk about Courtney Hamilton?" Malone asked. "She told us she spoke to her husband in the afternoon. She was very nonchalant about that call, which was made at a time when her son was technically missing, and her husband had issued a public statement about the son that we've since learned was misleading. To our knowledge, Josh Hamilton is not on any medication that would affect his behavior."

"In general, I thought her behavior was odd," Avery said. "Remember how she referred to Hamilton as the man who *raised* Josh? Isn't that a bizarre way to refer to her son's father, even if the child was adopted? Would you guys ever refer to yourselves as the people who *raised* Scotty?"

Seeing that question had infuriated Nick, Sam answered for them both. "Never. We'd describe ourselves as his parents. What do we know about her?"

"I looked into her background last night," Avery said. "She's from a wealthy Connecticut family. Her maternal grandfather was the governor of New York in the sixties. The family is well regarded. She met Hamilton at a dance on Long Island the summer between her junior and senior years at Vassar. They were married one week after she graduated from college. He had just joined the Bureau and was on the rise. They lived for a time in the San Francisco Bay area, where they had a son, Mark, and a daughter, Maura, eighteen months apart. Mark is a board-certified neurosurgeon in Chicago. Maura is a partner in a Boston law firm. Their son Josh was born five years after Maura, at the end of Hamilton's tour in Knoxville. Courtney told us he was adopted. She said he was the son of the administrative assistant in the Knoxville office, and they'd taken him in because she couldn't afford to care for him on her own."

"In the time I spent with him, he never said anything to me about being adopted nor did he mention it to Detective Cruz, who would've passed that along," Sam said. "In fact, Josh made a point of telling me he'd never fit into his accomplished family.

"Courtney told us Troy didn't want Josh to know he was adopted, so they never told him."

Sam shook her head in disbelief. "The poor guy. They kept him in the dark about everything."

"So we're operating under the assumption that Hamilton's murder and the son's kidnapping-adoption-abduction are related?" Tyrone asked.

"How can they not be?" Sam said. "The timing is not coincidental." She thought for a second and came to a decision. "I want everyone looking for Josh Hamilton. As far as we know he's still alive, so he's the priority. Talk to his coworkers, his friends, his neighbors, dig into every corner of his life. If we find him, we may find whoever killed his father too."

"I agree with the lieutenant's approach," Malone said.

The agent working the front door admitted Gonzo and Freddie.

"Where'd you guys come from?" Sam asked, thrilled to see them, even if Freddie still looked dangerously pale and Gonzo seemed incredibly wired.

"I apologize for missing the calls last night," Gonzo said to her and Malone. "Won't happen again."

"You're authorized and encouraged to take bereavement leave," Malone said.

"Not necessary," Gonzo said. "Other than the required appointments with Trulo, I'm back to work."

"Me too." Freddie wore a bandage over the cut on his forehead. "I got sprung an hour ago. No concussion, so I'm back to full duty. What can we do to help find Josh?"

Sam and Malone handed out assignments to every member of the squad and sent them on their way with orders to report in hourly.

"Our flight is at two," Avery said as he put on his coat. "The first return flight we could get was at one o'clock tomorrow afternoon, so pack a bag. I'll meet you at Reagan?"

"I'll be there."

"Let me know what you find out," Malone said as he took his leave.

"Seriously?" Nick said when they were alone—or as alone as they ever were these days.

"Let's go upstairs to have this fight in private." Sam headed up the stairs, prepared to do battle if necessary. In their bedroom, she turned to face him, watching as he closed the door that had played a pivotal role in last night's activities. Though his posture was casual as he leaned against the door, looks could be deceiving.

"There's no need for you to go on this trip."

"There's *every* need for me to go. This is *our* case."

"You're suspended, Sam!"

"Exactly! And this is something I can do to help out while I'm suspended."

"Avery can handle it on his own."

"And when he gets a big break, do you think he'll call us or his own people first?"

"I don't want you spending a night away with that guy."

Infuriated by the insinuation, she approached him, stopping when she was a few inches from him. "What do you think will happen, Nick? Are you worried that I'm going to sleep with him or something? Is our relationship so fragile that you'd actually be *worried* about such a thing? Do you have so little trust in *me*?"

"He's the one I don't trust, and no, our relationship is not fragile."

"Then what's the problem?"

"I don't like it."

"I don't like that Melinda stares at your ass when she's supposed to be watching all of you. I don't like that she's wondering how big your dick is every time she looks at you! Guess what? There's nothing I can do about it. He's a *colleague* and my *friend's* fiancé. That's all he'll ever be to me. I don't know how many times or ways I have to say that to get it through your thick skull that *I am not interested in him*!"

"Melinda doesn't wonder how big my dick is."

"Figures that's all you heard. You don't think so?"

"She's a professional."

"She's a *woman* who knows a hot guy when she sees one."

"And Avery is a man who knows a hot woman when he sees one, and he wants you. I don't care what you or anyone else says. He wants you, and you're handing him a golden opportunity."

"For what? To *have* me? Fuck you." She pushed him off the door and went across the hallway to pack for the night away.

The closet door slammed shut, and she spun around

to find him advancing on her, a look of fury on his face. "*Fuck me? Really?* Is that how we fight now?"

"That's how we fight when you insinuate that I'm unable to spend a night out of town with a colleague without being unfaithful to you."

Even with his hands on his hips and his mouth set in a mulish expression, he was still the most gorgeous man she'd ever laid eyes on. Even if she currently wanted to punch his lights out. He stared at her for a long, charged moment before the starch seemed to leave his spine as he exhaled. "I trust you."

"Then we don't have a problem." She packed a clean pair of jeans, a sweater to wear tomorrow, underwear, pajamas and socks into an overnight bag. Then she changed into a pair of black dress pants and a silk blouse to wear to the White House.

"Why're you getting dressed up to go on a trip with him?"

"I'm getting dressed up to go to the *White House*, you ass."

"I don't want you to go with him."

"I don't want you to go to Iran." Sam brushed by him as she left the closet and crossed the hall to the bathroom to pack a small cosmetic bag. When she was finished, she went into the bedroom where he was sitting on the bed watching her. "I'll see you tomorrow?"

"I guess you will."

She didn't want to leave it like this, but she was as mad at him as she'd ever been. "Tell Scotty I'll call him tonight."

"Okay."

Apparently, he was mad too, or he would've told her to be careful. He would've said he loved her. But he didn't say anything and neither did she. Checking the time on her phone, she saw that she had thirty minutes to kill before the pickup for the meeting with her White House staff—a meeting she wished she could cancel in light of her argument with the vice president.

After unlocking her bedside drawer to retrieve her weapon, badge and cuffs, she went downstairs, put on her coat and left the house with a heavy heart. She and Nick didn't fight like that. Ever. Her eyes burned, and she blinked back tears that she attributed to the cold.

She took the ramp to her dad's house and went in without knocking. "Hello?"

"In here, honey," Celia called from the kitchen.

Sam entered the kitchen where Celia hurriedly gathered up paperwork that had been spread out on the table. Since this was the second time she'd come upon them obviously trying to hide something, she said, "What gives?"

"Nothing," Skip said gruffly.

"Are you guys having financial issues? Tell me the truth."

The look that Celia gave her father confirmed it for Sam.

"What's going on?" Since she had time and didn't want to be at home, she took a seat at the table.

"We're handling it," Skip said.

"Skip—"

"We're handling it, Celia. That's the end of it."

"That's not the end of it." To Sam, Celia said, "Insurance only covered a portion of your father's surgery. We owe the rest."

"How much?"

"Two hundred thousand."

"What?" Sam asked, shocked. "Have you talked to the union?"

"We're not talking to the union." Skip's mulish expression told Sam he'd had this same argument with Celia. "My injury has already cost them enough. Everyone's premiums have gone up because of me."

"Who told you that?"

"No one had to tell me. I know how much all this costs."

"You were injured *on the job*. No matter what it costs, they owe it to you to find a way to pay for what you need. That surgery wasn't elective. It was lifesaving."

"I don't want to talk about this," Skip said.

"We have to talk about it," Celia said.

"We'll get a second mortgage on the house," Skip said.

"Dad, let me talk to the union, will you please?"

"No. I don't want charity."

"It's not charity! You were shot in the line of duty. You nearly gave your life for this city, and you're stuck in that chair for the rest of your life because of your service. It's the least they can do to help offset the cost. Please. Let me run it up the flagpole and see what can be done." She hated watching his eyes fill with tears. Covering his right hand, the one that retained sensation, with hers, she said, "Let me help."

"Okay," he said begrudgingly, "but make sure you tell them I didn't want to ask."

"I will. I promise."

"Thank you, Sam," Celia said, blinking back tears of her own.

"I don't want you guys suffering in silence over something like this, and Trace and Ang wouldn't either. We want to help, but you have to tell us when you need it."

"I hate that I need help for everything."

"I know you do," Sam said, feeling teary-eyed herself now. He'd always been so fiercely independent and vital. She never got used to the sight of him in the chair where he would spend the rest of his life. While the surgery had removed the bullet and restored some sensation to his extremities, it had caused secondary issues with pain that they were still contending with months later. He was better than he'd been, which was something to be thankful for, but it broke her heart to think of him and Celia stressing out about medical bills.

"This isn't why you came over," Celia said. "What's going on?"

"I'm heading to Knoxville for the night."

"How come?" Skip asked.

"Hamilton investigation."

"What happened to being suspended?" Skip asked.

"I'm still suspended. I'm going on my own time and dime to talk to someone we feel might have information about how Josh Hamilton came to be in the custody of Troy and Courtney Hamilton. Courtney says he was the son of Troy's administrative assistant who couldn't care for him. She still works in the office where Hamilton was assigned in the eighties, so Hill and I are going to talk to her."

"You and Hill?" Skip said, raising a brow.

"It's our case, Dad. We need someone there, and we're short-handed as it is, so I volunteered to go."

"And Jake signed off on that?" he asked, referring to Malone.

"He did."

"We couldn't believe the news about the FBI director," Celia said. "He didn't have security?"

Sam shook her head. "He declined it."

"Like someone else we know," Skip said pointedly.

"And Freddie," Celia said, "he's all right?"

"He's back to work with a lump on his forehead, no worse for the wear."

"Thank God for that," Celia said.

"No kidding. My squad has been through enough since losing Arnold. We can't take any more."

"Not to mention what nearly happened to you," Skip said.

"Not to mention."

"How's Tommy?" Celia asked. "I think of him so often and what he has to be going through."

"He was at the house this morning and is working the case. He didn't say much, but he seemed a little better maybe."

"It's going to take time," Skip said, speaking from experience. "The rest of his life really."

"He's talking to Trulo, so hopefully that helps him come to terms with it. He blames himself because he let Arnold take the lead for the first time, and this is what happened."

"It's such a terrible thing," Celia said. "For everyone. I think about AJ's poor parents and sisters too."

"I know," Sam said with a sigh. "I talked to his mother last week, and she's so strong. I don't know how she does it. I'd be a disaster."

"How are your boys feeling?" Skip asked.

"Scotty is back to school today, and Nick is... Well, he's pissed at me."

"Because you're going on this trip with Hill," Skip said.

"Yeah. He's being completely unreasonable."

"Is he?"

"Yes! Does everyone think I'm going to *cheat* on my husband the second his back is turned? That I can't control myself for one night away with a colleague?"

"A colleague who's made no secret of his affection for you."

"That's *his* problem, not mine."

"Listen to me, baby girl, and hear me when I say it's your problem too. It's your problem because Hill's affection for you makes your husband uncomfortable. After Steven died," he said of his partner who was killed years ago in the line of duty, "I was so intent on caring for Alice that I totally neglected your mother. I let her think someone else's wife was more important than mine. I regret that."

"This is different, Dad. He is nothing to me but a colleague and my friend's fiancé. That's it. And Nick knows that."

"Doesn't matter. He's threatened by the guy, and you need to respect that."

"What do you think?" Sam asked Celia.

"I agree with your dad. He's often talked about how his attention to Alice ruined his marriage, and I know he regrets that your mother felt neglected."

"Nick is *not* neglected. He's the *opposite* of neglected."

"He's threatened by Hill's interest in you, Sam," Skip said. "That's all you need to know."

"I would never, ever, ever, *ever* cheat on Nick. *Ever.*"

"And he knows that, but it doesn't make him any less threatened by Hill," Celia said gently.

"You guys are supposed to be on my side at all times," Sam said, making them laugh.

"We *are* on your side, baby girl, which is why we're

giving you this advice," Skip said. "We love you, we love Nick, we love the two of you together. Just because something seems preposterous to you doesn't make it less real for him."

"I get what you're saying, even if I don't like it." She checked her watch. "And I've got to run. Lilia is sending a car to pick me up for a meeting at the freaking White House."

"When do we get to see your speech?" Celia asked.

"I haven't even seen it yet, but I'll email a copy to you when it's ready."

"I can't wait to see it," Celia said, "and in case I haven't told you, I think it's amazing that you're going public with your fertility struggles. It'll help so many people."

"Thanks." She rubbed her belly, which fluttered with anxiety. "I just hope I can do it without making a fool of myself."

"You'll be great," Skip said. "I have no doubt. I can't wait to watch it on C-SPAN."

The reminder that her speech would be televised didn't do a thing for her nerves. She gave them each a kiss. "See you tomorrow."

"We'll be here," Skip said. "Safe travels. Love you."

"Love you too."

With her dad and Celia's thoughts about the situation with Nick and Hill heavy on her mind, Sam went outside to find a big black SUV waiting for her. One of the Secret Service agents on Nick's detail held the back door for her.

"Thank you, Nate."

"Yes, ma'am. Have a nice day."

"You too." She glanced at her home as the car pulled away, wondering if Nick was watching her leave and whether he was still angry. Though she still felt hurt by his insinuation that she would cheat, she had new perspective thanks to what her dad and Celia had said. When she had the chance, she would talk to him about it and hopefully fix the damage they'd done this morning.

CHAPTER TWENTY

GONZO COULDN'T FIND a parking space in freaking George-
town where Trulo's office was located. Since Christina
was joining him for this session, they'd chosen to meet
Trulo here rather than at HQ, where everyone would
know their business.

He was a full five minutes late by the time he sprinted
up the stairs to the second floor, taking a minute to catch
his breath and gather his composure. He would need all
the composure he could muster to get through the next
hour. When he felt as ready as he'd ever be to rip the
scab off the wound on his soul, Gonzo raised his hand
to knock softly on the door.

Trulo opened it and gestured for him to come inside
where he found Christina seated on the sofa, looking
tense and anxious. He'd done that to her. In the year
they'd been together, she'd gone from free and unencum-
bered, to insta-motherhood and partner to a wreck of a
man. On many a day lately, he wondered why she stayed
when she certainly didn't have to.

Gonzo took a seat next to her, attempting a reassur-
ing smile that apparently fell flat. She didn't look reas-
sured at all. Rather, she looked as if she were about to
jump out of her own skin.

"Sorry I was late. Parking is a bitch around here."

Christina reached for his hand. "It's okay."

Trulo zeroed in on Gonzo. "Christina filled me in on some of what's been going on at home."

Gonzo felt his face heat with embarrassment and shame over what he'd put her through. "She's a saint to stay with me."

"I believe she stays because she loves you."

"She's a saint for that too."

"Why would you say that?" she asked, her voice catching. "I'm exactly where I want to be, with the man I wish to be with."

Gonzo withdrew his hand from her grip and bent forward, elbows on knees. "It's not really fair to you. It hasn't been from the beginning. We were barely dating when I found out about Alex, and we went from a twosome to a threesome practically overnight. Then his mother was murdered and everyone thought I did it." He ran his hand over the jagged scar on his neck. "I got shot and nearly died. My partner got shot right in front of me and actually died, when it should've been me in his place. What woman in her right mind would stay with someone after all that shit in just over a year?"

Trulo turned his attention to Christina. "What do you have to say to that?"

She sounded unusually composed when she said, "What about all the time in between those events? What about all the days and nights the three of us spent together as a family? Doesn't that count for anything?"

"It counts for everything, but you can't deny I've put you through a lot in our short time together."

"You've also shown me love like I've never known. You've shown me it's possible to love someone else—two someone elses—more than I love myself. You've given me the family I always wanted, and even in the worst of times, I'm happier with you, Tommy, than I ever was without you."

Though he'd come in here hoping to convince her that she could do better than him and the insanity of his life, her words cut straight to his heart, reminding him of what they'd had and who they'd been before it all spun out of control.

"Tommy?" Trulo said gently. "What do you think of what Christina said?"

"I think…" He closed his eyes, took a deep breath and fought through the emotional reaction her words had stirred in him. "I'm a lucky man to have someone like her feel that way about me. But what about her? What about what she deserves?"

"Doesn't she get to decide that?" Trulo asked. "Doesn't she get to say what works for her and what doesn't?"

"Yes, of course she does." Uncomfortable and on the spot to talk about things he'd prefer to keep private, he ran his fingers through his hair, trying to buy himself some time.

"One of the things I preach to people in situations like yours is that crisis is never the time to make big decisions. You've been through a lot in the last year. Any one of those things would be enough to test a person's mettle. Added together they become overwhelming." Trulo leaned forward. "As hard as it is to believe now, you won't always feel the loss of AJ as acutely as you do today."

Gonzo huffed out a breath. "I doubt that."

"Remember the day you found out about Alex?"

"What about it?"

"Did you feel shocked? Sucker punched? Stunned? Confused? Overwhelmed? Enraged that his mother had kept him from you?"

"All those things and more."

"Over time, did most of those emotions fade away and leave you with other more manageable feelings about your son?"

"Yeah, I guess."

"It may take a year or two or perhaps even three, but one day you'll wake up and your first thought won't be about your murdered partner. Your first thought will be about your son or the woman you love or maybe both of them. When that day comes, I want you to be able to look over in bed and still see the same person lying next to you who you loved before your partner was murdered. I want your son to be sleeping in the next room, hopefully past 6:00 a.m.," he added with a small smile. "I don't want you to wake up alone, filled with regret over what you let get away at a time when you were traumatized."

As much as Gonzo hated to admit it, Trulo's words made sense. "You're right. You're absolutely right. But I can't get past the feeling that I'm being completely unfair to Christina to force her to stick with me while I take years, possibly, to come to terms with Arnold's death."

"From what she's said, it would be far more unfair to her if you were to end your relationship because you're having trouble coping with the death of your partner and friend."

Christina's soft sob broke him.

"Please don't cry. I'm sorry. I'm an asshole." Gonzo put his arm around her and drew her in close to him, holding her while she wept silently. He had no idea how long they stayed that way before she lifted her head from his chest and tried to regain her composure.

"You're not an asshole," she said softly. "You're heartbroken. I only want to help."

"I know, baby. I just… I don't know how to let you help me. I feel like no one can help me."

"That too will pass," Trulo said. "In time." After a pause, he said, "Christina?"

She swallowed twice and looked up at Gonzo with liquid blue eyes, her nose red and her skin blotchy from crying. It broke his heart to know he'd done that to her, to know it was the least of what he'd done.

"I'll stand by you for as long as it takes," she said. "If it takes years for you to feel like yourself again, I'll be there. But…"

Gonzo steeled himself to hear what came next.

"If you try to push me away again, Tommy, like you did the other night, I'm gone. And I'm taking Alex with me. If we go, we won't be back. I can take all the rest of it. That I can't handle. I just can't."

A heavy silence fell upon the room, making it hard for him to breathe.

"Tommy? Do you understand what Christina is saying?"

"Yeah."

"And?"

"What happened the other night won't happen again. I promise."

Her relief was so obvious and so profound that it cut through the numbness inside him, making him ache for what he'd put her through.

He reached for her and she came willingly into his arms.

"We've got a lot of work to do together," Trulo said. "But today was a good start."

Gonzo buried his face in the sweet fragrance of her hair, taking comfort in her familiar scent. They broke apart reluctantly. He was nowhere near done holding her, and he sensed she felt the same way.

Trulo saw them out. "I'll see you next week at the same time."

"Thanks, Doc," he said as he guided Christina through the door with a hand on her lower back. He kept it there until they were on the sidewalk and she turned to look up at him.

"Are you going to work?"

"Malone encouraged me to take a few more days to get my head together. He told me to come back Monday."

"You must not have been happy to hear that with such an intense case underway."

He shrugged. "If there's one thing I know for certain, there'll be another hot case right around the corner. It won't kill me to sit one out." Though it did make him feel guilty to sit one out while Sam was suspended. "How'd you get here?"

"I took a cab. I figured parking would be tough."

He put his arm around her. "I'll give you a ride."

They were quiet on the way home. He thought about the session with Trulo and could only assume she was doing the same. They climbed the stairs to their apartment, their footsteps heavy against the treads. Everything felt heavy these days.

"What time do we have to get Alex?" he asked, taking her coat to hang it next to his in the closet.

"Angela has him until four," she said of Sam's sister, who watched Alex for them occasionally.

He forced a smile, trying to act the way he would have before. "That's like two and a half hours from now."

"Uh-huh."

Not that he felt that he had the right after the way he'd

behaved, but he went to her anyway, put his hands on her hips and drew her in close to him.

Sighing, she looped her arms around his neck and rested her head on his chest.

Holding her this way reminded him of how perfectly they fit, like she'd been made for him and vice versa. "I'm sorry, baby. If I could take back what I said the other night, I would. I hate that I hurt you."

"I know it wasn't you talking. It was the grief."

"Still…that's no excuse."

She raised her head from his shoulder to offer a smile, but her eyes were still sad, and he hated that. "You're forgiven."

"You're better than I deserve."

She shook her head. "No," she whispered, drawing him into a kiss that went from soft and gentle to desperate in a matter of seconds. "I love you so much, Tommy," she whispered against his lips. "You'll never know how much."

Her words, words he didn't feel he deserved after the things he'd said to her, moved him deeply. Keeping his arms around her, he walked her backward toward their bedroom and came down on top of her on their bed. It had been weeks since he'd touched her this way, and all the love and desire he'd always felt for her came roaring back to life in a flashpoint of heat that left him breathless.

He'd been so numb, so broken, that it was almost painful to feel so much all at once. And then to realize what could've been lost forever… He dropped his head to her shoulder, breathing through the ache inside him.

She ran her fingers through his hair as she sprinkled kisses on his face. "Make love to me, Tommy. I've missed you so much. I've missed *us*."

He pushed up her sweater and helped her remove it, then she did the same for him. Reaching behind her, he unhooked her bra and pushed it aside, revealing sweet pink nipples. As he bent his head to tease one of them with his tongue, it occurred to him that Arnold would never have this. He'd never fall in love or make love to the woman he adored. He'd never know the joy of fatherhood. He would never again have anything. Ever.

Those few thoughts were all it took to extinguish his desire.

Dropping his head to Christina's chest, he fought through the tsunami of emotions that hit him every time he remembered what had happened to his partner.

"Tommy? What is it?"

"I…" His throat closed and his voice broke. "I can't. I can't do this."

"It's okay." She tightened her arms around him. "We don't have to do anything. I'd be perfectly happy if you held me for a little while."

As he wrapped his arms around her, he felt like a total failure—as a partner to her and to Arnold, as a cop, as a father, as a man. Trulo had said those feelings would fade in time. He only hoped that would happen before Christina wised up and realized she could do a hell of a lot better than him.

THE SUV DELIVERED Sam to the West Wing entrance, where Lilia waited for her wearing a classy red dress with a black blazer. "You look nice," Sam said, grateful she'd taken the time to change before her trip to the White House. "I feel like an amateur next to you."

Lilia laughed. "You look great as always. Come on in." She said that so casually, as if she weren't inviting

Sam into the most famous house in the world. "How's the suspension going?"

"It's been eventful, as I'm sure you know. I'm headed to Knoxville this afternoon to follow a lead in the Hamilton case."

"So you're working the case even though you're suspended?"

"Shhh," Sam said with a grin.

"I should've known. The West Wing has been buzzing all morning over the death of Troy Hamilton."

"What're people saying?"

"They're shocked. He was so larger than life and so respected."

"Yes, he was." It was all Sam could do not to tell Lilia the rest of the Troy Hamilton story. But that would come out in time, if Josh turned out to be Taylor Rollings.

"The morning shows were one big tribute to him," Lilia said. "People are stunned that someone like him could actually be murdered. It reminds me of how I felt when I heard Senator O'Connor had been murdered."

"When someone seemingly untouchable is taken from us, it's a reminder that we're all mortal."

"Yes, exactly. I hope you find the person who did it very soon."

"I hope so too." As they reached her suite of offices, Sam's phone rang and an out-of-state number appeared on the caller ID. Her heart leaped at the realization that the call was from Franklin, Tennessee. "I'm sorry, but I have to take this."

Lilia gestured to Sam's office. "Please. Take your time."

"Thanks, I'll be quick." Closing the door behind her, she flipped open the phone. "Holland."

"Detective Watson from Franklin."

"Do you have news for me?"

"I do. It's a match. We've had two independent experts confirm it."

All the air left Sam's body in a big exhale. While she'd expected the news, it was still a shock to have confirmation that the late FBI director had raised a kidnapped child as his own.

"As you can imagine," Watson said, "we're extremely eager to reunite Taylor with his family."

"Yeah, about that… He's, um… We don't know where he currently is. We're looking for him—"

"What do you mean you don't know where he is?" Watson asked, his tone tight with frustration that Sam could certainly understand. She'd be fucking furious if she were him.

"After his father was murdered last night—"

"His father was *murdered*? Who was his father?"

Sam released her hair from the clip she'd secured it in earlier and ran her fingers through it, trying to collect her thoughts. "The man who raised him was FBI Director Troy Hamilton."

"You're serious."

"Dead serious."

"Jesus Christ."

"I told you this case would be too hot to handle if the DNA was a match."

"There's hot and then there's thermonuclear."

"We were moving Josh Hamilton to a secure location last night when he and one of my detectives were overtaken by three men with assault weapons. They were taken from the scene in a van. We were able to trace the plates on the van and recover my detective, who'd been beaten. Josh wasn't with him. We're continuing to search for him."

Watson's deep sigh echoed through the phone line. "Did you get the guys who took them?"

"We have three men in custody who are demanding lawyers before they'll talk to us. We're hoping to learn more from them today. I promise you we're doing everything we can to find him."

"If we've come this far only to lose him now…"

"We're not going to lose him," Sam said with more confidence than she felt. "We're going to find him, and we're going to give the Rollings family the reunion they've been praying for the last thirty years."

"If it's just the same to you, I'm going to refrain from telling them he's been found until we know where he is."

"I think that's a wise move."

"It kills me to keep this from them."

"I understand. We're working as fast as we can to locate him and to figure out how he ended up in Hamilton's custody."

"Hamilton's murder has to be related to the kidnapping," Watson said.

"We're operating under that premise. I'm heading to Knoxville later today to speak to a potential witness."

"What witness?"

"I'm not at liberty to disclose that yet." The last thing she needed was Watson beating her to the punch with the administrative assistant in the FBI's Knoxville office. "I will as soon as I can."

"The kidnapping is my case, Lieutenant. If you have information that I should be aware of, it's professional courtesy to share it."

"I'll share it as soon as I have something. You have my word."

"I suppose I'll have to be satisfied with that for now, but I'm not going to sit on this news for more than twenty-four hours. The Rollings family has a right to know their son has been found."

"Agreed. I'll be in touch." Sam ended the call, her chest tightening with stress. No pressure much. Sam placed a call to Malone.

"Didn't I just see you?" he asked.

"The DNA is a match."

"Hot damn."

"The detective in Franklin is giving us twenty-four hours to locate Josh before he tells the Rollings family. It's killing him to sit on it that long."

"I understand. We're doing everything we can to find him."

"That's what I told him."

"Let me get back to it. Keep me posted."

"You do the same."

Sam closed her phone, put it in her pocket and took a series of deep breaths to ground herself in the moment, to remember why she was in her White House office and what needed to be done before she left for Knoxville. She went to the door and opened it. "Ready whenever you are."

CHAPTER TWENTY-ONE

SITTING ALONE IN her office, Sam read the speech her staff had drafted for her, dabbing at her eyes when the emotion behind the beautifully crafted words made her throat tighten. How would she ever say these beautifully crafted words out loud in front of two thousand people in a few short days?

Good morning, and thank you for inviting me to be your speaker today. I have to say at the outset that the subject matter I'm covering today is very difficult for me to talk about as I'm sure it's difficult for a lot of you to hear. I know that so many women have traveled a path similar to mine, and I'm here today to shed some light on the need for greater understanding of the challenges many women face in achieving what should be the easiest and most natural thing we'll ever do. For many of us, myself included, there is nothing easy or natural about having a baby.

I've had a lot of titles in my life—Samantha, Sam, Ms. Holland, Lieutenant Holland, Mrs. Cappuano, Second Lady. But only recently did I have the most important of all titles bestowed upon me—Mom. I am mom to my son, Scotty, the thirteen-year-old Vice President Cappuano and I adopted earlier this year. Scotty had spent the last seven years, since his mother and grandfather died months apart, as a ward of the Commonwealth of

*Virginia. My husband met Scotty on a campaign stop
at the home where he lived, and their bond was instan-
taneous. It took a while for the three of us to realize we
were slowly but surely becoming a family. Last summer,
Scotty took a tremendous leap of faith by leaving his
longtime home to come live with us. His adoption was
finalized in December, and we're delighted to be his parents. Being Scotty's mom is the greatest joy of my life.*

*My journey to motherhood was long and perilous,
filled with more lows than highs. The first time I became pregnant—accidentally—as a college student, I
still believed that it was a matter of when not if I'd have
a baby. I wasn't ready to be a mother then and went to
a clinic intending to end that pregnancy. I look back at
that decision now with the wisdom and hindsight of ma-
turity and wonder how I ever could've been so cavalier
with something so precious. My husband and I support
a woman's right to choose and the rights of all women to
control their bodies and their fertility. I was grateful then
and I'm grateful now that there are services in place to
help women who aren't able—for whatever reason—to
take on the enormous responsibility of bringing a child
into this world.*

*I miscarried that baby before I could decide not to
have it. That was the first of four miscarriages, one
of them ectopic and so severe I nearly bled to death.
After my third miscarriage, doctors told me I most likely
wouldn't conceive again. I believed them and resigned
myself to the reality that I would be the best aunt ever to
my beloved nieces and nephews and that would be more
than enough for me.*

*Until Nick Cappuano came back into my life six years
after I first met him, and resurrected my desire for a*

family—mostly because he'd never had much in the way of family growing up. My infertility struggles took on new meaning after we were married. I desperately wished the doctors had been wrong, that I might conceive after all.

Sam wiped away tears that flowed freely down her cheeks as they usually did when she thought or talked about this subject. She was thankful that Lilia and the others had left her alone to read the speech for the first time. Wiping her eyes with a tissue, she forced herself to continue through the most difficult part of her story, the devastating miscarriage she'd suffered last winter in the midst of the Lightfeather investigation.

Here I thought I couldn't get pregnant, and I was miscarrying again, before I'd even officially confirmed I was pregnant. That was a tough one. Perhaps the toughest of all. But there was a silver lining, if you can call it that. The doctors had been wrong. I could conceive again—and if I'd done it once, chances were I could do it again. The aftermath of that fourth miscarriage was one of the lowest points in my life. While mourning the loss of a baby I wanted desperately, I faced a tremendously difficult decision—should I try again, one more time, knowing the odds were stacked against me, or should I accept that it just wasn't in the cards for me to carry a child of my own? I thought about this dilemma constantly. I worried I wouldn't bounce back from another devastating loss, so I feared taking the risk. Nick and I talked about it, and as always, he said he'd go along with whatever decision I was most comfortable with. He's been amazingly supportive on this subject from day one. I've never felt any pressure from him. Before we adopted Scotty, he said he'd be completely satisfied if our family was only the two of us. Our family feels far more complete with

Scotty now part of it, and since he came to live with us, I've found myself thinking about my own fertility struggles far less often than I used to.

I shared my dilemma with my stepmother and sisters, who counseled me to try one more time or spend the rest of my life wondering what might've happened. I listened to their advice and decided to let nature take its course. So far we haven't been successful, but we sure are enjoying all the practice.

Sam smiled, imagining the frenzy that line would unleash, but appreciating the moment of levity.

Some of you may wonder why the vice president and I would choose to publicize our fertility struggles this way, and let me say, it certainly doesn't come naturally to either of us to air out our personal business in public. However, we realize we are in a unique position to bring light to issues that have touched our lives and shaped who we are. In addition to fertility, we care deeply for people, like my father, who live with spinal cord injuries. We are committed to my brothers and sisters in blue who sacrifice so much to keep our communities safe, and to children who struggle with learning disabilities, such as the undiagnosed dyslexia that plagued my childhood.

Despite the office my husband holds, we are regular people just like the rest of you. We have had our struggles, our share of joy and heartbreak. We both come from humble beginnings, so we relate to the concerns of middle-class families who are trying to make ends meet. We've been where you are. We understand and we want to help. I hope we can begin a national dialogue on these and other issues that matter to us and to so many of you too. We hope that by sharing our story, we can bring comfort to others who face similar chal-

lenges. And we hope that by bringing attention to these matters, we'll see an increase in federal funding to effect real and lasting change.

Thank you for having me today, and thank you for listening to my story.

Sam blew out a deep breath and wiped her eyes again. Thankfully, she hadn't bothered with mascara this morning or it would be all over her face by now. Lilia and the staff had done a brilliant job of capturing the story she had conveyed to them, but it was never easy to relive her devastating losses. She also appreciated that they'd managed to tell the story without mentioning her first husband, as she'd requested.

When she'd gotten herself together, she went to the door to invite in the staff. They filed in, gathering in the sitting area.

"Well?" Lilia asked, taking a close look at Sam. "What did you think?"

"It's brilliant. Thank you."

"Oh, that's wonderful to hear! Most of the credit goes to Andrea," Lilia said of Sam's communications director.

"I'm so glad you're happy with it," Andrea said. "We can make any changes you need—"

"I wouldn't change a word," Sam said, dabbing at her eyes again. "My only concern is how I'll get through it without bawling my head off."

"Practice," Keira said. "You may cry the first few times, but maybe you'll get it out of your system before Friday."

"I'll try that."

"Do you want to practice on the teleprompter?" Andrea asked.

"There's going to be a *teleprompter*?"

"Unless you'd prefer to memorize it?"

"Yeah, that's probably not happening by Friday."

"With the teleprompter," Andrea said, "you can look out at your audience as you speak. It makes the talk more personal and engaging."

"I suppose I should practice since I've never used one before."

Andrea got up from her seat. "Give me five minutes, and I'll set it up in the briefing room."

Sam rubbed a hand over her belly. "This is very big-time."

"Well, it is the White House, after all," Lilia said with a teasing smile.

Sam laughed. "I keep forgetting that."

"For what it's worth, I think you're going to be a huge hit, and people will love you for sharing your story—more than they already do."

"Not sure how I feel about that."

"It's a good thing," Lilia assured her.

"We're still being overrun with interview requests for you," Mackenzie said. "People are in love with you after the inaugural parade, as well as the interview you did with the vice president on the *Good Morning* show. I expect your popularity will soar even higher after this speech."

Sam grimaced at the thought of more attention. She'd managed to fend off most of it in the weeks since the inauguration, but everywhere she went people said something about her crowd surfing stunt. The way she saw it, she'd just been doing her job. That she happened to do it before an international audience was unfortunate for someone who preferred life below the radar.

Andrea returned, and she and Lilia walked Sam to the White House briefing room.

"I recognize this room," Sam said.

"You probably see it every day on the news," Andrea said. "It's where the White House press secretary—and occasionally the president himself—briefs the press." She took Sam to the podium and pointed out the screens on either side that contained the text of her speech. "You want to run through it once to get a feel for the teleprompters?"

"Um, sure, okay." Sam managed to get through most of it without getting emotional, but the part about losing Nick's baby had her throat closing. She cleared the lump from her throat and took a second to get her bearings before continuing.

"That was great," Lilia said when she had finished. "Really excellent delivery to say you aren't a seasoned public speaker."

"I'm hardly seasoned. I'm more like a quivering virgin."

Lilia and Andrea laughed and then went silent when Nick stepped into the room.

"Good afternoon, Mr. Vice President," Lilia said.

"Good afternoon, ladies. Would you mind if I had a word with my wife?"

"Of course," Lilia said.

"You did great," Andrea said with a smile for Sam before she followed Lilia from the room.

"I have to agree," Nick said. "That was fantastic."

"How much of it did you hear?"

"Enough to know you'll knock the cover off the ball on Friday. I'm so proud of you, Samantha. I know how difficult this subject is for you to talk about in private, let alone in public."

Unnerved by his unexpected appearance as much as his praise, she gathered up the pages Andrea had put on the podium. "Hopefully it'll do some good."

"It'll do a lot of good."

"What're you doing here?"

"I work here." He held out a hand to help her down the stairs from the podium. "And my reason for an extra sick day left with you."

Though she didn't need the help, she took his hand anyway. "I'm sorry I told you to fuck off."

"I'm sorry I gave you reason to."

She smiled up at him, instantly relieved.

He put his hands on her shoulders and gazed down at her. "I know I can trust you, Samantha. I *know* that. My issues on this topic are not about you."

"I wish there was some way I could make you see that you have nothing to worry about. I don't want anyone but you. I can't control what other people do or feel or say any more than you can. We can only control whether we let other people's crap touch us."

"You're right, and I'm going to try harder not to let that particular pile of crap touch us, but that doesn't mean the thought of you away with him for the night doesn't make me crazy."

"I'm not going to be *with him* overnight."

"If you'd get a freaking smartphone, we could Face-Time."

"And then you could confirm that I was alone in my room," Sam said, irked by the insinuation.

"No, then I could see your gorgeous face when I'm forced to go to bed without you."

She scowled at the smoothly delivered line. "Whatever you say."

He put his arms around her and kissed her forehead. "I couldn't let you go with the way we left things at home. I love you too much not to tell you so before you leave."

Sam curled her arms around his waist, inside his suit coat. "I love you too, even when you're irrational."

His huff of laughter made her smile as she breathed in the familiar scent of home. The thought of even one night without him was almost unbearable. "I've got to go."

"I know," he said, but he made no move to release her. Rather, he held her closer. "Be careful with my wife. She's everything to me."

"I will. I promise."

He pulled back to kiss her for real, lingering for only a second or two in light of where they were. "I guess that'll have to hold me over until tomorrow."

"Somehow you'll find a way to survive."

"Just barely."

He walked her back to her office to get her things and then saw her off in the same car that had delivered her to the White House, giving her one last kiss after he belted her into the backseat. "Call me later?"

"I will."

"Safe travels, babe."

She patted his handsome face. "I'll be back before you miss me," she said, quoting his words when he left for Afghanistan with the president.

"Doubtful." Smiling, he closed the door and waved as the car began to move.

CHAPTER TWENTY-TWO

RELIEVED TO HAVE put things back on an even keel with Nick, she placed a call to Malone to see where they were in the investigation.

"We're following a lead on Josh's possible whereabouts," he said briskly. "We got a tip from security at a hotel in Beltsville that a man matching Josh's description was seen entering the hotel last night with another man. We're knocking on doors now."

"God, I wish I was there."

"Don't punch people, and you won't be sidelined."

"Yeah, yeah. I'm on the way to the airport. Keep me posted?"

"Yep. Gotta go."

Sam closed her phone and put it in her coat pocket. It truly sucked to be suspended when an investigation of this magnitude was heating up, but at least she could help by taking the trip to Knoxville with Hill. The car dropped her off at the departure level at Reagan National Airport.

Hill was typing on his phone while he waited for her inside the terminal.

Sam took note of the tense expression on his face. "Everything okay?"

"Shelby's unhappy about this trip."

"So is Nick." Sam immediately felt disloyal to her husband for admitting that.

"Honestly, they act like we had some sort of affair or something."

Sam wasn't sure how to reply to that. She had never known what to say or do in the face of his obvious crush on her. She'd done nothing to encourage it, and the last thing she wanted to do now was acknowledge it.

Eager to get away from him after one minute in his presence, she said, "I'm going to pick up my ticket."

"Already done." He handed her the ticket.

"Who paid for this?"

"I did."

"Avery!"

"Relax. You can pay me back later. I did it to save time. The plane is boarding in fifteen minutes. Let's go."

As they went through security, Sam's stomach began to ache for a whole other reason. The only thing she hated worse than flying was needles, and she'd seen more than her share of them in the last couple of years. It didn't help her nerves that the sky had darkened with storm clouds as the day progressed. The thought of flying through stormy weather made her break out in a cold sweat.

Of course Hill noticed. "What's the matter with you? You're all pale and pasty."

"I hate to fly. Like hate it with a capital *H*."

"Now you tell me."

"Don't worry about it. Not your problem." As they walked to their gate at the end of the concourse, Sam filled him in on what was going on in Beltsville. People pointed and stared at her when they recognized her. Sam ignored the attention as she always did. More than a few people took notice of her with a man who wasn't her husband. She wondered if pictures of her and Avery would be all over social media before the day was out. Wouldn't that be fantastic? "Any word on Jacoby?"

"Nothing. It's like he dropped off the face of the earth. People within the Bureau are worried that he's dead too. They can't think of any other reason we wouldn't have heard from him after Hamilton was killed. They were the best of friends as well as colleagues."

"So there's no chance he was the one who killed Hamilton?"

"*What?* No. No chance at all."

"Just asking the question." After an uncomfortable pause she said, "You have to admit the timing of his disappearance is curious."

"Curious. In what way?"

He had to be in denial if he needed it spelled out for him. "Well, Hamilton is murdered, his son is abducted at gunpoint while in police custody and Jacoby goes missing. All on the same day. It's curious."

"The only way it's related is if Dustin was killed by the same person who killed Troy and took Josh."

"If you say so."

"I say so."

"Okay." She raised her hands to fend him off. "Don't get hostile."

"You don't know these people like I do. It would be like me asking you if Conklin is capable of killing Farnsworth."

"And I would tell you after years of working Homicide, I've learned that everyone is capable of murder if they have the right motivation."

"So Mother Teresa could've been a murderer? The Pope could be a murderer? The President could be a murderer?"

Sam shrugged. "I'm saying that everyone has that kind of rage inside them under the right circumstances."

"I disagree. There's nothing that could make me want to take another person's life."

"So if someone raped and murdered your three-year-old daughter, you wouldn't want that kind of vengeance? Never say never, Avery."

Her example made him recoil. "You're not right in the head, you know that?"

"You think that's the first time I've had someone say that to me? Admit it, under those circumstances, you could kill someone." Before he could reply, her phone rang and she took the call. "Holland."

"It's Malone. We've got Josh, but he's in bad shape."

"How bad?"

"EMTs couldn't say, but he's been knocked around pretty hard, and he's unconscious. They suspect he's been drugged."

"Great, so he can't tell us who took him."

"We think they intended to kill him with whatever they gave him. He's being transported now, and we're notifying his mother."

"Maybe you ought to hold off on that."

"On notifying the mother?"

Working a hunch, Sam said, "Yeah. I mean what if she's in on it in some way? You guys said she was weird last night. I just have a feeling all is not as it seems there."

"So we let her think he's still missing?"

"For now."

"I've learned to trust your gut, so we'll hold off for now. But if he takes a bad turn, we'll have to call her."

"Understood. Let's see what we find out in Knoxville and go from there."

"Call me after you talk to the admin."

"I will."

They boarded the plane a few minutes later, and when Sam realized it was one of the smaller commuter jets, she began to feel nauseated on top of anxious. She checked the seat-back pocket to make sure there was a barf bag in there. Just in case. She nearly asked to be removed from the plane when the pilot informed them that he expected a bumpy flight and as such there would be no beverage service.

"Oh my God." She wondered if it was too late to get off.

"What?" Avery asked, looking up from his phone.

"Did you *hear* what he said? The flight is going to be so bumpy they aren't doing beverages."

"If it wasn't safe, they wouldn't let us go. It'll be fine."

"Easy for you to say," she muttered.

Closing her eyes, Sam focused on the breathing exercises Trulo had taught her when her anxiety had been at an all-time high after Stahl attacked her. Trulo had suggested that she take a low dose prescription to fend off the anxiety, but she'd resisted, a decision she regretted as the plane taxied toward the runway. Her hands were sweaty, her stomach was doing somersaults and suddenly she had to pee. Urgently.

The plane lifted into the air, rocking and rolling. Sam gripped the armrest and closed her eyes tight against tears that appeared out of nowhere.

Avery's hand covered hers. "Sam. Breathe. *Sam!*"

She took a deep breath and then another, battling her way through the unreasonable fear. Everyone told her it was safer to fly than to drive, but even knowing that was true didn't do a damn thing to alleviate her fear.

"Are you okay?" Avery asked.

"Mmm."

"You don't look okay. You're kind of green."

"Can't talk." Sam pulled her hand out from under his and crossed her arms. She'd never understand how anyone managed to sleep on an airplane.

"You want to hear about the worst flight I was ever on? This one is nothing compared to that. It'll make you feel better."

She shrugged. She didn't really want to hear about it but was desperate for any sort of distraction.

He told her about flying into a typhoon in the South Pacific, how the plane was repeatedly struck by lightning and how he'd been certain they were all going to die. At one point the plane lost ten thousand feet in altitude in the span of three seconds. People were screaming, stuff was flying around in the cabin and the pilots were urging everyone to remain calm.

"As if," he said. "We were anything but calm." He continued to regale her with hideous flying stories from his years in the military as they climbed to cruising altitude, where they found slightly smoother air. His South Carolinian accent was nothing short of lyrical, and listening to him gave her something to do besides freak out.

Sam was amazed to realize she had calmed down somewhat as he described the many ways the flight could be worse. "Thanks," she said, looking over at him tentatively.

He studied her with honey-brown eyes that were filled with concern and affection. She wanted neither from him, so she sat up straighter in her seat and turned toward the window rather than look at him. Thankfully, he took the hint, and they passed the remainder of the flight in silence.

Sam had never been so glad to get off a plane in her life, including the thirteen-hour flight to Bora Bora. She choked back a groan thinking of how she'd be doing that flight again at the end of the month. At least they'd be on Air Force Two, which was a much bigger plane, and she was never as frightened to fly when Nick was with her.

They walked up the Jetway and into the terminal, where a woman let out a shriek at the sight of her. Fantastic.

"You! You're the second lady! *Oh my God, Henry! Get the camera.*"

Sam kept walking, but the woman gave chase and took a photo of her that had to include Avery as he was walking right next to her. Doubly fantastic. Thanks to the scene the woman had made, other people jumped on the bandwagon, snapping photos and screaming and yelling and other obnoxious things that made her grimace.

"There goes our element of surprise," Avery said with a droll smile.

"Sorry."

He waved off her apology and followed the signs to the rental car area. Twenty minutes later they were headed into downtown Knoxville, the GPS guiding them to Dowell Springs Boulevard. When they arrived, they parked and walked into the office together, badges at the ready. The main door to the office had been outfitted in black bunting in deference to Director Hamilton. A photo of him hung in the main lobby, and it too had been veiled in bunting.

"Let me take the lead," he said. "These are my people."

Though she usually hated to cede control of an interview, in this case, he was right. "I'm along for the ride."

The first person they encountered was one of Sam's favorite things—a receptionist. Avery presented his badge at the reception desk. "I'm Special Agent-in-Charge Avery Hill, Criminal Investigative Division in D.C. This is Metro PD Lieutenant Sam Holland."

"Oh, Agent Hill," the woman said. Sam figured her to be in her mid to late fifties. "We didn't know you were coming—and with the vice president's wife!"

Sam wanted to groan and punch her. She did neither. Her days of punching people were over. For now, anyway.

"I didn't tell anyone I was coming. I'm looking for Danielle Koch. Is she here?"

"I… I'm Danielle. Why are you looking for me?"

"Is there somewhere we could talk? In private?"

"I, um… Sure, I guess. Let me get someone to cover for me." She made a call and spoke softly to the person on the other end. A minute later, another woman appeared to take Danielle's place at the reception desk. She eyed Avery with suspicion and Sam with recognition.

"You're—"

"I know." Sam followed Danielle and Avery into the office, past cubicles of agents working on computers and telephones, to the conference room located in the back of the space.

"What's this about?" Danielle asked, the moment the door shut behind them.

"Director Hamilton."

Her eyes filled with tears. "It's so awful what happened to him. We're beside ourselves, especially those of us who knew him personally and worked with him." She wiped away tears.

"Before we go any further, I need to be assured of your discretion," Avery said. "Nothing we say here can be repeated to anyone. Do you understand?"

She nodded. "I'm under an NDA, so I get it."

"We're investigating the possibility of his son Josh's involvement in his father's death."

Danielle's face went slack with shock at hearing that. "No."

"You seem certain. Did you know Josh?"

"Not personally, but the director was such a good man. How could his own son possibly kill him?"

"It happens all the time in families. You should know that after years of working in law enforcement."

Sam had so many questions, but she bit her tongue and forced herself to stay silent while hoping Avery had an actual plan here. She would've started by asking Danielle why she'd given her baby to the Hamiltons to raise.

"Mrs. Hamilton told us Josh was adopted during the time her husband worked in this office. Do you recall the Hamiltons adopting him?"

"I do. I remember that very well. Mrs. Hamilton was actually back in Virginia with her older children by the time Josh joined their family, but Troy was still here."

"She also told us that the baby was actually yours. Is that true?"

Danielle's eyes widened and her mouth fell open before snapping shut. *"Mine?"* she asked in a squeaky voice.

"That's what she said. Is that true?"

"I... I've never been pregnant." The statement led to more tears. "My husband and I, we wanted children. Very badly. But the Lord never saw fit to bless us in that way."

"Was there another receptionist in the office at that time?"

"No, I was the only one."

Avery glanced at Sam.

"What can you tell us about Director Hamilton's relationship with his wife and with Deputy Director Jacoby during the time they were in Knoxville?" Sam asked.

"Troy and Dustin were best friends. They were inseparable. Courtney and Troy had their ups and downs as people do when they're parents of young children."

"What do you mean by ups and downs?" Sam asked.

"They... For a time they were separated, but they later patched things up."

"Do you know why they separated?"

"I don't. He didn't talk about it, and I never asked."

"How long were they separated?" Avery asked.

"About six months. Courtney took the children and went home to Virginia to be with her family while Troy stayed here."

"Was this before or after they adopted Josh?"

"Before."

"You seem fairly certain about a timeline that took place thirty years ago," Sam said.

"I remember it vividly. It was a difficult time for Troy, being separated from his family that way. We all thought it was somewhat cruel of Courtney to take his children away from him for so long."

"What role did this office play in helping to investigate the kidnapping of Taylor Rollings in Williamson County?" Avery asked.

She seemed stunned by the question.

"Mrs. Koch?" Avery asked. "Are you all right?"

"What does that have to do with Troy's murder?" she asked softly.

"We aren't sure. That's why we're asking."

"We supported law enforcement in Williamson County. For weeks, every agent assigned to this office worked that case, but we never found any sign of that poor baby."

"We've found him," Avery said.

"What? Where? Where is he?"

"I have to say again that what I'm about to tell you is highly confidential. It's critical that you refrain from telling anyone."

"I won't say a word. I promise."

"The baby who was taken from the Rollings family thirty years ago was raised as Josh Hamilton."

She shook her head, horror stamped into her expression. "No. That's not possible. There's no way Troy Hamilton could've been involved in something like that. He was *heartbroken* for the Rollings family. He spent *hours* with them, consoling them and offering whatever comfort he could. It's just not possible."

"I'm afraid the DNA has confirmed it."

She shook her head and blinked back tears. "I can't believe this," she whispered. "Why would Troy have done something like that to those poor people?"

"That's what we're trying to figure out."

"If there's anything you remember from the weeks before and after the kidnapping that you could share with us, no matter how small or insignificant it might seem, it could help us get to the bottom of this," Sam said.

The other woman seemed to think hard about that, and they gave her the time and the silence she needed.

"There was one thing that stands out in my memory," she said haltingly.

It was all Sam could do not to pounce, to tell her to spit it out already, and she sensed similar tension coming from Avery.

"Something wasn't right between Troy and Dustin. They were arguing a lot. At the time, I assumed it was because everyone was upset about the baby being kidnapped, but now… Now I'm not so sure."

"Is there anyone else in the office who was here when they worked here?"

"One other person. Dale Owens. He's one of the agents."

"Is he here?" Avery asked. "Could we speak to him?"

"Yes, let me get him."

"Remember," Avery said, "not a word about Josh to anyone."

Nodding, she left the room.

"What's your take?" Sam asked.

"I have no fucking idea what the hell is going on here. I can't get a read on this case."

"Me either. It's been a mind bender from the first second I met Josh."

"I feel the same way she does about the possibility of Troy having been involved in something so sinister. It flies in the face of everything I knew about him, the things he believed in as a leader and law enforcement officer. All I can think is that if he was involved, someone had something huge on him, and he had no choice but to go along with it."

"Could that someone have been Dustin?"

"I can't imagine that either."

CHAPTER TWENTY-THREE

DANIELLE RETURNED WITH a man with white hair, blue eyes and a kind face. He wore a cheap-looking lilac dress shirt with a matching tie, the kind discount department stores sold as a set. Danielle introduced him to Sam and Avery.

"What can I do for you?" Dale asked as he took a seat next to Danielle.

"Everything we speak of is confidential, understood?"

Dale nodded. "Been in this business since before you were born. I know how it works."

Ignoring the sarcasm, Avery said, "We're here about Director Hamilton's murder. We understand you worked with him and Deputy Director Jacoby while they were in this office."

"I did. That was a long time ago."

"Thirty years, to be exact."

"Sounds about right. We were heartbroken to hear of the director's death and the deputy director's disappearance. Is there any news about Dustin?"

"Not yet."

"And the director's son. Has he been found?"

"He has."

"Is he a suspect in his father's case?"

"Everyone is a suspect," Sam said. "It's a very active investigation."

"What do you remember about Hamilton's relationship with Jacoby or their time here in Knoxville?" Avery asked.

Dale blew out a deep breath. "Well, like you said, that was a long time ago. I'm sure Danielle mentioned there were some issues in Hamilton's marriage while he was here. The Mrs. went home to Virginia with the kids for a while there. Troy was a disaster over it."

"Do you remember anything specific about what he said or did in regard to his wife and the separation?"

"He was mad as hell," Dale said. "I remember that. We all gave him a wide berth after she left."

Avery took notes as Dale spoke. "How long was he wound up? Days, weeks, months?"

"Long time." Dale looked to Danielle for confirmation, and she nodded. "Months. Really let himself go to hell in a handbasket too. Stopped shaving, stopped sleeping, started drinking. We covered for him with D.C.— remember, Danielle?"

"Yes, I do. We filed reports for him that he didn't even know about. Things like that. We protected him."

"Where was Jacoby in all of this?" Sam asked. "Did he help to protect Hamilton too?"

They both took a second to think about that.

"I don't remember him being part of us protecting Troy," Dale said. "They'd had some sort of falling-out over something. Never did know what. Just that they weren't close like they once were. Jacoby kept his distance from Troy, if I recall correctly."

"That's what I remember too," Danielle said. "It was very tense around here with the two of them circling each other like a couple of rabid dogs."

"Did you ever think there was a connection between

the falling-out Hamilton had with Jacoby and the one he had with his wife?" Avery asked before Sam could.

"Ahhh, no," Dale said. "That never occurred to me."

"Me either," Danielle said, seeming intrigued by the suggestion.

"Can you tell us where the Hamiltons lived when they were here?"

"Their place was over in Lake Ridge, wasn't it, Dani?"

She nodded in agreement. "I babysat for the older kids a couple of times. Before they had Josh."

"They had that barbecue for the office that one time," Dale said. "Right before the Mrs. took off to go home."

"They were fighting that night," Danielle recalled. "Everyone was uncomfortable. The party broke up early."

"Do you remember what the fight was about?" Avery asked.

"I don't, just that they were very obviously in the midst of some sort of marital meltdown, and we were there to witness it," Dale said. "My Mrs. predicted they were going to split, and sure enough, they did a couple days later."

"How long were they apart?" Avery asked.

"The last six or so months he was here," Danielle said. "Not sure what happened when he transferred to head-quarters, but they got back together at some point and then we heard they'd had Josh."

"So that news came after he was in D.C.?" Avery asked.

"A short time before he left," Danielle said. "We were all surprised because they'd been separated awhile by then. We figured Courtney must've been pregnant when she left here, but later we heard they'd adopted Josh."

"This has been very helpful," Avery said. "Thank you both for your time."

"Could we get the address of where the Hamiltons lived when they were here?" Sam asked, working a hunch.

"I'll check the files," Danielle said. "Give me a minute."

They left the office a few minutes later with the address in hand.

"What're you thinking?" Avery asked.

"That it might be worth knocking on some doors to see if anyone in the old neighborhood remembers the family. And I don't know about you, but I have more questions for Courtney Hamilton."

"You read my mind."

"I'll call Malone, tell him what we've got and ask him to go back to her mother's place. I don't think we ought to wait on that. If she's involved, it would be easy for her to disappear."

"Agreed."

Sam placed the call to Malone and waited for him to pick up. When he did, she first asked about Josh's condition.

"I don't know yet. The paramedics were tight-lipped, and we're waiting on the doctors."

"Avery and I interviewed two people who worked with Hamilton and Jacoby while they were in Knoxville." She related what they'd learned and their concerns about Courtney Hamilton being a flight risk. "Is there any way you can track her down and maybe bring her in? You could use the pretense of precaution because people are attacking her family members. I've got one of my feelings about this, Cap. We need to act fast."

"I'm on it. Keep me posted on what else you find out."

"Anything back from the lab yet on the prints found on the golf club?"

"Not yet. We're leaning on them. And Lindsey is wrapping up the autopsy report too. Should have more on all of it soon. I'll let you know."

Sam ended the call with Malone and saw that Avery was on a tense call of his own. From the sound of it, he was being grilled by someone above him in the Bureau.

"Yes, ma'am. As soon as I have anything, you'll be the first to know." He rolled his eyes at Sam and made a moving-right-along gesture with his hand. "Of course. I understand. I'll be in touch." He jammed the phone into his pocket. "They're melting down at headquarters. That was the acting director."

"Still no sign of Jacoby?"

"Nothing. It's like he vanished."

"And he'd know how to do that, wouldn't he?"

"Yeah, he would," Avery said tightly. "Just like you and I would if we needed to. They're also fuming that I called you guys in before I called them when I found Hamilton's body, but I stick by my decision on that one."

"You handled it by the book, which is what you should've done."

"Try telling the acting director that. I'm sure there'll be hell to pay for me when the dust settles."

The GPS took them to the subdivision the Hamiltons had called home during their time in Knoxville. Avery brought the car to a stop outside a raised ranch that had seen better days. The exterior was right out of the eighties with faux brick siding and rusting metalwork around the windows. Abandoned plastic toys littered the front yard, and a half-built hot rod sat on blocks in the driveway next to a sedan with two flat tires.

"Nice place," Sam said.

"I bet it was back in the day."

"Let's see if anyone remembers them."

After knocking on a dozen doors and nearly being attacked by a Rottweiler, they hit pay dirt six doors down from the Hamiltons' old house. Mildred Spires, an eighty-year-old widow and mother to a friendly poodle, spoke in a lovely Southern accent and remembered the Hamilton family well.

"Come in," she said, after they'd shown their badges and identified themselves.

Sam was thankful that Mrs. Spires didn't seem to recognize her.

They were shown into a charming home, decorated in country style. A painted heart on the wall declared Home Is Where You Hang Your Heart. She offered tea, which they declined. When they were seated in the room Mildred referred to as her parlor, she lowered herself slowly to her recliner. The dog jumped into her lap and made itself at home. "What do you want to know about the Hamiltons?" she asked. "I saw the news about Troy this morning, and my heart about stopped! He was such a nice young man, so good-looking and hardworking. I told Courtney she'd be a fool to let that one go."

"So you were close to them?" Avery asked.

"Oh yes! I was like an extra grandma to Mark and Maura when they were little."

"How did you meet the family?"

"I heard through the neighborhood grapevine that they were in need of a cleaning lady, so I went by to see if I could help out. I cleaned for a number of people in the neighborhood back then." She held up twisted fingers. "Before my arthritis forced me into early retirement."

"Do you know why Courtney took the children and went home to Virginia?" Sam asked.

"Oh, well… Marriage is such a difficult thing sometimes. Are you married?"

"I am," Sam said, giddy on the inside that this lovely woman had no idea who she was. Since that happened so rarely these days, she decided to enjoy the anonymity.

"And you?" she asked Avery.

"Engaged."

"Then you know. You both know that relationships have their ups and downs. Courtney and Troy hit a rough patch where they couldn't seem to see eye to eye, so she took the children home to her mother's for a little cooling-off period. They were back together a few months later. They had their other son, Josh, and I still get Christmas cards from them to this day."

"So you don't know of any specific incident that caused them to separate?" Avery asked.

"No, like I said, it was a buildup of things, and Courtney thought it best for the children if they spent some time apart because they were fighting so much. She was quite sad about leaving. She had a nice circle of friends here, a bridge club and a book club and the country club. She was a joiner, that one. And the kids were doing well in school. It wasn't easy for her to decide to leave, because she loved her husband. I never doubted that." She offered a coy smile that lit up her eyes. "He was a good-looking devil. Like you, Agent Hill."

"Oh, um, well, thank you, ma'am."

"Before she left, I told her, don't let that man get away. You'll regret it down the road. I'm glad she listened to me, and they patched things up. My heart has been breaking for her since I heard the news about Troy last night. I can't imagine what she must be going through."

"Did you ever see the Hamiltons again after they left the area?" Sam asked.

"Not in person, but Courtney and I kept in touch by letters and the occasional phone call. It's dwindled to Christmas cards in recent years, but I do remember them fondly."

"This has been very helpful, Mrs. Spires." Avery rose and handed her his card. "If you think of anything else from back in the day that you think might be helpful, you can call me anytime. My cell number is on there."

"I'll do that." To Sam, she said, "I feel like I know you from somewhere."

"Not sure where. I've never been to Knoxville before. Do you get up to D.C.?"

"Oh, not in years and years. When my Tim was alive, we used to go for a weekend every now and then to see the monuments and the pandas. It's been more than twenty-five years since I was there."

"You mentioned the clubs that Courtney was a member of," Sam said as another thought occurred to her. "Were any of the other neighbors in those clubs or friends with her?"

"The only one still here would be Nancy Dumphries. She lives on the next street over." She gave them directions and sent them on their way.

"Nice lady," Avery said as they walked around the corner and down the block. The day was overcast and chilly, but warmer than D.C. by at least ten degrees.

"Very."

"I was trying not to crack up when she said she felt like she knew you."

"I enjoyed the rare moment of anonymity. I miss that."

"Sometimes I wonder how you manage to do your job when everyone in the country knows who you are."

"Not everyone."

"Okay, ninety-nine-point-nine-nine percent of the nation's population would recognize you."

"I just do my thing and try to ignore that crap. Most of the time it's fine. Since the inauguration, it's been a little harder, but that'll pass."

"No, it won't," he said with a laugh. "People are more fascinated by you than ever after you dived into the crowd at the parade."

"I couldn't let the guy who killed Arnold get away. He was standing there, right out in the open, almost daring me to notice him. What else was I supposed to do?"

"You did what any of us would've done. Unfortunately for you, the whole world was watching."

"It was worth it to nail that scumbag."

"How do you think Gonzo is doing? Really?"

"I don't know," Sam said with a sigh. "He's not saying much to any of us, and his attendance has been an issue for the first time ever. Malone gave him the rest of the week off to get his shit together. I hope he can come back from it. He's one of the best."

"That's a tough thing to come back from, especially the way it went down."

"Yeah. Happened to my dad when he was in Patrol. His partner was gunned down in a drive-by when he was standing a couple feet from my dad."

"Oh damn. Did they get the guy?"

"Nope. Took my dad a long time to get back in the game after that. He'd tell you himself he was never the same—as a man or a cop."

"How could you be?"

"As much as I'm worried about Gonzo, I've got my eyes on the rest of my squad too. After something like this, it's not unusual for people to decide it's not worth the potential sacrifice."

"You picking up any vibes?"

"Here and there. Nothing solid. Not yet anyway."

"I have every faith that if anyone can get them through this, you can."

"That's nice of you to say, but I'm fumbling my way through it just like they are. First time I've lost someone close to me on the job, and it's hard."

"It will be for a while."

"So we're told by the counselors they've sent to talk to us. I'm also under pressure to fill the spot that's now open in my squad, but it feels too soon to be talking about that."

"You'll know when the time is right."

"I guess." Eager to change the subject, she pointed. "That's the house."

CHAPTER TWENTY-FOUR

As they crossed the street, Sam took a call from Nick. "Hey, what's up?"

"I just got a visit from Derek Kavanaugh," he said of their close friend, who was also deputy chief of staff to the president.

"How are Derek and Maeve?"

"They're good, but this wasn't a social call. Apparently, the Oval is in full panic mode over Hamilton's murder, and the White House press corps is foaming at the mouth. The president's staff wants information, and they want it now."

"Don't we all," Sam said with a sigh. "So they put Derek up to asking you to pump me for information."

"Something like that."

"You can tell them we're working the case and making progress. That's all I've got for right now."

"I had a feeling you'd say that, so that's what I told him. I also might've mentioned that I resent being used for my connection to you."

Sam smiled. "Good."

"I guess Nelson is also furious that the Feds aren't running the investigation, even though the AG has explained about conflict of interest and jurisdiction."

"You can tell him the Feds don't have jurisdiction for the same reason they didn't have it when John was killed at the Watergate." The murder of Nick's boss and best friend, Senator John O'Connor, had brought Nick back into her life six years after she first met him. "Our city, our case."

"I'll pass that along. How's it going there?"

"Slow but good. We found some people who knew the Hamiltons when they lived here. Got some insight, but nothing huge yet. More like pieces in the puzzle."

"You'll put the picture together, babe. You always do."

"I hope you're right. Call you later?"

"I'll be waiting. Love you."

"Um, you too."

He was laughing when he ended the call, and Sam immediately felt bad for not saying it back to him. After a year of marriage, she was still navigating the work-home dynamic, and telling her husband she loved him in front of a colleague, especially this particular colleague, was a challenge for her. Maybe she should make saying it any time she damned well wanted to a goal for year two.

"The White House is unglued over Hamilton's murder," Sam said.

"You can see why they would be."

"They're also screaming about jurisdiction when we all know that's a nonstarter."

"You can't blame them for trying."

"Sure I can," she said with a cheeky grin.

Sam and Avery approached a yellow ranch house with a well-kept yard and mulched flower beds that were dormant now but would probably be extraordinary in the spring and summer. Avery rang the doorbell.

A woman in her mid to late fifties came to the door. She was petite with short dark hair and a friendly, if wary, smile.

They held up their badges. "Special Agent Avery Hill, FBI, Lieutenant Holland, Metro D.C. Police. Could we please have a moment of your time?"

She did a double take when she heard Sam's name. *"You're the second lady!"*

"Yes, ma'am."

"Oh my goodness! Come in. Please!"

Sam rolled her eyes at the grin Avery sent her way. It was too much to hope that she'd go unrecognized twice.

"What an honor to have you here! My husband and I are huge fans of your husband. We hope he goes all the way."

It was on the tip of Sam's tongue to say he goes all the way quite regularly, but she kept the thought private. "Thank you."

"And what you did at the parade! Oh my Lord! You're like a superhero!"

As the woman went on and on, Sam began to sweat while Avery became more amused.

Sam cleared her throat. "So the reason we're here—"

"Where are my manners? Can I offer you something? Some coffee or tea or iced tea or *anything*?"

"We're fine, thank you," Sam said as Avery said, "Some coffee would be wonderful."

She wanted to stab him through the heart with her famous rusty steak knife. The bastard was enjoying this far too much.

"Coming right up! My friends are never going to believe this! Can we take pictures while you're here? If we don't take pictures, everyone will think I made it up!"

"We'd be happy to do that," Avery said, pouring on the Southern charm.

Squealing, she went into the kitchen to make his coffee while Sam stared daggers at him. *"Really?"*

"Sorry. This has been such a shit day. I couldn't resist
some comic relief."

"At my expense."

"I'm very sorry about that."

"No, you're not!"

"My apologies."

Nancy returned with a tray containing coffee for both
of them, a plate of delicate cucumber sandwiches and
lemon cookies that looked homemade. Was there anything quite like Southern hospitality? Because she knew
it would mean the world to this very nice woman, Sam
poured some cream into her coffee and took two of the
tiny sandwiches.

"I wish I'd known you were coming. I would've made
something better."

"This is very nice of you," Avery said. "Now about
the reason we're here. You were friends with Courtney
Hamilton while she lived here in Knoxville?"

"Yes, I was, and I'm devastated for her today. Troy
was such a lovely man, and they were a beautiful family. My David and I had so many good times with them.
Our children were roughly the same ages, and we spent
many a weekend night playing cards and having a few
drinks while the kids played. Those were good times."

"Did Courtney confide in you when things between
her and Troy began to fall apart?" Sam asked.

"She did," Nancy said. "She was heartbroken over it,
and she struggled with the decision to leave."

"Did she say why they were having problems?" Avery
asked.

"She never came right out and said it, but I got the feeling that one of them might've had an affair. Now mind you, I couldn't figure out when either of them would've had the time. They were so busy with work and the kids and the house and all the stuff young parents deal with. David and I speculated endlessly about what might be going on, but we never did know for sure. It's further proof that the only two people who truly know what goes on in a marriage are the two people in it."

Wasn't that the truth. "When they lived here and you were socializing with them," Sam said, "did you ever meet his colleague Dustin Jacoby?"

Seeming startled by the question, Avery shot her a look.

"I met him a couple of times. They ran around together, and he joined us for cards sometimes. Dustin was single, and I got the feeling that they were like his family away from home. They did holidays together, that kind of thing. She joked about them being her two husbands."

Sam's skin tingled with the sensation she often got when she was on to something in an investigation, but this time her ears were buzzing too, which was odd.

"Was there ever any sense of something more than friendship between either of the Hamiltons and Dustin?" Sam asked.

"I don't think we need to go there," Avery said, scowling at her.

"Not that I ever saw," Nancy said. "They were the best of friends."

"This has been very helpful," Avery said. "Thank you for your time."

Nancy whipped out her phone. "How about a photo?"

Sam wanted to run for her life, but she smiled and nodded. "Sure."

Avery seemed to take great pleasure in dragging it out, taking multiple shots until he got one he was happy with.

"I will treasure this always," Nancy said, hugging Sam.

Trying not to bristle, Sam said, "Um, thank you." She couldn't get out of there fast enough.

"Why are you dragging Jacoby into this?" Avery asked the second the door closed behind them. "We've got nothing to tie him to any of this."

"Except for the fact that he's gone missing at the same exact time his boss was murdered and his boss's kidnapped son was kidnapped again. There's nothing curious about that to you?"

"It's far more likely that Jacoby is a *victim* in this than a perp."

"You say that with such certainty. The same certainty you had that there was *no way* Hamilton could possibly be involved with a baby's abduction. Remember that? Your exact words were *no way*, and now the DNA says *yes way*."

"I know what the DNA says. I still say Hamilton didn't know that baby was Taylor."

"And I call *bullshit* on him not knowing. He was involved in the investigation. How could he *not* know?" All of a sudden, her brain began to swim, the buzzing in her ears got louder and the ground tilted. What the hell? She stopped walking and bent in half, hands propped on knees, breathing through the dizziness.

"Sam? What's wrong?"

"I don't know." Despite the chilly bite in the air, her body felt hot, and her stomach wanted to reject Nancy's delicate cucumber sandwiches. Ugh. She forced herself to stand upright and instantly regretted it. The world was now actively spinning, and only Avery's quick thinking and his arm around her shoulders kept her from keeling over.

Shit, fuck, damn, hell, she had the goddamned flu.

THIS HAD TO be what it felt like to die. Sam wasn't sure which was worse, the chills, the constant puking or the fact that she'd actually needed Avery Hill's help—desperately. Everything was a blur from the time they left Nancy's house until he somehow got them into a hotel room where she'd done nothing but puke since he half walked, half carried her in there.

"Sam, I think we ought to call EMS," he said after another vicious bout of vomiting.

Curled into the fetal positon on the bathroom floor, she shivered violently as she tried to control the nausea long enough to speak. "Go. Away. Avery."

"I can't leave you alone like this."

"Go!"

She didn't know if he stayed or left because she couldn't move to find out. In fact, if she never had to move again, that would be fine with her. The next time she woke up it was dark, she was in bed and he was asleep in a chair in the corner. Sam realized she'd been awakened by her ringing cell phone.

Avery stood. "I'll get that for you."

Sam summoned the last of her energy to lunge for the phone. "No." Though she was sicker than she'd ever been, somehow she knew that if she let him answer that phone she'd have the biggest problem of her life. She fumbled with the phone and managed to flip it open before her eyes closed again.

"Sam!" Nick's cry got her attention. *"Samantha."*

"Sick."

"What? Honey, what's wrong?"

"What you had."

"Oh my God, baby. Where's Avery?"

"Won't go away."

"Let me talk to him."

Sam was on her way back to sleep. "Sam! Let me talk to Avery, honey."

She held up the phone. "Talk to him." She fell asleep to the lyrical sound of Avery's accent, which was strangely comforting under the circumstances, conveying the details of their afternoon and evening to Nick. Until she remembered that Nick hated Avery, who was now alone in a hotel room with her. Nick would be mad about that, but she couldn't keep her eyes open long enough to deal with it.

She dreamed about the case, about Arnold, Gonzo and Scotty. Where was Scotty? Did Nick have him? Sam woke up sweating, thrashing at the blankets that were wrapped around her legs, her anxiety spiking when she couldn't remember who had Scotty.

"Scotty. Where's Scotty?"

"Home with his dad."

Sam's eyes flew open to see Avery Hill wearing a T-shirt and sweats. He was seated on the edge of her bed.

"You need to drink some water so you don't get dehydrated." He held a cup of ice water and helped her sit up to take a sip.

The cold water sliding down her throat was the best thing she'd ever experienced. He forced a few more sips into her before Sam couldn't hold herself up any longer. She was asleep before her head hit the pillow and woke to the sound of men's voices. Sam thought she was still dreaming when she heard Nick. She had to be dreaming. He was in D.C. She was somewhere with Avery. Where were they again?

Tennessee.

She was in Tennessee, and her husband was in Washington. But then she heard him say, "I'll take it from here." The door to the room clicked shut, and she forced her eyes open to see if she was hallucinating. She had to be dreaming this.

Nick leaned over the bed to kiss her forehead, his familiar scent letting her know she wasn't imagining him. He'd really come. His thumbs on her cheeks wiped away dampness. "I'm here, baby. Everything is okay now."

"Are you mad?"

"What? Why would I be mad?"

"Avery," she said, swallowing a new wave of nausea. "He was here. In my room."

"He made sure you were okay until I got here." His fingertips on her face brushed away the hair that had stuck to her sweaty forehead. "How could I ever be mad about that?"

"He makes you crazy."

"He took care of you for me. It's okay."

Sam wanted to ask how he'd gotten there so fast and who was with Scotty and what was happening with the case, but she couldn't stay awake any longer. She drifted off only to be awakened sometime later when a wave of nausea had her sitting up in bed.

Nick was there, holding a bucket or maybe it was a trash can while she vomited. He held back her hair until it was over. The cool washcloth he used to wash her face felt like heaven. And when he got back in bed and put his arms around her, warming her chills with the heat of his body, she began to feel the tiniest bit better.

"Who's with Scotty?"

"Shelby. She was happy to stay since Avery is here."

"How'd you get here so fast?"

"It wasn't fast. It took interminable hours."

"Still, it seemed like you appeared out of nowhere. How'd you do that?"

"For the first time since I accepted this promotion, being vice president finally came in handy. You see, I have this plane on standby that I can use when I need to get somewhere fast."

"Brant must've had an embolism."

"I think he might be starting to get used to us."

Sam tried to smile but everything hurt, even her face.

"Go to sleep, babe. I'm right here if you need me."

Comforted by his presence as much as his sweet love, she curled her hand around his bicep and let sleep drag her into oblivion.

CHAPTER TWENTY-FIVE

JAKE MALONE ENDED the day as he started it—frustrated and infuriated with the interference coming from the FBI, which seemed to be one step ahead of them at every pass. And now he was hearing that Holland was down hard with the flu in Knoxville. What else could go wrong? This case was a freaking nightmare.

He made his way to the chief's office, waving to Helen, the chief's admin, on the way by. Her sympathetic smile didn't do much to assuage his shredded nerves.

"Whose idea was it to suspend Holland right before the FBI director got himself offed?" Malone asked.

Farnsworth poured him a shot of the whiskey he kept in his bottom drawer for nights that followed days from hell.

Silently, Malone took the glass from the chief, toasted him and downed the shot.

"What've you got?" Conklin asked from his seat in front of the chief's desk. He too held a glass in hand.

"Not enough." Malone dropped into the other visitor chair. "The Feds are making things very difficult in the field." He filled them in on what Holland and Hill had learned in Knoxville, including their interest in speaking with Mrs. Hamilton again. "The Feds have put a protective barrier around Courtney Hamilton and won't let us near her."

"It's still our case, Jake," Farnsworth said. "If we need her, we can take her into custody."

"That may be true, but we'll need a SWAT team to get her. The mother's house in Chantilly is a fortress. Her older children arrived today from Chicago and Boston. The family is expressing an interest in seeing Josh, who's still unconscious from a nearly lethal dose of phenobarbital."

"What're the doctors saying?" Conklin asked.

"That it's a waiting game at this point. Any word from the lab or Crime Scene? We need something to go on. The gunmen who took Cruz and Josh gave us dick earlier."

"The lab said they'd have something in the morning," Conklin said, "and we sent Crime Scene back in for another sweep. Carlucci and Dominguez interviewed the eyewitness, who didn't have anything more to add to what he'd already given us. He saw a person of average height and build running from the vicinity of the Hamilton home on Sunday afternoon around three-thirty. He couldn't describe the clothing or any other distinguishing features, so that's more or less a dead end."

"Did we get video from the surrounding homes? In that neighborhood, everyone has security."

"Archie's team is combing through that now," Conklin said.

"And still nothing on Jacoby?" Farnsworth asked.

"Not a trace."

With his elbows on the desk, Farnsworth leaned forward. "Finding him is going to be the key to this case."

"What makes you so sure?" Malone asked.

"Think about it. He was in Knoxville with Hamilton at the time the Rollings child went missing. He's second in command to Hamilton in the Bureau and falls off the grid at the same exact time that Hamilton is murdered and Josh is abducted. How could his disappearance not be related?"

"I think it's time we played hardball with the gunmen who abducted Cruz and Josh Hamilton," Conklin said. "Let's really go at them, make them think the others are rolling and see what we get. They're something we have that the Feds don't, so let's use them to our fullest advantage."

Malone got up and put his glass on the desk. "I'm on it."

"Jake, if you need to sleep, get on it in the morning," Farnsworth said.

"We'll do it now, and then call it a day."

"Keep us posted," Conklin said.

Malone waved to indicate he'd heard him and headed for the detectives' pit where Carlucci and Dominguez were working on reports. "Ladies, we're going to talk to our gunmen again, and here's the plan." He mapped out the strategy of making the others believe that one of their associates had started talking and it would go bad for the others unless they fessed up right away.

"They're going to want lawyers present," Carlucci said.

"We'll tell them we can absolutely get their lawyers here, but that might take until morning, and things are happening right now. It's up to them as to whether they want to cooperate. We want to know if any of them have info about the whereabouts of Dustin Jacoby or have had any contact at all with Courtney Hamilton in the last week."

Dominguez nodded. "Let's do this."

Malone handed each of them a case folder, keeping

one for himself, and called downstairs to the sergeant working the desk in lockup, asking to have the three men brought upstairs to interrogation rooms. "We'd prefer if they didn't see the others being moved."

"You got it, Cap. We'll have them upstairs in five minutes."

It'd been a while since Malone had done an interrogation on his own. He hoped he hadn't forgotten how it was done.

He'd taken Chris Kinney for himself, because they'd agreed earlier that he seemed to be the ringleader. Kinney had a rap sheet that dated back to high school when he'd been involved in an armed robbery at a convenience store in Southeast that put him in jail for five years. Since getting out four years ago, he'd stayed off the radar until now.

Kinney was stocky but muscular. He had close-cropped blond hair and a scar that slashed through his bottom lip. His arms were crossed, his expression defiant. "I got nothing to say."

"Well, you might want to listen, then. Here's what's going on. Your buddies are talking."

"No fucking way they're talking. They know better."

"I guess the thought of a long stretch in federal prison has them reconsidering their stance."

"Nice try, but I ain't buying."

"Does the name Dustin Jacoby mean anything to you?" Malone asked, playing a hunch.

Kinney didn't say anything but his body went rigid. Bingo. Interrogation was just like riding a bike, Malone decided. The skills came back when you needed them. He took a seat, keeping his posture relaxed and his tone amicable. "Here's what we think happened, and you can feel free to tell me I'm wrong. Something went down years ago between Jacoby and his boss, Troy Hamilton." Malone was grasping at straws with this theory, but Kinney didn't know that. His reaction to Jacoby's name was all Malone needed to head in this direction.

"We think it involved Hamilton's son Josh. Maybe Jacoby had something big on Hamilton, something he held over his head for years while they both rose in the ranks within the Bureau. But then the secret went public, and everyone's in cover-their-ass mode, including Jacoby, who's fallen off the radar. Now maybe, just maybe, Jacoby decides that his old buddy Troy has got to go before he can spill the beans on the whole scheme.

"So now we've got Troy out of the way, what do we do with the son who caused all this trouble in the first place? We can't have him running around telling people his parents *stole* him from another family. If we take him out of the picture, then everything is so much cleaner than it would be otherwise. And that, my friend, is where you come in." Malone paused for effect. "It was a good plan, except you got sloppy and forgot to take the plates off the van. Oh, and did I mention that Josh didn't die? Yeah, that's a bummer, because the doctors say he's going to survive, and when he starts talking, *whoa*, I want to be there for that. You feeling me?"

Kinney squirmed ever so slightly, but Malone saw it and pounced, leaning in so he was halfway across the table—right in the other man's face. "I'm giving you ten minutes to make your deal or I'm offering it to one of your pals." He stood and turned to leave, making it to the door before Kinney stopped him.

"What're you offering?"

"Depends on what you're giving."

Kinney sighed. "What if I could tell you where Jacoby is?"

"That'd be worth a conversation about lesser charges with the AUSA," Malone said. "It's the U.S. Attorney's call at the end, but I'd recommend leniency for your cooperation."

"I want to talk it over with my lawyer first."

"I'll get you a phone, but that'll take a few minutes. You should know that your friends are being offered the same deal as we speak. First come, first served." He made to leave the room again. "Let me see about that phone."

"Wait."

Malone smiled before he turned, losing the smile as he did. He remained stubbornly silent for a long moment before he checked his watch.

"All right. I'll take the deal."

"Excellent, give me a minute to let the others know." Staying in character, he stepped outside and stood there for five minutes before he went back in. Someone had once said there's a lot of acting in detective work, and tonight was a prime example of that. It was nice to know he hadn't lost his mojo since leaving the field to ride a desk.

Returning to the room, he produced a pad and pen. "Let's go through it from the beginning."

MALONE LEFT THE interrogation room twenty minutes later with a treasure trove of information from Kinney. He went directly to the chief's office where Farnsworth was also pulling an all-nighter. *We're getting far too old for this shit*, Malone thought as he knocked once before showing himself in.

"That went well," he said. "Kinney rolled on the others and identified Jacoby as the mastermind. He paid Kinney to help him take out Hamilton and to grab Josh."

"Jesus H. Christ. The deputy FBI director killed the director?"

"That's what he said."

"Did he say why?"

"Kinney saw dollar signs and didn't ask questions, but he said Jacoby was flipping out—his words—about getting it done fast. Things were falling apart, or so he said."

Farnsworth sat back in his chair to think that through. "So the release of that age-progression photo was like a fuse under a keg of dynamite."

"That's my thinking too. They sat on this for thirty years until that photo ruined the whole thing. No one ever would've known they had anything to do with taking Taylor if it wasn't for that photo."

"Why take out Hamilton and abduct Josh?"

"Kinney didn't know the why of it. He only knew that he was being paid to get rid of them both." Malone handed the chief a slip of paper. "That's Jacoby's second cell phone, the one he used to keep in touch with Kinney over the weekend. He doesn't know if it's still in service, but if it is, it could lead us to Jacoby."

"Let's get IT on tracking it."

"On my way up there from here. Before I go, though, I'm having another thought. Holland and Hill reported there was tension in the Hamilton marriage while they were in Knoxville, at the same time Jacoby was there and Taylor was kidnapped. Courtney left, took the children back to Virginia. I'm thinking she knows a lot more than she let on about what happened to her husband and how that baby came to live in her house."

"Agreed."

"The Feds have her surrounded. There's no way we can get to her."

"No, but I know who can." Farnsworth picked up the receiver on his desk phone, flipped through an old-fashioned Rolodex and placed a call. "Pat, Joe Farnsworth, sorry to wake you up. We have a situation and could use the assistance of the Virginia State Police." He laid it out for his old friend, giving him the full story on their belief that Jacoby was involved and that Courtney Hamilton had information relevant to the investigation. "I need you guys to get her out of her mother's house and bring her here." Joe laughed at whatever his friend had to say and then nodded. "Thanks a lot. I owe you one." He put down the receiver and grinned up at Malone. "Nothing cops love more than a good old-fashioned turf war. They're all in."

"Excellent. Let me get this number up to Archie's crew and see if we can locate Jacoby."

"I've forgotten how fun this can be."

"I was just thinking that myself. Doesn't seem fair that Holland usually gets to have all the fun while we toil away at desks."

"The old guys still got game."

"You know it." Filled with a new burst of energy, Malone took the stairs two at a time and went into the IT area, which was largely deserted at this hour, except for several third-shift detectives who were sifting through surveillance video from the Hamiltons' neighborhood. Malone wasn't surprised to find Lieutenant Archelotta at one of the terminals, working right alongside his team.

"What can we do for you, Cap?" Archie said when he saw him coming.

Malone handed him the piece of paper. "I need a trace on a phone number."

"Sure thing."

"I was told the location we're looking for might be in the mountains."

"If it's putting out a signal, we'll find it."

"The sooner the better. This is as hot as hot gets."

"Let me figure out who the carrier is and request a warrant. Give me thirty minutes."

"Thanks, Archie."

"They got you working for a living this week, huh?" Archie asked with a cheeky grin.

"Very funny. I'm going downstairs. Come find me if you get anything."

"You'll be the first to know."

Malone went down the stairs, intending to try to catch a cat nap in his office, but when he was paged, he ducked into Holland's office to take the call. "Malone."

"It's Nick Cappuano."

"Mr. Vice President. What can I do for you?"

"I'm in Knoxville with Sam. She's really sick, but all she wants to know is if you've got Mrs. Hamilton or if you've found Jacoby."

"You can tell her we're getting closer on both of them, and one of the gunmen rolled and gave us Jacoby."

Nick put the phone on Speaker, conveyed that information to Sam, and naturally, she had more questions.

Malone filled them in on what they knew so far, and what was currently being done. Ten minutes later, she ran out of questions—and, from what he could hear, steam.

"I appreciate your time, Captain," Nick said. "Perhaps now my wife will actually go to sleep and stay asleep."

"I live to serve."

"We'll be back in the city tomorrow. I assume you'll hear from my lovely bride."

"I shall eagerly anticipate her return."

Nick snorted with laughter before the phone went dead.

Malone grunted out a laugh as he hung up the phone. Classic Holland. Sick as a freaking dog and still on the job. He'd no sooner had that thought than Cruz and Gonzales appeared in the doorway. "What're you guys doing here?"

CHAPTER TWENTY-SIX

"COULDN'T SLEEP," CRUZ SAID. "I can't stop thinking about Josh, so I went by the hospital to see how he's doing. No change."

"I couldn't sleep either," Gonzo said. "I figured there might be something I could do to help."

"Right now, we're waiting on Archie to tell us where we might find Dustin Jacoby, who's apparently smack in the middle of this whole thing—whatever this whole thing might be."

"So we're actually about to go after the deputy director of the FBI in relation to the murder of the director?"

"And possibly the kidnapping of the child the director raised as his own."

"At least there's never a dull moment on this job," Cruz said, his expression incredulous.

"Shoulda gone into banking or insurance or something predictable and boring," Gonzo said as he took a seat and put his feet on Sam's desk.

Cruz took the other seat and put his feet up too.

While the cat was away…

"You really think you could be happy doing something else?" Cruz asked Gonzo.

"I've started to think maybe I could," Gonzo said, keeping his eyes down as he spoke.

"Are you making conversation or telling me something, Sergeant?" Malone asked.

"Right now? Making conversation."

Cruz stared at Gonzo. It was no secret the two men were close friends outside of work. "Are you seriously thinking about leaving?"

"I'm seriously thinking about all my options, up to and including a career change."

"What does Trulo say about that?" Malone asked.

"I got the speech about time being the great healer of all things, the same thing he always says, along with how important it is not to make any big or hasty decisions while I'm grieving."

"It's good advice," Cruz said. "After I got shot, he told me it would be a while before I could hear a car backfire and not think it was happening again."

"Including your own car?" Gonzo asked with a ghost of a smile that filled Malone with an unreasonable amount of hope. If he could make a joke, maybe he might actually survive the loss of his partner.

"That's hilarious. Ha. Ha. Actually, he meant *other* cars, and it turns out he was right. It took six or eight months, but I didn't jump out of my skin every time I heard a loud noise anymore."

"I was in a high-speed crash when I was in Patrol," Malone said. "Rolled over three times, busted a couple of ribs and my collarbone. Took me a year before I could drive over fifty miles an hour, which made it tough for me to do my job. My partner did all the driving for a while, but anytime we had to chase, I'd close my eyes and break into a cold sweat until it was over. Every damned time, I expected the car to roll over." He could still remember the sickening fear that made him feel weak and ineffective.

"I've never heard you were in a crash," Cruz said.

"Was a *long* time ago. More than twenty years. You never forget it, but you do figure out a way to cope." He fixed his gaze on Gonzo. "In time."

"I'm sensing a theme here," Gonzo said with a small grin. "I hear what you're saying—what everyone is saying. I'm not planning any hasty decisions. I'm only thinking more and more about the possibility of doing something else, not acting on it."

"I don't think you're alone in that after what happened," Cruz said.

"What do you know?" Malone asked.

"Tyrone," Cruz said somewhat reluctantly. "He's not taking Arnold's death well at all—not that any of us are—but he's… He's messed up over it."

"I'll ask Trulo to talk to him," Malone said.

"I think he already has," Cruz said. "I shouldn't even be saying anything because he confided in me, but I'm worried about him."

"You absolutely should say something," Malone said. "We can't help him if we don't know he's having trouble."

"Still… I don't want him to think I came running to you."

Malone understood where he was coming from. "I got ya. I'll keep an eye on him." He leaned forward, elbows on the desk. "The loss of Arnold was a blow to all of us. I remember vividly how devastated everyone was, myself included, when Steven Coyne was killed in a similar fashion, and I hadn't worked that closely with him. Everyone felt it, just like we all feel the loss of Arnold. It's a horrible reminder that we put ourselves on the line every day out there."

"And most of the time, no one gives a shit," Gonzo said.

"I still believe more people do than don't, regardless of what the media would have us believe," Malone said.

Lieutenant Archelotta appeared in the doorway. "I've got your location. He's in the mountains in West Virginia, and we've got him on the footage from the hotel in Beltsville where Josh was found."

FREDDIE RODE WITH Malone and Gonzo in a department SUV, following the MPD SWAT unit that was deployed to assist the West Virginia State Police. Everyone was tense. They anticipated that Jacoby might fight back and fight back hard. With everything on the line, he had nothing to lose.

Organizing the operation to go after Jacoby in the mountains had taken a couple of hours and a lot of coordination with West Virginia State Police, which had to be convinced that it was actually in their best interest to help the MPD track down the missing FBI deputy director.

It also took some doing to keep the Feds out of the loop. The last thing they needed was interference that would allow Jacoby to get away.

The Virginia State Police had been successful in removing Mrs. Hamilton from her mother's home and now had her in custody. McBride and Tyrone were on their way to pick her up and bring her to HQ.

On the tense, quiet ride north, Freddie texted Elin to let her know where he would be for the next couple of hours.

Why do you have to go?

Because this is our case and he's a person of interest.

I don't like it.

Ever since Arnold was killed in cold blood on a city sidewalk, she'd been a lot more nervous about his job. Then he'd been abducted at gunpoint and knocked around, which sent her nerves into the red zone.

I'll be fine. Try not to worry. This isn't our raid. We're just along for support. I won't be out in front.

Not this time anyway, but there'd be plenty of other times when he and his team would be leading the charge. He hoped that she would eventually relax a little but didn't think it would happen anytime soon.

The conversation with Malone and Gonzo earlier had brought home how deeply the suffering ran in their small, close group within the Homicide squad. Not only had his death affected each of Arnold's colleagues profoundly, it was also taking a toll on their loved ones.

Please be careful. Love you so much. Can't take any more near-misses.

Freddie blew out a deep sigh. He hated that he put her through so much and couldn't imagine what he'd do if it finally became too much for her. How would he go on without her? He couldn't even bear to think about a life that didn't include her. Love you too, baby. Don't worry.

His phone dinged with a new text from Sam. What's happening there?

He filled her in on where they were going and why. I'm so pissed to be sitting this one out. Be back soon to help out.

We've got ya covered. No worries. How you feeling?

Like death.

Ugh. Sorry. I'll let you know what happens.

Please do.

VA SP has Courtney Hamilton in custody. More to come on that too. And we've got Jacoby on the security film from the hotel in Beltsville where Josh was found.

It's all coming together. Any word on how Josh is?

Last I heard he's the same, but doctors are optimistic that he'll pull through.

I've got to give Franklin police something in the AM. They're anxious to tell Taylor's parents that he's been located.

Hopefully we'll have some good news for them soon.

Hope so.

Freddie looked out into the dark of night, thinking of Josh and people in Tennessee that he'd never met, but who were about to get an answer to all their prayers. He could only hope—and pray—that the son they'd missed for so many years would live to be reunited with them.

AFTER THE EXCHANGE with Freddie, Sam put down her phone and tried to fall back to sleep. Though she felt worse than she ever had in her life, she was wide-awake and buzzing with adrenaline after hearing her people were hot on Jacoby's trail. She'd give anything, well, almost anything, to be with them when they took him in.

She sat up slowly, her head spinning from even that small movement. The bedside clock read four-thirty.

"What're you doing?" Nick asked.

"I'm coming out of my skin being here when things are going down at home."

"You're sick. Even if you were there, you wouldn't be working."

"Still…can we go home?"

"Right now?"

"Didn't you say the plane is on standby whenever you need it?"

"Within reason."

"Will you check? Please?"

Sighing, he got out of bed, turned on a light, pulled on a pair of sweats and went to the door.

Sam heard the low murmur of voices but couldn't make out any specifics of what was being said.

The door closed and Nick came over to sit on the bed. "They'll see what they can do."

"Thank you."

He tucked her hair behind her ear. "You're sure you feel up to traveling?"

"I never feel up to traveling, but I'm losing my mind, in addition to my lunch, being here. I want to go home."

Nick reached for the cup of ice water he'd put on the bedside table earlier. "Drink. Stay hydrated so you don't end up in the hospital like I did."

She did as he asked, her stomach gurgling in protest at the cold liquid. For a second, she feared the water would come right back up. But it stayed down. The battle let her know she wasn't as over the flu as she'd like to be. She sank into the pile of pillows, breathing through the nausea. "This sucks balls."

"Yeah, it really does. I can't remember ever feeling worse in my life."

"Because you're superman. You never get sick."

"Whatever you say, babe."

A soft knock on the door had him crossing the room for an update. "Thanks so much, Brant. We'll be ready." He closed the door and turned to face her. "Wheels up in one hour."

"Thank God." Then she thought of Avery. "Um, what do we do about, um, Avery?"

"What about him?"

Sam rolled her eyes at the testy way he said that. "Would it be possible to offer my colleague, who was so amazingly helpful to me when I was sick, a ride back to D.C.?"

"Yes, it would be possible. Do you want me to call his room and see if he's interested in joining us?"

"It's very nice of you to offer, but I'll call him." She found his name on her list of contacts and placed the call.

"Hill."

"It's me. Sam."

"How're you feeling?"

"Better. We're going home. You want to hitch a ride with us?"

After a long pause, he said, "Um, sure. I need to return the rental car, though."

In consultation with Nick, they discussed logistics and agreed that they'd pick him up at the terminal in forty minutes.

"See you then," Avery said before the line went dead.

"Look at us," Nick said as he put on jeans and a sweater. "One big happy family."

"There may be hope for you two yet."

"I wouldn't go that far." He came around the bed to help her up, holding her until she got her bearings. "Take it slow. You were really sick last night, and you're going to feel weak and dizzy for another day or two." He placed his hand flat against her forehead. "You're still warmer than you should be too."

"I'm okay." She kissed his cheek and went to find her suitcase. By the time she brushed her hair and teeth and put on some clothes, she was completely drained of energy. A dizzy spell had her gripping the bathroom sink so she wouldn't fall.

Nick's arms came around her from behind. "Easy, baby."

She rested against him, letting him hold her up when it was too much to do it herself. Sam slept through most of the ride to the airport in the pearly dawn light and woke when they stopped to pick up Avery. The Secret Service handled everything with their usual dispatch and they were loaded onto *Air Force Two* a short time later.

Sam insisted on walking up the stairs to the plane herself, which, in hindsight, was a mistake.

Nick belted her into her seat and sat next to her.

Avery sat across the aisle from them.

Though she kept her eyes closed, Sam heard the stewards offering food and beverages and Nick encouraging Avery to have whatever he wanted. Both men ordered breakfast and coffee. Nick asked for ginger ale and water for her.

Sam hoped she could handle the smell of the food.

That was the last thought she had before the wheels touching down at Andrews Air Force Base jarred her out of a sound sleep.

"Welcome back, babe." Nick offered a glass of ice water, and she took a greedy drink.

"I can't believe I slept through an entire flight. I need to get sick more often if that's what it takes to sleep when I fly."

"You've got a little more color in your cheeks than you had earlier."

"I actually feel better."

"I'm so glad to hear that."

Surrounded by Nick's detail, they got off the plane and into one of the ever-present black SUVs for the ride into the city.

She fired off a text to Freddie. What's going on?

Waiting game. Everyone is in position. WVSP is calling the shots, so we're on standby.

Ugh.

No kidding. Cold up here.

Sam closed her phone but kept it in hand in case there were updates.

"Anything new?" Avery asked.

"Nothing yet."

"Other than the fact that you have the director's wife in custody, or I suppose that doesn't count as anything."

"I figured you already knew that, so it would be redundant to mention it."

"What do you hope to gain by taking her in?"

"Information about her relationship with her husband, among other things."

"What other things?"

"After what we heard yesterday, you have to ask? We want to know the true nature of her relationship with Jacoby too."

"What're you suggesting?"

"Nothing. Yet." As she said the words, another thought occurred to her. How old were Mark and Maura Hamilton when their younger brother became part of their family? What did they remember from that time? She couldn't wait to get back on the job.

Avery clicked away on his phone for a few minutes before sending her an angry glare. "Were you going to tell me that you guys have Jacoby's house in the mountains surrounded?"

"No, I wasn't, because we have jurisdiction over this case, and everywhere we go, you guys show up, acting as if it's actually your case. How do you know about Jacoby?"

"Because he put out the word to the Bureau that he's in need of assistance at his getaway, where he's been on a hunting trip since the weekend."

"And you buy that shit? You buy that the deputy director of the FBI would go completely off the grid without telling anyone he's doing that? Really?"

"There's probably a perfectly good explanation."

"How about the fact that the thugs who took Cruz and Josh *told* us Jacoby hired them?"

"And you're taking their word for it?"

"How would they have his private cell phone number if he hadn't hired them?"

"Sam," Nick said, taking her hand. "Don't get worked up."

"Look," Sam said in a calmer tone, "I know you don't want to believe that men you looked up to were involved in something so sinister, but all the evidence is pointing in their direction."

"Granted, but you and I both know that doesn't mean it's a slam dunk."

"Never said it was."

They existed in uneasy silence the rest of the way into the city, where they dropped Avery off at home.

"Thanks for the lift."

"Avery."

"Yeah?"

"Thanks for what you did for me yesterday," Sam said. "I appreciated it."

"As did I," Nick said.

Avery's face was expressionless when he said, "Sure. No problem."

The door closed and the Secret Service agent who'd gotten out to open it got back in the front seat.

Sam waited until the car was moving again to ask the question she'd been dying to ask since they landed. "So what happened between you two while I was out cold on the plane?"

CHAPTER TWENTY-SEVEN

"WHAT MAKES YOU think anything happened?"

Sam shot him a look. "Because I know you. Spill the beans."

"We talked about you."

"Um, you're going to need to elaborate on that."

He took her hand and kissed the back of it before turning it to press his lips to her palm. "We talked about how amazing you are, how strong and loyal and supportive of your friends and colleagues, how you're tireless in your efforts to get justice for victims of the most violent of crimes, how you're the most incredible wife and mother."

Stupefied, Sam stared at him. "You did not talk to him about that stuff."

"Actually, I did talk to him about that and how much I love you and how nothing and no one will *ever* come between us. I was pretty adamant about that last part."

"Tell me you're joking."

"I'm dead serious, Samantha. We had a man-to-man conversation, and I think we understand each other a lot better than we did before."

"What did *he* say?"

"He didn't have much to say other than he agreed with just about everything I said about you. Of course he has no way to know what kind of wife you really are. If he did, well… Let's just be glad he doesn't know what he's never going to get to experience firsthand because he'd be *so* bummed."

Even though her entire body went hot for reasons that had nothing to do with fever or the flu and everything to do with his ridiculous possessiveness, she couldn't let him know that it turned her on. "I'm going to kill you, and I'm going to make it hurt."

"Sweetheart, I'm surrounded by Secret Service agents. I'd like to see you try."

"You're not surrounded by Secret Service when you're sleeping."

"Ah, duly noted. Will sleep with one eye open from here on out."

"So basically you had Avery Hill all to yourself for two hours and you tortured him."

"I wouldn't go so far as to call it *torture*. I'd say it was more of an information session."

"You're a dead man."

"You won't kill me. You like the sex too much."

"It only took one year of marriage to create a monster."

"You love me."

"I don't love you having a 'talk' with Avery."

"It was a good thing. We cleared the air."

"What would his side of the story be?"

"I imagine he'd say the same."

"Let me ask you something."

"Anything you want."

She glanced over at him, not sure if it was wise to ask the question that had been on her mind since he appeared in Knoxville the night before. "Why did you come to Tennessee? Was it because I needed you or was it because I was alone in a hotel room with Avery?"

Nick's eyes went wide with surprise and then narrowed with anger. "Are you really asking me that?"

"Yeah, I guess I am."

"I came there," he said in a tight, furious-sounding tone, "because you were sick and needed me."

"And not because Avery was taking care of me?"

"That had nothing to do with it."

Sam remained skeptical but kept her thoughts to herself, as they arrived at home, where they were greeted by Secret Service Barbie, who was working the door. Of course she was.

"Good morning, Mr. Vice President, Mrs. Cappuano."

"Good morning, Melinda," Nick said with a polite smile.

Sam swore the woman all but swooned from being on the receiving end of that smile. She was only human, the poor thing. "Maybe I need to have a 'talk' with her about the greedy way she looks at my husband's sexy ass," she whispered as he hung their coats in the closet. "I could tell her how big your dick really is. Give her something to fantasize about."

"Or not."

Chuckling at his predictable reply, she headed for the stairs, eager to shower and change and get to the hospital to check on Josh.

"Um, where do you think you're going?" Nick asked twenty minutes later when she emerged from her closet dressed and ready to go.

"To the hospital to see Josh."

"You've been sick, Samantha. You need to take it easy today, or you're going to relapse."

"I'm fine. I'm only going to the hospital where I'll also

get something to eat." She patted his face and went up on tiptoes to kiss him. "You can go to work. You're off duty."

He lifted her sweater, which covered the service weapon strapped to her hip. "If you're just going to the hospital, why're you bringing the hardware?"

"Because I never leave home without it, as you well know." She kissed him again. "I swear I feel fine. Tired and a little achy, but otherwise fine. I need to check in on Josh and get things moving with the Franklin police who are waiting for my okay to tell the Rollingses that he's their son. I can't bear to make them wait another day for that news."

"Fair enough. Just promise you'll come home as soon as you can."

"I will. I promise."

He leaned in to kiss her. "And for the record, I went to Knoxville because I couldn't bear the thought of you feeling so crappy without me there to take care of you. Not for any other reason."

"That's a pretty good reason. Thanks again for coming. It meant everything to me to have you there."

"You mean everything to me." He kissed her once more. "Be careful out there."

"Always am."

Sam went outside and was surprised to realize her car was parked in its usual spot, even though she hadn't left it there. Nick must've arranged to get it home from HQ. The keys were in it, which was another benefit of the security afforded by the Secret Service. They did have their uses.

Feeling light-headed and nauseated, she started the car and headed for the checkpoint, taking it slow. She desperately wished she were still in bed, but with so many threads needing to be pulled in the case, she'd never sleep anyway. She may as well do what she could to help out.

On the way to the hospital her phone rang with a call from Detective Watson.

"Good morning," Sam said.

"What's the status?"

"As far as I know, Josh's condition is unchanged. I'm on my way to the hospital now to see him."

"I want to tell the Rollingses that we've found him."

"Will you also tell them that he's gravely injured or who had him all this time?"

"I'll tell them everything I know."

She could hear the fierce determination in every word he said, and frankly, she didn't blame him. She would feel the same way in his place. Locating a child who'd been missing for thirty years would be cause for huge celebration in the Franklin police department.

"Do I have your okay to proceed?" Watson asked.

"Yes, go ahead."

"They'll want to come there."

"We'll do everything we can to accommodate them."

"Um, pardon the question, but it's my understanding that you're currently suspended. Is that true?"

"Heard about that all the way down there in Tennessee, huh?"

"Everyone has heard about that."

"I'm suspended for one more day but still actively engaged in the case. I'll personally make sure the Rollings family is treated with the dignity and respect they deserve when they come to my city."

"Thank you for that. I can't believe I actually get to go tell them this news. If it gets any better than this in a career, I'm not sure when."

"You've worked hard for a long time to be able to give them this news. I'm only sorry we were unable to keep him safer. We're in the midst of a truly baffling case here with his abduction and his father's murder."

"Are there any suspects?"

"One and you won't believe who."

"I'm all ears."

"The deputy director of the FBI."

"Holy shit. Really?"

"Yep."

"Wow, well… I'll let you get back to that mess while I go tell Mr. and Mrs. Rollings that their prayers have been answered."

"You enjoy that, and let them know that from everything we're being told, he's expected to recover from his injuries."

"They'll be glad to hear that. I'll be in touch."

Sam closed her phone and tried to imagine the reaction of the Rollings family to hearing their child had been found. If nothing else came of this nightmare case, at least those poor people would have closure on their son's disappearance. They'd get to meet him and get to know him and perhaps, over time, build a relationship with him.

At GW, she asked for Josh at the reception desk and was directed to the sixth floor. Patrol officers were stationed outside his door, and they seemed surprised to see her in light of the suspension, not that they'd ever ask why she was there.

Because they were required to ask for identification, even if they knew the visitor, she showed them her badge.

"How is he?"

"Doctors are in there now, Lieutenant. As far as we know, there's no change."

"Help you with something?" a man asked. He was in his thirties with dark hair and intense eyes. In him, Sam saw Troy Hamilton.

"And you are?" she asked even though she already knew.

"Mark Hamilton. This is my brother's room."

Sam showed him her badge. "Lieutenant Holland, Metro PD."

"What do you want?"

Okay, Sam thought, *so that's how we're going to play it?* "I've been involved in your brother's case for days now. I wanted to check on how he's doing."

"By involved do you mean how you allowed him to be kidnapped at gunpoint and taken hostage?"

"I understand that you're upset, Mr. Hamilton—"

"You don't understand anything. My father has been murdered, my brother has been viciously assaulted and my mother has been arrested. You don't have the first clue how I feel!"

"Could we go somewhere and talk? Please? I have information I think you and your sister would want to know."

For a second she thought he was going to say no, but then his shoulders sagged and he turned to walk away.

Sam grimaced at the Patrol officers and went after him. They ended up in the waiting room where a woman who bore a striking resemblance to him was bent over her phone.

"Maura, this is Lieutenant Holland from the Metro PD. She says she has info we need to know."

Maura looked up from her phone, and Sam could tell that Maura recognized her, but she didn't mention it. "What kind of information?"

"The kind that will be difficult to hear." Sam closed the door and sat across from them.

"More difficult than our father being murdered or our brother being abducted or our mother being arrested?" Maura asked.

Sam had to remember she was dealing with a lawyer in addition to a bereaved daughter. "Yes, possibly."

"So what is it?" Mark asked.

"Thirty years ago this week, a baby was kidnapped from a hospital in Tennessee."

"What does that have to do with us?" Maura asked.

"That baby is your brother Josh." She watched as two intelligent, accomplished people tried to wrap their brains around what she was telling them.

They exchanged glances.

"That can't be true," Maura said. "Mother had him when we moved back to Virginia. He wasn't even born in Tennessee."

"Do you remember your mother being pregnant and having a baby?"

"I remember it vividly," Mark said. "Her belly was huge. I remember being afraid she was going to break open."

"I remember that too! Her skin was so tight and stretched."

Sam reeled as she listened to them. So Courtney had been pregnant when she left Knoxville to go home to Virginia? Neither of her friends had mentioned that.

"So there's no way the baby that went missing could be our brother," Mark said.

"Actually, it is him. We have DNA evidence linking him to the father of the missing baby."

"Are you insinuating that our parents had something to do with taking that baby?" Maura asked.

"I'm insinuating that they raised a kidnapped baby as their own. What they knew and when they knew it is something we'd all like to know."

"They couldn't have possibly known he was kidnapped," Mark said. "My father devoted his entire life to truth and justice and the law. If you go public with these insinuations, we'll sue your ass off, and we'll go after your badge too."

"Feel free to do whatever you need to do, but this information will be going public probably today when the Rollings family in Tennessee finds out that their prayers have been answered and their son has been found."

"This can't possibly be true," Maura said with a whole lot less conviction than she'd had at the beginning of the conversation.

"I'm sorry. I know how difficult it has to be for you to hear this, but it is true, and we believe that Dustin Jacoby killed your father and abducted your brother because he was afraid of what would happen when the truth came out."

They stared at her as if she had two heads.

"He was my father's *best friend*," Mark said. "He's like an uncle to us. He would never harm my dad."

"Look, I get that this is extremely shocking to you, but everything I'm telling you is true. The West Virginia State Police and the Metro PD have Jacoby surrounded at his cabin in the mountains. We have footage that shows him with your brother at a hotel in Beltsville after your brother was abducted at gunpoint and fed a nearly lethal dose of phenobarbital. We have the gunman who orchestrated the abduction telling us that Jacoby hired him and two of his associates to help him kill your father and abduct your brother, who was kidnapped from a family in Tennessee as an infant." Sam paused, took a moment to look at both of them. "Now, hearing all that, do you *honestly* believe that I could make up a story this crazy?"

"What could our mother possibly have to do with any of it?" Maura asked.

"We're not sure, but we're hoping to find out. The FBI wouldn't let us near her, so we had no choice but to take her into custody so we can speak to her about some questions we have."

"What kind of questions?"

"Things about her marriage and her relationship with Jacoby."

"They were friends."

"Right."

"Are you insinuating they were more than friends?" Mark asked.

"I'm not insinuating anything other than we want to talk to her again."

A nurse came into the waiting room. "Your brother is awake. He's asking for you."

Mark and Maura took off toward Josh's room. Sam followed, hoping she'd be allowed in to see him.

CHAPTER TWENTY-EIGHT

"Do we know why he was taken?" one of the patrolmen working Josh's door asked.

"We do," she said.

"Did we get them?"

"Most of them. We're working on bringing in the ring-leader now."

Half an hour after they went into the room, Mark and Maura emerged. She was tearful. He was pissed.

"Josh wants to see you," Mark said. "You've got five minutes."

Though Josh had described his family as not particularly close, Sam was glad that his siblings seemed to care so much about him. He was going to need their support in the days and weeks to come as his new reality set in.

Sam went into the room, wincing at the sight of his bruised and battered face. His upper lip was grossly swollen and one eye completely closed. He had a bandage on his forehead and another on his chin, through both of which she could see sutures.

"How're you feeling?" she asked.

"Great…"

"I'm so sorry this happened, Josh."

"How's Freddie?"

"Better than you. Banged up but back to work today."

"That's a relief. He was super cool. He told me to do

whatever I was told and stay alive. Just stay alive, he said."

"That was good advice."

"It was Dustin. I couldn't believe it when I saw him there—at the house where they took us."

"Did he say anything to you?"

"Just that he was sorry. He was really sorry, but he had to do it." Josh tried to sit up and groaned, his hands covering his head. "God, my head is killing me, and they said he drugged me."

"He gave you phenobarbital, enough to almost kill you."

"How could he try to *kill* me? He's known me all my life."

"We think he also killed your father."

"*Why?* Why would he do that?"

"The DNA results are back, and you're a match to Mr. Rollings." Sam said it quickly but succinctly. "Detective Watson from the Franklin police department in Tennessee is notifying the Rollings family as we speak. He said they're going to want to see you. How do you feel about that?"

"I… I suppose it's fine. They've waited a long time."

"Yes, they have."

"So what does that have to do with Dustin and my father's murder?"

"We think something went down thirty years ago in Knoxville when your family and Dustin lived there."

"They never talked about living in Tennessee. I didn't even know they did. Is that weird?"

"It is, but it was also a difficult time in your parents' marriage. Did you know they separated for about six months?"

"No, I've never heard that either, and it surprises me. They were always so solid, or at least they seemed that way to me."

"And your siblings never talked about Tennessee or your parents living apart?"

"No."

"Your mother came right out and admitted to us the other night that you're adopted. They never told you that?"

"Nope," he says with a bitter laugh. "I guess I was living totally in the dark in that family."

"The odd thing is, Mark and Maura remember your mother being pregnant around that time, when they left Knoxville to move back to Virginia."

"So what happened to that baby?"

"That's a very good question."

THE WAITING FOR something to happen was utter torture. Freddie was freezing, starving and exhausted. This totally sucked, especially because they had no control whatsoever over any part of this mission. It was being run by the West Virginia State Police, who were operating with an overabundance of caution in light of the fact that their person of interest was the FBI deputy director.

And as if there weren't enough law enforcement officers here already, the Feds had shown up half an hour ago, demanding to know why their deputy director's vacation home was surrounded by armed officers.

Thus, the standoff continued unabated in the fifth hour.

"How long are we going to stay here, Cap?" Gonzo asked, giving voice to Freddie's most pressing question.

"I don't know," Malone said with a sigh. "It's turned into a three-ring circus."

Another half hour passed in eerie, tension-filled silence before the incident commander from the West Virginia State Police left his post to come talk to them. He was halfway across the snow-covered yard when a shot rang out, striking the officer and knocking him off his feet.

All hell broke loose, with people shouting and return fire shattering the silence.

The officer who'd been hit crawled across the snow to where Freddie and the others from the MPD dragged him to safety.

"Hit my vest," the man said through gritted teeth. "I'm okay."

They propped him up against their SUV. He reached for his shoulder mic to check in with his team.

"Tell them we want Jacoby alive," Malone said.

The officer conveyed the message. His radio crackled to life.

"Do we have the green light to go in, Cap? We've got a clear line on the back of the cabin, and the shot came from the front."

He looked up at Malone who nodded. "We're not getting anywhere waiting him out," Malone said.

"Go," the captain said into the shoulder mic, grimacing with pain.

From their position, they couldn't see the action, but they could hear it. Shattering glass, wood splintering, shouts, gunshots. The whole thing seemed to happen in slow motion, but it only took about thirty seconds from the order to the report they'd been waiting for:

"We've got him."

A few minutes later, Dustin Jacoby was marched from the cabin in handcuffs and leg chains and delivered to them over vociferous objections from the shell-shocked Feds.

Freddie wasn't sure what he'd been expecting, but Jacoby was smaller than he'd thought he would be—maybe five-ten with a lean build and graying dark hair.

Ignoring the Feds, Malone and Cruz loaded Jacoby into their SUV for the ride back to the city. The West Virginia State Police team came to collect their captain.

Malone shook hands with the injured man. "Thanks a lot for the help. We owe you one."

"Anytime," he said, his face twisted in obvious pain.

As Freddie got into the backseat next to their prisoner, his phone chimed with a text from Elin.

They're reporting shots fired outside Jacoby's place. Tell me you're all right.

I'm good, and we got him. On the way back now.

Thank God.

Freddie's next text was to Sam. We've got Jacoby. On the way back now. Got a little hairy there for a minute or two. He fired on the WVSP and it went downhill fast from there.

Anyone hurt?

Their incident commander was hit in the vest. He's ok.

So Jacoby actually fired on you guys?

Yep.

Nothing says 'I'm guilty' quite like firing on law enforcement.

No kidding. I get to sit next to him on the ride back. Good times.

Can't wait to hear what he has to say for himself. BTW, Josh is awake and I got to talk to him. He's confused about why Dustin would've taken him or killed his father. I told him about the DNA. The poor guy has a lot to contend with.

For sure. I'm glad he's awake anyway.

Yeah… Tell Malone to call me before he talks to Jacoby. I've got more.

Ok.

They rode back to the city in silence. Jacoby stared out the window the whole way and didn't utter a word to any of them, and Freddie fully expected the deputy director wouldn't willingly say anything to them. Ever.

"I DON'T UNDERSTAND why I'm here," Courtney Hamilton said. "My husband was murdered, and I'm being arrested? I was in Virginia all day Sunday. I had nothing to do with it."

"We have some questions for you, and the Feds wouldn't let us near you," Jeannie McBride said. "They gave us no choice but to take you into custody."

"I spoke to **Agent** Hill and your chief the other night. I told them what I know."

Working from the notes Sam had supplied from her trip to Knoxville, Jeannie said, "You didn't mention that you and your husband were separated for a time thirty years ago."

"What in the world does that have to do with him being murdered?"

"I'll get to that. Why did you separate from your husband and take your children home to Virginia while he stayed in Knoxville?"

"That's our personal business, and it was thirty years ago. What does that have to do with anything?"

"We ask the questions, Mrs. Hamilton," Tyrone said. "You answer them. That's how this works."

"I don't understand what our temporary separation has to do with Troy's murder, but I left because we weren't getting along, and I didn't think it was good for my children to see us constantly fighting. We needed a breather."

"And you were pregnant when you left Knoxville?"

Judging by the stunned expression on her face, she hadn't expected that question. "I… No, I wasn't pregnant."

"Your children told our lieutenant that they remember you being pregnant when you moved back to Virginia," Jeannie said.

"They're wrong. They were four and five years old."

"They have distinct memories of you being pregnant with their younger brother Josh, but you told my captain and chief the other night that Josh was adopted. Can you explain that discrepancy?"

"I… Do I need a lawyer?"

"I don't know, Mrs. Hamilton, do you?"

She thought about that for a long moment, long enough that Jeannie began to believe she would lawyer up, effectively ending the conversation until her lawyer arrived. "I… I was pregnant," she said softly. "I miscarried at six months."

"And this was after you left Knoxville?"

She nodded. "The loss was devastating. Until yesterday, I'd never experienced anything so painful or heartbreaking. Thank goodness my mother was there to care for Mark and Maura because I couldn't do it. For a long time, I couldn't do a thing for them."

Jeannie waited to see if she would say more, and her patience was rewarded.

"Troy knew how upset I was to have lost the baby, so when the admin in his office got pregnant out of wedlock he offered to adopt the child."

"The administrative assistant in your husband's Knoxville office was Danielle Koch, is that correct?"

"Yes, Koch. That was her last name. I'd forgotten it."

"Mrs. Koch told our officers this week that she's never been pregnant. She and her husband were unable to conceive."

Courtney's mouth opened, and her lips twitched. "That… That's not possible. Josh, he was hers. He was Danielle's."

"He was not Danielle's child. She's never given birth."

"That's what she wants people to believe! She was ashamed. You aren't going to take her word over mine, are you?"

"Um, yes, Mrs. Hamilton, we are. She would have no reason to lie to us about whether she'd ever given birth to a child."

"What reason do I have to lie to you?"

"I'm not sure, but I do know who actually gave birth to the child you raised as Josh."

"Who?"

"Chauncey and Micki Rollings."

"Who are they?"

Jeannie placed copies of several newspaper articles about Taylor's abduction on the table in front of Mrs. Hamilton and let them speak for her.

Courtney scanned the headlines before looking up at her, affecting a perplexed expression. "I'm afraid I don't understand. Troy and Dustin worked that case when they were in Knoxville, but I never met those people."

"You raised their son."

She recoiled in horror.

Jeannie couldn't tell if it was real or faked.

"You… That… That's not true! They looked for that baby everywhere for weeks. Troy and everyone in his office put in more than a hundred hours *straight* working that case. They didn't sleep or shower or eat. All they did was look for that baby!"

"Who was never found until this week when an age-progression photo was released to mark the thirtieth anniversary of the abduction." Jeannie put that photo down in front of Courtney, who blanched at the sight of her son looking up at her. "Your son saw the photo and put two and two together to get the possibility that he might be Taylor Rollings."

"What're you saying?" she asked softly, her lashes glistening with unshed tears.

"I'm saying that the child who was taken from the Rollings family was raised as Josh Hamilton. We'd like to know how he came to be in your custody."

Jeannie watched as the other woman searched the ar-

chives of her life, as if looking for an explanation that
Jeannie would believe.

"He… I… I'd like to call my lawyer now, please."

CHAPTER TWENTY-NINE

SAM WAS GETTING ready to leave the hospital to head home when her phone rang. Eager for news about the case, she took the call.

"Lieutenant Holland, I'm calling on behalf of U.S. Attorney Tom Forrester. He would like to see you in his office today at noon. Are you available?"

Sam swallowed hard. "Yes, I can do that. Do I need a lawyer?"

"That might be a good idea. We'll see you then."

The chipper-sounding woman was gone before Sam could reply. Fuck. She found their lawyer friend Andy Simone's phone number in her list of contacts and made the call. When your husband is the vice president, receptionists tended to give your call higher priority, which is how she ended up speaking to Andy a minute later.

"Sam, this is a nice surprise."

As he was a close friend of Nick's, they socialized with Andy and his wife, but Sam didn't have a regular reason to call him on her own. Not like Harry, who she had on speed dial. "I need a lawyer, Andy."

"What's going on?"

"The U.S. Attorney would like to see me today at noon to discuss the possible assault charges he's going to file against me."

"Ah crap, so he's actually going through with that?"

"Apparently. Are you available?"

"This isn't my specialty, but I'll get someone from my firm and meet you there. Let's say eleven forty-five in the lobby so we can talk for a minute before the meeting."

"Thank you so much. I appreciate this."

"It's no problem. And try not to worry—he'd be crazy to file charges when you and your husband are the most popular couple in America. He'd get run out of office."

"I hope you're right about that."

"We'll do everything we can. I'll see you soon."

"Thanks, Andy." She checked the time on her phone and saw that she had an hour before she had to meet him, so she went to the hospital cafeteria and choked down some tasteless scrambled eggs and toast. The food made her feel slightly less awful, but the curious stares from the other people in the cafeteria had her taking the weak tea she'd bought out to her car where she sat to kill time before the meeting.

She thought about calling Nick or her dad or her sisters or Malone or someone who could talk her down off the ledge, but she didn't call anyone. Rather, she watched the minutes go by on the dashboard clock, trying to remain calm ahead of the meeting.

Her phone rang and she took the call from Detective Watson in Tennessee. "Holland."

"It's Watson. I've just come from the Rollings home."

"How'd it go?"

"There were a lot of tears. It was… It was the coolest thing I've ever been part of in all my years on the job. To be able to give them this amazing news… Well, you know, we don't deliver good news very often."

"No, we don't."

"As you can imagine, they're very interested in seeing

him. Mrs. Rollings's elderly mother lives with them, so they need a day or two to make arrangements."

"That'll give him some time to recover from his injuries before they see him. He's rather banged up."

"I hope you don't mind that I told them you're involved in the investigation, and naturally they said they'd like to meet you too and thank you for your help in finding their son."

"I didn't do much of anything. He was the one who made it happen."

"Still, I think it'd mean a lot to them to meet you."

"I'll make that happen. Keep me posted on when you're coming, and I'll let Josh—or I guess it's Taylor—know."

"How is he coping with everything?"

"As well as can be expected under the circumstances. It's a lot to take in."

"He's going to adore Chauncey and Micki. There's nothing not to love about them. They're great people."

"That'll make it easier for him, I'm sure."

"I've taken enough of your time. I'll call you when I have flight information."

"I'll look forward to hearing from you. I'm really glad you called. This feels like a win for all of us, which is not something I say very often in my line of work."

"Trust me, I get it. Talk soon."

Sam closed her phone and thought about the parents in Tennessee getting news they'd waited thirty long years to hear. She couldn't imagine how they must be feeling after learning their son was alive and mostly well after so many years of wondering what'd become of him. The not knowing had to be the purest form of hell on earth for a parent. She hoped she never found out what that was like. The very thought of it made her shudder and reach for her phone to text her son.

Just saying hi and I love you.

You're not supposed to text me in school, but I love you too.

Sam smiled at the predictable reply that provided an unreasonable amount of comfort in light of her troubling thoughts. He was such a good boy, and they were so blessed to have him in their lives, even when he chastised them.

At eleven-twenty she left the hospital and drove to the federal building on Fourth Street Northwest. She'd been there often on official business but never on business that involved the possibility of her being brought up on charges. By the time she parked, ran a comb through her hair and applied lipstick to bring some color to her hideously pale face, she had minutes to spare before she was due to meet Andy and his associate.

She ran up the stairs to the imposing building and nearly ran smack into Detective Ramsey as he emerged from the main doors.

He wore a thick plaster cast on his arm and a nasty scowl on his face. "Fancy meeting you here, Lieutenant."

"Hey, Ramsey, how you doing? Good to see you up and about."

"Fuck you."

"You have a nice day now."

"You're going *down*, Holland."

She waggled her brows at him, talking over her shoulder as she moved past him. "Already did last night. My husband *loved* it."

"Whore."

Sam laughed and kept moving. He wasn't worth her time, but the encounter hadn't done much for her already-rattled nerves. Andy waited for her in the busy lobby with another man in a suit. Both were consulting their phones when she approached them.

"Hey," she said. "Thanks for coming."

"Hi, Sam." Andy leaned in to kiss her cheek. "This is my colleague, Kurt Hager. He works on the criminal side of the house and is better versed in these sorts of things than I am."

"Pleasure to meet you," Kurt said as he shook her hand. "And an honor to be of assistance."

"We'll see if you're still saying that in an hour," Sam said in a dry tone that made them laugh. "Listen, here's the deal, I laid the guy out. He said something extremely shitty to me, and I let him have it. The blow knocked him down the stairs, and he suffered a concussion and broken wrist. I just ran into him outside, and he's still pissed. If he's been here, clearly he's putting the pressure on the USA to charge me."

"What did he say?" Kurt asked.

Sam sighed, hating to relive anything having to do with the hideous incident with Stahl that had led to her current predicament. "He asked me if I'd had a nice vacation after I came back from the thing with Stahl. I told him to fuck off and he said he was sorry that Stahl hadn't taken the starch out of me, or something equally offensive. I didn't think. I just acted. I punched him and I walked away. Next thing I knew I heard he was in the hospital."

"Well," Kurt said, "it's definitely an assault but with extenuating circumstances. Let's see what the USA has to say."

They took the elevator to Forrester's office, where Sam was given VIP treatment, right down to the offer of a beverage.

"I'd love some water, please," she said since they were offering.

Andy and Kurt settled on coffee, which they enjoyed while they waited for Forrester to join them. He came in a short time later, moving swiftly into the room. Tall with silver hair and shrewd blue eyes, he projected an air of confidence that Sam appreciated when they were on the same side of a case. Today his confidence only added to her nerves.

"Lieutenant," he said, shaking her hand when she stood to greet him.

"Good to see you, Tom."

"Likewise," he said, his New York accent coming through loud and clear in the single word.

"This is Andy Simone and Kurt Hager, my attorneys."

He shook hands with both of them. "Pleasure." Forrester took the fourth seat in the grouping of chairs and poured himself a cup of coffee. "Heck of a bind you've put me in, Sam."

"I realize that."

"Your colleague is pissed, and rightfully so."

"I understand."

"I assume you're aware of the circumstances under which Detective Ramsey was assaulted," Kurt said.

"I am," Forrester replied, "and his choice of words was indeed unfortunate."

"Unfortunate," Sam said with an ironic laugh. "That's one way of putting it."

Forrester put down the coffee and leaned toward her, elbows on knees, colleague to colleague, or so he wanted her to think. "Look, I'm in a really tough spot on this one, Sam. I'll be honest with you. The only reason my office hasn't already filed charges is because of who your husband is and because the president himself has asked me not to."

"Don't let that stop you," Sam said, earning scowls from Andy and Kurt. "Seriously, if you feel you have a case, charge me. If you don't, then don't. But don't base your decision-making on who I'm married to. Neither of us would appreciate that kind of special treatment."

"I get where you're coming from, and I respect that you're not asking for special treatment when most people in your position would." He paused and looked directly at her. "I'm not entirely sure I can successfully prosecute these charges, Lieutenant, so I'll be taking the case to the grand jury. I'll let the people decide."

"Oh, well..." As Andy and Kurt exchanged smiles, she realized Forrester had found a way out of pressing charges, and Andy and Kurt had figured that out before she did. He was counting on her popularity—and Nick's—to get them both out of the bind they were in.

"It'll take a couple of months, but as soon as I know whether there'll be an indictment, I'll let you know."

Sam exhaled a deep breath she'd been holding since she got the call from his office earlier. "Thank you."

"I want to be clear about something. I'll do this once. And only once. The next time something that should result in clear-cut charges comes across my desk, I'll handle it the way I would for anyone else."

"Understood."

"Great." Forrester stood, indicating the meeting was over. "Thanks for coming in." He shook hands with each of them and sent them on their way.

They didn't speak until they were in the elevator.

"He's smooth," Kurt said. "He found a way to get you off the hook and save face for his office at the same time."

"I won't be off the hook until the grand jury rules," Sam said.

"The likelihood of them bringing charges against a popular vice president's equally popular wife are slim to none," Andy said. "And Forrester knows that."

"You should be prepared for a firestorm in the media," Kurt said. "When it gets out that Forrester is taking the case to the grand jury rather than moving forward with charges, your boy Ramsey isn't going to take that well."

"I can handle it," Sam said.

"It's apt to get really ugly," Andy said. "For you and for Nick."

Sam hated to be the source of trouble for him, but she knew what he would say if he were there. "Nick agrees that Ramsey had it coming after what he said to me, and I have to believe that most rational people would've done what I did in the same situation."

"I guess you'll find out," Andy said, holding up his phone so she could see the headline on his screen.

U.S. Attorney Meets with Vice President's Wife Ahead of Assault Charges. The story was already on the *Star*'s website. She zoomed in for a closer look and saw that one of Darren's colleagues had written it.

"*How* do they already have that?" Kurt asked.

"Ramsey," Sam said. "He saw me coming in here, knew why I was here and went straight to the media with it." Sam's phone rang, and when she saw Freddie's name on the Caller ID, she said, "I've got to take this. Thanks again for coming."

"Anytime, Sam," Andy said.

"Keep us posted," Kurt said as he walked away with Andy.

"What's the latest?" Sam asked.

"Jeannie and Tyrone went hard at Mrs. Hamilton," Freddie reported. "They and everyone who watched aren't sure if she knew that Josh was Taylor Rollings. When they asked how Josh came to be in her custody she clammed up and asked for a lawyer. The guy she wants is in New York and can't get here until tomorrow, so she'll be spending the night."

"And Jacoby?"

"Lawyered up. His guy is in court today, so he's a guest of the city for the evening too."

"Excellent, which means they're all mine when I get back tomorrow."

He snorted with laughter. "We predicted that's what you'd say. Since most of us have been working since Sunday, they sent us home until zero seven hundred when we'll pick it back up."

Her phone rang with another call, this one from Nick. "Get some sleep, and I'll see you then," she said to Freddie. "Thanks for the update." She hoped she was hitting the right button to take the other call. "Hi, there."

"Something you want to tell me, babe?"

"It's good news actually."

"Not according to the *Star*."

"You gonna believe them or me? I was the one in the meeting with Forrester."

"What'd he say?"

"He's taking it to a grand jury."

"So that means…"

"He's hoping there won't be an indictment because of who I am and because of who you are."

Nick's low whistle echoed through the phone. "Crafty."

"We thought so too."

"We?"

"Andy and his friend Kurt, a criminal defense attorney, who came to the meeting with me."

"How come I didn't know there was going to be a meeting?"

"I only found out myself an hour ago, and I didn't want you to worry until there was something to worry about. Turns out, there probably isn't."

"Still, you should've told me only so I could reassure you and tell you everything would be okay. That's my job, so you've got to let me do my job."

Sam smiled as she walked out to her car. "It's very sweet of you to want to reassure me. Thank you for that."

"How're you feeling?"

"Shitty, so I'm heading home. I'll see you there?"

"As soon as I can possibly get out of here. Get some rest and dream of Bora Bora."

"Mmm, I can't wait."

"Won't be long now. Love you, babe."

"Love you too. Wake me up when you get home."

Sam hadn't expected to drive home from her meeting with Forrester with a smile on her face, but Nick's call had cheered her up considerably. The best news of all? Tomorrow she could go back to work and hopefully close this baffling case once and for all.

CHAPTER THIRTY

GONZO STOPPED FOR flowers on the way home. He asked the florist for something exceptional, and she'd come through with a huge bouquet that was so fragrant, he'd had to open the car windows so he could breathe. By the time he reached the landing outside their apartment, the grand gesture felt silly rather than romantic. As if a bunch of smelly flowers would make up for the shit he'd put her through.

He was on the verge of taking them downstairs to trash them on the street when the door flew open.

"I thought I heard you out here."

Keeping the flowers behind his back, he said, "How'd you know it was me?"

"I've listened for you for more than a year now. I recognize what you sound like coming up the stairs."

"And I'm supposedly the detective."

"I've got mad skills," she said with the flirty smile that reminded him of life before disaster struck. "What're you hiding?"

"Oh. Right." He unveiled the flowers and held them out to her, feeling like an idiot until he saw her face light up with pleasure.

"Tommy… They're beautiful! Thank you."

He followed her to the kitchen where she found a vase and arranged the flowers to her liking.

When she was finished, she turned to find him watching her. "What?"

"Nothing. Just enjoying the view. It's nice to see you smiling."

"You make me happy when you bring me flowers for no reason."

"They're not for no reason. They're for a million reasons." He went to her, put his hands on her shoulders and gazed down at her gorgeous face. "They're because you stayed when it would've been easier not to. They're because you love my son like he's your own. They're because you love me even when I don't deserve it."

She started to shake her head, but he stopped her with his fingers on her chin.

"Yes, Christina, sometimes I don't deserve your love, but I'm always so damned thankful to have it."

Curling her arms around his neck, she went up on tiptoes and kissed him. "Remember the night we met?"

"Of course I do. What about it?"

"I was such a mess that night. John O'Connor had been killed and my heart was broken into a million pieces. I'd been so crazy about a man who'd never thought of me the way I thought of him."

"He was the crazy one. Look at what he missed."

She gazed up at him, a smile curling her lips. "One hour after I met you, I knew everything would be all right. That's all it took, Tommy. One hour to fix everything that was broken inside me."

"You give me way too much credit," he said, humbled by her unwavering love for him.

"And you don't give yourself enough. When you look back at the last year, all you see is the hard stuff. You don't see the wonder, the joy, the magic. You don't see everything you've given me. I have a son because of you. I have a life that I never could've dreamed of when I was working sixteen hours a day and thinking I had a great life when it was empty and meaningless."

Gonzo ran his fingers through her hair and kept his gaze fixed on hers as he kissed her. "The night I met you was the luckiest night of my life."

"I'm glad you think so."

"How long has Alex been asleep?"

"About thirty minutes."

"Mmm," he said, nuzzling her neck, "that gives us about ninety minutes before he wakes up."

"We could watch a movie."

"We could. Or… We could finish what we started yesterday."

"You'll have to refresh my memory—"

He picked her up, making her squeal with surprise. "Shhh, don't wake him up. We've got stuff to do." Gonzo carried her into their bedroom and shut the door. He put her down next to the bed and tugged her sweater up and over her head, leaving her in a sexy, lacy pink bra that did wondrous things for her breasts. Bending his head, he nuzzled the plump tops, earning a moan from her. He reached behind her to unhook the bra and pushed the straps off her shoulders.

She unbuttoned his shirt and flattened her hands on his chest before sliding them down to unbutton his jeans.

Her touch resulted in a predictable and welcome reaction, and he made a conscious effort to stay focused on the here and now, to give her a fraction of what she'd given him by not letting his demons derail him again. She unzipped him carefully, working around the bulge that got bigger by the second.

And when she dropped to her knees to work his pants and boxers down over his hips, the weeks without her, without this, nearly resulted in a premature finish. Thankfully, he was able to control himself long enough to experience the sublime pleasure of her tongue on his cock, the heat of her mouth and the tight grip of her hand. She effectively cleared his mind of every thought that wasn't about her and the way she made him feel when she touched him this way.

"God, *Chris*..." His head fell back and his knees buckled. "Baby, wait. Let's do this together." He reached for her, helped her up and brought his lips down on hers. He'd missed this so much. He'd missed *her*. He'd had no idea how much until right now. They came down on the bed in a tangle of limbs, desire pounding through him like an extra heartbeat.

"Tommy, I want you. Now." She helped him get rid of her yoga pants, and he yanked on the tiny panties that barely covered her. The fragile fabric ripped in his hand, baring her to him.

She took him in hand and guided him to where she wanted him most, to where he wanted to be more than he'd wanted anything in weeks. The sweet relief flooded his system, the powerful punch of emotion nearly reducing him to tears. He'd come so close to losing her too.

Gonzo gathered her in close to him, holding her tight while he throbbed inside her.

She ran her feet up the back of his thighs and wrapped her legs around his hips.

"Love you, baby. I love you."

"I love you too, Tommy. More than anything."

"It's going to be better. I promise."

She buried her fingers in his hair and kissed him again,

her mouth opening to the deep thrusts of his tongue. They moved together in a familiar rhythm, seeking reunion as much as release. He broke the kiss to take her nipple into his mouth, sucking and biting down just hard enough to get her attention. Her internal muscles contracted tightly around his cock and she cried out when she came, fisting his hair and digging her nails into his ass, which triggered his release.

Afterward, he came down on top of her, aware as always of how much bigger than her he was, but unable to move. Not yet. Not when it felt so damned good to be with her this way. He wasn't ready to let go of the small taste of heaven, to return to the nightmare in progress.

In the gray afternoon light, lying in the arms of the woman he loved, his son asleep across the hall, Gonzo found a small measure of acceptance. His partner was gone. No amount of wishing or hoping or begging would ever change that simple fact, and nothing he could do would ever bring him back. For whatever reason he'd been spared, and it would be up to him to live for both of them.

He would never forget the young, earnest, smart, eager, often-annoying, but incredibly sweet man who'd taken a shot that technically should've killed Gonzo. Intellectually, he knew it wasn't his fault. He hadn't pulled the trigger to fire the bullet that killed his partner. But emotionally… He would always blame himself for putting Arnold in the position that had led to his death, and somehow he had to find a way to live with that.

"What're you thinking about, Tommy?"

"I'm thinking about acceptance and finding a way to go on that honors my partner rather than disappoints him."

"You could never disappoint him. He worshipped you."

"It would disappoint him if I let his death ruin my life, if I quit a job I used to love because he was killed, if I became a drunk or worse. Any of that would disappoint him."

"You could never be or do any of those things."

"I don't know… I was well on my way to all of them before the coffee table shattered and woke me up to what really matters."

"And what's that?"

He turned them over so she was on top of him and ran his hand down her back. "You, Alex, our family, my squad. The people I love, the people who love me. That's what matters."

She lifted her head off his chest to look him in the eye. "You matter, Tommy. You matter so much to all of us." Leaning forward, she kissed him softly. "It's nice to have you back."

"We'd been talking about getting married before everything happened."

"We'll get there. When the time is right, it'll happen." Hands propped on his chest, she sat up and began to move her hips, which was all it took to restart his motor. "The first time only took fifteen of our ninety minutes. How about we see how much we can get done in our remaining seventy-five minutes?"

The sexy gleam in her eye made him smile even as he realized how close he'd come to losing her. "I'm down for that."

SAM WOKE TO a dark bedroom and soft lips on her back.

"Shhh," Nick whispered. "I told Scotty I was coming up to wake you for dinner." He cupped her ass and squeezed. "Are you recovered enough for a quickie?"

"Mmm, yes please." Languid and relaxed after a great nap, she floated on a cloud of contentment as he shed his clothes and resumed the sensual massage, his hands and lips coasting over her back and bottom.

"Your skin is like silk, Samantha."

She squirmed, trying to get closer to him, to find some release from the throbbing pressure between her legs. "You said we had to be quick."

"We do."

"Come on then."

His soft chuckle irritated and amused at the same time. He loved to torture her, to make her beg, to make her come like she never had before him. His fingers dug into her hips as he lifted her to her knees and moved her legs apart. "I can't wait until next week when I can worship this sweet ass for an hour before I do this." He slammed into her, stealing the breath from her lungs and wrenching a sharp cry of pleasure from her lips.

"Shhh."

"Don't do that and then tell me I have to be quiet."

His hand came down on her ass, drawing another moan from her. Then he picked up the pace and reached around to caress her clit. The combination had her on the verge of release within seconds. Normally, when they had time to spare, he'd back off and make her wait, but tonight he didn't make her wait, driving her to an explosive release that had her biting the pillow to keep from screaming.

"Yes," he whispered. "Just like that. Ah, God, Samantha..." He came as hard as she had, his fingers digging into her flesh as he heated her from the inside. "I can't wait to have ten full days in bed with you."

"Is that all we're going to do?"

"That's it. Every minute of every day for ten beautiful days."

"I can't think of anything I'd rather do." She squeezed the hand he'd placed over her fast-beating heart.

"And that, my love, is why you're the best wife I've ever had."

Sam snorted with laughter. "I'm the only wife you're ever going to have."

"In that case, thank God I got it so very, very right the first time around." He took a nibble of her shoulder and soothed the sting with his tongue. "Now get your lazy ass out of bed so we can have dinner with our son."

RECHARGED AND READY for battle, Sam arrived at her office at six-thirty the next morning to go over the reports that had been filed in her absence. Technically, her suspension didn't end until zero seven hundred, but no one was around to snag her on the thirty-minute technicality.

Before she dug into work, she took a moment to fire off an email to the president of the Fraternal Order of Police union about the bills her father had been hit with after his surgery. He responded right away, pledging to look into what they could do, and Sam thanked him. She hoped they could do something to help with the bills.

With that taken care of, she focused on the autopsy report for Troy Hamilton, which confirmed the blow that caved in his skull had ended his life. Approximately twenty other hits had been redundant and were indicative of the murderer's rage. Fingerprints found on the golf club belonged to Hamilton, the man who served as his caddy and Jacoby, who often played with Hamilton. Avery had noted in the file that Jacoby's prints on the club didn't mean he was the murderer. Records at their exclusive club put Jacoby on the golf course with Hamilton at least fifteen times in the last year alone.

He could've held the club for Hamilton while he tied his shoes, for example, Hill had written in the notes.

"Still in denial, are you, Avery?" she muttered.

"Not so much anymore," Hill said from the doorway, startling her.

"Good morning to you too."

"Nice to see you back where you belong."

"Nice to be here."

"Hell of a scrum outside."

Sam shrugged off the comment. "That's what you get when the USA considers charges against the VP's wife."

"What's up with that anyway?"

She told him about the grand jury decision and watched his eyes widen with realization of what the USA hoped to achieve.

Nodding, Avery said, "The grand jury gets him off the hook, and he's hoping they won't indict."

"Something like that. I wish he'd said I'm not going to file charges and that would be the end of it, but I realize he has to pacify Ramsey and everyone else around here who thinks I get special treatment."

"It's a wise move on his part." He took a closer look at her, and Sam had to fight the urge to squirm.

"What?"

"You look better. You feel okay?"

"Still tired and a bit achy, but much better than I was." Embarrassment heated her face. "Thanks again for the assist. You went way above and beyond."

"It was no problem."

Sam stood, eager to get away from him and his golden-eyed gaze and the ever-present weird vibe he put out. "I need to update my murder board and get ready for the morning briefing."

"I'll give you a hand."

"Great," she said with far more enthusiasm than she felt. "What's the word coming from the Bureau?"

"Stunned disbelief. Troy is dead, Dustin's a suspect, Courtney's in custody. Everyone is trying to get their head around the fact that our revered director raised a kidnapped child as his own, and we're holding our breath waiting for that to become public. Do you know when that's going to happen?"

"I expect to see Detective Watson and Mr. and Mrs. Rollings sometime today when they arrive to see Taylor. We'll work with Watson on a joint statement once we've had a chance to speak with Jacoby and Mrs. Hamilton."

"He's hired Tim Russo to represent him," Avery said.

"I like that guy. I remember when he refused to represent Elle Jestings in the Vasquez case because she owed his firm fifty grand. She was so mad." The memory made Sam smile months later. She loved when arrogant murdering assholes got their comeuppance.

"At least he's a straight shooter, unlike our old friend Bill Springer."

"That's true." The name *Springer* alone was enough to give Sam nightmares, so she shook off the reference and focused on the updates to the murder board Malone had kept in her absence. He'd done a good job, but he was no Sam Holland. She filled in the new information that'd come in overnight and tried to ignore Avery to the best of her ability.

"Lieutenant."

Sam turned to face Detective Carlucci.

"Nice to have you back."

"Nice to be back."

"Gigi and I finished going through the phone records, and we found something interesting." Dani laid some papers on the table and pointed to the highlighted outgoing call recorded on Jacoby's personal cell phone on Sunday at 2:20 p.m. "That's the landline number for Courtney Hamilton's mother's house."

"And the call came in roughly one hour before Troy Hamilton was murdered." Sam's body buzzed from the burst of adrenaline that came from pulling threads that led to connections. "Excellent work." She added the information to the murder board under the photo of Courtney Hamilton and drew a red line with an arrow on it to Jacoby.

Malone came into the room, looking sharp-eyed and well rested. "Courtney Hamilton's attorney is here, and she's ready to talk."

"Excellent," Sam said. "I love to talk."

Malone rolled his eyes. "Welcome back, Lieutenant. I'd say we missed you but you didn't give us the chance to miss you."

"Aww, Captain." She dabbed at her eyes dramatically. "You're so sweet."

"Let's get the AUSA here," Malone said, "and then see what's on Mrs. Hamilton's mind."

CHAPTER THIRTY-ONE

WITH CHIEF FARNSWORTH, Avery Hill and AUSA Hope Dobson observing from the next room, Sam and Malone stepped into the interrogation room where Courtney Hamilton sat at the table with an older man with gray hair. He was the picture of a distinguished esquire, right down to the aura of self-importance he projected—and that was before he opened his mouth and confirmed he was a pompous ass.

"Mrs. Hamilton has agreed to speak willingly, and we fully expect that her cooperation will be taken into consideration."

"That, of course, depends on what she wants to talk about," Sam said with a big, friendly smile that resulted in a nasty scowl from his royal highness. "And I didn't catch your name."

"It's John Tillinghast Esquire." He put a business card in front of her and another in front of Malone. They ignored the cards.

"Any relation to Brad Tillinghast? Lobbyist who got into a little scrape with the law last year."

"He's my nephew," John said tightly, as if he'd tasted something rancid. "And as you well know, he was never charged with anything."

"Cavorting with prostitutes and 'appetites' his wife found offensive," Sam said with a cluck of disapproval that made John's face turn bright red. "That was some nasty business. Is he still married?"

"How is that relevant to the business before us?"

"Oh," Sam said, full of innocence, "I thought we were still in the get-to-know you stage of the interview. My apologies. Please proceed."

"I see your reputation is well earned," he said in a low growl.

"That's so nice of you to say."

Malone coughed to cover a laugh, and Sam decided this was going to be a very good day.

"My client would like to cooperate in your investigation."

Sam leaned in, elbows on the table, rapt attention. "In what way?"

"She has information about Dustin Jacoby that she believes will be relevant and helpful."

"We're listening."

"First, we'd like to know what accommodations will be made to protect her."

"From what?" Sam asked, genuinely baffled.

"Prosecution, for one thing."

"Has she committed any crimes?"

"Her actions would probably put her firmly in the area of accessory."

"To murder? To kidnapping? Or the always-popular option C, all of the above?"

"Both," he said, scowling again. "But without her, you'll never get Jacoby on either of those things."

"Like I said, we're listening."

"Like *I* said, what're you offering?"

"Depends on what she has to say."

"I don't operate that way. I want guarantees."

"You said my reputation precedes me, but apparently you haven't heard that I don't give guarantees. Now, either your client has something useful to tell us for which we may or may not recommend leniency when it comes to charges, or you're wasting our time. And if you're wasting our time, that's not going to help anything because we've got a lot to do today."

The lawyer seemed frozen with indecision.

Sam stood, prepared to walk away if he couldn't move his fat ass and get this show on the road.

"Wait," Courtney said. The single word sounded torn from her soul. "I'll tell you what you want to know. I'll tell you everything."

"Courtney—"

"Shut up, John. I'm all done keeping secrets. It's gone on long enough."

Here we go, Sam thought as she returned to her seat. It was all she could do not to rub her hands together with glee. She pressed the record button on the device on the table. "This interview is being recorded as part of the Hamilton investigation." She listed the time and date and who was present in the room. "Mrs. Hamilton?"

"Troy met Dustin in law school at Northwestern in Chicago," she began in a soft tone, her gaze fixed on the observation window behind Sam. "They were closer than brothers. The night I met Troy, I also met Dustin. We were at a summer home on Long Island that belonged to the parents of one of their law school friends. I'd been invited by friends of mine from home who were renting a house in the Hamptons for the summer. Troy and I hit it off immediately that night. We had a lot in common. We both came from high-profile families and were often burdened by the weight of their expectations. Dustin, he was a different story. He'd been raised by a single mother in the projects in Chicago and had gone to Northwestern, undergrad and law, on scholarships." She took a sip from her glass of water. "I'm not sure how long Troy and I dated before I realized if I got one, I also got the other."

"How do you mean?"

"I rarely had dinner alone with him, for example. Dustin was always there."

"Did they live together?"

She nodded. "But it was more than that."

"Were they lovers?"

She hesitated before she nodded again. "But I didn't know *that* until after Troy and I were married."

"I'm afraid I don't understand," Sam said, legitimately baffled.

"I didn't either," Courtney said.

John handed her his monogrammed handkerchief, and Courtney accepted it with a grateful grimace that might've been a smile under other circumstances. She dabbed at her eyes. "I caught them. In our bed."

Sam tried to imagine... No. Just no. "How long had you been married?"

"About two months."

"Troy was mortified, but Dustin... He said it was better to get the truth out in the open now rather than drag it out indefinitely."

"And what was the truth?"

She swallowed and gripped the handkerchief in her closed fist. "They were in love and they wanted to spend their lives together."

"So why did he marry you?"

"Because they couldn't spend their lives together and have the careers they wanted too. Not back then. No,

they decided because Troy was the better connected of
the two that he needed a wife and a family. The deal was
that Troy would bring Dustin along with him."

"You were duped."

"Yes, but the kicker was, Troy said he loved me too,
that everything he'd ever said to me was true."

"He loved you both."

"Yes, but that wasn't all."

Sam was literally on the edge of her seat waiting to
hear the rest.

"They…they wanted our relationship to include all
of us."

"You wanna run that by me one more time?"

"Our marriage was, for many years, a ménage."

Sam had heard a lot of crazy shit on this job, but this
was by far the craziest thing she'd ever heard. The FBI
director—and his deputy—had been part of a ménage
à trois marriage? Judging by John's expression, this
was shocking news to him, as well. "Did that mean you
were…intimate…with both of them?"

"Yes," she said, her face flushing with what might've
been embarrassment or maybe it was shame. Sam
couldn't tell. "And they were with each other too."

"Your children?"

"Were Troy's. They look just like him. There was
never any doubt about who their father was."

"But it was possible it could've been either of them?"

"Yes," she said softly.

"How did you get away with this among your family
and friends?" Sam asked, fascinated more than anything.

"Most of the time we were together, we lived away
from our closest friends and family."

"What happened in Knoxville?"

Courtney continued to knead the poor handkerchief, making a mess of the fine linen. "Dustin and I… We became exceptionally close during those years. Troy was on the rise and was often called to Washington, sometimes for as long as a month at a time. Dustin… He was there for me, you know?"

Sam didn't get it. She didn't get how any woman handled two men, when she more than had her hands full with one.

"We… Troy, he came home early from a trip, and he… He caught us together."

"That wasn't allowed?"

She shook her head. "The agreement we had was that I was only supposed to be with Dustin when Troy was there too. He was so angry and so hurt. He felt like we'd betrayed him. He ended it with both of us and sent me and the children home to Virginia."

"Did he know you were pregnant?"

She shook her head. "Not at first. But a month or so after we left, he came to see the kids, and I couldn't hide it anymore."

"And the baby was Dustin's?"

Courtney dabbed at her eyes with the handkerchief. "Things between Troy and I had been tense for a while. I had only been with Dustin. The baby was his."

"Did Dustin know?"

"Yes," she said with a small smile. "He was so excited to have a child of his own."

"What happened?"

"I… I miscarried at six months, which was utterly devastating."

Sam ached at the thought of going so far in a pregnancy only to end up empty-handed at the end. Except that's not what happened to Courtney.

"Dustin was beside himself. He came unglued. I'd never seen him like that."

"Like what?"

"Out of his mind with grief and rage at the hand he'd been dealt. He was in love with me and with Troy, and because he was acting so unstable, Troy wanted him out of our lives, going so far as to try to have him fired from the Bureau. It was a nightmare." She dropped her head into her hands. "We were wrong to ever think an arrangement like what we had with him could work long-term, but we'd never had any reason to believe he was mentally unstable until he turned up at my mother's house with a baby he said he'd adopted to replace the one we'd lost."

"Holy…" Sam realized she'd said the word out loud.

"He told me the baby had been born to their receptionist in Knoxville, and when she couldn't afford to keep it, he'd offered to take the baby." She wiped her eyes and dabbed at her nose. "He said it would be like our baby had never died."

"Did you tell Troy?"

"I did, and he realized right away that the baby had been taken from a family in Tennessee."

"And he told you that?"

Nodding, she said, "We were horrified. We had no idea that Dustin was capable of such a thing, but losing the baby had done something to him. He'd snapped. He told us he'd ruin us if we ever said a word about where that baby came from. He would tell the world how we'd lived, and Troy's career would be ruined, our family would be homeless when Troy went to jail for kidnapping. Dustin had been clever. He'd set up the whole thing to look like Troy had done it. He said we were going to continue on like nothing had happened, or he'd ruin us both and our children would end up in foster homes."

"Let me get this straight," Sam said, her mind whirling. "He basically blackmailed a fellow FBI agent and his wife into raising a kidnapped child—a child you both knew had been kidnapped—as your own. Is that right?"

"Yes," she said, "and you have to believe me. Troy and I were horrified. He'd worked the Rollings case and had been heartbroken for them."

"So why didn't he return their child when he realized what Dustin had done?"

"Because he'd lose everything he'd worked so hard for if he did, and we'd both go to jail. We had three children to consider, and we chose to stay quiet even if it slowly killed us."

"Did you know Troy knocked your son around every chance he got?"

"That's not true! Who told you that?"

"Your son did."

"Troy loved him! Keeping this secret nearly killed us. Troy developed ulcers that plagued him for the rest of his life. I had migraines, and when that picture came out and it looked just like Josh, Troy said he was going to come clean and tell the truth. Dustin said we couldn't let that happen. That's why he killed Troy. To keep the secret long enough to get out of town. Except I couldn't leave my mother and my children…"

Sam slapped her hand on the table, making Courtney and John startle. "Screw you and your ulcers and your migraines! *You took their child.* Do you have any idea what you put those poor people through for *thirty years* while you were enjoying a life of prosperity and success?"

"Technically, my client didn't take their child."

Sam lacerated him with a look. "Screw you too. No deal." Speaking directly to Courtney, she said, "You'll be charged with accessory to kidnapping after the fact, and I hope you serve one day for every day that child spent in your family when he should've been with theirs."

"I was honest with you!" Courtney cried. "You'd never have gotten all this from Dustin. I gave you the *truth*!"

"Too bad it was thirty years too late for the Rollings family—and for Taylor." She walked out of the room and went straight to her office, slamming the door behind her. As she released the clip that held her hair up, she realized her hands were shaking. And the stomach she'd thought cured was looking to unload its meager contents.

Placing her hand over her mouth, she breathed through her nose until the nausea subsided, leaving her with a sick feeling that went bone deep. The men Avery had so revered were monsters, and Courtney was every bit as bad for keeping their secrets for so long.

Three decades. That's how long a mother in Tennessee had longed for the child who was being raised by the director of the FBI and his wife and his...whatever Dustin had been to them. It was sickening. When she'd regained her composure, she checked her phone and found a text from Watson letting her know they'd arrive at the hospital around two. The Rollings family was looking forward to meeting their son—and her.

I'll be there, Sam replied, and just for shits and grins, she'd see if she could bring her husband, the vice president. She fired off a text to him asking if it could be arranged.

I'll see what I can do, babe. Would love to be there.

A soft knock on the door had her spinning around. "What?"

The door opened and Avery Hill stood there, his face ashen with shock and disgust. "I don't even know what to say."

"There's nothing to be said other than case closed."

"What about Dustin?"

"What about him? We've got more than enough to charge him with two counts of kidnapping, murder for hire, assaulting a police officer. The list goes on and on."

"So we don't need to talk to him?"

"Sam's right," Hope said when she joined them, looking pale after what she'd heard. "We've got enough to charge them both." Of the three identical triplets who served the District as Assistant U.S. Attorneys, Hope was the only one who was a mother, which had probably made Courtney's sordid tale that much more difficult to hear.

"If no one objects," Avery said, "I'd like the supreme pleasure of telling Dustin Jacoby that he's totally fucked."

"I'm all for that," Sam said.

The others nodded in agreement.

"Someone will need to brief the media," the chief said. "I think they're giving birth to each other outside."

"I'll do it," Sam said, salivating at the thought of shredding the vaunted reputations of Hamilton and Jacoby, "and then I'm going to the hospital to be there when Taylor sees his parents for the first time in thirty years."

CHAPTER THIRTY-TWO

SAM WENT WITH Avery to speak to Jacoby, who was pacing the interrogation room when they walked in. He seemed startled to see Avery.

"What're you doing here?" Jacoby asked, his dark eyes narrowing with displeasure.

"I volunteered to be the one to tell you that you're being charged with murder, two counts of kidnapping and felony assault of a police officer, among other things. In other words, you're totally and completely fucked."

"Mr. Jacoby is willing to cooperate with your investigation in exchange for leniency," his lawyer said.

"Thanks," Avery said, "but we're good. Courtney Hamilton told us everything we needed to know to put the pieces together."

"And you're going to believe her over your own deputy director?" Jacoby said with a malicious smirk that Sam wanted to smack off his smug face.

"You bet your goddamned kidnapping, murdering ass I am."

"You obviously don't care too much about your career, Agent Hill."

Hill stepped around the table to face off with Jacoby directly. "Are you still under the illusion that you have any power over me, my career or anything having to do with the Federal Bureau of Investigation? You and Hamilton are a disgrace to everything we stand for as federal agents, and I plan to enjoy every second of your downfall, which will begin when Lieutenant Holland briefs the media in five minutes. She'll be sharing the security video we have from Hamilton's house that shows you wielding the golf club that ended his life."

Sam waved to Jacoby, who stared daggers at her, giving her no doubt that he was more than capable of everything he was being accused of.

"Mr. Jacoby should be given the right to tell his side of the story," the lawyer said.

"He'll have his day in court," Avery said. "After which I'll look forward to seeing you rot in prison for the rest of your life."

"Me too," Sam said. "Looking forward to that tremendously, but now I need to get out of here because the media is waiting and the baby you stole thirty years ago is about to be reunited with his real parents. We've got far more important things to do with our time than spend it with the likes of you. Are you coming, Agent Hill?"

"Yeah," he said, glaring at Jacoby, "I'm finished here."

Sam preceded him out of the room. "You okay?"

"I've been better."

"You were great in there. I enjoyed that very much."

The compliment earned her the hint of a smile from Avery.

She handed him a piece of paper.

"What's this?"

"A check for what I owe you for the Knoxville trip."

"Oh. Okay." He stashed it in his back pocket. "Thanks."

"Listen, Avery… So Nick told me you guys talked on the flight home, and I just wanted to say that I'm sorry if he made you feel uncomfortable or—"

"It was fine, Sam. He said some things I needed to hear and reminded me of how lucky I am to have a woman like Shelby who wants to marry me. It's all good."

"I'm glad to hear that," she said, sighing with relief. "It'll save me the bother of stabbing him in his sleep."

Laughing, Avery shook his head. "He sure is a lucky guy."

"I know. I tell him that every day. Now, what do you say we go make the day of all the reporters who're waiting for the dirty details of this case?"

"I say lead the way."

THE REUNION OF Taylor Rollings and his parents was everything Sam had hoped it would be for them and far more emotional for her than she'd expected. They'd been thrilled to meet her and Nick, who'd rearranged his schedule to be there for her as much as the Rollings family.

He stood now with his arm around her shoulders watching Chauncey and Micki Rollings talk to their son like he was an old friend rather than the son they'd given birth to and then lost two days later almost thirty years ago. Micki continued to dab at her eyes more than an hour after they arrived. She said she'd probably be crying tears of gratitude for the rest of her life now that her beloved son had been found.

For his part, Josh, who'd asked to be called Taylor going forward, took it all in, beaming with pleasure from the attention and unconditional love he felt from Chauncey and Micki as well as their other children, Sue, Will, Michael and Chauncey Junior. Taylor had been their third child, after Sue and Will and before Michael. He closely resembled his brothers, who'd been consulted by the artist who worked on the age-progression photo of Taylor.

"Here I always thought I was the baby of the family, and I'm a middle child," he said, soaking it all in.

Before the Rollings family had arrived, Sam and Avery had briefed Taylor on the outcome of the investigation and answered his many questions about the role his "parents" and Jacoby had played. He'd been stunned but resigned to move forward and not dwell on the past.

The bruises on his face weren't quite as angry as they'd been yesterday, and the swelling around his eye had abated somewhat. Micki didn't seem to care about his bruises. She couldn't stop touching his hand, his face, his hair, as if to confirm he was real. Every so often she would stop herself and offer a chagrined smile. "I'm sorry. I can't help myself."

"It's okay," Taylor said. "I understand."

Sam began to feel as if they were intruding. "We're going to go," she said to Watson, who wore a euphoric expression that Sam suspected was rare for him.

He shook her hand and then Nick's. "It was an honor to meet you both. Thank you for everything."

Micki and Chauncey hugged her. "We'll never have the words to properly thank you for what you've done," Micki said.

"All the credit goes to your son," Sam said. "He's the one who sounded the alarm, and he's the reason your prayers were answered."

Micki's eyes lit up with joy as she looked at him. "I'm so excited to get to know him. We have so much time to make up. I have thirty years of Christmas and birthday gifts for him." She wiped away tears. "I'm sorry. I'm a mess today."

"With very good reason." Nick made Micki sigh when he kissed her cheek. "Enjoy every moment with him and your family."

He held the door for Sam and followed her out to the hallway where his detail waited for them. Nick put his arm around her to draw her in close to him. "Thanks for asking me to come," he said in a soft tone that only she could hear. "I'll never forget that."

"Sometimes this job doesn't totally suck."

"Most of the time it does."

Sam laughed at his emphatic reply. "Yeah, but today it didn't suck. Today was a very good day."

SAM PRACTICED THE speech at least a hundred times. Maybe two hundred times. Nick had listened to it and coached her on delivery and pausing for impact and other tricks he'd learned on the campaign trail. Scotty listened and offered suggestions. Even Shelby, Skip and Celia had weighed in. Over the last couple of days, if Sam hadn't been dealing with the paperwork and the press in the wake of the Hamilton case, she'd been practicing her speech.

In the end, it was a good thing she'd done all that practicing because when the big moment came and she stood at the podium with two thousand sets of eyes watching her expectantly, her dyslexia kicked in, making the words on the teleprompter scramble in an unreadable pattern.

As she broke out in a cold sweat, she forced a smile and shook her head at the irony. "I'm here to talk about my infertility challenges and guess what? My dyslexia has decided today would be a great day to rear its ugly head." A soft wave of nervous laughter greeted the comment. She leaned forward on her elbows, determined not to embarrass herself or Nick, who was in the audience somewhere. She hadn't wanted to know where, so she wouldn't lose her concentration.

"Since I can't read the teleprompter, I guess I'll have to wing it. It's my story, and I know it by heart, but my wonderful White House staff wrote a beautiful speech that I'll make sure is released so you can see what I was supposed to say today." The audience laughed again, and she relaxed ever so slightly when she realized they were friendly and rooting for her to succeed, not hoping she'd fall flat on her face.

Sam tried to pretend she was talking to a group of old friends as she started at the beginning, with the unexpected pregnancy in college and took them through her infertility journey, culminating with the miscarriage she and Nick had suffered last year. As always when she got to that part, her chest tightened and tears threatened. But she battled through to the finish, to the most important part about how she and Nick wanted to make a difference for people struggling with infertility and other issues that mattered to them.

"Nick and I want you to know we understand the challenges those suffering from infertility grapple with on a daily basis. We want to help, and if hearing my story makes even one of you feel less alone with these challenges, I'll be satisfied. Thank you for your time and attention, and when you read the speech I was supposed to give, you'll see just how brilliant my staff really is. Thank you for having me."

Sam couldn't believe her eyes when every one of those two thousand people stood to clap. The roar of applause was nearly deafening and totally overwhelming. And when Nick walked onto the stage carrying a bouquet of red roses, the crowd truly went wild. Sam had never been so happy to see him.

Smiling, he kissed her cheek. "You were amazing, babe."

Though she had two thousand people applauding her, his praise trumped a standing ovation any day.

They stood together for another couple of minutes, smiling and waving to the crowd, before he guided her off the stage, with his hand on her back.

"Fancy meeting you here," she said when they were offstage.

"I hope it was okay to join in your thunder."

"My thunder is your thunder."

"Is that a come-on?"

Sam laughed and went up on tiptoes to kiss him. "Thank God that's over."

"I almost died when you mentioned the dyslexia. Way to punt."

"You couldn't tell I was sweating?"

"Nope. You were calm, cool, collected, funny, touching, poignant and incredibly sexy. They loved you, and I do too."

"I'm really glad you were able to be here while I lost my public-speaking virginity."

"I won't always be able to come, but I wouldn't have missed this one. Not only because it was your first time, but because of the topic."

"Yeah, it's a tough one."

"I'm so damned proud of you, Samantha." He kissed her forehead and then put his arms around her. "You'll never know how many people you touched today by sharing a piece of yourself with the rest of the world."

"Feels good to be able to help people. Maybe your

job won't totally suck if we can do stuff like this once in a while."

"No, it totally sucks. Not as bad as yours, but it definitely sucks." They were still laughing when Sam's staff found them.

"You were *amazing*!" Lilia said, grinning widely.

"I'm already getting emails from other organizations who want you to speak to them," Andrea said, holding up her phone.

Grimacing, Sam looked up at Nick, who beamed with pride. *"Great..."*

"Welcome to the big time, babe."

SAM SPENT THE rest of the day finishing the reports on the Hamilton investigation and attending yet another press briefing about the case. People were riveted by the salacious details of the Hamiltons' "arrangement" with Dustin Jacoby and the sinister plot behind Taylor's kidnapping. For days now, it had been the lead story in every newspaper and on every TV newscast and entertainment show.

The news of Forrester's plans to take Sam's case to the grand jury had barely made a ripple thanks to the frenzy surrounding the Hamilton case. Sam had heard through the grapevine that Ramsey was furious with Forrester for being a "pussy" about charging her, and he'd been whining about her getting special treatment. It gave her a perverse thrill to hear he was pissed, but she was wise enough after what'd happened with Stahl to keep a close eye on Ramsey. She had a feeling her troubles with him were far from over.

She got home at five-thirty, an hour before her mother was due to arrive for the get-together Angela had ar-

ranged. Sam had spoken before two thousand people earlier in the day but was far more nervous about seeing her
mother than she'd been about the speech.

When the Secret Service agent working the door admitted her, Scotty ran over to hug her. "I watched the
playback on C-Span, and you were awesome. Were you
freaking out that you couldn't read the teleprompter?"

"You know it. I started to sweat."

"Well you'd never know. You were so good, Mom.
Really, really good."

Hearing him call her Mom never got old. "Aww,
thanks, buddy. Means a lot coming from you."

"I'm still mad that I had to go to school and couldn't
go with you."

"I know. Sorry about that. It would've been a lot more
fun with you there."

"Of course it would've."

Sam laughed and hooked her arm through his. "So
come sit with me for a minute. I want to talk to you about
something."

"Whatever it is, I didn't do it."

"Said the future politician."

"You really think I could be a politician?"

She ran her fingers through his hair, earning a predictable scowl. "I think you, Scotty Cappuano, could be
anything you want to be as long as you work hard and
do well in school."

"Why'd you have to ruin it by bringing school into it?"

Sam laughed because she'd felt exactly the same way
at his age, not that she could tell him that.

"What do you want to talk to me about?"

"Remember how you asked me about my mother and
why we don't see her?"

"Uh-huh. You said you have a complicated relationship with her."

"Right. After what happened a couple of months ago," she said, knowing she didn't need to clarify what she meant, "I started to think it might be time to 'uncomplicate' that relationship. She wants to see me, so Ang and Trace are bringing her over in a little while."

"Will I get to meet her?"

"Absolutely. That's one of the main reasons she wanted to see me. She wants to meet her new grandson."

"That's cool. Are you… I mean… Are you weirded out about seeing her?"

Smiling at his choice of words, Sam said, "Not really. It's time to let bygones be bygones, you know?"

"I guess. Mrs. Littlefield always used to tell us it takes far less energy to forgive than it does to hold a grudge," he said of his former guardian at the state home in Virginia.

"Mrs. Littlefield may very well be the wisest person in the entire world."

"She totally is. If I'm going to meet my grandmother, I probably need a shower cuz I stink after hockey practice."

"You don't stink, but that's not a bad idea."

He ran for the stairs. "Let me know when she gets here."

Sam watched him go, bursting with pride and gratitude for every minute she got to spend with him.

Shelby emerged from the kitchen and handed Sam a glass of chardonnay. "I figured you might need this after the day you've had."

"You know me so well. Thank you."

Shelby took a seat on the sofa and curled her legs under her. "Your speech was spectacular. I loved it."

"Thanks. It was *this* close to being a spectacular disaster. Freaking dyslexia."

"Not only did you give hope to women with infertility, you also showed people with dyslexia that they can overcome any obstacle and be successful."

"And I showed people who puke under pressure they can overcome that too."

Shelby dissolved into giggles. "Thank goodness that didn't happen."

"Can you even imagine? Hi, I'm the second lady. Barf."

They lost it laughing.

"I already had enough barfing for one week," Sam said. "And for what it's worth, you should know your guy holds up well in a crisis."

Shelby curved a hand over her rounded abdomen. "It's worth a lot, especially in my current condition. He said you were scary sick."

"He was a trouper." Sam glanced at her friend. "I hope you don't think…"

Shelby held up a hand to stop her from going there. "It's all good. Avery and I talked the other night, and he reminded me again that he's engaged to the woman he loves. That's all I needed to hear."

"*Awww*, isn't he sweet?"

Shelby waggled her brows. "He really is."

"Barf."

"Like you're one to talk about being schmoopy when you're all moon-eyed over your man."

"I am not *moon-eyed*. Whatever that even means."

Shelby batted her eyelashes and went into a series of swoons that seemed more like convulsions to Sam.

"If I ever act like that, I invite you to stab me with my own rusty steak knife."

Shelby lost it laughing again.

"How's he doing anyway?" Sam asked.

"Who?"

"Avery. This case with Hamilton and Jacoby was hard on him."

"It really was," Shelby said with a sigh. "In addition to the nightmare it's been for the Bureau, he's so disillusioned by what they did. It's sickening. Those poor people and Josh… Or I mean Taylor. To find out his entire life was a lie…"

"The Rollingses are such good people. They'll get him through it, and he'll feel like a part of their family in no time."

"Still… They'll never get back the thirty years that were taken from them."

"That's true."

Shelby made a big production out of getting up from the sofa. "I'd better get my portly self home."

"There is nothing portly about you. In fact, you're the most adorable pregnant woman in the history of pregnant women."

Shelby blinked repeatedly.

"If you cry, I'll take it back."

"Okay. I won't cry, then. I'll just say thank you for the kind words, and I'll see you tomorrow."

"I'll be here. Thanks for everything. You're the glue that holds this entire operation together."

The statement resulted in more blinking.

"Go!"

"I'm going."

Shaking her head, Sam laughed at Shelby's out-of-control emotions. None of her pregnancies had lasted long enough for the crazy hormones to kick in the way they had for Shelby. She couldn't help but wonder if she'd be like that too. Maybe one of these days she'd get the chance to find out.

CHAPTER THIRTY-THREE

ANGELA AND TRACY arrived a few minutes later, exchanging greetings with the agent working the door.

"How do you deal with having all these hot guys underfoot all the time?" Angela whispered. "That guy at the door is *ridiculous*."

"Easy, married cougar."

"Being married doesn't mean I'm dead. My eyes work just fine, and that guy is *smoking* hot. What's his name?"

"I think it's Zach."

Angela fanned her face. "Zach. I like that."

"I'm telling Spencer," Tracy said.

"Oh please. Whatever. Like you weren't wiping up the drool too."

"He can probably hear you guys talking about him," Sam said.

"Good," Angela said with a sly smile.

"Not to change the subject, but you have to help me figure out what the heck I'm going to get Nick for an anniversary gift."

"First anniversary is paper," Tracy said.

"Huh?"

"There's a theme for every year," Angela said.

"Who decides this shit?" Sam asked, flabbergasted. "Does someone sit around and make these decisions for everyone?"

Laughing, Angela said, "It's long-standing tradition. And hello? Weren't you married before?"

"I certainly never stressed out about what to give him for an anniversary gift. We just went out to dinner or something."

"And now you care enough to at least ask what you should get for him," Tracy said. "That is just one of the many ways your second marriage is a huge improvement over the first."

"There's no comparison," Sam said. "I want to get it right like he always does. So what do I give him?"

"It doesn't technically count as paper, but a Brazilian would make him happy," Angela said, snickering.

"How do you know?" Tracy asked, slightly horrified.

"I'll never tell."

Tracy pounced. "Have you had one?"

"Maybe."

"This I need to hear," Sam said. "Do tell."

Lowering her voice so there was no chance Zach could overhear, Angela said, "After Ella was born, I was feeling kinda…I don't know, frumpy, I guess. I have horrible stretch marks, and my belly looks like a war zone. I was afraid Spence wouldn't want me anymore."

"Which you know is insane," Sam said. "That man worships the ground you walk on."

"Still… After one of my friends put the idea of getting waxed in my head, I couldn't get it out, so I decided to try it."

"And…" Tracy raised her brows in inquiry.

"He freaking *loved* it. Went *nuts* over it. Spent *hours* down there. Needless to say, after that, I wasn't worried that I'd lost my appeal anymore."

Sam fanned her face. "Wow. That sounds hot. Did the waxing hurt?"

"Like a motherfucker. But it was so worth it. If you're interested, I've got a girl who's great."

"In light of who I'm married to," Sam said, "I can't just go to a salon and ask to have my hoo-ha waxed."

Tracy and Angela dissolved into laughter. "I can have her come to you. She'd be thrilled."

"Not sure how I feel about knowing there's a random woman out there who'd be *thrilled* to wax my unmentionables."

"Trust me, when you're all out and proud, you want someone working down there who knows what she's doing. You want me to set it up?" Angela leaned in, lowering her voice. "He was down there for *hours*…"

"How do you have time for *hours* of that?" Tracy asked. "You've got two little kids."

"Who are in bed by seven o'clock every night," Angela said, winking at Tracy.

The thought of surprising Nick with something so unexpected for their getaway was too appealing to resist. "I'll do it," she said before she could change her mind.

"You will *not* be sorry."

"Somehow I doubt that."

"Now I want it too," Tracy said.

"I'll ask about a two-for-one," Ang replied.

"I'm not doing this with her," Sam said.

"What've you got against my hoo-ha?" Tracy asked indignantly.

They were pissing their pants laughing when the door opened to admit Nick and his detail. He stopped short at the sight of the three of them, sprawled on sofas, laughing their asses off. "Do I even want to know?"

"Oh yeah," Angela said with a dirty smirk. "You want to know."

"Shut up, Angela!" Sam said, tossing a pillow at her sister. "It's a surprise!"

As he did every night the minute he walked in the door, Nick unknotted his tie and unbuttoned the top two buttons on his dress shirt. "I'm on fire with curiosity."

"You'll be on fire all right," Tracy said, reducing her sisters to hysterics once again.

Sam got up to kiss him. "Stop torturing my poor husband."

"Yes, stop torturing me, and tell me the big secret."

"Not happening," she said, patting his handsome face. "It's for us to know and you to find out."

"When? When will I find out?"

"On the trip."

His sexy hazel eyes went hot with desire that almost made Sam forget they weren't alone. "I suppose I can wait a few more days. What time is your mom coming?"

Sam's stomach dropped, and the hilarity was forgotten. "Any minute now."

"Let me run up and change." He kissed her forehead. "I'll be right back down."

Sam returned to her seat on the sofa. "Why am I so nervous about seeing her?"

"Because it's been a long time since you willingly invited her into your life, and you're afraid it'll be awkward," Tracy said.

"Yes, that's it exactly."

"You don't have anything to worry about," Angela said. "She's thrilled to be invited into your home, and she can't wait to meet Scotty and get to know Nick. And she's very excited to be with you too. It'll be fine, Sam."

Angela snapped her fingers. "I have the perfect idea of what you should do for an anniversary gift."

As they talked about Angela's idea for Nick's gift, Sam tried to stay focused on that rather than the visit with her mother. Despite her sisters' assurances, her mother's arrival a few minutes later had the butterflies in her belly doing backflips.

Brenda Ross had cut her hair since the last time Sam saw her, and the new style made her look even more youthful than usual. Though her dark hair was now shot through with gray and there were new lines around her brown eyes, Brenda looked great for her age. She wore a huge smile as she hugged Sam.

"Thank you so much for seeing me."

"Um, sure. No problem. Come on in. Can I get you something to drink? Some wine or something stronger?"

"I'd love a glass of wine."

"Coming right up." Sam went into the kitchen to get it for her and took a moment to calm her nerves before returning to the living room with the bottle and glasses for her sisters too.

Wearing jeans and a sweater, Nick was coming down the stairs as she returned and his warm, private smile went a long way toward putting her at ease. Everything was easier to face when he was there to share the load.

"Brenda," he said, kissing her mother's cheek. "It's great to see you again."

"You too, Nick. Or should I call you Mr. Vice President?"

"Not if you want him to answer," Sam said, drawing a laugh from the others.

"What she said," Nick said with a smile. "I'm just Nick."

"It's a huge honor to be the mother-in-law of the vice president. I'm very proud of you both. Your speech was amazing, Sam."

"Oh. You saw that, huh?"

"I think most of the country has seen it by now."

"Awesome," Sam said with a lack of enthusiasm that made the others laugh.

Nick squeezed her shoulder. "Sam is still getting used to being famous. We both are. It's not all it's cracked up to be sometimes."

Scotty came running down the stairs. "Is she here yet?" He stopped short when he saw Brenda sitting with his parents and his aunts. "Oh, sorry. I'm Scotty."

Amused, Brenda stood to shake his hand. "It's so nice to meet you."

"You too."

"I've heard so much about you from your aunts. They're your biggest fans."

"They only say that because I keep their kids under control."

"That's true," Angela said. "That's the only reason we keep you around."

"Very funny," Scotty said.

"No, it's true," Tracy said, grinning at her nephew.

"Um, what should I call you?" Scotty asked Brenda.

"How about Brenda? Does that work?"

"Works for me."

Scotty's natural ease with new people went a long way toward calming Sam's nerves. It was hard to stay wound up when he made it look so easy.

They chatted with Nick and Scotty for half an hour or so and then Nick suggested he and Scotty go watch the Caps game upstairs. Sam appreciated the way he smoothly gave her time alone with her mother and sisters, but not until he was certain she was comfortable.

Brenda got up to hug them. "I hope to see you again soon," she said to Scotty.

"Me too."

After they'd gone upstairs, Brenda said, "I'm so glad to meet your amazing son, Sam, and for the chance to get to know Nick a little. His public persona, which is quite impressive, doesn't do him justice."

As far as compliments went, Sam had to admit they were pretty good. "Thanks. I like them."

"I can see why. And your home is lovely."

"That's all Nick. He's the one with the style."

"I figured it had to be, because you never cared about such things when you were younger."

"I still don't."

"You should see what we go through when she has to be turned out for something formal," Tracy said, rolling her eyes. "First we have to pry the handcuffs out of her hand and then—"

"That's enough out of you."

Laughing at their banter, Brenda said, "I'm so happy that you girls are close to each other. When you were fighting like tomcats growing up, people would tell me you'd get over it and be best friends someday. I had my doubts."

"We definitely got over it," Sam said. "I'd be lost without them."

"As would we without you," Tracy said.

"Although we would spend less time at the emergency room without you," Angela said to more laughter.

"What can I say? Shit happens."

"Shit happens to you far too often," Tracy said.

"While we're on the subject of shit happening," Brenda said, "I wanted you to know…I've been diagnosed with stage one breast cancer." Before Sam could react or begin to process the news, Brenda continued. "It was caught early and the prognosis is very good, but my doctor said it's important for my daughters to understand that me having it puts you at greater risk for developing it at some point."

"I'm…I'm sorry to hear that," Sam said.

"I'm having a lumpectomy in two weeks, and if that goes well, I shouldn't need more treatment. I'm very cautiously optimistic."

"That's good news," Sam said. "But I'm sorry you have to go through all that."

"I've made up my mind to remain positive and to be thankful for the early diagnosis and that it's treatable."

"We've talked her into having the surgery up here so we can take care of her afterward," Tracy said. "She'll be staying with me."

"I've actually been thinking about moving back to D.C. permanently," Brenda said, taking all three of her daughters by surprise. "My grandchildren are growing up too fast, and being so far from my family gets kind of lonely sometimes." The man she'd left Skip for was long gone, and Sam had no idea if there was someone else in her mother's life. Apparently not if she was lonely.

The news that her mother was moving home would've knocked her for a loop only a few months ago, but now… It was fine with her.

"I promise not to cramp your style too badly," Brenda said. "It'll be nice to have you all close by." To Sam, she said, "I'm sure you must be thinking that I have a lot of nerve coming here after all these years to tell you bad news and that I'm coming home."

"That's not what I'm thinking."

While they waited for her to say something more, Sam tried to get her thoughts together. "I've regretted that so much time has gone by and that we've been out of touch for so long. I... I've come to realize there was a lot more to the story of what happened between you and Dad than I knew back then. And...it's probably time to put the past where it belongs. I want you to know Scotty and Nick, and me too, I guess."

"I'd love that, Sam," Brenda said softly as she dabbed at her eyes with a tissue. "I'm sorry for the way I left and for what happened with Jerry. I never should've let that happen while your father and I were still married. That was wrong, and I'm sorry I hurt you—and your dad. You all deserved better from me."

Sam had waited nearly twenty years to hear her mother express regret over what'd happened the day after Sam's high school graduation. And after carrying deep-seated resentment for all those years, she was surprised at how a few sincerely spoken words could effectively dispose of the anger. "Apology accepted."

"I also want you to know that I've been to see your dad and Celia, and we had a nice talk. It was good to see him, and to have a chance to talk to her. He seems to be doing well, all things considered."

"He's better than he was," Sam said. "We've learned to be grateful for small victories."

The four of them chatted for another hour before Brenda got up to leave. "It was so nice to see you, Sam. Thank you for having me."

Sam hugged her mother, holding on for longer than

she'd intended. When she pulled back, there were tears in her eyes and her mother's. "It was good to see you. Keep me in the loop on the surgery and everything."

"I'll do that." She hugged and kissed Angela and Tracy and thanked Zach, who held the door for her.

"That went well," Angela said.

"Very well," Tracy added. "How do you feel about it, Sam?"

"I feel…relieved and concerned for her and for us in light of her diagnosis."

"Knowledge is power," Tracy said. "Now that we know, we can be proactive. That's how I'm choosing to see it."

"That's a good way to look at it," Sam said.

Her sisters left a short time later. Sam went upstairs to look for Nick and Scotty and found them lying on their bed with the Caps game on much louder than she would have it. She crawled in between them and straight into her husband's arms.

"I'm outta here if you start anything," Scotty said.

"He's such a buzz killer," Sam said. "What we were thinking adopting him?"

"You were thinking you're the luckiest parents ever."

"You know it, buddy," Nick said with a chuckle.

"Pizza's here!" Scotty bolted from the room and flew down the stairs.

"How does he know that?" Sam asked.

"There's an app for that."

"He's got a *pizza* app? For real?"

"Yep, and it comes in handy at times like this. How'd the visit go, babe?"

"Good. Really good, actually."

"What did she want to tell you?"

Sam sighed. "She's been diagnosed with stage one breast cancer. Very treatable, great prognosis."

"That's too bad."

"It is. For her—and for us. It puts us at higher risk."

"I sure do hate to hear that."

"Like Tracy said, it just means we have to be more proactive. It's nothing we can't handle."

"I've begun to think there's nothing you can't handle."

Sam raised her head off his chest so she could look into his eyes. "As long as I have you, I can handle anything."

"Since there's nowhere else in this world I'd rather be than with you, then I guess you're all set."

Smiling, she leaned in to kiss him and didn't stop until Scotty's loud groan ruined the moment.

"I swear to God I'm going to ground you guys if this kissing stuff doesn't stop." He'd brought the pizza, paper plates and a roll of paper towels upstairs with him.

As Nick bit his lip to keep from laughing out loud, Sam sat up and took the pizza box from Scotty. "We're living for the day you get your first girlfriend. I hope you're prepared for a lifetime of revenge."

"To quote my mom, the badass cop, 'bring it on.'"

Laughing, Sam dished out the pizza and settled in to enjoy the picnic with her two favorite people. For once, everything in her world was perfect, and she intended to enjoy the peace while it lasted.

EPILOGUE

"WHEN DO I get my surprise?" Nick asked when they were on the plane heading for ten days alone together in Bora Bora. They were curled up on the sofa in his private cabin, away from the prying eyes of his detail and the flight crew.

"What surprise?" Sam asked, intentionally playing dumb while tingling with anticipation. She knew exactly what he was talking about and had endured the epic humiliation of bikini waxing to make it happen. She'd be having nightmares for years about the entire thing.

"Don't pull that crap, Samantha. You and your sisters have had my imagination working overtime for a week now, and the fact that I haven't been allowed to touch you for two whole *days* hasn't helped."

"I'll give you your surprise as soon as we get there," she said, intentionally squirming so her back side pressed against his erection.

Groaning, he said, "Fine, if you're going to be that way about it."

"Patience, my love."

He took hold of her hand and ran his lips over her knuckles. "I'm out of patience because I'm so excited to have ten days alone with you."

"You think Scotty will be okay while we're gone?"

"He'll be fine. He'll get tons of attention from Shelby

and your dad and Celia and Tracy and Angela. They told us not to worry. *He* told us not to worry. So we should relax and enjoy every minute."

"I feel kind of guilty going somewhere without him."

"I think that's called parenthood, babe." He leaned in close enough to nuzzle her neck. "Just think...*ten days* with no one telling us to quit kissing so much."

"Mmm, that will be nice."

"Let's get some sleep so we can fully enjoy every minute in paradise."

Sam took the hand he offered and let him help her up. They took turns in the tiny bathroom and then crawled into bed. "It's kinda funny how different everything is this time than it was last year when we had to fly commercial like regular people do."

"And yet some things are exactly the same as they were then," he said with a meaningful smile.

"The most important things."

She rested her hand flat against his bare chest, feeling his strong heartbeat beneath her palm. "I'm not afraid to fly when I'm with you."

"Then I guess you shouldn't fly without me ever again."

"We both know that's not always going to be possible."

"I'll go whenever I can," he said, sounding sleepy.

Sam closed her eyes and tried to settle in, hoping he would get some much-needed rest.

The next thing she knew they were being awakened by an announcement from the cockpit, letting them know they'd be landing in forty-five minutes.

"I can't believe I slept on an airplane—again," she said.

"You might be getting over your fear of flying."

Her meltdown on the flight to Knoxville was evidence to the contrary, but she didn't feel like talking about that today. Not when paradise awaited.

With their usual efficiency, the Secret Service got them off the plane and into an SUV for the ride to the resort.

"Where will they be while we're here?" she asked of the detail that included Melinda, much to her dismay.

"In villas on either side of us."

"So they'll be spying on us?"

"No, they won't be *spying*," he said, laughing. "They'll be close by if we need them, but mostly out of sight."

"What does this mean for my need to skinny-dip?"

"It puts a damper on that, but everything else involving nudity is recommended and allowed."

They were given a VIP welcome at the resort and shown to the same villa they'd occupied last year. After Nick had a brief conversation with Brant, the agent left and Nick locked the door behind him.

"Alone at last," he said.

"Whatever shall we do?"

"I can't think of a thing I want to do."

"God, one year of marriage and we're already so bored. What does that mean for the other seventy years you're going to be stuck with me?"

"It means," he said as he put his hands on her hips to draw her into his embrace, "I'm the luckiest bastard in the universe."

"We're both lucky. So lucky." With her hand curled around his neck she drew him into a kiss. "You want that surprise now?"

"More than I've ever wanted anything. Ever."

"That's a whole lot of want."

"You have no idea."

"If you undress me, you'll find it."

The dress she'd bought for the trip flew over her head. Her bra came off next and then he was on his knees before her, sliding panties down her legs and gasping at the sight before him. "Are you freaking kidding me?"

"Good surprise?"

"I won't know for sure until I get a closer look."

He lifted her right off her feet and carried her to the huge bed they'd all but lived in last year. Something told her this year was going to be more of the same, and that was fine with her.

"Samantha…" He licked and worshipped her, making her tremble from the sensations that were a thousand times more intense than usual.

Angela had forgotten to tell her to expect that.

"Just when I think you can't possibly get any sexier than you already are, you blow my fucking mind." He sucked hard on her clit, and she came instantly, crying out with the abandon that came from being completely alone with him and not having to worry about making too much noise.

His body came down on hers, hot and hard and heavy. Grasping her hips, he pushed into her, the tight squeeze triggering another release for her.

"So you like my surprise?"

"I fucking love it, and I love *you*, so much."

She ran her fingers through his hair. "I love you too. You, this, us…it's everything."

"Mmm, yes, it is."

Sam had no idea how much time passed before they wore themselves out. The bright sunshine had given way to twilight that shimmered over the surface of the bluest water she'd ever seen. "As amazing as our loft is, there's no substitute for the real thing."

"I want to come here every year until we're old and gray and too decrepit for anything more than a peck on the lips."

Sam laughed at the picture he painted. "You will never be that decrepit."

"Will you still love me if I am?"

"I'll always love you."

"You want your present?"

"Hell yes, I want my present."

As he got out of bed and walked out of the room, Sam enjoyed the view of his spectacular ass. He returned with a cardboard box. "Did you know the first anniversary is paper?"

"My sisters told me that." She reached for the package she'd stashed next to the bed when they first arrived. "Which is why I got you this."

"And here I thought you'd gone with wax over paper."

She snorted with laughter. "I did both."

"You first."

Sam tore into the box and found a smaller box on top of a layer of tissue paper. Inside she found a gorgeous platinum bracelet on which he'd had the words "The first of many" engraved. "It's so beautiful! I love it." She put it on and held up her arm for him to see.

"It matches the one I got you for the inauguration."

"I see that. It's perfect." She leaned in to kiss him. "Thank you."

"There's more, and in case you're wondering, the tissue paper is my contribution to tradition."

Under the layer of bright red paper were a treasure trove of intimate goodies, including massage oil, lubricant, a vibrator and a couple of odd-shaped objects she couldn't immediately identify. Her body flushed with heat and desire, but before she could indulge the desire, she had questions. "How in the world does the vice president of the United States make a purchase like this and get away with it?"

"Carefully," he said with a chuckle. "I had it shipped to Shelby's."

"So *she* knows about this?"

"She has no idea what was in the box, just that I needed to have it sent to her so you wouldn't know. I made a joke about being married to a detective."

"Wow, I'm impressed and intrigued. Now open yours."

He tore the paper off the framed collage she'd made at Angela's suggestion of her favorite pictures from their first year of marriage, including their wedding, honeymoon, Scotty's adoption, the inauguration and group shots with the people they loved best.

"This is fantastic, Sam."

"It's not as exciting as massage oil, but—"

"It's amazing. What a year this has been. I love it, thank you." He put down the frame and moved the box to the floor so he could hold her. "What do you suppose our second year will be like?"

Resting her head on her favorite chest, she said, "Probably a lot like the first—chaotic and busy and crazy and absolutely incredible."

"I don't know about you, but I can't wait for every minute of it."

Smiling, she kissed him, lingering over the sweet taste of his lips. "As a very wise boy once said, *bring it on.*"

* * * * *

Dear Reader,

Thank you so much for reading *Fatal Identity*! I hope you enjoyed catching up with Sam and Nick and the rest of the Fatal characters. If you want to read more about Sam getting a bikini wax or how they made use of Nick's gifts on their trip, join my newsletter mailing list at marieforce.com to receive a link to the added extras. If you're already on the list, watch for a link to the bonus content in the release week newsletter. You can also download my Marie Force App at Apple and Android to receive occasional bonus content. Join the Fatal Identity Reader Group at www.facebook.com/groups/FatalIdentity to chat about the book with spoilers allowed and encouraged as well as chances to win release week giveaways. Make sure you're also a member of the Fatal Series Reader Group at www.facebook.com/groups/FatalSeries to be among the first to hear news about the series.

Fatal Identity marks a turning point in the Fatal Series. It's the first time in the series' six years that the book is being released in all formats at the same time. It's available in ebook, print and audio, and I couldn't be more excited that readers and listeners of all formats can get it on the same day. Thanks to the HQN team for making that happen and for the brilliant new Fatal Series covers. I hope you love our Sam and Nick as much as we do! Thank you to my editors, Margo Lipschultz and Alissa Davis, as well as my agent, Kevan Lyon, for their work on the Fatal Series.

My appreciation goes to Captain Russell Hayes of the Newport, Rhode Island, Police Department, for answering my many questions as I wrote this book. As always, Russ is an outstanding resource to me, and I wouldn't want to write the Fatal books without him at the other end of an e-mail. Thanks also to Christopher Burnette, forensic specialist, for his help with the DNA storyline in this book.

Special thanks to my amazing team that works behind the scenes to keep me sane—Julie Cupp, CMP, Lisa Cafferty, CPA, Holly Sullivan, Isabel Sullivan, Nikki Colquhoun, Cheryl Serra, Ashley Lopez and Courtney Lopes. Thank you, ladies, for all you do every day! Love you all!

And to my incredible readers who make this journey so much fun, thank you for your support of my books! I appreciate each and every one of you more than you'll ever know.

xoxo
Marie

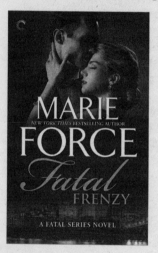
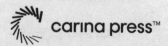

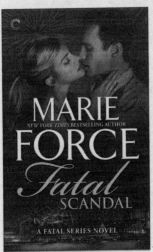
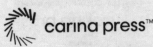

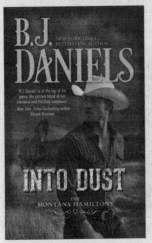

USA TODAY bestselling author

SARAH MORGAN

**introduces _From Manhattan with Love_,
a sparkling new trilogy about three
best friends embracing
life—and love—in New York!**

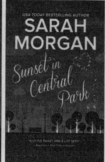

Order your copies today!

"Morgan's brilliant talent never ceases to amaze."
—_RT Book Reviews_

REQUEST YOUR
FREE BOOKS!

2 FREE NOVELS
FROM THE SUSPENSE COLLECTION,
PLUS 2 FREE GIFTS!

YES! Please send me 2 FREE novels from the Suspense Collection and my 2 FREE gifts (gifts are worth about $10). After receiving them, if I don't wish to receive any more books, I can return the shipping statement marked "cancel." If I don't cancel, I will receive 4 brand-new novels every month and be billed just $6.49 per book in the U.S. or $6.99 per book in Canada. That's a savings of at least 18% off the cover price. It's quite a bargain! Shipping and handling is just 50¢ per book in the U.S. and 75¢ per book in Canada.* I understand that accepting the 2 free books and gifts places me under no obligation to buy anything. I can always return a shipment and cancel at any time. Even if I never buy another book, the two free books and gifts are mine to keep forever.

191/391 MDN GH4Z

Name _____ (PLEASE PRINT) _____

Address _____ Apt. # _____

City _____ State/Prov. _____ Zip/Postal Code _____

Signature (if under 18, a parent or guardian must sign)

Mail to the **Reader Service:**
IN U.S.A.: P.O. Box 1867, Buffalo, NY 14240-1867
IN CANADA: P.O. Box 609, Fort Erie, Ontario L2A 5X3

Want to try 2 free books from another line?
Call 1-800-873-8635 or visit www.ReaderService.com.

* Terms and prices subject to change without notice. Prices do not include applicable taxes. Sales tax applicable in NY. Canadian residents will be charged applicable taxes. Offer not valid in Quebec. This offer is limited to one order per household. Not valid for current subscribers to the Suspense Collection or the Romance/Suspense Collection. All orders subject to credit approval. Credit or debit balances in a customer's account(s) may be offset by any other outstanding balance owed by or to the customer. Please allow 4 to 6 weeks for delivery. Offer available while quantities last.

Your Privacy—The Reader Service is committed to protecting your privacy. Our Privacy Policy is available online at www.ReaderService.com or upon request from the Reader Service.

We make a portion of our mailing list available to reputable third parties that offer products we believe may interest you. If you prefer that we not exchange your name with third parties, or if you wish to clarify or modify your communication preferences, please visit us at www.ReaderService.com/consumerchoice or write to us at Reader Service Preference Service, P.O. Box 9062, Buffalo, NY 14240-9062. Include your complete name and address.

SUS15R

MARIE FORCE

00415 FATAL AFFAIR	__$7.99 U.S.	__$9.99 CAN.
00416 FATAL JUSTICE	__$7.99 U.S.	__$9.99 CAN.
00417 FATAL CONSEQUENCES	__$7.99 U.S.	__$9.99 CAN.
00418 FATAL FLAW	__$7.99 U.S.	__$9.99 CAN.
00420 FATAL DECEPTION	__$7.99 U.S.	__$9.99 CAN.
00421 FATAL MISTAKE	__$7.99 U.S.	__$9.99 CAN.
00422 FATAL JEOPARDY	__$7.99 U.S.	__$9.99 CAN.
00408 FATAL SCANDAL	__$7.99 U.S.	__$9.99 CAN.
00410 FATAL FRENZY	__$7.99 U.S.	__$9.99 CAN.

(limited quantities available)

TOTAL AMOUNT	$_____
POSTAGE & HANDLING	$_____
($1.00 for 1 book, 50¢ for each additional)	
APPLICABLE TAXES*	$_____
TOTAL PAYABLE	$_____

(check or money order—please do not send cash)

To order, complete this form and send it, along with a check or money order for the total amount, payable to Carina Press, to: **In the U.S.:** 3010 Walden Avenue, P.O. Box 9077, Buffalo, NY 14269-9077; **In Canada:** P.O. Box 636, Fort Erie, Ontario, L2A 5X3.

Name: _____
Address: _____ City: _____
State/Prov.: _____ Zip/Postal Code: _____
Account Number (if applicable): _____
075 CSAS

*New York residents remit applicable sales taxes.
*Canadian residents remit applicable GST and provincial taxes.

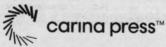

carina press™

www.CarinaPress.com

CARMF0716BLR